PRAISE FOR LUANNE RICE
and
LAST KISS

"A very potent mix of mystery, romance, and suspense that makes the pages fly by." —*Connecticut Post*

"A poignant story about love...love lost, love found, true love, old love, family love. There's not a heartstring it doesn't tug, though it's never maudlin.... While little shore towns may seem sleepy, Rice feels there's always a lot going on...that undercurrent.... The novel...has a *Practical Magic* feel to it...and a touch of the film *Ghost*." —*New Haven Register*

"Rice's fans will rejoice as she revisits her beloved beach community in this engrossing story of love and redemption." —*Booklist*

"Rice makes a solid return visit to the Hubbard's Point, Conn., setting of *Beach Girls*....An element of supernatural whimsy, a dark secret involving a trust fund, and a disturbing question...add complexity, while cameos from other *Beach Girls* characters contribute an engaging, homey touch."
—*Publishers Weekly*

"Luanne Rice finely crafts the best of the genre of 'chick books.' The talented writer can make you laugh and make you miserable, then make you glad she did....The story is...oh, so satisfying. Go ahead, smile and cry and stay up all night to finish a chapter. It's a good sensation." —*Oklahoman*

"Readers can count on Rice for a book that bares the emotions of her readers, as well as of the characters in her novels." —*Brazosport Facts*

"An exciting investigative romance with a touch of the paranormal and a feel of homecoming...a deep character-driven thriller." —*Midwest Book Review*

"Rice's novels are romantic even though they're not exactly romances.... They sometimes feature mystery elements but they certainly aren't suspense novels. They're really just terrific stories about complicated and believable people.... This one is a sort of sequel to [Rice's] warm and memorable *Beach Girls*...a mystery and a potential romance in a novel that isn't bound by category rules, and is all the richer and more satisfying for that."
—*Sullivan County Democrat*

More Critical Acclaim for
LUANNE RICE

"A rare combination of realism and romance."
—*New York Times Book Review*

"Luanne Rice proves herself a nimble virtuoso."
—*Washington Post*

"Few writers evoke summer's translucent days so effortlessly, or better capture the bittersweet ties of family love." —*Publishers Weekly*

"Ms. Rice shares Anne Tyler's ability to portray off-beat, fey characters winningly."
—*Atlanta Journal-Constitution*

"Rice has an elegant style, a sharp eye, and a real warmth. In her hands families, and their values... seem worth cherishing." —*San Francisco Chronicle*

"What a lovely writer Luanne Rice is."
—DOMINICK DUNNE

"Luanne Rice has enticed millions of readers by enveloping them in stories that are wrapped in the hot, sultry weather of summer.... She does it so well."
—*USA Today*

"[Luanne Rice's] characters break readers' hearts... true-to-life characters dealing with real issues—people following journeys that will either break them or heal them." —*Columbus Dispatch*

"A joy to read." —*Atlanta Journal-Constitution*

"Addictive ... irresistible." —*People*

"None of Luanne Rice's characters love halfheartedly.... Rice writes unabashedly for women, imbuing her tales with romance and rock-strong relationships. However, the stories she crafts lift themselves above the typical escapist romance novels. Rice's characters grapple with the weighty issues that come with loving other people. Her stories are for women who face trying relationships with their own husbands, daughters, or paramours." —*Chicago Sun-Times*

"What the author does best: heartfelt family drama, gracefully written and poignant." —*Kirkus Reviews*

"Rice is a master of...emotional intensity."
—*CinCHouse.com*

"Few...authors are able to portray the complex and contradictory emotions that bind family members as effortlessly as Rice." —*Publishers Weekly*

"Rice, always skilled at drafting complex stories...reveals her special strength in character development."
—*Newark Sunday Star-Ledger*

"Rice...breathes life into poignant tales not only about love but also about forgiveness." —*Booklist*

"Rice's ability to evoke the lyricism of the seaside lifestyle without oversentimentalizing contemporary issues...is just one of...many gifts that make...a perfect summer read."
—*Publishers Weekly* (starred review)

"Rice, as always, provides her readers with a delightful love story filled with the subtle nuances of the human heart." —*Booklist*

"Luanne Rice touches the deepest, most tender corners of the heart." —TAMI HOAG, author of *The Alibi Man*

"Pure gold." —*Library Journal*

Also by Luanne Rice

LUANNE RICE

Last Kiss

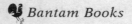

Bantam Books

Last Kiss is a work of fiction. Names, characters, places, and incidents either are the product of the author's imagination or are used fictitiously. Any resemblance to actual persons, living or dead, events, or locales is entirely coincidental.

2009 Bantam Books Mass Market Edition

Published in the United States by Bantam Books, an imprint of The Random House Publishing Group, a division of Random House, Inc., New York.

BANTAM BOOKS and the rooster colophon are registered trademarks of Random House, Inc.

Originally published in hardcover in the United States by Bantam Books, an imprint of The Random House Publishing Group, a division of Random House, Inc., in 2008.

This book contains an excerpt from the forthcoming book *The Deep Blue Sea for Beginners* by Luanne Rice. This excerpt has been set for this edition only and may not reflect the final content of the forthcoming edition.

ISBN 978-0-553-58976-4

Cover design: Shasti O'Leary Soudant
Cover photograph: © Goodshoot/Jupiter Images

Printed in the United States of America

www.bantamdell.com

9 8 7 6 5 4 3 2 1

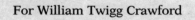

For William Twigg Crawford

Last Kiss

PROLOGUE

THE WATER WAS GLASS-CALM AND PITCH-black, reflecting the summer constellations and the lights of the houses along the coast. Green light illuminated the chart table down below, but Gavin Dawson didn't need to look at charts. Not once he'd passed the light at Race Rock: these were his home waters.

His trip had been long. He'd been in Maine, resting up from a long case involving old Seal Harbor money, when he'd gotten the call: all the way down east, in a hidden harbor ringed by pines, where his only clock had been the sun and the tides. The message had been left with his service. He'd returned the call, listened just long enough to know he wanted to take the case, told his new employer they'd decide on terms once he had the chance to assess the situation.

Then he'd started the engine, hauled anchor, and headed south. The weather had been fair; he'd skirted the tail end of a storm moving out to sea. His boat, the

Squire Toby, didn't mind one way or the other—she got the job done. She was as old as he was, thirty-three feet long, and tough as hell. The rebuilt twin 350 Crusaders throbbed belowdecks, better than music.

Entering Long Island Sound, he was coming home. He found himself thinking of old friends, old faces. He thought of Sheridan. His skin started prickling; he thought about turning back. But he'd given his word, signed on for a job, so he kept going. Past Mystic, Noank, and Groton. He heard the engine of a small plane, watched it fly overhead and land at Groton–New London Airport. He saw the big stone buildings at UConn's Avery Point campus, dark for the summer.

He passed Ledge Light, the square brick lighthouse at the mouth of the Thames River; New London; Waterford. Once he saw the big ugly stack of Millstone Point, he knew he was practically there. Cruising past the power plant, he glanced over. Sheridan had always hated the place; she'd spent one summer protesting, a completely useless enterprise, just bobbing in her rowboat and holding up a big sign: YOU ARE HURTING THE SOUND.

She cared, he gave her that. The way she'd sit there all day, getting sunburned and thirsty. She wrote a song about it. Everyone else was out making money, having fun. He remembered waterskiing by her one day, slaloming behind Tommy Mangan's Boston Whaler, jumping the wake to impress her and spray her while she sat in the hot sun, holding her sign.

"Thanks for cooling me off!" she'd yelled.

"No problem," he'd called back.

He put the memory behind him as he rounded the headland and crossed the mouth of Niantic Bay, past Black Point and Giant's Neck. Hugging the coast, he avoided the shoals he knew like the back of his hand. He and his friends had gone fishing here—either off the rocks with rod and reel, or spearfishing down below the surface.

The ones with rich parents had scuba equipment and fancy fishing gear. The ones without rich parents just snorkeled or held their breath or fished with cheap poles. Either way, it didn't matter; they'd spent hours here, season after season. Ed Moriarty had pointed a speargun at Gavin's head once. Only once, and just as a joke; even so, Gavin had broken his wrist. Anger, his old demon.

He slowed down, staring at this stretch of coastline. This was the east side of Hubbard's Point, a rocky peninsula that jutted into Long Island Sound. The shingled cottages looked the same as ever. Their lights shone on the water, crazy orange and yellow lines scoring the black surface.

The tide was low; he could smell the seaweed and marshes. Taking the last turn around the Point, he puttered between the big rock and the breakwater, skirting the raft twenty yards from the beach, next to the rock. He maneuvered between two other boats moored by the breakwater: a sloop and a fiberglass speedboat. Then he dropped anchor and turned the engines off.

His ears rang from the long hours of engine

sounds. He walked to the stern, stared across the water. Facing northeast, he saw Little Beach, dark and deserted, off to his left, then the thick woods, and then Hubbard's Point Beach, the long strand of sand reaching toward the rocky Point.

The longer he stood there, the more his hearing came back. He heard small waves slapping the hull, seagulls crying from their rookery on North Brother, kids laughing. He glanced at Little Beach, realized teenagers were still being teenagers: they were partying on the sand, behind the rock still painted with shark's jaws, graffiti that had been there nearly thirty years. The kids held his attention for a few seconds, then he turned back to stare at Hubbard's Point.

His gaze went to the Point, the actual granite point that gave the beach its name. There were several houses built along its crest, some thirty feet up from the water. There were lights on in her house. One light upstairs, one downstairs. His hand closed around the binoculars, but he didn't raise them to his eyes. Not yet. He pulled a deck chair close to the rail and sat down. The boat moved on the tide, straining against the anchor line. He barely noticed.

There was food down below, and ice, and scotch. He'd go get some or all of it eventually, but not now. First he had a job to start.

He watched.

PART ONE

CHAPTER 1

NELL KILVERT LAY BACK ON THE GRASS, hearing the breeze rustle the leaves overhead. Her bikini was salt-and sun-faded, a pretty shade of rose; around her waist she wore a beach towel, still damp from her last swim. Around her ankle she wore a strip of cloth, so ragged it looked ready to fall off. Charlie had tied it there three hundred and fifty-something days ago, just before leaving Hubbard's Point for college, at the end of last summer.

Her long hair was dark brown. She had cat eyes: green, almond-shaped, unblinking. Right now there were tears pouring down out of them, into her ears, as she stared up at the gorgeous blue sky.

"It's so beautiful," she whispered.

"I know. So why are you crying?"

"Because he can't feel it . . . he'll never feel summer again."

"Why do you come here?"

"So I can be near him."

The boy—his name was Tyler—stared at her. She knew he was there, kneeling beside her, but she blocked him out. She focused completely on Charlie. Closing her eyes, she could imagine him right here with her.

The cemetery was quiet. Located behind Foley's Store, right in the middle of Hubbard's Point—between the train bridge that separated the beach from the rest of the world, and the Sound—it was filled with tall trees. And it was filled with graves. One of them was Charlie's.

Nell lay on the ground by Charlie's headstone. She came here often, at least once a day, before or after work at Foley's, carefully timing her visits to avoid seeing his mother. Not that she didn't like Charlie's mother—Nell visited Sheridan often. They would sit quietly in the dark house, sometimes talking, sometimes not. Nell would look at the silent guitars and remember how when Charlie was young, his mother had filled their house with music. Nell craved those times with Charlie's mother, her companion in grief. But here at the grave, Nell knew Sheridan needed her own time with her son.

"Don't you ever get spooked here?" Tyler asked, so close she could feel his breath on her forehead.

"Why would I?" Nell asked.

"Well, because it's a graveyard."

"Once someone you love dies, you're not scared of graveyards," she said.

"Huh," he said, sounding unconvinced. An old tree creaked in the breeze, making him jump. She knew he'd like to book out of there, head down to the sun and fun on the beach, but he wouldn't leave her.

Nell had an effect on boys. It mystified her. It had started with Charlie, of course. She'd loved him as long as she'd known him. They'd spent the last few summers together, right here at Hubbard's Point. He was the wildest boy at the beach, like a mustang running free. No one had been able to tame him, no one but Nell. That's why he'd called her the Boy Whisperer. . . .

It still fit. Even though the beach boys all knew she was still in love with Charlie, they wanted to be with her. They wanted to tell her their secrets. She thought maybe it was the whisper of tragedy that surrounded her. Her mother had died when she was young. Her father had lost it big-time, until Nell had brought him together with Stevie Moore, the artist most people considered a witch. Now Stevie was virtually Nell's stepmother, and the beach boys probably thought her witchiness had rubbed off on Nell. They dreamed of sex spells. And after Charlie's murder, the boys had come flocking even more.

But Charlie had had the magic, too. He was the great-grandson of Aphrodite, the doyenne of Hubbard's Point beach magic. Her magic book had been the source of many of Charlie's mother's best songs, but not the inspiration for the film Charlie had wanted to make. As much as he disavowed it, Charlie had inherited his family magic; Nell used to tease him, that he had it in his kiss. The other beach boys wanted to make Nell forget Charlie's kisses. . . .

Nell lay beside his headstone, staring down her right leg at the strip of beach towel he'd tied around her ankle last summer. It was all she had left of him. She wondered how he'd feel to know about the other boys. He'd never been the jealous type in life. He hadn't needed to be, and he still didn't now. He was her only one.

She closed her eyes, and even with Tyler beside her, she let herself dream of Charlie. He'd been so comfortable in his own skin, in his own life. He'd wear jeans and a T-shirt, even when they were supposed to get dressed up for candlelit beach dinners at their parents' houses. Well, his mother's. His father was a no-show.

That's what Charlie had called him. Just one of those dads who bailed on their kids, no real explanation other than the fact they didn't feel like showing up to raise their children—the opposite of Nell's dad. Charlie was casual, tough, a little hardened by growing up without a dad. He'd had to figure things out by himself.

But oh . . . he'd figured them out so well.

He was competent. Nell found it sexy as hell, too—the way he could do anything he set his mind to. He could fix her car, catch huge stripers, identify raptors, film equally well using digital or Super 8. He had an artist's eye but a rugged soul. His mom had gently steered him into therapy, to deal with his father's absence, and Nell knew he'd gotten into the habit of figuring himself out. He was rigorous with himself.

He'd been so practical, while his mother and her family had been so driven by magic. His mother was in touch with the spiritual, but Charlie had insisted on staying real, right in the world as it is. It was how he'd survived the disappointment of missing a father he never really knew. His mother had made up for it the best she could, trying to heal Charlie's deep scars. And they were deep, Nell knew—but he'd learned to take care of himself.

He'd think about things. That might sound so normal, so regular, but what eighteen-year-old boys do that? He'd really consider his choices, and if he did something he was sorry for, he'd always make it right. He was introspective while at the same time being tough. He was very physical, ran cross-country in school. He'd been captain his senior year, and he was known for taking the team on adventures.

He'd run the team into Cockaponset State Forest, straight into the sixteen thousand acres of woods, made them find their way out. Another time he'd led them across the Connecticut River, over the catwalk beneath the Baldwin Bridge, one hundred feet up above the water.

He'd loved the woods, he'd loved rivers, he'd loved running. And he'd loved Nell.

They'd kiss. He'd make her tell him what felt good to her. She liked having her hair brushed, and he'd done that for her. Her big, muscular boyfriend had sat next to her, on the mattress in the attic, brushing her hair. She could almost feel it now, the way he'd kiss her neck while he was doing it. The memory made her tremble, because it felt so real and she knew it wasn't, and she knew she'd never feel it again.

"Oh," she whispered.

Tyler leaned over, touched her lightly. He stroked the inside of her left arm, but that's not what gave her goose bumps.

"What are you thinking?" he asked.

"I can't talk about it," she said.

"Charlie, right?" he asked, sounding disappointed.

"Of course.... And about where I have to be," she said, sitting up.

Grabbing Tyler's wrist, she checked the time on his watch. Nearly four. That gave her an hour to get to her appointment—five o'clock, an hour from right now. She'd timed it for her day off from waitressing at Foley's. She'd seen the big boat come in last night. Partying at Little Beach with the other kids, she'd watched it round the Point and drop anchor off the breakwater.

She stood up, brushing dry grass from her sweaty skin. Tyler put his arm around her, but she gave him a look and he dropped it. He stepped back, giving her a moment. She stared at Charlie's headstone, at the name and dates. It seemed impossible in ways too huge to grasp, that last summer he had been her boyfriend and so alive and so strong, and that this summer he was buried in the ground, and all that remained were words carved in stone. The breeze made her shiver.

The shiver went deep, into her bones. She backed

away, then headed toward the gravel path with Tyler, toward the beach and the boat and what she hoped would turn out to be the answer.

SHERIDAN WORE HER OLD straw hat and yellow gloves, kneeling in the garden and digging in the earth. The soil was stony, but things grew anyway. It amazed her, the way the most beautiful flowers could take hold of so little, bloom all summer long. She grew roses and morning glories, clematis and delphinium. Day lilies, orange and yellow, bloomed along the privet hedge.

Her favorite patch was the least showy: the herb garden. A raised stone circle, no bigger than a beach umbrella, was filled with rosemary, sage, wild thyme, mint, lemon verbena, lavender, and burnet. Her grandmother had used these herbs to make magic. Blind and unable to read, she had gotten Sheridan and her sisters to read the spells from her magic book. So many of the spells had involved plants right here in the round garden.

Some of the herbs came back year after year: reseeded themselves, survived the harsh winter and salt wind. Others Sheridan would replant—she'd take trips to the farm stand, buy flats of herbs, and bring them home.

Long ago, Charlie had helped her in the garden. Those times were engraved in her memory—even now, she could feel him right here with her—four years old, digging in the soil with his little spade. She could see him so clearly, laughing and pretending he was a pirate burying his treasure.

No, sweetheart, she'd say, watching him empty his pocket, pour pennies into the hole he'd just dug. *Don't bury your ice cream money. Plant the herbs instead.*

But, Mom, he'd say, *pirates always bury their treasure.*

Then what will they do when they want a Good Humor?

They'll ask their mothers to get them one!

He'd thrown his arms around her, streaking her with mud. She hadn't minded at all. She could say that for sure—getting dirty in the garden was part of the fun. Letting him plant his spare change—it had been so adorable. They'd dig and plant and water, wedge his nickels and dimes and pennies into the soil, and then they'd head down to the beach, dive into the waves, let the salt water wash them clean.

Or was that true? Hadn't she gotten the tiniest bit impatient with him? Maybe more than a tiny bit? Had she spoken sharply about the value of everything, wanting him to appreciate what he was given? And most of all, to grow up to be different from his absent father? She'd wanted him to know, to really understand, that people worked hard for their wages. She'd wanted him to learn to value what was important— and certainly not just money.

Once when he was a teenager, he'd accused her of turning everything into a lesson. *Why can't things just be?* he'd asked. *Why does everything have to add up to some big message? Does every story have to have a moral?*

"Every story doesn't have to have a moral," she said out loud now, pulling up weeds. A seagull perched on the peak of the roof, letting out a raucous cry. She ignored it, focusing on the garden.

If anyone should know about stories not needing morals, it was Sheridan. Her songs, inspired so much by her grandmother's bright arts—love magic, the opposite of the dark arts—were about moments in time. Today, yesterday, this second, last night: specific moments of love and connection. Aphrodite's book of spells had been about lightning bolts of love: not about the whys or what-ifs.

Her cottage overlooked the beach and bay; she had her back to the blue water. It was a bright summer day, but she couldn't wait for nightfall. Days were hard. Her son should be home for the summer, having completed his freshman year of college.

They had loved their summers here at Hubbard's Point, and her body was still on Charlie-time. She couldn't help it; mornings, she'd wake up thinking she had to get him up for his summer job as lifeguard. He'd taken his responsibility seriously—keeping his eyes on all the swimmers. He'd especially watched all the little kids, and once an old man had needed reviving, and Charlie had resuscitated him.

Sheridan had known what a huge heart Charlie had, and how much he wanted to help. It was almost as if his father's inattention—his abandonment—had brought out every bit of kindness and care in Charlie's being. Sheridan worked overtime to make him feel loved, trying to make up for the fact his father had never been there. She'd poured all her love into her son, so badly wanting him to turn out well adjusted, happy, self-confident, and kind. She knew how kids with absent fathers fought an uphill climb in life; the hole in their hearts where their fathers' love should have been was almost impossible to fill. She knew that such kids were at risk for bad relationships, for not being able to bond.

But that wasn't Charlie.

Noontime, on his break from lifeguarding, she would head for the kitchen to make him a sandwich; now, instead, she'd pour herself a drink. Afternoons, she'd think about heading down for a swim, figuring she'd see him sitting on the lifeguard chair, watching out for the swimmers. Or taking a break, racing Nell out to the raft. More drinking, less thinking.

"Hey there."

Looking over her shoulder, Sheridan saw Stevie Moore coming up the hill, carrying a cloth-covered wicker basket. She wore a paint-streaked smock, which, as voluminous as it was, couldn't quite cover her pregnant belly.

"What are you doing out on such a hot day?" Sheridan called.

"All I want to do is walk," Stevie said. "It's the strangest thing."

"Maybe that means it's almost time . . ."

"I'm not due for another four weeks, but have you ever seen anyone so huge?"

Sheridan tried to smile, moving her trowel and watering can, giving Stevie a hand so she could settle herself onto the herb garden's low stone wall. Reaching into the wicker basket, Stevie pulled out an old-fashioned jar.

"Beach plum jelly," she said, handing it to Sheridan. "I've been putting up preserves."

"Thank you," Sheridan said. Her mind raced, zapping through memories of her own pregnancy, when she'd suddenly gone cooking-crazy. She'd started collecting recipes, when previously she'd hardly ever looked at one. She'd canned all the tomatoes in the vegetable patch; she'd made jam from late summer peaches, blackberries, and beach plums. Touching the cool glass jar made her remember so vividly, she nearly moaned.

"Nell's been helping me," Stevie said.

"She's a great girl," Sheridan said.

"She . . . mentioned how much she likes visiting with you."

"It's good of her to stop by. She . . . misses Charlie."

Stevie nodded. "He was a wonderful boy."

"Well, you were like an unofficial aunt to him," Sheridan said. "From the time he was born."

"Whenever Jack went away, I could always count on Charlie to help me out. Stretching canvases, hanging paintings . . . all of it. I was so happy when he and Nell started . . ." Stevie trailed off. "Sheridan, I brought you something else . . ."

Sheridan watched Stevie's hand inch into the

wicker basket again; she saw the edge of a small canvas. Suddenly she knew what else was in the basket.

"No," Sheridan said.

Stevie's hand stopped, but not before Sheridan registered everything about the small, exquisite portrait: Charlie's blond hair, bright blue eyes, the expression so full of love and humor.

"No," Sheridan said again.

"I sketched him last summer, before he left," Stevie said. "I did the painting last month, and I wanted..."

Sheridan closed her eyes and shook her head. Back and forth, back and forth, hard. If she did it long enough, she could make Stevie and the portrait disappear. All the beach kids had used to call Stevie a witch, but they'd been wrong. Stevie's magic was nothing compared to Aphrodite's. Sheridan and her sisters came from a lineage of true power. Their grandmother had taught them how to make things happen. And make other things stop.

Right now, shaking her head, saying the word "no" over and over, she was sending Stevie away. She wasn't ready to see a portrait, in oils, of her only son. Her only child, her boy Charlie. She couldn't bear seeing him captured on canvas, couldn't stand the idea of seeing him again, the most alive she'd seen him in months, brought to life by paint and the hand of an old friend...no, Sheridan couldn't stand that.

"All right, then," she heard Stevie say. "I'm so sorry, Sheridan..."

"No, no, no, no," Sheridan kept whispering, her

eyes shut so tight she saw little white stars in the purple dark.

No, no, no, no, no . . . the word sounded so hollow and empty, but somehow beautiful, like the inside of a bell. It soothed her, the way the best incantations did. It gave her power, that single word. The book of spells had an entire chapter on the word "no."

When she opened her eyes, quite a few minutes later, Stevie was gone—as Sheridan knew she would be. The seagull on the roof's peak had flown away. Sheridan glanced at the jar of beach plum preserves; her hand closed around it, and she threw it as hard as she could. The glass shattered, and the dark red jelly splashed all over the granite ledge.

The sun had moved in the sky. Afternoon was dragging on, but evening would be here soon enough. With night came peace. Sheridan could pull the shades and block out the stars and moon. She and Charlie shared the same darkness.

Digging in the herb garden, she felt close to him again. He was in the earth now. She pulled off her yellow gloves, got dirt under her fingernails. She dug out weeds, tossed them aside. The herbs' fragrance rose and surrounded her. She smelled thyme and mint. Charlie had loved to chew on mint leaves. The smell brought him back to her, and just then her fingers closed around something flat and hard.

She knew before she pulled it out: a penny. The copper was green and thin with age. Holding the coin in her hand, she flew back in time. Ten years, twelve years, fourteen years: back to when Charlie was a four-year-old pirate, burying treasure in the herb garden.

Mom, she wanted to hear him say.

Charlie, I'm here, she said, her voice thin in the salt breeze blowing up from the beach, just in case he was listening.

CHAPTER 2

NELL DITCHED TYLER AND RAN DOWN THE
seawall alone. Her best friend, Peggy McCabe,
met her at the end of the beach. They tried to
schedule the same shifts at Foley's, and generally
succeeded. Peggy sat just below the high-tide line,
wearing her yellow bathing suit and a Red Sox cap,
staring through binoculars out at the boat anchored
near the breakwater. Her nose and shoulders were
streaked with zinc oxide. Every inch of her body was
covered with freckles, and she jumped up as Nell approached.

"He's out there," Peggy said. "On the deck of his
boat."

"I know," Nell said, squinting out across the
sparkling bay. "We said five, and it's almost five."

"I can't believe he even came. Do you think he can
help?"

"We'll see," Nell said. She checked for the plastic

bag she'd tucked into the side of her bathing suit. Then she started walking toward the water's edge, followed by Peggy. But when they were ankle-deep, Nell stopped her friend. "I have to go alone."

"I'm not letting you," Peggy said stubbornly.

"Charlie will be with me," Nell said.

"Look," Peggy said. "I know you believe that—and I'm happy to indulge you most of the time, but not now. You're not swimming out to a stranger's boat alone. You're not."

"Peggy, this is for Charlie. It's..." Nell hesitated. She had to find a way to word it that Peggy would understand and accept. "It's the last thing I can do for him...and I have to do it on my own. I know it will be fine. You can watch through the binoculars, okay?"

Peggy, stubborn Irish girl that she was, started to shake her head no, but Nell grabbed her wrist and gave her "the look." It was dagger-sharp and no-nonsense; Charlie had never argued with it. Her father and Stevie wouldn't even try. Peggy opened her mouth, but then just shrugged.

"If anything happens to you, I'll never forgive myself."

Nell nodded, kissed her cheek. Wedging the plastic bag more securely into the side of her bikini bottom, she dived into the water. It felt cold and bracing, but couldn't push away Peggy's words: *If anything happens to you, I'll never forgive myself*. Nell thought of Charlie and knew how that felt. It was the most terrible feeling in the world. If she had gone to New York that weekend, everything might have been different.

She swam hard, letting the cold water and exertion numb her body. The tide was starting to go out; she rode the current a little, reaching down to check that the plastic bag was still there. She was an expert swimmer; like Charlie, she had grown up loving the water, feeling almost as at home in it as on dry land. She felt him swimming beside her now, could practically feel his leg brushing hers beneath the surface.

But Peggy's words clung to her; they haunted her, worse than any ghost. *If anything happens to you, I'll never forgive myself....* That's why Nell was swimming now, why she had made these plans, why she had a plastic bag filled with ten twenty-dollar bills shoved into her bathing suit, why she could barely sleep at night. She couldn't forgive herself, and the reality hit her just about midway to the big boat.

She hadn't been with Charlie that late summer day when he'd died; after a season of constant togetherness, of barely letting each other out of their sight, he'd finally pried himself away to start college. *One year,* he'd said, holding her; *we'll be apart your senior year, but you'll apply and get in and...* The rest was understood: *and we'll be together.*

But they weren't. And that wasn't him swimming beside her: he was dead, in the ground. All she felt was the tide, the current, the quick brush as she passed a school of minnows. Her arms felt as if they were filled with sand, but she forced herself to keep going.

* * *

GAVIN SAT ON THE *Squire Toby*'s deck, feet propped on the rail, watching the beach. The plan had been to meet at five; it was ten after the hour, and he saw no sign of approaching boats. Someone was swimming; he watched for a minute, admired the stroke, looked toward the shore again. He checked his cell phone in case he'd missed a message—nothing. He thought about checking with his service, but he knew if the client had called to change plans, they'd track him down.

Maybe the whole thing was a hoax. Could it be possible? He'd feel pretty stupid, coming all the way down from Maine, if it was. He'd been dog tired after his last case, divorce among the old guard of Mount Desert Island; old money never died, it just went to the lawyers and shuffled through bank accounts.

Gavin glanced up at the small gray cottage—there was nothing stopping him from walking up the hill to say hi. He'd been up since dawn, had swum in to the beach and taken a run. He'd gone past her house. When he'd gotten right in front, he'd slowed down, thought about running straight up the hill. But his feet had kept moving.

Five-fifteen. Gavin went down below, got a cold Heineken, came back on deck. The sun felt hot on his head, and he took a long drink, draining half the bottle. Killing time, he glanced around for the person he'd seen swimming earlier, but there was no sign. He began to scan the horizon for approaching boats.

Gavin didn't like to be kept waiting. He started to feel annoyed, drank some more.

"Hey. Hello."

He heard a voice, breathless. Looked around, didn't see anyone.

"Hello, have you got a swim ladder?"

He looked over the port side, saw a sleek head, huge green eyes peering up at him as she trod water. He gestured toward the mahogany boarding ladder in the stern and watched the young woman swim to it, then pull herself up; he gave a hand, helping her aboard.

"Gavin Dawson?" she asked.

"Yes," he said. "But you should have asked my name before you climbed onto a stranger's boat."

"I knew it was you," she said. "It had to be. You described yourself perfectly."

"Huh," he said. What had he told her? *A grizzled old detective.* He'd been being charming and self-effacing. "So. You're Nell Kilvert?"

"Yes," she said. She smoothed her long dark hair back, then reached down into the hip of her bikini bottom. She pulled out a Ziploc bag full of money and tried to hand it to him.

"Hang on," he said. "Let's not rush things. Let me get you a towel, and you can pick up where you left off on the phone."

"I'll take one of those, too," she said, pointing at the Heineken.

He didn't even bother replying to that. He went below, pulled a fresh towel out of the locker, got himself another Heineken and her a nice can of root beer. When he returned to the deck, he gestured at the two chairs. She wrapped the towel around her and sat down, accepting the soda without comment.

Gavin stared at her, and he felt his own Hubbard's Point past coming to meet him.

"You look just like Jack," he said.

"My dad," she said, taking a slug of root beer. "Although a lot of people think I look like my mom."

"Emma," he said. "I knew her well."

"You were part of the old crowd," she said, and it wasn't a question. "I've heard all about you."

"Is that why you called me?"

She nodded. "Yep."

"Well, that's flattering, but I know there are people right here who could help you."

"I know," she said. "My best friend Peggy McCabe's uncle Joe is an FBI guy, and there's Patrick Murphy, a retired cop, and others, and everyone knows them all, but none of them are right for this."

"No offense, Nell, but how would you know that? You're how old?"

"Eighteen," she said.

"And you think Joe and Patrick aren't quite up to the job?"

"That's right," she said.

"Why's that?"

"Because they follow the rules," she said.

Gavin stared at her as she gazed off the stern at a patch of rough water. He tracked her gaze. There was nothing visible on the bay's smooth surface, but he knew a school of something had just passed beneath. When he looked back at Nell, he found her staring at him.

"You don't," she said. "Or at least you didn't when you were a kid here."

"Guess I still don't," he said. "Much."

"I think that's why Charlie's mother liked you so much. And Stevie, too."

"Stevie?" he asked, just because he wasn't sure he was ready to discuss Sheridan.

"Stevie Moore," she said. "She lives with my father. And me."

"Stevie was a free spirit," he said.

"She still is," Nell said. "And so is Charlie's mom. Her music is amazing. Or it used to be...until Charlie died. Now she doesn't write or play at all. She hardly does anything. She visits his grave..."

Gavin let that sink in.

Nell closed her eyes for a long moment, then opened them. "Honestly, I didn't really expect you to come. The thing is, I didn't know where else to turn. No one's doing anything." She sat still in the canvas deck chair, staring across the placid water. She was the picture of calm, except for the tears that had begun to stream down her face.

Gavin stared at her. In his work, he faced a lot of emotional people; he was good at hardening his heart against stories of betrayal, lust, and marital intrigue. But watching this girl, her expression impassive, tears leaking from her green eyes, made him

have to look away. He went down below, came back
with a handful of paper towels.

"What should people be doing?" he asked.

"Investigating more."

"The papers said he was murdered."

"Yes."

"What happened?"

"He was in New York, and got mugged, and the
cops said it was random..." She broke off, her face
crumpling. Gavin took a breath, knew he had to slow
her down if he wanted her to get through it.

"Why was he in New York?" he asked.

"He moved there last August, a year ago... to start
his freshman year."

"College?"

Nell nodded. "NYU. He wanted to be a filmmaker,
and they have the best program anywhere. It's hard
to get in there, and Charlie didn't have, well, the most
straightforward academic record. He was so smart,
and athletic—but sometimes he had a hard time concentrating in school. He always wanted to be *doing*
things, not just sitting and studying. But he was so
talented, he really had a vision, even though he was
so young. The admissions people couldn't not let him
in when they saw how passionate he was...."

Passionate. Sheridan's son; not a surprise. Gavin
filed the information away, then backtracked.

"What do you mean, he didn't have a straightforward academic record?"

"Well, he went to a few different schools, depending on where his mom was recording. They lived in

Nashville, then New York, then back to Nashville, and then senior year here at Hubbard's Point. He was a year ahead of me, but we were at the same school . . . Black Hall."

Gavin nodded, wondering about Sheridan, trying to imagine what had made her come back here to Hubbard's Point year-round—this had always been her summer place. He'd been used to seeing her in beach weather; but he remembered the December he'd stood with her in the cold, the snow falling around them, and he'd loved her more than ever. Over eighteen years ago now . . .

"His grades were okay, not great," Nell continued. "Charlie loved living life, not studying it. That's why he was out so late that night. The cops acted almost as if it was his fault, going down by the river . . ."

"The river?"

Nell nodded. "The East River. That's where he was murdered."

"You said it was late?"

"Three a.m."

Gavin looked at her. He thought of a young kid in Manhattan, out doing whatever, wrong place–wrong time. Tenderness wasn't his strong suit. But she had mentioned Sheridan a few moments ago, Sheridan not making music, just visiting her son's grave, and Nell herself looked so haunted and vulnerable, so Gavin made his voice gentle.

"The cops think he was mugged?" he asked.

"Yes, but he wasn't!" she said vehemently.

"Why do you sound so sure about that?"

"Because of Charlie," she said. "If you knew him..." She looked down at her knees, pulling words together. "He was...you'd just, if there were any choice, any choice at all of people to mug, he wouldn't be the one you'd pick."

"Was he big?"

"Well, sort of," Nell said. "But that wasn't it. He was tall, muscular, really lean from running. But it was more the way he moved, and the way he could look at you. As if he could see through you, read your mind, and know everything you wanted, all at the same time."

Gavin listened. She wasn't convincing him. The rough water moved closer to the boat, and Gavin saw flashes of silver: a school of bait closely followed by something bigger. He registered the dark horizontal lines of a big striper. It rose, then disappeared, and he stared at the patch of water where it had been.

"He'd spent time in cities his whole life," she said defiantly.

"Well, that doesn't make him immune." He wanted to give her some words of wisdom about young men thinking they're invulnerable, about Charlie having been out late in a place he probably shouldn't have been, but she cut him off.

"It would be like someone mugging you," she said.

That got his attention. "What do you mean?"

"Like what I said before: if a mugger had the choice, do you think he'd pick you?"

"No," Gavin said, not immodestly. He was six

three, one-ninety, all muscle, just like the striper, and not lean like a runner, not to mention licensed to carry and unlicensed to do a good deal more. "But then again, I'm not lean."

Nell peered at him, frowning with displeasure. "Who cares how big you are? If the guy wants to kill you, the way they did with Charlie, you think your big football shoulders are going to stop him?"

"It wasn't football," Gavin said.

"Well, whatever sport. The point is, I'm talking about a look in your eyes. Kind of like a force field . . . somewhere between a laser and a razor, and Charlie had it—it was, it was like an aura of danger. It came from either not caring or caring too much—I was never sure exactly which. Charlie was badass; you wouldn't mess with him. You just wouldn't."

Gavin suddenly knew what she meant—"the look." He'd seen it in the mirror, and he spotted it on the street. He was surprised she could put it into words, this young girl from the beach. What did she know about badass?

"The police investigated?"

"Yes," she said, sounding sullen.

"You think they got it wrong?"

"I *know* they got it wrong," she said.

"Why was he down by the river?"

"Who knows? If you knew Charlie, you'd realize that he went where he wanted. It was a hot summer night, and he was probably trying to catch a breeze." Her throat caught. "He loved rivers, but he was probably wishing he were here at Hubbard's Point, at the beach..."

"Who was he there with?"

"No one. I told you—it was hot. He loved being by the water. Here, even in Nashville—the river there. Going to the water inspired him. He was already working on a documentary, even though his classes hadn't really started yet. Maybe he was thinking about that, trying to clear his head."

"What was he making the documentary on?"

"His father, sort of, but not really," Nell said, impatient. She wanted to tell the story in her own way. But just hearing the words "his father" got Gavin in the fighting spirit.

"What made him want to do a documentary sort-of-but-not-really about his father?" Gavin asked. "Is his father dead?"

"No," Nell said.

Too bad, Gavin thought, staring at the water. His gaze lifted toward the Point. Here he was, anchored off Hubbard's Point after a long trip south from Maine. Nell was watching him, waiting for him to tell her whether he'd take the job or not, whether he'd keep the soggy bag of money she'd brought as his retainer.

He'd already signed on—from the moment in Maine he'd heard her say the words "Sheridan Ross-lare's son." The rest of it didn't much matter. Gavin had heard about Charlie's death right after it happened. He'd thought of it every day since then, thought of Sheridan. He'd written her a hundred notes, ripped them all up. He would have sent flowers, but he had the feeling that wouldn't have helped Sheridan. She had made her wishes clear that snowy day nearly two decades ago, and he'd worked hard to find an uneasy peace and respect those wishes.

As hopeless as he thought the case was—pretty clearly a straightforward mugging—he knew he'd be getting police reports, interviewing witnesses, talking to the cops and whatever assistant DA had been assigned to the crime. He turned to look at Nell. She might be his new client, but he wouldn't be doing the work for her.

"What does his mother think?" he asked.

"Charlie's mother?"

He nodded. "Yes. Sheridan."

"Think of . . . what?"

"Of your calling me."

Nell paused. "She doesn't know."

That brought him up short. "Then how did you contact me?"

"Not through her," Nell said quietly but sharply. "From what Charlie said, your name wasn't to be mentioned in the house. I found you because I remembered some things Charlie told me about you—his aunts told him you and Sheridan used to be together. But you broke up, right?"

"Something like that."

"They said you almost got married."

"Aunts don't always know much."

Nell snorted. "Trust me, Charlie's aunts know everything, especially Agatha. She's a one-woman Psychic Friends Network. Spooky..."

Gavin smiled, remembering Agatha and her more suburban-styled sister, Bunny. Sheridan had certainly had a colorful family. "Okay, so what did Charlie tell you his aunts told him about me?"

"Well, that you're a detective doing private investigations for some big-deal divorce lawyer, that you live on your boat wherever the work takes you, and that you have an answering service in Hawthorne."

"Close enough."

"He thought you sounded cool."

"That's me," Gavin said. "Cool."

She smiled. He saw her staring down at a scrap of towel tied around her ankle. As she gazed at it, her eyes filled again with tears.

"I should have been there," she whispered.

"With Charlie?"

She nodded. "It was so hard for us, being apart; we'd had the whole school year and summer together, and seeing him pack up to go to college—it was crazy-terrible. He'd only been gone a week; he called me, and we talked about my heading into the city for the weekend."

Gavin was silent, waiting.

"I should have gone in. But it was so hot," she said, crying softly. "The last weekend of summer, and a heat wave hit, and I wanted to stay at the beach. Why didn't he get out of the city? I wanted him to take the train back out here... We argued about it."

"But he was trying to settle into college."

She nodded, wiping her eyes.

Gavin knew about forks in the road. Going left, and only later realizing that if you'd gone right everything in your life would have been different. Split-second decisions—or ones you had the chance to consider for years. The choice of who to love, what to do, whether to stay together...

He closed his eyes for just a few seconds, picturing Sheridan in the snow. He could see the curve of her pregnant belly, the way she'd cradled it with her arms. She was wearing a down parka, sitting on a big chunk of granite, one of the many rocks in her grandmother's yard. The way her arms had encircled her belly, as if she were holding not herself, but her baby. He was already so real to her; she'd loved him so much.

Gavin stared at Nell Kilvert, waiting for her tears to stop.

She looked up at him, eyes still damp but defiant.

"So, you'll take the case?"

Gavin nodded. He reached into his wallet and handed Nell his card, complete with all his contact info. She tried to hand him the money again, more insistently. He shook his head.

"Keep it," he said. "I'll bill you later."

"What's your rate?"

He shrugged, staying silent as the sound of the water played against the hull of his boat.

"Come on. I want to make sure I can afford you."

"You can. I'm cheap," he said, gazing across the bay and up the hill toward Sheridan's house again. He saw someone standing outside, near the herb garden. Or maybe it was just a shadow. The sun was bouncing off the bay, and the light was in his eyes.

CHAPTER 3

THE ROSSLARES' HILLTOP COTTAGE WAS DIF-
ferent in many ways from any other house at
Hubbard's Point. From the outside it might have
looked the same: set between the road on one side
and the beach on the other, perched on the granite
ledge, built of salt-silvered shingles with white shutters and a blue door, with green window boxes overflowing with petunias, and a brick chimney on the
north side. It was pretty and sweet, a typical New
England seaside cottage.

But inside was another story. The Rosslare women
had had witch powers through the generations. Sheridan Le Fanu Rosslare, the current owner, was a singer-
songwriter who had for years divided her time between
New York and Nashville, summering in Hubbard's
Point. Her powers were concentrated in the music
she wrote, and the rooms overflowed with sheet music, CDs, notebooks, acoustic guitars, electric guitars,
amps, headsets, and, recently, bottles of bourbon.

Sheridan's music equipment was layered over her mother's and grandmother's belongings. Eccentricity and witchcraft had basically skipped a generation in her mother, Clio, a good mom who had lost her husband too young to cancer, then put herself through teacher's college while raising Sheridan and her two sisters. Clio's contribution to the décor included books, more books, and many more books.

The grand matriarch, Sheridan's grandmother, was known by a single name: Aphrodite. She was Irish with a brogue so thick few Hubbard's Pointers could understand her. She'd been born blind outside Dublin, grown up in the Wicklow Mountains—in the town of Glencree, so small it didn't even have a sign, now known for its international center of peace and reconciliation, located in former British barracks. Her town was an axis of both peace and violence, and it seemed to spawn witches: her grandmother, mother, and aunts all practiced a form of magic called *Aphrodeen*—white witchcraft found mainly in Ireland, devoted to filling the world with love. Aphrodite was named after the Irish witches' patron, the goddess of love.

From a young age, although blind, Aphrodite had been gifted with second sight. Aphrodite could see with her heart. She had an instinct for love, and her mother and grandmother taught her which herbs to grow, which spells to chant, how a well-placed snippet of hair could make two people fall in love with each other, how patience and the willingness to listen could help a person see the truth in all things.

She inherited a collection of books containing spells and enchantments; there was always someone who would read them out loud to her.

Aphrodite had another gift: the ability to call the dead. She had been taught by her mother and grandmother that love never dies, and that the living need help contacting their beloveds who'd gone before them. They'd told her she'd refined her other senses, including the one that didn't have a name, the sixth sense that allows connection with those who have passed on. Growing up in the rugged Wicklow Mountains, along the Military Road and the site of so much bloodshed, she had found that long-dead soldiers wanted to talk to her.

Walking through the thick heather of Wicklow's moorland, she would often have company: the ghosts of rebels who'd been killed in uprisings, both men and women, asking her to lay flowers on the graves of their sweethearts, asking her to give messages to their children and grandchildren. And Aphrodite would always do her best to do as they asked.

One of the ghosts had a grandson, James Rosslare. He was a wild boy, prone to dares and risk-taking. Growing up in the mountains, he'd scale any peak, jump the widest fissures, inch along crumbling ledges, dangle off cliff edges. One time he'd broken into St. Kevin's 110-foot-tall round tower at Glendalough, climbed the corkscrew stairs to the top, then exited through a narrow window and tried to scale the very peak using mountain-climbing gear. He would have succeeded, except the caretaker spied him hanging from a rappelling line and called the police.

Aphrodite found James the next day, to give him the message from his grandfather.

The police had released him with his promise never to try such a thing again, and he and Aphrodite had sat together, under a tree in his backyard. She'd tried to explain the impossible—that James's long-dead grandfather was worried about his pranks.

"Not just because you could fall from such a great height," Aphrodite had explained, "but because it's not right for you to climb Saint Kevin's holy tower . . . it's sacrilegious."

"Saint Kevin didn't seem to mind," James had said, laughing. "Only the caretaker did."

"The caretaker and your grandfather," Aphrodite had said gently. "He told me to say this to you: 'Seamai, have more respect, will you?'"

"He called me Seamai?" James had asked, pronouncing it "Shay-mee," the affectionate way his grandfather always had. His laughter stopped.

"Yes."

"He was the only one who did."

"He also told me with all that sugar you put in your tea, it's a wonder you can't—"

"Fly," James had said, growing pale. "He said that? You heard him?"

"He did, yes. And yes . . . I heard him."

"He used to tease me about that."

Aphrodite nodded. "He said you'd fly all the way to—"

"America," James had said, shocked. "He wanted me to go there."

"Then maybe you should put your energy into that, instead of climbing sacred towers," she said.

A year later, Aphrodite and James got married. And a year after that, moved to America. James used his daredevil ways to find work at the power company—a lineman who'd scale phone poles and work in any weather. He made more in overtime than anyone on his crew, and within five years, he and Aphrodite had bought this salty, rustic cottage in Hubbard's Point.

Americans were less open to the sixth sense, the one located in the heart. They'd always been suspicious of witches. Hubbard's Point was just a state away from Massachusetts, where women had been burned and hanged as witches just for living unusual lives.

Time went on, and their daughter and granddaughters helped her grow herbs in their seaside garden. Aphrodite would teach them spells, encourage them to believe in love and express their feelings about things that mattered. Sheridan had learned the lesson as a child, grown up weaving her love and beliefs into her songs.

She remembered sitting on her grandmother's lap, being held and rocked. Aphrodite was barely five two, no more than ninety pounds. But when Sheridan sat on her lap, it felt like the whole world. Sheridan would lean back into her grandmother's arms, feeling safe and protected. Aphrodite would sing softly, teaching

Sheridan songs as they rocked on the porch. That was how Sheridan learned to harmonize.

The song she wrote that started her career, "Annie Glover," was about the last woman hanged as a witch in Boston. Annie was an Irish washerwoman, sent to Barbados as a slave by the Englishman Oliver Cromwell in the 1650s. Her husband died there, and she and her daughter were then sent to Boston, to work for the John Goodwin family.

In 1688, four of the five Goodwin children became ill. Witch fever was in full swing, and when a doctor concluded "nothing but a Hellish Witchcraft could be responsible for these Maladies," they looked to Annie. She was a practicing Catholic—had refused to renounce her religion. And she had recently been accused of stealing laundry from the family, and was therefore suspected of harboring a grudge against them.

Reverend Cotton Mather interrogated her; Annie spoke in her native Irish, refusing to answer him in English. Reverend Mather—later of the Salem witch trials—condemned her to death by hanging, saying, "The court could have no answer from her but in Irish." In his *Magnalia Christi Americana*, he called her "a scandalous old Irishwoman, very poor, a Roman Catholic, and obstinate in idolatry." And on November 16, 1688, Annie Glover was hanged in Boston. They called her a witch, but her greater crime had been a refusal to give up what mattered most to her: her religion, her language, the things she believed in.

Sheridan had been so moved by the story, and the

way her grandmother told it. She'd always known
that magic didn't come from outside: it came from
your heart, from the strongest beliefs, from love.
When she was sixteen, she wrote a song from the per-
spective of Annie's daughter:

> *My mother told the truth, in the language she*
>   *loved*
> *Their minds were made up, she was already*
>   *wrong.*
> *The men of Boston hanged Annie Glover*
> *They didn't understand, so they killed my*
>   *mother. . . .*

Sheridan's mother was so proud, she recorded the
song on a cheap tape recorder, entered it in the Newport "new talent" folk song competition. Sheridan
won. The whole family went to Newport for the day.
The festival was held at Fort Adams, a Revolutionary
War installation on the edge of Narragansett Bay.

With the backdrop of Newport Harbor—the water
so blue, with boats with white sails skimming in and
out, around the headland, with the lights of the long,
graceful bridge starting to twinkle in the rose-amber
twilight, they saw Sheridan take the stage with her
acoustic guitar—a used dreadnought with a ragged
hole in the front.

Sheridan looked so small, nearly overwhelmed by
the guitar. Her reddish-blond hair glinted in the
dying sunlight, and her blue eyes looked fierce and
bright, searching for her family in the large crowd.

Standing at the microphone, she spoke: "I'd like to dedicate this song to my mother and grandmother, and to Annie and her daughter, and to the misunderstood everywhere." Her courage came from learning to sing for someone else, one boy back at the beach. . . .

She began to sing—with passion, straight from her heart—and the crowd didn't move or breathe until she was finished. Then everyone gathered at Fort Adams broke into a wild cheer. She was only sixteen, but already she understood love down to her bones. A star was born, and she'd never looked back.

Sheridan's family supported her. She finished high school, but instead of going to college, she moved to New York to play punk and new wave. Later she signed with a record label and went to Nashville to start recording. Everyone in the family took turns heading south to visit her, keep her grounded in the family—her mother, grandmother, and both sisters. Between recording sessions, she'd always return north, home to Hubbard's Point.

When Aphrodite died—a year after her daughter Clio, who'd had a sudden heart attack while, blessedly, listening to Mozart at an afternoon concert—she'd left her magic things to her three granddaughters. Her gardening equipment had all gone to Floribunda, or "Bunny." Named after a rose, Bunny had the gift of a green thumb; her Black Hall house was the pride of the local garden club, always a favorite on the annual spring house and garden tour.

Many of the magic books, her white crockery mortars and pestles, and her black iron cauldron had gone to Agatha. Agatha had always loved to cook and bake, and of all the sisters, she had been the most avid about magic. She lived in a cottage behind the Renwick Inn, and she'd hung out a shingle offering *Love Spells and Other Magical Thinges*. Bunny scolded her, saying there was no such word as "thinges," but Agatha didn't care—she did a land-office business every summer.

With three girls and only one house, arrangements had to be made. Agatha and Bunny both lived in town. But Charlie loved it at the Point, and Sheridan couldn't stand to let go of her grandmother's cottage. So she'd bought her sisters' shares, and now owned the Rosslare cottage and the rest of Aphrodite's belongings—including her book of spells, a deep and powerful source of inspiration for Sheridan's songs.

Sheridan sat in the living room now. The shades were drawn; the setting sun's light hurt her eyes, and the luminosity of twilight was almost too much to bear. She heard crickets in the garden, birds calling from the trees. Her eyes fell on her Gibson acoustic, on the mother-of-pearl inlay along the fret board. A line of light came through a crack in the shades, making the inlay glint. Her fingers twitched, but she couldn't pick up the guitar.

This was where she had written that first song, "Annie Glover." The air of Hubbard's Point was filled with beautiful noise. She remembered sitting here with her grandmother, Aphrodite teaching her to quiet down and listen. The waves rolled in perfect rhythm, more steady than any metronome. Bees would swarm the honeysuckle vine growing out front, their electric hum coming through the screens.

Sheridan and her grandmother would sing, sometimes soft like a lullaby and sometimes exuberant and loud. Aphrodite would let Sheridan look through the magic books for spells, and she'd turn them into lyrics about love and loss and hope and dreams. They'd sing the songs she wrote, harmonizing with each other's voices.

They'd sing for each other, for Sheridan's mother and sisters, and for everyone they'd loved who had died. Aphrodite told her that the more beautiful the music, the higher it could reach toward heaven. Sheridan had written with one boy in mind: some of her language came from the book, but all of her feelings came from him. That was so long ago; he had long since been gone from her life.

Now a brass clock ticking on the mantel was the only sound. The air felt still and warm, the dark shades blocking the sea breeze. Sheridan sat on the loveseat with her eyes closed, an almost-empty glass of Wild Turkey in her hand. In a few minutes, when the sun was officially down, she'd refill her glass. But it bothered her, drinking in the near-dark, wondering what her grandmother would think to see her now.

The light faded slowly, the sharpness of lines coming through the cracks dimming and softening until finally the whole room was in shadow. The sun-faded coral and teal slipcovers were now gray; the bright hooked rugs were as dull as sand; the colorful book spines were just one solid wall of muddy nothing.

Sheridan sat in the darkness. She reached onto the shelf beside her, pulled a framed photo close, held it against herself, glass side pressed to her chest. She couldn't bear looking at the actual picture—couldn't take seeing Charlie's eyes.

She thought about lighting a candle. She sometimes did at this time of day. Growing up, there had always been candles burning, not for the light they gave, but for remembrance. Her grandmother used to say the flame honored a person's spirit, reminded the living that the dead were never really gone.

But they were; Charlie was gone. Sheridan wished her grandmother were still alive so the two of them could sing to Charlie. They could harmonize, sing the most beautiful song there was, send the notes up to heaven for Charlie. But that was crazy, and she knew it. Charlie was gone, and he'd never hear her sing for him again.

Holding the picture, Sheridan refilled her glass. Bourbon warmed her and made her thoughts fuzzy. She savored the smoky taste; it brought back feelings of being in the South, driving on back roads in a pickup truck, singing songs—writing them as she drove, words and lyrics straight from her feelings. The landscape was gentle, bluegrass and knobs and limestone quarries, smoke drifting up from chimneys in the hills. When it rained in Tennessee and Kentucky, the mud was full of chalk, swirly and white, runoff from the limestone.

When Charlie was little, she'd have him with her in his car seat. Well, most of the time. When she wasn't recording or touring... Sometimes, not often, he'd stay with one of her sisters or her mother and grandmother, right here in this very house. The tour bus of a Nashville almost-star had been a tough place for a little boy. Taking him on the road had been difficult, but she'd needed him near her. She'd had to overcome the fact his father had never been a part of his life.

But he'd had a grandmother, and a great-grandmother, and aunts, and near-aunts who'd loved him. Sheridan's friends at the beach—Stevie, Maddie, Rumer, Dana, Bay, Tara—they'd all pitched in with one another's kids. That's the kind of place Hubbard's Point was, Sheridan thought, taking another sip. A place so full of love and care it could almost make up for other emptiness...

She thought of Charlie's last year. They'd spent it right here in this house; Sheridan had taken the time off from recording. She'd needed something she wasn't getting—from the studio, the road, her fans. New York didn't have it, and neither did Nashville— so she'd come home. Enrolled Charlie in Black Hall High for his senior year; he hadn't minded being uprooted from his friends in Nashville because it had meant him being closer to Nell. They'd been best summer friends, with romance gaining intensity once they'd hit sixteen. After that, no one could keep them apart.

Just then she heard a creak—someone walking on

the porch. Boards groaning under human weight—not a ghost, that's for sure. Even so, she felt spooked. No one visited her—she'd let people know that visitors were not welcome. Not that she didn't love her friends, she always would, but she just didn't want to see them anymore. The days of hanging around with friends were over.

Three things:

First, she saw the silhouette of someone tall and broad standing at the door. He was backlit by the fading light of the summer day, and she saw his shape through the thin cotton curtain hanging on the small square window of the back door.

Second, he knocked. Actually, he tapped. Just the lightest pressure of knuckles against glass. Staring at his outline, she watched how tentative he was. She had the feeling he didn't want to disturb her; even more, she had the sense he knew that she couldn't take noise. Anything loud, a harsh rap or a real knock, would make her jump out of her skin. So whoever the stranger was, he was considerate.

Third, he wasn't a stranger. She knew him instantly. Even though she couldn't see his face, couldn't get a clear look at his hair or eyes or mouth or anything, and although she hadn't seen him in nearly twenty years, she knew it was Gavin. She just knew.

He knocked again, no louder than the first time. Sheridan pushed herself off the loveseat, drifted toward the door. She didn't make a sound, didn't want him to know she was home. She stood in the middle of the room, not even breathing.

"Sheridan?" His voice came through the glass.

She didn't move. She didn't want to see or talk to him. But if she had, she'd probably want to ask him what had taken him so long. Where had the twenty years gone, where had he been all this time?

"Sheridan?" he asked, knocking again.

Standing still, Sheridan felt his presence through the door. It was a current passing through wood and glass, into her skin and bones, as if she'd bumped into an electric fence. She leaned into it, feeling as if it were holding her up.

One last knock, and then he walked away. She heard his footsteps on the porch. After they faded, she walked to the door, drew back the curtain and gazed out. Her knees were shaking. The sky was dark blue, filling with hot stars. Her yard needed mowing, and the tall grass was alive with fireflies, their liquid gold-green neon lighting up the night.

The big man stood on the rock ledge. At first she thought he was gazing down the hill, toward the beach. But then she realized he was bent over from the waist, picking something up. Glass glinted—the jar of Stevie's preserves that Sheridan had smashed on the rocks. Gavin was gathering up the bits of broken glass.

When he was finished, he walked down the hill to the garbage can behind the garage. She heard the tinkling of glass as he dumped it in. Peering out the window, she figured he'd walked away.

But no—he came back up the hill, went to the rock ledge, and sat down. And just sat there in the darkness, surrounded by fireflies. She stood mesmerized, the aftereffects of electric shock, staring.

She leaned against the kitchen door, separated from Gavin by an inch of wood and a pane of glass, and closed her eyes and felt her heart trying to break out of its cage.

GAVIN KNEW SHE WAS INSIDE. Not that he saw or heard her—he just knew. Her spooky blind Irish grandmother had supposedly had some weird sixth sense, but so did Gavin. His came in the form of superfine instincts, valuable for detection and crime solving. He had eyes in the back of his head. He had the vision of a hawk and the hearing of a panther. Did panthers have good hearing?

The problem was, his instincts had failed him just now. So attuned to Sheridan hiding in the dark, inside her closed-up house, he'd missed the fact a goddamn broken jar was lying right on the rocks. He stepped smack on the upraised jagged edge, and it had cut clear through his goddamn deck shoes. The sole of his right foot was bleeding like crazy.

Sitting on the rock, he pulled off his ruined shoe and inspected the damage. Bugs were buzzing around his head, damn fireflies. He swatted one but good, got glow juice on his fingers. He tried to see his foot in the dark—the cut looked deep, but he'd been sliced up worse. He was glad for the chance to sit down, have an excuse to stay in Sheridan's yard a little longer. If she came out to yell at him, he'd tell her it was the least she could do, considering he'd sliced his foot open on her smashed jelly jar.

His fingers were sticky from the jelly and from his blood. He wiped them on the granite and instantly cut his finger on a tiny shard of glass left behind. This was not his night . . .

Or maybe it was. He hadn't been this close to Sheridan in over eighteen years. He felt rocked; their last meeting had been right here—in her grandmother's yard, on this very boulder. The evening had been freezing cold, snow starting to fall, and they'd sat huddled together. She'd had something to tell him, and he'd had something to tell her right back.

He'd wanted to put his arm around her, to keep her warm, but she wouldn't let him. She was pregnant, and had broken up with him already—what had made him think she would change her mind?

Tonight was warm, but he felt frozen in place. He couldn't have moved if he wanted to. The sound of waves hitting the beach drifted up the hill. He stared down at his boat, moored out by the breakwater. Hard to believe it was just hours earlier he'd talked to Nell Kilvert.

He wondered whether Sheridan had somehow found out—maybe she'd spotted his fine Chris-Craft and been inspired to pick up binocs to check it out, seen him conferring with her son's girlfriend.

Or maybe she had no idea he was in the area. Either way, it didn't much matter—he wasn't going anywhere. He heard a door creak open behind him. The fabric of a long dress swished through the tall grass, sounding just like the breeze. She stood behind him, and he heard her breathing.

"What happened to your foot?" she asked.

"Cut it on broken glass," he said. "Maybe you shouldn't go throwing jars at the rocks."

"That's what you get for trespassing in the dark."

"You got me there," he acknowledged.

He still hadn't turned around, and he couldn't. He wasn't afraid of much, but he was afraid to look into her eyes. She handed him a wet cloth; he took it without looking over his shoulder.

"Thank you," he said.

"Could you please not sit on that rock?" she asked.

"This—"

"I don't like seeing you on that rock."

He nodded; so she was remembering that winter day, too. They had sat right here, with snow falling on them and the rock. . . . He stood, and it hurt to put weight on his foot, but he wasn't going to let her see that. When he turned around, she was standing right there.

Small, slim, with the same thick mane of hair she'd always had. In his memory, and on the covers of her CDs, her long hair was auburn, touched with glints of gold. But here, even in the dark, he could see that it was now pure white.

"I went gray overnight," she said, seeing the shock in his eyes. "It's not an old wives' tale; it really does happen."

"I'm sorry," he said.

"That I have white hair?"

"No," he said. "About Charlie..."

She shook her head and put her hands over her ears. "Shh, shh. Don't say his name," she said. "Not after dark, not with blood on the rock."

He stared at her, wanting to take her thin wrists in his hands, pull her to him and hold her and rock her and not say his name.

When they were young, he'd sometimes laughed at her grandmother's old-world ways, at her superstitions and magic, at the way she'd tell them to never step over a broom, to never pick a rose in the fog, to never speak a name of the dead between twilight and midnight. He'd always known that Sheridan believed in her grandmother's powers.

Sheridan lowered her hands, bent from the waist to look at Gavin's foot. Without facing him, she started leading him toward the house.

"You'd better come inside and wash that off," she said. "I wouldn't want you to get an infection and blame me."

"No," he said. "We wouldn't want that." He hobbled and hopped his way through her yard. She walked ahead, not helping him.

When they got to the porch, she stopped and turned, looked him in the eye for the first time. He smelled bourbon, but she didn't seem the least bit unsteady. Her expression was wild, though; he thought she was about to scream. Their eyes locked for ten, fifteen seconds, the words trapped in her throat. He thought she was about to break in half. But then she calmed herself.

"After I wash the blood off, you'll have to go," she said.

"Whatever you say," he said.

She led him to a kitchen chair. He looked around; he was in a time machine, back to their youth. Everything looked the same: the cracked linoleum floor, the wooden table and chairs painted with so many different coats of paint he could see a lifetime of Rosslare décor in the layers; bouquets of herbs upside-down and drying from the rafters; shelves filled with jars of dried and powdered herbs, seashells, channeled-whelk egg cases, mice skulls, owl pellets, birds' eggs, goldfinch and blue jay feathers.

"Nothing has changed," he said as she filled a basin with warm water. She didn't reply, and suddenly he heard the harshness she must have heard in his words: *everything* had changed. "Well, what I mean is, success hasn't spoiled you. Big-time Nashville recording star, and you still don't live in a mansion."

"Not so big-time," she said.

"C'mon," he said. "I hear you on the radio."

She tested the temperature. He watched her, wondering what she'd say if he told her he had all her CDs, that he'd gotten an iPod just to listen to her in remote locations. He kept his mouth shut. She crouched down, soaked a cloth in the water.

"Hey," he said, "is this going to hurt?"

"Probably."

"Could I have a drink?"

She stared at him, obviously wanting to find a way to wiggle out of it. But instead she stood up, filled two glasses from the bottle of Wild Turkey on the counter, and handed him one. They clinked and drank it down.

"You ready?" she asked.

"Yep," he said.

She washed the cut. It was wide and deep, and even though her touch was soft, it seared like hell.

"You should get stitches," she said, drying his foot and opening a tube of ointment.

"It's not that bad," he said.

"Well..." she said, dabbing on the ointment. When she was finished, she wrapped his foot in a piece of gauze and taped it. "I think you should probably get stitches anyway."

"Okay, Dr. Rosslare," he said.

Now that she had finished with his foot, she sat back on her heels and looked up at him. Taking stock, maybe. He knew he looked weathered, older. Some guys got soft as they aged, but Gavin had hardened. Not just from his workouts, but from what he'd been through along the way. He'd found little to love in life; he figured she could see that just by looking at him.

Sheridan, on the other hand, looked beautiful. Loss and grief had given her a porcelain-type breakability that made him want to pick her up and hold her. Her white hair looked almost silver in the kitchen light; it was shocking next to her fine skin and clear blue eyes, mysterious and sexy. There were a few lines around the corners of her eyes, reminders of when she used to laugh.

"Sheridan . . ." he said.

"Well, I guess you're all patched up now. Except for your shoe; I'm sorry about that."

"Don't worry about it." He stared at her, wondering what to say next. He was almost never at a loss for words. She stared back; he could feel her wanting to ask why he'd come, but she held back.

"You know why I'm here?" he asked, meeting her more than halfway.

She shook her head.

"I've come to find out what happened."

She just stared, her blue eyes glinting. "Happened?"

"To Charlie," he said.

"Oh God, I told you. Stop."

She jumped up, and in the kitchen light he saw the agony in her eyes and knew that the prohibition had nothing to do with magic or superstition or the hours between sunset and midnight: it was just because she missed her boy so much. Or maybe an old reason: because having Gavin here reminded her of all that had been between them, and all the chances he'd blown.

"Sheridan, I'm sorry . . ."

"I didn't ask you," she said, pacing. "I didn't call you here, and I don't want anything from you."

"I realize that," he said.

"Then go, okay? Just stop whatever you think you're doing to help, and go. That's what will help."

"I can't," he said.

"What do you mean?"

"As you said, you didn't ask me. You're not my client."

"Jesus, someone hired you?"

He nodded. He waited for her to ask him who, and he was ready with his standard "I'm sorry I'm not at liberty to divulge" disclaimer. But she didn't ask. She just stood in the middle of the room, looking as if language, heart, and everything else had just deserted her. Then she picked up the bottle of Wild Turkey.

"Sheridan," he said.

"You didn't know him, Gavin," she said. "He was . . . he was so beautiful. Just a beautiful, wonderful boy."

"I'm sure that's true," he said. "He was your son."

"I don't know why you think finding out 'what happened' will make a difference, will make anything better. I already know what happened. My son was killed."

"I know," Gavin said. "I'm so . . ."

"So sorry," she said, nodding. She spoke with a soft voice, and a slight but noticeable—although he hadn't heard it earlier—Nashville accent.

"Sheridan, I am."

"Thank you. I do appreciate that. Now, if you'll excuse me, I'm going to turn in. It's getting late, and I'm, I'm just so tired. I've . . . it's been good seeing you again, Gavin. Thank you for coming by."

"Coming by?" he asked quietly. Did she think it was a social call, that it was anything less than the most important thing he'd done in years?

"Yes."

"Sheridan..."

"Gavin," she said, desperation showing in her eyes. He knew she was about to shatter, that she couldn't take this anymore.

"Okay," he said. He took a step forward, feeling a pull to hug her. But she turned her back, walked out of the room still holding her bottle of Wild Turkey.

She'd said it was getting late...it was eight-fifty. Did she really go to bed at this hour? He followed her into the living room. She didn't notice, but just walked up the wooden stairs, as if she were a ghost or a sleepwalker, leaving him to stand alone in the middle of the room.

Gavin looked around. He knew there was plenty to learn about Charlie Rosslare, right here in this room, information that could help him investigate. But all his attention was on the staircase. Sheridan had been right there, and now she was gone. He heard her footsteps on the floorboards up above. He stared at the stairs' well-worn treads and polished oak banister, trying to will her to come back down.

But she didn't, so he left. He limped out of the house, leaving his ruined deck shoe and a bunch of bloody footprints behind. Sheridan had said he should get stitches, but she hadn't offered to drive him to the hospital. And he didn't have a car.

There was one person he could call—his old friend, partner in crime and crime solving, and quasi-boss—but he wasn't in the mood. He thought about heading back to the boat, but that seemed too far away.

The first time he'd seen Sheridan in close to nine-teen years, he couldn't quite bear to leave her. So Gavin limped back to the rock ledge in her yard, sat down, and stared back at the lightless windows of her dark house.

CHAPTER 4

H E WORE A PIN-STRIPED ITALIAN SUIT, drove a Bentley, and had perfected the finest sneer the shoreline had ever seen. He was as tall as Gavin, with a leonine head and mane of wavy hair. He owned a classic sailing yacht and belonged to the Hawthorne Yacht Club and was one of the few people not in the Navy who could get away with wearing epaulets. His wife, Laney, was a peach, and he didn't deserve her. He walked with his head held high among people who loathed and feared him. People called him "Jaws" because of the human detritus he left behind. He was Vincent de Havilland, divorce attorney.

When Gavin called, Vincent came. Picked him up in the Bentley—with a worried glance at the bloody foot, but nary a warning about keeping it off the white leather upholstery...that's the kind of friend he was. They'd met as kids, right here at Hubbard's Point.

They'd grown up together, summer after summer at the Point. Vincent had started life as a nerd—he wasn't ashamed to admit it. Gavin had defended him against those who'd thought they'd have some fun at Vinnie's expense.

As time went on, their friendship stayed strong. Gavin had been working with the beach crew; Vincent had been interning in his father's law office. While the other beach kids had spent their summers enjoying the sun and fun and innocent pleasures of Hubbard's Point, Gavin and Vincent had seen the same dark spark in each other's eyes: a profound mistrust of the world and its people.

"How was it?" Vincent asked the minute Gavin emerged from the ER and slammed the car door shut.

"Which part?"

"Meeting your client."

"Bullshit," Gavin said. "That's not what you want to know."

Silence as Vincent drove. Gavin could almost see the wily wheels turning as he tried to cover his curiosity.

"Okay. Seeing Sheridan," Vincent said finally.

"It was all right."

Vincent threw a look at Gavin's foot. "Your first time seeing her in all these years, and you need an ER?"

"Fuck you."

"You say that, but the last time something about Sheridan upset you, you put someone else in the hospital and got yourself kicked out of the Navy. I make my money on divorce work, Gavin—I don't want to be having to defend you in court again. Now tell me what happened—"

"I don't want to talk about her."

"Fine."

Gavin stared out the window; he knew Vincent was being protective, was worried about him. Gavin's temper had gotten him in trouble before, gotten him sent to anger management. Count to ten; picture a beautiful scene; take a deep breath, then another, another, another. Right now, anger was the farthest emotion from his mind. He was just sad; he couldn't stop thinking about Sheridan.

And about Charlie.

"You okay?" Vincent asked a few miles up the road.

"I'm good," Gavin said.

"Well, you're obviously not. So let's talk shop, take your mind off her," Vincent said. "People are blithe."

"Yeah?" Gavin said.

"You know it. Don't tell me you don't. It's what keeps us both in business. Let me tell you my latest case."

"Start with the assets," Gavin said, because that's what Vinnie loved most.

"Eighteen mil."

"You never take a case under five—you're doing good with this one."

"I upped my minimum to ten," Vincent said. "But

this one's a bit higher. Family money on his side. We have a trust to break."

"Why'd you say 'blithe'? Which one's blithe?"

"They both are," Vincent said, snorting. "Forty years old, went to college together, three kids, big house in Black Hall, winter place in Vail. She believes the diamond ads, that love is forever, he believes in *GQ*, that he deserves a hottie on the side."

"They're both living the American Dream," Gavin said.

"Like I said: blithe."

"Let me guess: she read his e-mail."

"Text messages," Vincent said, laughing. "The greatest gift ever given a divorce lawyer: the electronic age. Why don't these idiots realize that once you write it and send it, it never goes away? We have him cold. Beautiful, tender messages about what she did to him last night, when can they meet again, how the youngest kid is almost through high school . . ."

Gavin laughed. "He's dead. So, is he going to settle?"

"I hope not."

"Right. That would cut down on legal fees. Also, it would cut down on pain and heartache for your client and the kids. . . ."

Vincent shrugged. He did have a conscience, but he was a practical man with a big nut to cover. Collecting art, buying real estate, and a penchant for custom-made suits meant he had to keep the money coming in. Gavin had worked with him on many cases—and he based his own international operation, including his answering service, out of the de Havilland Law Practice, LLC, Hawthorne, Connecticut. Gavin himself was based here, although work often took him out of state.

"She came in saying she loved him, that even though she wanted a divorce, she hoped to wind up as friends," Vincent said. "For the sake of the kids and all...little Johnny and Morgan and Monique. That was three months and two depositions ago. He's hiding assets. Turns out his girlfriend's been around a lot longer than my client thought. Also there's porn on his computer...Internet porn—the divorce lawyer's second-best friend."

"Who's his lawyer?" Gavin asked.

"Tripp Long."

Another paper-hanger—a lawyer who filed motion after spurious motion, clogging up opposing counsel's fax machine and the court calendar with motions.

"So you're going to trial?"

"Or right down to the wire. My client's a sweetheart, and her husband is trying to screw her over. I can't let that happen."

"You're a superhero," Gavin said as they pulled up in front of the converted stable that housed Vincent's office.

"You eventually going to talk to me about your case?"

"Yeah," Gavin said. "But don't push me."

Vincent nodded. Gavin's foot was bandaged, numb from the novocaine they'd shot into his sole before stitching it up. They'd given him a prescription for Vicodin as well, but he'd ripped it up. He'd been down the painkiller road before. Limping into the office after Vincent, he said hello to Judy, receptionist-secretary and majordomo of both de Havilland LLC and Dawco.

"How's it going, Gav?" Judy said, standing for a kiss and handing him a pile of mail.

"Great, Jude. How about you?"

"I'm fine, happy to see you. I was all set to send the mail pouch to Maine when I found out you were coming."

Gavin gave her the patented Dawson squint—drove women crazy. He and Judy had been flirting toward an assignation for the entire ten years she'd been working here. The whole reason they got along so well was that nothing ever happened. They were the Bond and Moneypenny of southeastern Connecticut.

Limping into the inner sanctum—the windowless and fortified panic room, installed after one enraged husband had come calling with a shotgun—Gavin sat at the desk. He came to his office only sporadically; he operated better on the boat. The beauty of electronics made that possible—he could receive and transmit from anywhere in the world. Pain traveled, and so did Gavin. He worked for people who had lost everything. It was his job and mission to help them recover it again.

The lost item could be money, could be real estate, could be intellectual property, could be reputation, could be love: no job was too tough for Dawco. The work—and the desperate—paid well. He'd learned that long ago, when he'd cut his teeth as a private investigator for the most ruthless divorce attorney in the richest state in the union: his best friend, Vincent de Havilland.

He yawned; he'd stayed up all last night. He'd sat on Sheridan's rock until he was sure she'd fallen asleep. Then he'd hobbled down the stone steps to the beach, gotten sand in his cut, rowed his dinghy through the calm and starlit bay out to the *Squire Toby*.

He'd sat on deck the rest of the night, until the sun came up, watching her house with binoculars just in case she changed her mind and wanted to call him back to be with her. Not that he'd told her where he was staying, but he had the feeling she'd know that he was close by, that he'd be on a boat. He'd always spent as much time on the water as possible, and Sheridan knew him well enough to realize that wouldn't change.

So he stretched, trying to get some energy. He walked over to the coffeemaker, poured himself a cup. In spite of how tired he was, right now he had work to do—a two-part assignment, a two-part mystery.

First, his teenage client, Nell Kilvert, wanted him to learn the truth of what had happened to her boyfriend.

Second, Gavin himself had lost something and needed to get it back. It didn't have a name, wasn't even any one thing. But Sheridan was and had always been the only love of his life, and he knew that by solving the first mystery he'd be at least moderately on the way to solving the second.

"Fucking cosmic," he said, logging into his crime-solving network and typing out a coded message to his contact in the NYPD. Then he called Vincent into his office, to tell him what was going on.

WHY MEN PULL AWAY... *learn the secret to creating an attraction SO POWERFUL he'll never leave you!*

"Should we click on the link?" Peggy asked.

"It's pretty bogus, don't you think?" Nell asked.

"Maybe for you," Peggy said. "You don't want another boyfriend, but guys won't leave you alone."

"It's ridiculous," Nell said, pointing at the caption on the screen. "It's aimed at someone lame and desperate. People are either right for each other or they're not. When did Talk2Me become a dating site?"

"I'd like to know how to hold on to Brandon."

"Don't, Peggy—he likes you, it's obvious."

"Come on, I want to read what they say..."

Nell didn't reply. She lay on the twin bed beside Peggy, her laptop open as they checked their Talk2Me pages. Some kids liked to collect as many friends as possible, but Nell liked to keep it real.

It was called a social-networking site. People signed up to stay connected with real-life friends, and to connect with like-minded kids in cyberspace.

If you liked music, you could seek out musicians; if you liked sports, there were plenty of athletic types. In a way, it was just like high school—cliques, clubs, and loners.

Nell had seventy-two Talk2Me friends, and she had rules about who she accepted—she had to actually know them or know someone who knew them, or they had to send her a message that she really connected with.

Lately she'd been communicating with a guy, Laird. His screen name was Laird Vedder, in honor of the friendship between Laird Hamilton and Eddie Vedder. He was a big-wave tow-surfer from Half Moon Bay, and she'd met him through Charlie.

Well, she hadn't actually met him, and neither had Charlie—he was just a cyberfriend. But he had good energy and had written her beautiful words about Charlie and how life never ends, but is just like one wave following another. . . .

After tapping out a message to Laird, she closed out of her profile and clicked onto Charlie's. It did her heart good to keep it alive. She and Charlie had been so close, had no secrets; they'd shared playlists and passwords. She hadn't cared if he read her e-mail, and he'd liked the way she updated his Talk2Me profile, always including pictures of their life and times at Hubbard's Point.

Right now, staring at Charlie's profile, she felt a little faint. There was his face, smiling out from the screen. The picture showed him standing on the boardwalk, just before the beach movie was about to start: the sky was dark, and the flash was a little too bright, startling him.

Nell remembered that night so well—last summer, mid-July, hot and humid. The movie had been *Charlotte's Web*. They were too old for it, but they didn't care. Besides, it had been one of Charlie's favorite books as a kid—his mom had read it to him.

They'd put their blanket down and settled in, but they'd never gotten to watch. Thunderstorms had rolled off the Sound, driving everyone off the beach before the movie even started.

Nell and Charlie had scrambled under the boardwalk. Raindrops had come through the cracks, but they hadn't cared. They'd pulled their sandy blanket around them, kissed in the rain while people ran overhead, bare feet knocking sand and pebbles down on their damp heads.

"I'm going to do it," Peggy said now. "Click on the link and find out."

"Find out why men pull away?" Nell asked.

"Yes. And how to create an attraction so powerful, Brandon will never leave me...."

Nell smiled at her best friend. She knew how hard it was, both of them about to head off to different colleges—Peggy to Wellesley, Brandon to UConn. Nell had planned to apply to NYU early decision, so she and Charlie could be at the same school. She'd wanted to go into filmmaking, too, and work with him, and she'd loved the city, and most of all, she'd loved Charlie.

Now that was over. Nell wasn't going to college in

the city where Charlie had died. Last fall her father had encouraged her to look in and around Boston, but her heart hadn't been in it: Emerson, Boston College, Boston University, Regis. Good schools, varied in size, campus, and curriculum. Her father and Stevie wanted her to be excited about choosing Regis, but she felt dead inside.

She watched as Peggy peered at the screen, reading some craziness about always asking your man what he thought about everything, caring about his opinions, and respecting the kind of car he drove. Totally bullshit stuff that made Nell sad to think people actually believed it. She and Charlie hadn't needed any lessons or rules for staying in love. They would have loved each other forever. They would have grown old together.

Someone knocked on her bedroom door, and her dad stuck his head in.

"Anybody hungry? Stevie's shucking corn, and I'm about to start the grill."

"I'm starved," Nell said, smiling at her father, even though she wasn't hungry at all.

He looked into her eyes and smiled back. She knew he was worried about her since Charlie; his wife, Nell's mother, had died. Both he and Nell knew the truth, that you could love someone with all the power and force you had, but it couldn't stop death. And once you lost someone, it made loving everyone else both more precious and more impossible.

Nell had been a little depressed this past year. Okay, a lot depressed. She'd missed a few weeks of school. She hadn't shown any interest in the college application process, and her guidance counselor was "concerned."

Her father understood her. In fact, they supported each other. He was obviously excited about the new baby he was having with Stevie, but sad and disturbed by the fact Stevie didn't want to get married. Nell had noticed them not getting along so well. Her dad was having a tough year, too.

But even with his concerns about Stevie, he was completely there for Nell. He grieved along with her for Charlie—he'd loved him, too. He'd felt sad that Nell couldn't enjoy her senior year; he'd had to push her to go to college interviews, to make her fill out her applications, write her essays. He'd driven her to four colleges, all in Massachusetts. She both craved his attention and felt sad because she needed it so much.

"Come help Stevie," he said. "I know she'd appreciate it."

Peggy jumped up, ran into the kitchen. Nell just stared at her father, trying to smile. They'd been through so much together—the loss of her mother, and now the loss of Charlie. He wanted her to be happy.

"College girl," he said.

She kept the smile on her face, didn't feel it inside. She'd decided on Regis College, the opposite direction from Hubbard's Point than New York, the opposite in many ways from NYU. It was small, set on a beautiful campus a few miles outside Boston. It had an excellent library and a small museum on campus, and great professors. It was nurturing, the kind of place a person might come back to life. If only she believed that . . .

"You okay?" he asked.

She nodded. "You?"

"I know this is a tough time of year," he said. "Coming up on the anniversary . . ."

"It's always tough," she said. "Because Charlie's not here."

"I know."

"It was like this when Mom died," she said.

"Yes, it was. And we still love and miss her, but life got better. It will for you, too, honey."

"By 'better,' you mean Stevie, right?"

He nodded, but his eyes were so sad. Nell gave her father a hug. She loved Stevie, but couldn't understand why she was hurting him this way.

"Maybe she'll change her mind," Nell said.

"I have to be ready for the fact she probably won't," he said.

"Well, have hope," Nell said.

"I'd say the same to you," her father said. They gazed at each other, trying to smile. The words were so hopeful, but it was hard to take them to heart right now. For her father's sake, Nell nodded and gave him a smile.

She shut down the laptop. Her father patted her shoulder as she walked with him to the kitchen. She was picturing how this day could have been if only last August 31 hadn't happened: Charlie would be here for dinner, too.

He and Nell would sit together, holding hands under the table, dreaming of going to New York, starting their life together away from home. Maybe their love would even inspire Stevie to finally see the light and say yes to Nell's father. Love like Nell and Charlie's was so powerful, who knew what might happen. . . .

CHAPTER 5

SHERIDAN SAT IN THE LIVING ROOM WITH her two sisters, Agatha and Bunny. The sun was up, so the shades were down. Last night Gavin had been here, and she swore she could still feel his presence. He had sat on the rock ledge for hours, until she'd fallen asleep. When she'd woken up sometime before dawn, he was gone.

"What's the point of having a terrace if we can't sit on it?" Agatha asked.

"A lovely *bluestone* terrace," Bunny said, as if that made all the difference.

"Stop, will you please?" Sheridan asked.

"I don't see why depriving yourself of sunlight is helpful. Come on, honey . . . let's go outside," Agatha said. "I'd like to raid your herb garden, for one thing."

"Help yourself," Sheridan said.

"Have you ever considered what a waste it is, the

fact that you have Grandmother's herb garden, but that you don't believe?"

"She believes," Bunny said quietly. "And she doesn't try to profit from it, either. Look at you, marketing love potions and psychic readings to tourists and summer people."

"It pays my mortgage," Agatha said.

"I'm so glad you came over here to bicker," Sheridan said, standing up and walking into the kitchen. She reached for three glasses and the bottle of bourbon. Then she thought of last night, of how she had poured drinks for herself and Gavin. She knew she'd caught the alarm in his eyes, watching how fast she'd tossed hers down.

Instead, she went to the refrigerator and opened it. There always used to be a pitcher of iced tea in here. Her grandmother had started the tradition, brewing it with Barry's tea from Ireland and lemon verbena from the garden. Sheridan used to make sugar syrup, Southern style—she'd learned how in Nashville. Charlie had loved that.

Her sisters were still in the other room, arguing about whatever. Sheridan wasn't listening. She wondered why she hadn't told them that Gavin Dawson had stopped by. That would stop their squabbling, she was sure. At one time, they'd assumed he'd be their brother-in-law.

She noticed that one of her sisters had brought a plate of orange cookies, left it on the table. Charlie had loved his aunts' cooking. . . . Sheridan stared at the plate, feeling stabbed through the heart.

"Sheridan?"

"Bunny," she said, turning. "Why didn't I cook more?"

"Cook, honey?"

"He deserved a mom who stayed home and cooked. Like you do for your kids, like Aggie does for Louis."

"You made music," Bunny said, putting her arm around Sheridan's shoulders. "That was as good as any meal. Charlie loved your songs, he loved how he knew all the secrets in your lyrics. The rest of the country would be trying to figure out who you meant by 'Dark Heart,' which lover you were trashing, but Charlie would know you were talking about the mean guy at the gas station...."

Sheridan looked down; "Dark Heart" and all her love songs, even or especially love-gone-wrong songs, had been about one person. She'd only told Charlie they'd been about less dire situations like a mean man at the gas station.

"No music was ever as good as your orange cookies," Sheridan said.

"I didn't make these," Bunny said. "Ag did."

"But yours are great, too," Sheridan said, her eyes filling with tears. She couldn't say his name with many people, but she couldn't *not* say it with her sisters. "Charlie loved having aunts who baked."

Bunny stood there. She was small and round, with curly brown hair and big green eyes. She wore a periwinkle-blue sundress with pink scallop shells embroidered around the scoop neck. She adored the sun and loved getting a tan, but Agatha and Sheridan had convinced her to start using sunscreen after she got squamous cell skin cancer two years ago.

"His aunts loved baking for him," Bunny said.

Sheridan saw the tears in her sister's eyes and had to look down. She shook, thinking of how much Charlie had loved his Aunt Bunny.

He had adored Agatha, too, but in a different way. He'd gotten the hugest kick out of Agatha's eccentricities; Sheridan's grandmother had died when he was a baby, but she lived on in Agatha. Agatha wore black, chanted spells, gathered herbs, played Irish music on her fiddle.

Bunny was calm, gentle, suburban. The only mark she cared about making in this world was in loving her family. And Charlie had been her family.

"Why did he have to leave us?" Sheridan whispered.

Bunny couldn't answer; she stepped closer, put her arms around her sister. Sheridan leaned against her soft body, and they held each other. They'd grown up in this house, spent so many happy summers and fun times. They'd gathered round their grandmother, begged her to put spells on them. Later, when they were older, they'd sometimes laugh at the believers, even at their grandmother herself for the way she believed in her own gifts. But even so, they'd always loved reading to her from her magic books.

Agatha walked in behind them. She had lit a candle; Sheridan could smell the honeysuckle-scented smoke. If her sister started in on anything crazy, if she slipped too overtly into Irish-mystic or spiritualist mode, Sheridan would be out of there so fast.... But all Agatha did was put the candle down on the kitchen table, walk over, and slip her arms around Sheridan and Bunny.

"I heard what you were saying from the other room," she said. "And all I could think to do was light a candle for him."

"Thank you," Sheridan whispered.

"He's on my mind all the time," Agatha said, her voice breaking.

"It's why you baked the orange cookies, isn't it?" Bunny asked.

Sheridan felt Agatha nod. She must have been unable to speak, because no sound came out of her throat. The three sisters stood there holding one another. Bunny broke away first, reached down and lifted the plate, held it.

The smell of orange peel and vanilla bean was sweet and gentle, and reminded Sheridan of sitting on the porch, rocking Charlie in her lap while he ate one of his aunt's cookies.

"I'm going to tell you something," Sheridan said. "But I don't want to talk about it."

Her sisters listened.

"Gavin's here."

"Gavin Dawson?" Bunny asked, her eyes bright.

Sheridan nodded.

"Where is he?"

"On his boat," Sheridan said.

"But . . ." Bunny began.

"She told you," Agatha said sternly, but with light in her eyes. "She doesn't want to talk about it."

"Okay," Bunny said, reaching for a cookie as a warm smile overtook her. "This one's for Charlie."

"For Charlie," Agatha said.

Sheridan took one, held it in her hand. She couldn't take a bite, but she liked holding it. She stood in the sister circle, staring down at the old linoleum floor. She saw a rusty smudged bloody footprint she had missed wiping up, made last night by Gavin's badly cut foot. Seeing it somehow made her feel a little better. Not much, but a little. She nibbled the cookie's crispy brown edge.

"For Charlie," she whispered.

After another long hug, they pulled apart. Bunny drifted back to the table, picked up the box of gauze bandages.

"Who are these for?" she asked.

Sheridan shrugged, turning away to hide the color rising in her face. Something in Bunny's smile told her she knew they had been for Gavin. She thought about "Dark Heart," how she'd written it a year after she and Gavin had broken up, not long after Charlie was born.

But earlier in her songwriting career—at the very start, when she was a teenage girl with her first guitar—she had sat right here in this kitchen, picking out notes and writing lyrics to fit in sixteen-bar verses and eight-bar choruses, all of them about the bright wildness of falling in love with Gavin Dawson.

They had been beach kids together, just like Nell and Charlie. Gavin was different from anyone she knew. He was from the tough part of a small Rhode Island mill town; he'd gotten sent here to spend summers with his grandmother, to keep him out of trouble.

Gavin had a temper, got into fights with the other boys here at the beach. He'd get together packs of kids to go diving off the train bridge into Devil's Hole, or to dive from the breakwater and poach lobsters from the pots out there.

But with Sheridan, he seemed like another person. She gentled him somehow; even then she'd known she had that power. She'd be very still, just watching him, and he'd calm down. She'd see him for everything he was: a boy with a jagged scar on his cheek, with holes in his sneakers, who would dive deeper than anyone else, hold his breath, and steal lobsters. He was a daredevil, daring his own personal demons. Life had made him feel unsafe—at home, on the streets, everywhere. With Sheridan, it was different.

Sheridan saw the best in him, and something in the way she didn't look away, or judge him, or look down on him, made him lean into her. She didn't need spells or special herbs—but she'd exerted some kind of magic that made him want to be different around her. She made him want to be his best.

The sea breeze that swept through Hubbard's Point, the tides that rose and fell on the beach and the rock ledge, the phases of the moon that waxed and waned through each of the summer months:

those rhythms seemed to come not from nature, but from the love that grew between Sheridan and Gavin.

They had started as friends. He had been devoted to her—she'd known it before he'd ever said. She could tell by the way he looked at her, the way he'd flinch if anyone ever teased her. Once Ed Moriarty had made a comment about her freckles, and Sheridan had seen Gavin register the moment, store it up for later. He'd broken Ed's wrist, ostensibly over a spearfishing incident, but Sheridan would never stop believing the real reason had been because Ed had made the mistake of calling her "Freckle-face." There was danger in Gavin's devotion. Love with Gavin would always be a fine line between passion and ruin.

But oh, the passion. She'd first learned about it sitting beside Gavin when they were thirteen. It was the Fourth of July, and they'd gathered with a bunch of friends on the seawall to watch fireworks being shot off across the water, from a barge off Black Point. The display was extravagant—fountains, pinwheels, sky rockets. Sheridan and Gavin were side by side on the wall, arms and legs touching. Just the way his bare arm brushed hers was more heart-stopping than the fireworks. She'd felt stunned, frozen, unable to believe the intense feelings shooting through her body, coming straight from his.

His hand had brushed hers—was it on purpose? The idea it might have been made her feel faint. Her head was light, but she'd never felt more clear. The moment quivered, holding them close together. She never wanted the fireworks to end. The explosions echoed her heartbeats. The flashes made her blink, and when she turned to Gavin and saw him smiling at her, she couldn't turn away to look back at the sky.

Those feelings stayed with her all that summer, through the next winter. The following July, she counted days till the Fourth, her body trembling as she anticipated sitting next to Gavin on the seawall. She'd lie awake at night, her pulse racing, wondering whether he'd touch her hand again. But it rained. A deluge, remnants of a tropical storm, buckets of rain and galloping waves that kept the fireworks barge in port. All she had to do was mention to Gavin that she was disappointed the display had been canceled.

He misunderstood. Thinking she was upset because she'd wanted to see actual fireworks, not understanding that what she'd been longing for was a chance to sit next to him on the seawall, feel his closeness and the wild thrill of his skin brushing hers, he'd ridden his bike to a construction site in Niantic and stolen some quarter-sticks of dynamite.

He'd lit them off late the night of July fourth—throwing them into metal garbage cans beside the boardwalk, within sight of her bedroom window, while the rain poured down. She'd heard the wild booms—louder than the thunder that had been rumbling all evening—jolting her out of bed. Staring down from her room, she'd seen the bright, intense flashes—blue-white and crazy-close. There, silhouetted by the afterglow, was Gavin. He stood on the boardwalk, reaching his arms up as if he could touch or catch Sheridan.

She remembered staring down with horror. How could he put himself in such danger? The blasts had wakened the whole beach, and her mother and sisters stood by the window trying to see who was vandalizing the garbage cans. The police were called, their sirens screaming. Sheridan shook, not knowing what to hope—she wanted Gavin to get away, but she also wanted him to get caught, so he'd never do anything so stupid and destructive again.

They'd seen each other the next morning, at Foley's Store. Drizzle fell, soft and gray, cushioning the pain she felt inside. The police had missed Gavin—he'd spent the night running from them, hiding under various cottages. He obviously felt elated, seeing Sheridan walk in wearing her yellow slicker.

"Did you see?" he asked when she approached his table.

"I have to talk to you," she said, shaking. He noticed her expression, and his smile dissolved. Nodding, he followed her outside. A police car cruised slowly down the street. Together, without a word, they ran around the corner, ducked into the dark and narrow path that led into the cemetery.

"Why did you do it?" she asked as they hid behind the stone wall that encircled the graves.

"For you," he said. "You said you were sad about the fireworks being canceled, and I didn't want you to be sad."

"Gavin," she said, "you could have gotten your hand blown off. You could have gotten killed."

"No way," he said. "That would never happen to me."

"It could have," she pressed.

"I did it for you," he repeated, not understanding. She watched him go pale. He didn't get it, and truly, neither did she. They sat hunched under the dripping trees, so close together she could feel the warmth of his skin. It was even more intimate than the fireworks last year, and the way he was looking at her, the way his eyes looked so perplexed yet so washed with emotion, made her tremble.

"I don't want you to get hurt," she said.

"I won't," he said, and it sounded like a promise. "I can't."

"How can you say that?" she whispered. "You're fourteen. You're a boy . . . flesh and blood. That was too dangerous."

He shook his head, and she watched him bring his hand so close to her face, holding it just an inch from her cheek as if all he wanted to do was touch it, trace her cheekbone, bring his mouth close to hers.

"Don't you get it?" he whispered.

"Get what?"

They sat there, trapped in silence as grownup feelings and thoughts ran through them. She wanted something she couldn't put into words. If she could have, she would have crawled into his jacket with him. She would have pressed herself against his body, she would have made herself his other half.

She was shaking, and so was Gavin. It must have scared him, because he broke the spell.

"I'm invincible," he said, breaking into a grin.

"No," she said.

"Uh-huh," he said, nodding.

"How can you say that?"

"The cops didn't catch me, did they?"

"Forget the cops. You could have gotten killed."

"But I didn't. Sheridan . . ." He stared into her eyes, and the feeling began rolling back, like a huge wave all the way out at sea.

"What?" she asked, her voice a croak.

"I'm trying to tell you what it's like," he said. "I'm not afraid of anything. Dynamite, it's nothing. You just have to pay attention, lighting the fuse. I know what I'm doing. Do you believe me?"

She stared at him then, and the strangest thing happened. Her desire, all that passion pent up inside from last Fourth of July, turned into the most tender emotion possible. Instead of fire in her skin, she felt tears in her eyes. He was just a little boy, really. He came from a tough place, unlike anywhere Sheridan had ever been. They'd both lost their fathers, but the difference was, Sheridan had enough family love to hold her and keep her and make her want to be safe. She didn't trust that that was the case for Gavin, and she didn't even have to think about it: she just took his hand.

"It's okay, Gavin," she whispered, staring into his eyes, seeing tears pop over his lower lids. "It's really okay."

"I'll never get hurt," he said fiercely.

She just squeezed his hand, unable to respond.

And they sat there in the silvery-green gloom of the graveyard as police cars drove up and down the winding streets of Hubbard's Point, hiding from the law and hiding from whatever it was in Gavin that made him think it was okay to put himself in the gravest danger, that made him believe he wasn't worth treating with precious care.

That was the summer they were fourteen; it was the next year when everything had really, irrevocably changed. He'd put her on warning, shooting off the stolen dynamite, let her know that loving him came with the high price of worry and a certain insecurity—that he'd always take risks. But passion didn't come with brakes or caution.

She stood in her kitchen now, remembering that next summer. Her desire had had a whole other year to build, and so had his. It was late, after midnight. They were fifteen, and although it was past the curfew his grandmother had so ineffectively tried to enforce, he'd sneaked out to come up the hill and listen to her play her music. He'd been begging her to let him sit there and listen, and she'd told him she wasn't ready for an audience—even him.

Sheridan's family were all fast asleep. She'd been sitting right here, at the table, with the battered old guitar she'd bought at a tag sale, playing chords, trying to work out a song she'd been writing. Through the screen door, she heard crickets in the yard and seagulls crying across the water on North Brother,

off Black Point, right in the same bay where the fireworks were always held. Then she heard something
else:

"Shit!"

Jumping up, holding her guitar, she pressed her
face to the screen.

"Who's there?"

"Me," Gavin said, stepping out of the shadow of the
oak tree that had been there then. It had fallen in a
hurricane five years ago. He held up his foot. "Sorry—
I stubbed my toe. Keep playing."

"I told you—no one's allowed to hear," she said.

Even in the darkness, she'd seen him grin. "I
know," he said. "That's why I had to sneak out to
hear you. What's the song about?"

"Nothing," she said.

"Come on. Play it for me."

She remembered moths bumping into the screen
door, trying to get to the light. Her heart had felt like
that in her chest. If she let him hear, then he'd know.
She hadn't ever played in public, or for anyone but
her family—her performance at Newport was a year
away. Besides, the lyrics in this particular song were
very specific and personal, and Gavin would hear
them and realize how she felt. They played in her
mind, making her feel dizzy.

Without even planning, she felt herself slowly
opening the door, felt the cool night grass beneath
her bare feet. She held her guitar under one arm as
Gavin followed her to the herb garden.

Sitting on the wall, she felt Gavin sit beside her, so

close their hips were touching. Her pulse was racing so hard, and she adjusted her guitar, checked to make sure it was in tune. She'd glanced at him, seen him staring at her, his eyes blazing in the starlight. Her mouth was dry.

"I've only played for my family," she said.

"What am I?" he asked. "We've known each other forever."

She swallowed hard. It was true, all Hubbard's Point kids were like one another's family, but that wasn't what this song was about. When she played for her mother, grandmother, and sisters, she sang Irish songs, or traditional American songs, or classics like "Moon River." Or she and her grandmother would sing spells from the book.

"It's just a song," she said, giving herself an escape hatch. "It's not about anyone or anything in particular..."

"Okay," he said, sitting so close she swore she could hear his heartbeat.

She began to strum. Then she got her courage up and began to sing.

> *"Maybe some time, maybe some day,*
> *Maybe you'll feel the same way,*
> *I'll close my eyes, I'll think of this,*
> *You'll be there, and then we'll..."*

She stopped, unable to say the last word. Overhead the stars were tiny white lights in the black sky. She stared up, feeling embarrassed.

"Finish singing it," he said, gazing at her.

"It's not done," she said. "I don't have the last line."

"Please?"

"I can't."

"Will you tell me the title, at least?" he whispered. She shook her head.

"Please tell me, Sheridan . . . what's the title of your song?"

"'First Kiss,'" she whispered.

He nodded, staring at her. She felt herself shaking. She should never have done this. It seemed so forward, so crazy, as if she'd just decided to turn herself inside out right in front of him.

She'd never been kissed before, but she'd dreamed for so long about kissing Gavin; it had inspired her to write the song, and in spite of what she'd been thinking about escape hatches, there were none in sight.

"Sheridan," he whispered, putting his arm around her.

She'd been clutching her guitar, but he gently took it out of her hands. In her dreams since the fireworks two summers ago, she'd worried that she'd be awkward when it happened, but when he finally kissed her, she fell into the kiss and knew exactly what to do. His lips were cool, and the scent of the herbs surrounded them, so she thought kisses tasted of mint, verbena, and thyme.

Their hands were shaking, and Sheridan felt herself trembling, so she pressed closer against his body, to feel how strong and solid he really was. Their tongues touched, and it made her feel hot inside, and the song she'd been writing flew out of her head, and she learned in that instant something she would never forget: that songs could be beautiful, emotional, passionate, but nothing compared to real love.

Because it wasn't just a kiss: it was the start—or maybe the middle—of their love. Sheridan pulled back a little, to look into Gavin's eyes. They were staring at her, as if they'd always known her, could see inside her heart.

"Sheridan," he whispered.

She nodded, waiting.

"Did you write that song..."

"For you," she said.

And now, standing in her kitchen with her sisters, Sheridan thought back to that night when they were both fifteen, amazed at the way they'd laid it on the line. Neither one of them had pretended anything. They'd told each other the truth.

They always did, and it had been the truth, eventually, that drove them apart. Thinking about that, Sheridan soaked a sponge and wiped Gavin's footprint off her kitchen floor.

LOVE WAS STRANGE. Stevie Moore had always known it. She lived in her little house on the hill, just a couple of yards down from Sheridan Rosslare, and felt an ache in her heart. With dinner over, and the dishes done, she stood alone in her studio. Nell was in her room, and Jack had stalked out after dinner, going on one of his long, solitary walks.

Stevie gazed down the cliff at the wide crescent beach and the half-moon bay, at the gleaming white boat anchored just inside the breakwater. She knew that Nell had been out there—that, in fact, she was responsible for Gavin coming to town.

She paced her studio, stopping at her workbench. Maybe if she mixed some paint, she'd feel more centered. She squeezed cadmium red from the tube onto her palette. Staring at it, her vision blurred, and she felt dizzy.

The paint looked primal, like blood. It made her think of her heart, which was hurting. She sat on the window seat, hand over her heart, feeling it beat under her fingers. Down on the beach, the waves washed in one after the other, endless and without end. Her life source had always been right here: the beach, the waves, Jack.

She closed her eyes, thinking of him. How could love hurt so much? Sometimes it seemed the more you opened yourself up, the greater the pain. Wasn't it supposed to be the other way around? Wasn't closeness supposed to bring happiness, peace, joy, security? If that was true, why did Stevie feel as if she was tilting and falling, about to slip off the earth?

Jack seemed so unhappy. The worst part was, she had started it last night with one little touch. Jack had seemed so withdrawn lately. The way he'd sit at dinner, hardly able to smile. And the way he'd sleep on his side, facing away, as if he wanted to forget he was sharing a bed with Stevie. Last night she'd reached over with her foot, touching him with one tentative toe.

Sometimes she'd do that and he'd turn over, wrap her in his arms, kiss her with such passion she'd flood like a tidal creek. She'd overflow, unsure of where she ended and he began. They'd make love, and whisper secrets, and the tide would rise higher, and they'd float away together—right out of their bed, out the window, out of the world. On nights like that, they lived in their own sea. They were each other's boat, and they were each other's tide, and they were both the safety and the danger of a risky voyage.

But not last night. When she'd touched his leg with her toe, she'd wanted him to roll over and look at her. Even if he couldn't touch her, or tell her what he was feeling, or make love to her, she'd wanted to just gaze into his eyes. But Jack hadn't turned around. He'd just stayed very still, pretending to be asleep. Then he'd inched his leg away from her toe.

And that's when Stevie had lost it.

"You have to stop treating me this way!" she said, shaking him.

"Shh," he said. "It's late. Go to sleep, Stevie."

"Go to sleep? How can I, when I feel so rejected?"

"*You* feel rejected?"

"Jack, I love you. Just because I have doubts about marriage—can you blame me?"

Silence from Jack. Oh, long, terrible silence. No words, no sounds, but in the stillness he'd let her know that *he* wasn't the one doing the rejecting, *he* wasn't the one pushing her away. Sure, maybe he'd pulled his leg out of her toe's touch, but that was nothing compared to what she was doing to him. He did blame her for having doubts about marriage—that was very clear.

Arms wrapped around her pregnant belly, she stared out the window at Gavin's boat and rocked herself. She couldn't bear hurting Jack—but at the same time, she couldn't bring herself to do what he wanted.

And there she was, right back to thinking the same thing: love is strange.

She'd lived such a wild and colorful, such a vexing and perplexing, love life. She'd followed her heart for so long, with such disastrous results. Stevie had been like a tropical storm, just looking for landfall. She'd been through so much—and had put others through so much in her past marital mistakes. Some people's marriages ended in divorce. Sad, even tragic, but not the end of the world. But Stevie had had *three*. Three marriages, three divorces. She'd sworn she'd never get married again.

She knew the science of the human body: that it was ninety-seven percent water. That her veins were filled with salt water, just like the creeks in the tidal marsh. That once a month—well, before her pregnancy—her body's cycle echoed the moon's pull on the ocean's tides. She painted, and considered her art to be a force of nature—bigger than she was, and from sources she couldn't understand.

Jack Kilvert had been her harbor for so long now,

ever since they'd gotten together. He'd let her rest within the walls of his protected anchorage. He'd let her ebb and flow, he'd appreciated the intensity of her storms. He'd felt the force of her waves, and he'd slid into gentle pools illuminated by soft, yellow moonlight. He'd made her feel loved.

So why had it become so difficult?

She tried to track when the trouble had really started. After Charlie's death, certainly. Nell had been wrecked, and they'd had to help her through every day. This school year, she'd been hanging by a thread. Her grades had suffered; she'd seemed indifferent to her future. It had been such a struggle to get her to care about college; the whole process of looking seemed to remind Nell of how she wouldn't be joining Charlie at NYU, how she wouldn't be seeing him ever again.

Stevie had quit painting for a couple of months, just to give her extra attention. And Jack had scaled back his business travel, so he could be closer to home while his daughter needed him.

Stevie and Jack had pulled together for Nell. They completely had, no doubt about it. But losing Charlie had been wrenching for all of them. They'd loved him almost like a son—a boy they'd known forever, the son of one of their best friends. His death had knocked everything out of them.

Stevie had watched what it did to Jack. Perhaps the sudden violence of it had reminded him of Emma—losing his wife in the car accident. Once again, Jack had had to devote himself to helping Nell face the death of someone she loved. Charlie dying was another strong reminder that nothing lasted forever, that nothing in this world was permanent.

And then Stevie had gotten pregnant. She cradled her belly. Yes, that's when things with Jack had started changing. Maybe it wasn't the pregnancy alone, but coupled with losing Charlie—the two together were a one-two punch of love, destiny, and mortality, too much for Jack to withstand. He proposed—knowing how she felt about marriage—and he hadn't liked her answer.

And now nothing was the same, and Stevie wasn't sure they'd ever be able to go back to the way they were.

Why was every question a challenge? Why was every touch a line drawn in the sand? Why did their protected harbor suddenly feel about to be breached by the worst storm in the world?

Staring down at the beach, she saw Jack standing on the boardwalk. He stared out at Gavin's boat as if he wished he were on board and could cruise away. Stevie stared at the man she loved and wondered whether this was the summer everything she loved would collapse.

Because that's how it felt.

CHAPTER 6

THE *SQUIRE TOBY* TUGGED ON ITS ANCHOR
line in the outgoing tide, in the warm breeze of
the mid-August night. Gavin was down below, waiting for the rest of the fax to come through. His satel-
lite signal was strong here, and he could transmit
and receive just as fast as at the office.

Judy had offered to come aboard, to help him col-
late, but he'd said he thought he could handle it;
there was only one woman he wanted here. He
leaned against the chart table, keeping weight off his
foot. He had just started to read the first few pages of
the police report on the death of Charles Rosslare
when he heard, above the whirring fax, the soft
splashing of oars.

He climbed up on deck, looked across the water. A
lone figure steadily rowing an old wooden rowboat
came straight out from the end of the beach: Sheridan. He couldn't believe it; it was almost as if his feelings were so strong, he'd willed her to come. When

she drew alongside, he gestured for her to tie the line to the boarding ladder. He gave her his hand as she climbed aboard.

"How'd you know I was here?" he asked.

"It wasn't too hard," Sheridan said. "I knew it had to involve a boat, and this one arrived at Hubbard's Point exactly when you did. I can see it from my house."

"Hmm," he said, not mentioning that it worked both ways: he could see her house from here, and he'd barely taken his eyes off it.

"You always did love the water . . ."

"That's for sure," he said. "Well, welcome aboard."

"She's pretty," she said.

"Let me show you around," he said, taking her on a tour. He gave her the whole spiel, the fine points of his classic thirty-three-foot Chris-Craft Futura. They went below, and she admired the mahogany he'd recently finished stripping and redoing.

Sheridan glanced at the chart table, at the bookcases, at the teak floor. Standing in the galley area, she seemed to take notice of the fact he'd pulled out most of the cabinets to install more electronics—including the fax, still pumping out pages of Charlie's autopsy. Gavin slid them all under a chart before she could see what they were, steering her forward.

"This is where you sleep?" she asked, peeking into the v-berth built into the bow.

"Yes," he said. He watched her gaze sweep through the small space, coming to rest on a photo of her—a beautiful one, taken here at Hubbard's Point when they were still together—he always kept on the shelf within sight of his pillow. She immediately looked away, pretending she hadn't seen it. He felt himself redden, and limped awkwardly back through the cabin and onto the deck.

"You have a beautiful boat," she said, following him into the fresh air. He pulled out a chair for her, and one for him, and sat beside her under the stars. The sky was bright, but heavy air was moving in. Tomorrow would be muggy, with afternoon thunderstorms.

"Thanks," he said. He kept his face impassive, so she wouldn't get any idea of how often he'd dreamed of this moment, of her coming aboard.

"Must take a lot of work, keeping her up."

"Yeah," he said. "You've probably heard the jokes about owning a wooden boat: it's cheaper and easier to just stand in a cold shower all day, ripping up money. But to me it's worth it. Chris-Craft used to advertise the Futura as 'the Jaguar of the Cruisers.' She's a great boat, and my home."

"You live on board all the time?" she asked.

"Yes," he said. "Keeps me mobile—I can go wherever the work is. Might take me a few days, or more, to get there, but once I arrive, I've got my home base right there."

"No hotels for you," she said.

"Nope."

"What made you do it?" she asked.

"Decide to live on my boat?"

"I mean, become a detective. That's what you are, right?"

Gavin shrugged. "I put 'consultant' on my taxes. I'm a lot of things."

"You work for Vinnie?"

"Sometimes. You know I do," Gavin said patiently.

She glared at him. "What I mean is, do you *still* work for him?"

"Well, I still base out of his office, but I'm pretty much freelance."

They stared at each other. Sheridan had hired her old friend Vincent de Havilland to get her through what amounted to a messy divorce. She and Randy Quill, Charlie's father, were married for less than two years, but that didn't keep him from going after everything Sheridan had.

They had gotten together not long after Sheridan had broken up with Gavin. He gazed at her now, thinking of the million things he'd done wrong. To him, they were living proof that opposites attract.

Although they'd both lived on the same side of the railroad line in their summers here at Hubbard's Point, there was no question about him coming from the wrong side of the tracks. His father had joined the Navy, like his father before him, and had died suddenly, when Gavin was just six, of a burst appendix aboard ship. Gavin remembered his mother crying. He'd tried to comfort her, and deep down he'd remembered what his father had said, before leaving the dock in Newport—that Gavin had to be the man of the family while he was gone.

It hurt him, seeing how hard his mother had to work to take care of him and be able to keep their house, knowing how tired she was. They'd lived in a working-class neighborhood in Central Falls, Rhode Island, the top floor of a two-family house. The washing machine never worked, so his mother would send him to the Laundromat with all their clothes and a pocketful of quarters. He liked doing it, trying to help her.

When he was ten, an older kid tried to steal all his money. Gavin had seen him waiting at the corner, a cigarette cupped in one hand, his pocketknife in the other. Gavin knew he should just cross the street, but he wasn't built that way, and walked right by the kid. In spite of the weapon, Gavin had fought with everything he had. He'd wound up with two black eyes and his cheek sliced by a rusty Buck knife.

But worse than the physical wounds was the shame he'd felt, the sense of letting his mother—and father—down. The money was gone—three dollars that his mother had worked so hard for. That kid had taken it as if it was nothing—had just knocked Gavin down and stolen every last quarter. That school year, Gavin had seen the kid walking down the hall and had run at him, fists pounding, legs kicking. He was half the older boy's size, but he'd punched him in the face, broken his front teeth.

The next summer, his mother sent him to Hubbard's Point to spend summers with his grandmother. Gavin hadn't wanted to go—he'd been there before, but never for long. He begged his mother to keep him at home, telling her that his place was with her, that he'd made his dad a promise. But his mother had started seeing someone new, a man from New Bedford, and she told Gavin it was better for both of them if he went away.

Those words had hurt, almost more than the fights, or even having his money taken. His mother was sending him *away*—that word haunted him. He knew that as hard as he tried, he still got into trouble sometimes, and that that was hard on his mother, too. He almost couldn't blame her if she didn't want him, if he'd let her and his father down so badly, she just couldn't love him anymore. She drove him to Connecticut, dropped him off. He remembered standing in the front yard, watching her car disappear, wondering whether anything would ever feel right again.

But his grandmother was very kind, and she made him feel at home—and Hubbard's Point felt like heaven on earth. The beach, and the tennis courts, and all the gardens, and all the happy families, and, especially Sheridan. It took Gavin a while to stop fighting and suspecting everyone of wanting something from him. That had been all due to Sheridan. But then again, so had the fight.

He remembered the day it started. Kids had gathered on the beach. Gavin couldn't take his eyes off Sheridan—her tawny skin with its light dusting of golden freckles straight from the sun, and the way she smiled at him, as if she knew all his secrets. The strangest thing of all was how he found himself wanting to tell her—his secrets, his stories, tales about the places he'd been. His friends had told him her father had died, too. He knew she'd understand what that was like. They were the same age, and he had the crazy feeling he'd known her his whole life.

By that time, he'd been in trouble with the cops back home, had been warned that next time he could end up in juvenile hall. There was something so safe and special about Hubbard's Point—he both loved it here and yet couldn't stand another minute of it. He was afraid they would find him out, know he was a bad kid, send him away. But something in the way Sheridan looked at him made him believe that she wouldn't—she wanted him right there.

"You're going fishing?" she asked as the kids gathered their snorkels and equipment.

"Yeah," he said. "I guess so."

She nodded, smiling. He wished he didn't have to hang around with the boys; he wanted to swim with Sheridan, race her to the raft, lie next to her until the sun dried them off.

"Hey, Dawson," Ed called, wading into the water. "Quit talking to Freckle-face and c'mon. We got to get out there before the tide gets too high."

"Shut up," Gavin said, feeling the flashpoint his school counselor had warned him about. Seeing the hurt in Sheridan's face, hearing the cocky humor in Ed's voice, he felt himself about to blow. But Sheridan put her hand on his wrist.

"It's okay," she said. "Just have fun. I hope the water's clear, so you can see lots of fish. . . ."

Gavin had nodded, shocked by the feeling of her fingers on his hand. He'd shivered in spite of the hot sun, dived into the water after his friends. And the day had gone on.

They'd been spearfishing out at the breakwater, going after blackfish and eels. Gavin had caught the biggest fish, using Ed's spear. When they got to the beach, Ed—just a big, innocent rich kid with a fancy toy—had waved the spear around, kiddingly pointed it at Gavin's head. Without even thinking, he reacted, throwing Ed down on the ground.

Ed's wrist had snapped. Even though it was an accident, Gavin became a pariah. The other beach kids were frightened of him; he was even scared of himself, of what he'd felt inside at the moment he'd rushed at Ed. But Sheridan wasn't afraid of him. She'd sit beside him, when the other kids would edge away. She'd ask him if he wanted to go swimming, or for a walk over to Little Beach. He'd tease her, asking her to write him a song, and she'd tease back, saying she would.

One August night, the summer they were fifteen, she asked him to watch shooting stars with her; no one had ever asked him to do that before. It was the night of the Perseid meteor shower, and they'd lain together on the sand, staring up at the sky. He remembered he couldn't talk, and the feelings that poured through him reminded him of two summers earlier, when they'd watched fireworks together.

Lying beside Sheridan, he'd looked up, and he'd felt as if the stars were rushing at them. They burned his skin, made him feel alive, as if he mattered some-how. Then he felt Sheridan rest her head on his shoulder. It lasted just a few seconds. It wasn't ro-mantic, exactly, or only; it made him feel as if he was important to her, as if she was letting him know that they belonged to each other.

The next week, she'd played him her song, "First Kiss." And then he had kissed her.

Staring at her now, on the deck of his boat, that's what he was remembering... They were together after that. A couple, all through their teens and into their twenties, all through his years in the Navy and the beginning of her songwriting career. He'd joined the Navy because it was what men in his family did; they'd put him on a submarine, and he'd be gone for months at a time. *You're the man of the family*, his father had said.

He did one tour, then signed up for another before Sheridan could ask him not to. Sometimes he won-dered whether he hadn't engineered that perfectly—he already sensed she was getting really tired of waiting for him.

Gavin knew about dogs heeding the call of the wild—returning to their atavistic roots when set loose in the woods. That's how he'd felt in the Navy—as if the old neighborhood had reclaimed him. He could run from his rough beginnings, but he couldn't stay away forever. Loving Sheridan had kept him tethered to Hubbard's Point, but it was a sweet life that never felt quite right, that he didn't honestly feel he deserved.

The Navy fed his restlessness. He served aboard the USS *William Crawford*, a 688-class fast-attack submarine designed for stealth and speed while conducting ISR—intelligence, surveillance, reconnaissance—missions. Nuclear-powered, the *Crawford* could travel at top speed to trouble spots; there were a lot of seedy ports, with no shortage of drinking and brawling. In Kowloon, Gavin got tattooed while drunk—a heart with Sheridan's name in it.

He made friends with a really good guy, Joe Donovan from Bainbridge Avenue in the Bronx. Joe's dad was a cop, and that's what Joe would become when he got out of the Navy. On the ship, he kept an eye on Gavin. He pulled him out of a fight in Singapore, where the knife missed Gavin's heart by barely a single inch, got him back to the *Crawford* for medical care.

Joe also listened to Gavin talk about Sheridan—endlessly, miles under the sea, half a world from home.

During those long talks when Gavin would describe their times at Hubbard's Point, about lying on the beach and watching shooting stars with her, it had felt almost as if he was making it all up. As if he were telling Joe a story about another man entirely—someone who could love and be loved by a woman like Sheridan. Someone so different from Gavin . . .

Gavin drove her away. He knew that now. Maybe it went back to the day that kid had stolen his money, made him feel he'd let his parents down. Or when he stood by while the landlord ragged his mother about late rent, or the times they didn't answer the phone because of bill collectors. He'd felt like shit, unable to keep his promise to his dad. He hadn't been able to take care of his mother, be the man of the family. So how could he do that for Sheridan? They'd tried, done their best. But Gavin couldn't even count on himself to stay on the straight and narrow, and Sheridan knew that if she stuck with him, he'd always be going back to sea, leaving her alone on dry land.

After the breakup, Sheridan must have felt the need to rebound fast and big-time, because that's how it happened. She met Randy Quill in Nashville; he was new in town, not well known. He had written a few songs, played in a few bands. Sheridan, optimist that she was, had seen Randy's potential, wanted to record one of his songs—just as soon as he wrote one anyone could stand hearing.

Gavin would never forget the brain-searing moment he saw them together; his sub was in port in Virginia, and he took leave and hitched to Nashville. The breakup had been a huge wake-up call, and he was hurting. He knew what he had to do. He wanted to surprise Sheridan and ask her to come back to him.

She had a show at the Ryman Auditorium, and Gavin showed up with a big bouquet of roses, hoping to win her back, desperate for the chance to set things right with her. He never gave her the roses, though. Right after the show, he started toward the stage and saw Sheridan kissing someone else.

Turned out to be Randy. Gavin wheeled around, gave the roses to the woman at the ticket window, and hitchhiked back to Norfolk. He got arrested that night—bar fight at a dock near the shipyard.

Gavin got thrown into the brig for nearly killing the guy; he could barely remember what the fight was about. Some stranger had insulted one of Gavin's shipmates, but of course the real problem was that he'd seen Sheridan kissing another man, and his wild-dog, old-neighborhood self came out. He put the guy in the hospital and should have gone to jail for a long time, but instead—thanks to Vincent participating in his defense—he got kicked out of the Navy with a dishonorable discharge.

Meanwhile, Sheridan and Randy went on. He began accompanying her everywhere. Sheridan employed him, gave him the title of road manager. He had proposed and was angling to become her business manager when three things happened: she became pregnant with Charlie, they married, and then she caught Randy cheating.

By the time Sheridan called Vincent, she had had the baby and given Randy many more chances. Every time, he promised to be better, stop treating her badly, and every time, things got worse.

Sheridan left Randy for good. She'd offered him a generous settlement, just to make peace and because he was her baby's father—and because, in Gavin's opinion, she was more than honorable. Randy declined, deciding instead to sue her: for alimony, custody of the baby, a cut of her catalogue, and future earnings.

"I've never really thanked you for working on my case," Sheridan said slowly now.

"I'm glad I was able to," Gavin said.

"I wanted you to leave the Navy," she said, trying to smile. "Just not in the way you actually did."

"I know," he said. "Me neither. I pretty much wrecked my life, but Vincent hired me. He really took a chance on me."

"I remember he told me he was planning to use you, to investigate Randy."

Gavin nodded. "He told me you made it pretty clear you didn't want to hear any details of the investigation. At least any that involved me."

"It was tough," she said, softly. She stared at him, and just having her here, looking into her eyes, was turning him inside out.

"Tough how?"

"Well, knowing that you were working with my divorce lawyer; that you'd see the mess I'd made of things after . . ."

"After dumping me."

They both laughed. "Yeah," she said.

"Well," he said, "I didn't want you to be happy with any other guy, but you didn't deserve Randy."

"You must have done a good job," Sheridan said. "Randy dropped the suit pretty fast . . . and he set up that trust for Charlie."

"That's because of Vincent," Gavin said. "Best divorce lawyer you could have had."

"Maybe so, but we were losing every motion until you signed on. The judge had given Randy temporary support, plus visitation." She closed her eyes and shook her head. "He never planned to visit."

"No," Gavin said. "He wasn't much into his children."

"That's putting it mildly."

"Yeah," Gavin said. "Randy was a piece of work. All those working-class-hero songs he kept trying to get recorded, but guess what? He hardly ever worked."

"I figured that out," Sheridan said. "What did you get on him? Seriously. That made him go away?"

"Didn't Vincent tell you?" Gavin asked cautiously.

"Well, he told me about the affairs."

"Yeah," Gavin said. "That was it."

Sheridan nodded, but she peered at him through silver hair as if trying to see whether he was telling the whole truth, which he wasn't. Randy had been a serial bounder; he'd landed in Nashville about a year before Sheridan met him. Before that, he'd worked his way through Memphis, Miami, and Los Angeles. He targeted talented, successful women in the entertainment business.

When Vincent dispatched Gavin down to Nashville to look into Randy Quill's past, Gavin had expected to find the usual dirt: cheating, porn, and hopefully a thing for strippers. Randy had the trifecta, but he also had something else: a large bank account.

Gavin cut his teeth as a private investigator by

delving into Randy Quill. Because Randy had hurt
Sheridan, Gavin burned to discover every sordid fact
he could. The investigation let him satisfy his aggres-
sion without swinging a punch; he hung out in bars,
made friends with other roadies, dug into Randy's
business. He followed Randy into a small bank and
opened his own account there the next day. He still
remembered the account executive who'd helped
him: Lulamae Jennings.

Two dinners at the Black-Eyed Pea, and Lulamae
divulged that Randy was depositing large checks
signed by three different women in three different
states. He used three names with the same initials to
keep everyone off track: Randy Quill, Randecker
Quill, and Randall Quint.

Turns out Randy had been receiving spousal support from two past wives, and had received a healthy
financial settlement from an old girlfriend. The terms
of each of those court dispositions required that the
payments would stop if he ever remarried or received
spousal support from anyone else.

Gavin remembered it well and fondly, his meeting with Randy. They were in his double-wide, just
down the road from Opryland. Randy was tall, handsome, sensitive looking; he played the part of singer-
songwriter to perfection. Gavin could, grudgingly and
irritatingly, see why Sheridan had fallen in love with
him. Guitars were everywhere, and Sheridan's voice
emanated softly from the stereo.

"I love her, that's the thing," Randy said, sounding
heartbroken. "I can't understand why she'd do this to

me, to us . . . to me, her, and our baby. Can't you tell her I don't want to break up our family?"

"Well, Randy," Gavin said, sitting back in the leather armchair, "not much I can do about that; it's her decision."

Randy squeezed his eyes shut. Gavin watched him carefully, amazed at how he could turn so pale on cue, and how he could manufacture a tear so easily. He wasn't sure he'd ever met a true con man before, but this one was for real. Randy was top-rate, first-class, top-of-the-line; Gavin, at the start of his career as a PI, knew that he had a lot to learn from this guy.

"That sure upsets me," Randy said after a minute, wiping his eyes.

"Yeah," Gavin said. "Because you love her so much."

"I do."

"And because you want to be such a hands-on father."

"Damn straight."

Gavin took some papers out of his briefcase. He watched Randy watch him—apparently indolent, too bereft to really care what they were. Gavin knew he expected to sign papers settling the case in his favor.

Randy would forgo a custody battle and child support, and Sheridan would pay him a lump sum of two hundred thousand dollars. Randy had been specific about wanting the lump-sum payment instead of periodic alimony: because the IRS would consider it a property settlement, and therefore not taxable to him.

"Got a pen?" Gavin asked.

Randy nodded. He reached for a plastic pen with the same slogan as a poster on his wall: *Daltonville Speedway!* He dragged the papers across the table, as if they weighed a ton. Started reading. Gavin never once took his eyes off him.

"Huh?" Randy asked after ten seconds. He looked up from the page, eyes blazing. "What the fuck?"

"Maybe you shouldn't have known so much about tax law," Gavin said. "That was kind of a giveaway."

"The *fuck*?" Randy asked, slamming the pen down. "I'm not signing this!"

"Yeah, Randy. You are."

"I'm supposed to be getting two hundred grand—not paying it!"

"Well, we changed things up a little. We figured that since Sheridan is raising your son all by herself, the least you can do is put something in trust for his future. A nice round figure, like two hundred thousand dollars. With inflation and all, that should cover his college and grad school expenses, with a little left over to buy his mother something nice. A Mercedes, maybe. Like the one you have in LA."

"So what if I have a Mercedes?" he asked, his eyes slitting.

"Well, it's just, you didn't disclose it. Courts are funny about financial disclosure forms; they like them to be truthful and accurate."

"So I forgot about a fucking car."

"Yeah, you did. And you forgot about the fact you're receiving monthly payments from two other

women. That's probably where you got so knowl-
edgeable about the IRS. Vincent's sharp that way,
Randy. It really pricks his ears up when a roadie
knows so much about tax code."

Randy's pallor had increased, well beyond what
was touching and poignant. He looked close to losing
his lunch.

"Yeah, Randy. We know you haven't been paying
taxes. Haven't even been filing, have you?"

"I'm not good with paperwork," he said.

"Uh-huh. We figured that. Nice touch, having all
your mail go to a single postbox instead of your
many homes. Look, we don't want to make trouble
for you with the federal government. We really don't.
You got such a nice place right here . . . plus the one
in LA, and the condo in Miami. Why trade all this for
a lockup?"

"What do you want me to do?" he asked, his voice
flat.

"You're going to set up the trust for Charlie. Then
you're going to tell Marie and Jennifer it's time to
stop the spousal support. They're raising your other
kids, after all. Two boys. You never even bother to
visit your children, you miserable shit. We won't report you for triple-dipping, and we won't report you
to the IRS. This conversation will be our little secret."

"But—"

Gavin held up his hand. "We won't tell Sheridan
what you've been doing. Partly because I don't want
her realizing she was taken by a snake. She actually

loved you, feels sad you turned out to be such a disappointment. 'Music guys cheat,' that's what she told Vincent. As if you're part of some noble fucking Nashville tradition. She wants her kid to think he had a decent dad, though. That means a lot to her. And that's why you're getting off so fucking easy."

"Easy!"

"Yeah, asshole," Gavin said. He took one step across the trailer, lifted Randy up by his neck. He watched the pale face turn blood-red. Thinking of what this guy had done to Sheridan, Gavin wanted to kill him. Memories of the brig, the submarine, and the old neighborhood filled his mind. Instead of punching Randy, he grabbed his hand, stuck the pen in it.

"You're going to sign the trust document, and then you're going to call your bank and tell them to issue a check in Charlie's name."

"Goddamn you!"

"You're out a couple of grand, but your secret is safe with us. Me and Vincent. The IRS doesn't get a packet of your financials, and your exes' lawyers don't get calls giving this address."

"You're threatening me?"

"Uh, yeah. You're quick, aren't you?"

"I swear . . ."

"So. To continue. You sign, and the IRS doesn't get this address. Or the one in LA, or the one in Memphis . . . Memphis, you know, where little Jeffrey and his mother live?"

"Shut up."

"Clint and Jeffrey, your two other sons. Have you ever even met them?"

"I told you—shut your mouth!"

"You keep fathering kids just to get money out of their moms. The sad thing is, Jeff's mom doesn't even have that much. Her career's taken a downward turn since you—how can she sing about love when you trashed her so badly? You're a one-man scourge on country music, Randy. Her father has to help her with the payments. Nice, right?"

"That's not my fault, the way she went downhill ... she still owes what the court ordered her to pay."

"You want me to tell the IRS you said that?"

"Okay," Randy said, wrenching his hand away. "I'll sign."

Gavin should have waited till the documents were executed—that would have made everything so much easier. But Randy pulling back that way, trying to get some control after he'd already controlled so much and hurt Sheridan so badly, threw a switch in Gavin. And Gavin went a little crazy.

He'd had to hold Randy up in the chair, guide his broken hand across the pages. The check was stained rust-red from his broken nose. Funny, but the banker never even mentioned the blood spots.

"Well," Sheridan said now, gazing across the dark bay at the lights of Hubbard's Point, "I knew you had something to do with Randy setting up a trust for Charlie. It shocked me, to be honest. I had no idea he had that kind of money. He always seemed so broke."

"People can come up with all sorts of resources

when it's for the good of their kids," Gavin said steadily.

"He stayed out of Charlie's life as much as he could," Sheridan said. "Never sent him a birthday or a Christmas card. Never came to visit...Charlie invited him to his high school graduation, just a few months before..."

Before he died, Gavin knew she was about to say.

"But Randy didn't come. Charlie talked to him on the phone, though. They had a long talk..."

That got Gavin's attention. "Yeah?" he said, looking over.

Sheridan nodded. "It made Charlie so happy. He'd always wanted a relationship with his dad. He was such a sweet, sensitive boy.... He wrote songs, but his real passion was filmmaking."

"He was going to study it," Gavin said with a long look. "Nell told me."

"Nell?"

"She hired me. She's my client."

Sheridan stared, absorbing that fact. "She loved my son," she said with a small smile. "She can't let him go. I'm worried about her... She keeps watching the films Charlie made, and now this—hiring you."

"What films did Charlie make?"

"He wanted to do one about lost fathers."

"Did he approach Randy?"

"Yes," Sheridan said. "Charlie didn't really talk about it with me much. He knew how I felt about Randy; I didn't think Charlie would get very far with him."

Gavin watched her, the way her eyes flickered as she talked about her son.

"He'd just started college," he said.

"Yes," she said. "It was..." She paused. "I didn't know it would be so hard, having him leave home. We'd spent time apart, over the years. I was always on the road. And he liked to go places himself. I let him go to Bonnaroo when he was just sixteen."

"Bonnaroo?"

"The music festival...on a farm in Tennessee," she said, looking off into the distance. "I never worried about him, because he was smart. He was tough, like..." She trailed off, swallowing the rest. "Anyway. He knew how to have fun without getting in trouble."

"So New York..."

"I wasn't at all worried about him," she said. "And I didn't think I'd miss him the way I did. New York is just two hours away. I'd visit him, he'd come home. But seeing him head off with all his things...he was really leaving home." She hugged herself, eyes filling with tears. "I told myself I'd see him soon; he'd come back to see Nell—he could never stay away from her long. Or I'd see him at Parents' Weekend."

Gavin was silent, knowing what was coming.

"I never saw him again," she whispered, her voice breaking. "He never came home again."

"Sheridan," he said, reaching for her hand. She wouldn't give it to him.

Gavin stared at the water's glassy surface, reflecting stars and the lights from the cottages on the

Point. Sheridan took a deep breath, looked around at the calm water, the rocks and woods and the beach.

"This is beautiful," Sheridan said after a few minutes, gazing around. "I never come out here...And your boat is lovely."

Gavin looked at her; he didn't know whether she really meant it, or she just wanted to change the subject, stop talking about Charlie.

"Thanks," he said.

"How long have you lived on board?"

"This boat, five years."

"I used to hate thinking of you on that submarine," Sheridan said. "All cooped up in a tin can, down under the sea. But I know you needed it, somehow. I didn't like it, but I should have accepted it. I'm sorry about what happened between us."

He listened, electric.

"I wanted..." she began. "More than anything..."

"What?" He leaned toward her.

"Just, I wanted it to work out between us...I wanted us to be different from the way we were."

"I loved the way you were," he said.

She listened, then shook her head. "No," she said. "I couldn't handle waiting for you to tire yourself out."

"What do you mean?"

"You were in a fight," she said. "All the time."

"Yeah," he said. "I know."

"Not with other people, that's not what I mean. With yourself. You were in the ring with yourself. It was so hard to see—such a battle going on all the time. You had to be on board a submarine loaded with torpedoes because you were always ready to fire."

"At who?" he asked.

"Oh, I have some theories," she said.

"Tell me."

She gave him a long look through narrowed eyes. "The kid who stole your laundry money, for one," she said.

"How do you know about that?"

"You mentioned it once or twice."

He winced, wondering how often he'd told her that old story. And all the others... And why?

"You really think that's what went wrong?"

"I've had some time to think about it," she said.

She thinks about me, was the absurdly joyful thought that blasted through his mind. But he stayed silent, letting her continue.

"I think about it a lot," she said. "And sometimes I feel sad that I wasn't patient enough to wait for you to wear yourself down. I could see you were in a struggle; I just got tired of watching you. All your energy going into something you'd never be able to win."

"I don't want you to feel sad about me," he said.

"Thanks. We were together a long time."

"I know," he said, staring at her.

"I just... couldn't go on like that anymore. I couldn't keep hoping that things would get better. It hurt too much to get my hopes up every time. I began to see our problems as river rapids—just rushing and swirling, with rocks and white water, and you on one side and me on the other. And no bridge."

"Why didn't you tell me what you saw, the mistakes I was making?" he asked. "Even that night, when I came to see you here?"

"Would you have listened to me? Would you have believed me?" she asked.

He shook his head. No, he wouldn't have believed her. He would have tried to talk her out of it, convince her to see him as her protector, instead of someone who lived to get into bar fights, beat the living shit out of anyone who crossed him, get back—not so much at the people who'd given him and his mother a hard time, but the circumstances that had stolen all their hopes and dreams.

"I was just about eight months pregnant when you came to see me that last time. We sat on that rock outside the cottage . . . I told you about Randy; that it wasn't working out. I felt Charlie kicking inside the whole time."

"I wish I could have raised him with you," Gavin said.

"Shh," Sheridan said, looking away. "Stop now . . ."

He just stared into the night and felt glad she was here right now. She was so close, he could have reached over to take her hand. He glanced down, saw it resting on the arm of the deck chair. Her wrists and hands were so fine; her fingers were long and elegant. He'd loved watching her play guitar.

"Well, never mind all that," she said, breathing the

sea air. "That's ancient history. It's nice to be here on your boat now. Really nice."

"Thanks," he said. "I'm glad you came out. Would you like a drink?"

She shook her head. "I'm . . . I'm not drinking to-night."

"Okay," he said. For some reason, that made him happy.

"What's her name?" she asked.

"Her?" he asked. "There's no 'her.'"

She laughed, sounding a little nervous and embar-rassed. "I mean your boat. What's she called?"

"Oh. The *Squire Toby*," he said.

She was silent for a few moments. Small waves lapped the hull, and they heard the sound of a fish jumping out of the water. Did she know what it came from—did the name of his boat sound familiar? Sheridan was named for Sheridan Le Fanu, the Irish-man considered the greatest writer of ghost stories in Victorian times.

"*Squire Toby*?" she asked.

"Yeah," he said.

She nodded. He knew she got it. *Squire Toby's Will* was the title of one of Le Fanu's best-known works. He couldn't name his boat after the woman he loved, because she didn't love him. It wouldn't have been right. But naming his boat after a ghost story written by her namesake—what was wrong with that?

"My grandmother loved that story."

"Ah, Aphrodite."

"I miss her," Sheridan said.

"She and Clio were all right. I used to love going to your cottage when we were kids. Your grandmother once told me my father was standing right over my shoulder; that was the summer we were twelve."

Sheridan nodded, glancing over at him. "She told me. Your father was never far away from you. Even through all your trouble..."

"I loved your grandmother," Gavin said.

"Well, she loved you," Sheridan said.

"I thought that might get me farther than it did," Gavin said, trying to laugh. "With you."

"You didn't need any help," Sheridan whispered.

A power boat puttered in from beyond the breakwater, fishermen back from Wickland Reef. The *Squire Toby* swayed slightly in the wake, and Gavin caught Sheridan's wrist as her deck chair slid a few inches.

Her skin singed the tips of his fingers. He stared into her blue eyes, trying to read everything about her. The water rocked them, reminding him of when they were young and often on a boat. The way he felt about Sheridan was eternal, and he'd always known it.

"Sheridan," he said, wanting to pull her into his arms. "Remember that song, the first song you ever played me?"

She shook her head, but he'd never believe she could forget it.

"Maybe it's time to write another song. One that picks up where that one left off."

She shook her head hard. "No," she said. "No more songs, no more music...that's over."

Her suffering was in her eyes, in the air. Gavin wanted to reach for her and hold her, but he couldn't. She was missing Charlie so much, he could feel it himself, as if he and she shared the same heart.

"I have to go," she said, sliding her wrist away. "And I have to ask you a favor."

"What?" he asked, ready to promise anything.

"Leave me alone," she said.

They stood there staring at each other for a few more moments, then Sheridan climbed down the ladder, untied the painter, and climbed into the dinghy. Lifting her oars, she set them into the oarlocks; before starting to row, she leaned on the oars and looked up at Gavin. She opened her mouth for a second—Gavin swore she'd been about to say something else. But she didn't, not even a word. She just nodded and rowed away.

He stood at the rail, watching her go. He hadn't made any promises, and she'd asked him for the one favor he couldn't grant.

Her boat made ripples in the calm surface; their edges caught mysterious light. He listened to her oars pull and dip, pull and dip. He closed his eyes, wishing he could tell her: there was a rhythm to what she was doing, and it sounded like music.

And he wasn't going to leave her alone.

CHAPTER 7

SUMMER STORMS WERE THE BEST. THEY'D swirl into being over Southern waters, drawing strength from the warmth and moisture, charging up the coast. Lightning would streak through heavy air, and thunder would follow. The number of seconds between the lightning and thunder determined how far away the storm was.

Nell and Charlie had loved storms. One day—just before he'd left for college—while her father was at work and Stevie was painting in her studio, Nell had taken him up to the attic, to lie on an old mattress under the eaves. The rain pelted the roof and the wind shook the trees outside. She lay in his arms, staring up at the small window. Lightning flashed.

"One-Mississippi, two-Mississippi, three-Mississippi, four-Mississippi, five-Mississippi," he said, and then they heard the thunder crack, felt it in their bones.

"One mile away," she said, arching her back and kissing him.

His mouth was so hot, and he tasted so good. Every time they were together, every time they kissed, she felt both so happy and so...so something else. Not quite sad, not quite worried, but as if she were already missing him. As if she knew the kiss couldn't last forever, and that time would pass and she would have to go to work, or he would have to go home to dinner, or her dad would come home, or Stevie would call.

"Let's live up here in the attic," she said, holding him tighter.

"Right here?"

"Yes. And never leave."

"Okay," he said, pushing the hair back from her forehead, staring into her eyes. He brought his face close to hers, kissed her softly, then hard. Their bodies were so close, every possible inch touching. The rain drummed on the roof over their heads, and she never wanted it to stop. It felt like a cocoon, like a wet, silk, rainy chrysalis, and they were safely inside.

When they stopped kissing, she felt that weird not-sadness thing again.

"Oh," she said.

"What's wrong?"

"It's going to sound strange."

"Most things do," Charlie said. "Do you ever think that? Almost everything anyone says is really crazy? Unexpected, cool, and you have to wonder, why are they saying it?"

"Yeah," Nell said, smiling. She loved him so much,

partly because he "got it." He saw the world through the same kaleidoscope she did. Maybe it came from her mother dying when she was young, and his father staying out of his life, but Nell didn't want to think about those things. Bad stuff happened to everyone—it wasn't an excuse, just an explanation. That's why Charlie would make such a good documentary.

He kissed her again, running his right hand down her bare arm. She was wearing a bikini top and clamdiggers and his fingers felt so light on her skin, she arched her back and thought she might dissolve. But then they stopped kissing, and she had that standing-on-a-cliff feeling again.

"So," he said, "what's going to sound strange?"

"Oh," she said, "that I miss you."

He nodded. He was such a cute boy, Nell thought. He had big blue eyes and long light hair. He looked like a boy who could do absolutely anything, and be happy, and grow up to be the kind of man who looked much younger than his years. But right now, hearing Nell's words, he looked old. He had depth and wisdom and experience in his young eyes. . . .

"I miss you, too," he whispered.

"Why is that?" she asked, holding him tighter. "When we're right here together? And you haven't even left yet?"

"Because we know we can't live in the attic. You'll have to go downstairs eventually, and I'll have to go home, and then I'll have to . . ."

"Shh," she said. "Don't say . . ."

"Leave for New York."

Those words brought tears into Nell's eyes. She kissed his lips, touching her tongue to his, feeling how much she loved him. The truth seemed so cruel. Sometimes Nell felt she couldn't live another minute, facing all the goodbyes and loss that came with life.

Someday, though. Right? Someday? she wanted to ask. She wanted him to promise her, and her to promise him that they'd always be together. Next year she'd join him at NYU; they'd get an apartment in the Village as soon as they could convince their parents. They'd stay together, be faithful, never be apart. But something kept her from saying the words out loud; Charlie could never make her feel stupid, but she held the words in anyway.

The next time it stormed, they went back to the attic. This time Charlie had brought his video camera. He'd be leaving in a few days; he was going to turn eighteen at the end of the year, in December, and he'd be getting some kind of trust fund that would fund the documentary he wanted to make. His mother had let him get a really good camera, so he could start his filmmaking career.

Nell loved that about him. He was like her: a combination of wanting things to last forever, and a chafing to make things happen and get on with everything. That would happen at NYU. They'd learn everything there was to learn about writing a script, shooting a scene, editing the footage. Charlie was ahead of her, ready to start classes in just a couple of weeks. Even more, he had a great subject: lost fathers.

Having a father who was a total mystery was great for the film, but sad for Charlie. His mother never wanted to talk about it. Sheridan stopped short of really badmouthing Randy Quill—but she didn't have to. Charlie's aunts would do it for her. They tried to hold back, but once they got started, they couldn't restrain their anger at Randy for not being there for Sheridan and Charlie.

Nell knew how strange Charlie felt, having a dad like that. He was so sweet himself, so full of love, such a generous spirit. He couldn't fathom a man who would fail his family. And neither, really, could Nell.

He made a list of things he wanted to put in his film, shots he wanted to take, places he needed to visit. Nashville, of course; New York City; maybe Florida, Los Angeles, and Memphis, where Randy had girlfriends. He called his father. When he was younger, his father had been too busy to talk. Lately he'd been more voluble, told Charlie he had two other kids. Charlie had siblings.

But that stormy day, Charlie wasn't thinking of the film about his dad. He had another idea. They went up to the attic, with the idea of interviewing each other—something different, just for them.

He'd held the camera, asked her questions. Nell had giggled and felt nervous for about ten seconds. Then she'd blocked out the hardware in his hand, just talked as if they were having one of their normal conversations. Later they'd switched places, with her interviewing him.

How often had she watched the tape? Nearly every time it rained, she took it out. Right now the air was humid, thick with moisture. She felt it on her skin, a fine sheen of dampness. The windows were open, and outside she heard the first drops starting to tap the leaves.

She logged into his Talk2Me page. Keeping it going made her feel as if a part of him was still alive. She saw his picture, read through all his "favorites"— bands, books, movies, separated by category, each including a paragraph or two he'd written with his usual combination of passion and cool. Every entry reminded her of him. They had loved the same things: *To Kill a Mockingbird* was each of their top books.

Arctic Monkeys and the Hold Steady were Nell's current obsessions in the band department, but even though Charlie preferred Nashville music, he listed them as well—just as she'd listed some of his favorites on her page: Brad Paisley, George Strait, as well as Cumberland, the band he'd heard the night he died.

Nell copied the link to Charlie's Talk2Me page, e-mailed it to Gavin with a note: *You want to know who Charlie was, this will help....*

Writing those words, she felt her throat close tight. The ache was terrible, as if she'd swallowed broken glass. How sad it was, beyond belief, that the only way Gavin could get to know Charlie was through such meager means, by reading through paragraphs he'd written at least a year ago.

Charlie had been so young—his taste would have changed. Nell was wise enough to know that people didn't stay the same; the important, core matters would have remained, but other things might have shifted. In some ways, Charlie was trapped in amber, in the Talk2Me page he had created. Nell knew this, but still she couldn't bring herself to delete the account.

So she sent it to Gavin. She considered going down to the beach, walking in the rain. She liked that, the feeling of warm raindrops on her body. She could sit on the boardwalk, under the pavilion, and stare out at the gray water. But then she'd see Gavin's boat.

Nell had brought him here to investigate, but as far as she could tell, all he was doing was sitting out there. Every time she looked out there, he was on deck fishing or talking on his cell phone. She felt frustrated. Even though he hadn't taken her money, she was dying for him to do the job, to learn what had happened to Charlie.

So never mind going to the beach. Maybe something else . . . Putting Gavin out of her mind, she left her room. She headed down the cooler upstairs hall—no direct light penetrated, and a breeze wafted through from windows open in the bedrooms—to the attic stairs. As soon as she opened the door, she felt the heat—the attic was super-warm. But she didn't care . . . she wanted to feel close to Charlie, and this was where it was most likely.

She sat on the mattress where they used to lie together. Making sure the tape was in, she turned on the camera. Then she held it so she could see the monitor, and watched the interview she'd done with Charlie last summer, in this very spot. Sometimes she turned up the volume, to make it sound like his normal speaking voice.

Right now she watched without sound. The way he sat, so relaxed, his head resting back on the pillow against the sloping eaves. His sexy blue eyes, and the way his long blond hair fell across his face. Nell wished she didn't know the tape by heart, couldn't anticipate his every move. Like how he was going to brush the hair out of his eyes—now.

The rain started, and she turned up the sound. She heard her own question, off camera. "Why do you like storms so much?" And now Charlie answered, his voice filling the attic.

"Because of the energy," he said. "Because they can't stop themselves. . . . Summer storms especially. The named ones . . . hurricanes. They start down south . . . I started down south. . . ."

"Where?" asked off-camera Nell.

"Nashville. Nashville, Tennessee. It's different down there. The trees, the grass, the way music comes out of every window. Up here you look at houses at night and see blue light. TVs . . . Down there, you don't look so much as listen. You just hear music coming from everywhere."

"Tell me about you starting in Nashville. What do you mean?"

"I mean that's where my parents got together...."

"Who are your parents?"

"My mom is Sheridan Rosslare. Speaking of music, you know?" He smiled, played a little air guitar. Then his smile went away. "My father, well, he doesn't exist...."

"He must, if you're here."

"Really?" Charlie asked.

Nell froze the frame. She stared at Charlie's face. He was asking a rhetorical question, but she knew he meant it—she could see the pain in his eyes. Since his father wasn't in his life, did he really exist? What was he to Charlie?

The rain fell harder, and Nell played the rest of the tape. She loved the part at the end, where she'd set the camera on a stack of old books and gone to lie beside Charlie on the mattress. She sat still now, watching herself wriggle into his arms, lie against his tall, strong body. She watched his arms wrap her up, his hands tangle in her hair. She'd always loved the way he touched her hair....

"I love you forever," he'd whispered.

"So do I," she'd whispered back.

"I'd give you a ring if I could. But I don't have one. So..." He'd reached down next to the mattress, grabbed the old beach towel he'd dropped there. He bit the edge, tearing a strip of striped terrycloth. Sitting up, he'd leaned over to tie the piece of towel around her ankle.

"That's better than any ring," she'd said, pulling

him into her arms again, pressing her body against his.

"It means the same thing," he'd said.

"What is that?"

"That I love you, Nell. Always . . ."

Then they'd kissed and kissed, and whispered and whispered, never letting each other go, until the tape ran out.

They hadn't cared they were on tape. They'd been so carefree and careless, but they'd known, way better than most kids their age, that nothing lasted forever. They'd learned the hard way, the hardest way of all—by losing parents. Nell's mother had died, and Charlie's father had never even stepped up. But somehow, in those moments when the camera was running, they must have forgotten.

Because they looked so happy. Nell watched herself and Charlie kissing, and it hurt to see how happy they'd looked, and she still wore the cloth around her ankle.

Outside the small attic window, lightning flashed.

"One-Mississippi," Nell whispered, staring at her and Charlie on the screen. "Two-Mississippi . . ."

GAVIN SAT DOWN BELOW, oblivious to the storm outside. The wind had picked up, and the *Squire Toby* was rocking, pulling against the anchor line. Gavin ignored it, sitting at the chart table, staring at his computer screen. The police report lay on the mahogany surface, and he had the pages spread out and annotated.

Nell had included a link to Charlie's Talk2Me page, in case there were any clues about who he'd met that last night. The problem was, Gavin couldn't access it because, as he was cheerfully informed, *You're not a member yet!*

So he spent twenty long minutes he'd never get back registering at the site—giving them his e-mail address, thinking up a screen name—he picked the name Hubbard, because he was at Hubbard's Point and he was nothing if not original—and typing in a password.

He felt sleazy doing all this. It was creepy, a guy his age on a site like this. You read about it all the time, middle-aged men adopting fake screen names, trolling Internet sites for young prey. Once he logged on, he could see why they came here. The welcome page was filled with pictures of beautiful young people, male and female, with little cartoon balloons coming out of their mouths: "Talk to me!" "Talk to ME!" If these were his kids, he'd lock up their computers.

Finally all signed in, he went to the page Nell had sent him.

It was Charlie's. Gavin stared at the young man's photo, saw Sheridan in his eyes, the shape of his face, the lightness of spirit. He thought about the effort the boy had gone to, uploading photos and music, writing paragraphs about what mattered to him, including pictures and descriptions of Nell.

It felt invasive, reading through all the material. Gavin reflected on how open kids were, how much they revealed to the entire world. Who besides him might be reading Charlie's page right now, right this minute? And who had read it before last August 31? Who knew what danger lurked in the hearts of people trolling the Internet? It made Gavin shake his head, wishing kids would be more private.

Gavin scanned the comments left by Charlie's "friends." He couldn't tell which had been written by true acquaintances, which by total strangers. Every note on the page had a tone of closeness, of strange intimacy. The ones from Nell included her signature picture—a photo of her with Charlie. Even here, for her own signature, Nell had chosen to show herself with the boy she'd loved, as if they were one.

Staring at the picture, Gavin knew a little of what Nell was feeling. She still loved Charlie so much. The fact that he was dead did little if nothing to change that. Love was love. Gavin had felt it for Sheridan long after they had parted. They'd been together through their teens, into their early twenties. He felt it still.

Nell and Charlie hadn't had that long together. But still, gazing at their photo—arms draped around each other, Nell planting a kiss on his cheek—Gavin could see that the connection was the same. He bet they would have lasted—longer than he and Sheridan had, for sure. In the real world, too—in honest coupledom, not just in their minds.

He scanned Charlie's lists of "favorites." The kid

had had decent taste—or at least Gavin was able to recognize some of the books, movies, and music Charlie had cited. The one that really caught his eye, under "favorite bands," was Cumberland.

Gavin picked up the police report. He read the autopsy report first, saw what he already knew: that Charlie had died of a single punch to the side of his head. It had left knuckle prints and killed him instantly, and he'd apparently fallen to the ground right where he'd stood.

His body had been found in the dirt, just behind home plate at the ball fields—a city park all the way east on Houston Street. Blood had trickled from his nose and mouth, post-mortem. Along with Charlie's boot marks, there were fresh footprints of two other people. Among Charlie's belongings had been the ticket stub to a concert at Club 192 in the East Village, found in his jeans. The band playing that night had been Cumberland.

Gavin made a call on his cell phone, to Detective Joe Donovan, his old mate from the USS *William Crawford*—closer than a brother. Joe was his man in the NYPD.

"Hey," Gavin said when Joe picked up.

"So'd you get the fax or what?" Joe asked. "You can't be bothered to call and thank me? This isn't even my case, but I look into it just for you."

"Thank you. I have a question."

"You're welcome. Fire away."

"What about the band Cumberland?"

"Uh, what are you talking about?"

"The band Charlie went to see the night he died. What do you know about them, their fans, the people who were at the club?"

"Hmm," Joe said.

"Nice. You didn't look into them?"

"First, it's not my case, and second—why are you doing this?" Joe asked.

"Has your department caught the guy who did it?" Gavin asked, anticipating the long silence that would follow. "No, I know they haven't. So you know what that makes this? An unsolved case, a mystery."

"Unsolved case, yes; mystery, no. You know it, too, Gav. I hate to put it this way, because I know this is personal for you, but he was a young kid in the wrong place, and he got rolled."

"Listen," Gavin began.

"No. You're forty-four, forty-five now, and in your own way you've started playing it safe. Have you forgotten what it was like to go wandering at night? Used to happen to guys from the ship all the time, right? Foreign ports, we used to think we were the U.S. Navy, no one going to mess with us, right?"

"Right," Gavin said, reflexively running his hand over the scar slanting down his right side under his T-shirt.

"You got the scar to prove it," Joe said, as if they were video-conferencing. "All you had to do was give up your wallet, and you could have walked away. And, uh, I seem to remember another time, Norfolk, Virginia . . ."

"Okay, you made your point," Gavin said.

"You know, we're not supposed to give high-profile cases extra priority," Joe said. "But this one..."

"Sheridan Rosslare's son," Gavin said.

"Plus, she's your Sheridan."

"She's not 'my' Sheridan."

"Whatever."

"I'm serious—you know..."

"What I know is what I used to have to listen to, trapped in a sub with you, no escape. Sheridan, Sheridan, Sheridan..."

"Okay, shut up."

"So, what I'm saying is, we went the extra mile on this one. Trust me, Gav—you're not going to find anything more than what we already know. The best we can hope for is that someone knows something. Maybe our guy talked, or maybe the third party will get tired of protecting his friend."

"Third party?"

"Three sets of footprints in the dirt."

"All guys, all around the same size," Gavin said, looking at the police report. "Right?"

"Size 11, size 12 boots—Charlie's—and sneakers."

"What the hell's that mean?"

"Who knows?"

"It might not have been random, Charlie going to hear the band," Gavin said, staring at the profile still open on his computer screen.

"No?" Joe asked.

"Seems he was a fan of theirs."

"So were a lot of people. They're popular. My

daughter loves Cumberland. How do you know Charlie did?"

"I'm going to send you a link to his Talk2Me page," Gavin said.

"We check MySpace, Facebook, Talk2Me routinely," Joe said. "You're on there?"

"Yep."

"You're kidding me."

"Why would I kid?"

"Great. You're on Talk2Me. You and the pervs."

"Give me some credit," Gavin said. "I'm solving a case."

"I've heard that before," Joe said.

CHAPTER 8

A FEW HOURS AFTER THE THUNDERSTORM, Sheridan and Bunny sat on the bluestone terrace, drinking lemon verbena iced tea and gazing across the bay. It had stopped raining, and they could see patches of blue behind torn white clouds. Haze hung over the landscape, a gauzy film caught on the rocks and in the rosebushes, and Sheridan felt haunted.

"What a lovely boat," Bunny said, binoculars pressed to her eyes.

"Stop spying on him," Sheridan said.

"What's he doing? He keeps pacing around . . . is he on a cell phone? Who's he talking to?"

Sheridan ignored her sister, concentrating on the taste of the tea. It was light and refreshing, infused with mint and orange rind, the perfect summer drink. It would be so much better with some Wild Turkey poured in. But she was trying to make it two days in a row bourbon-free, so she just sipped the tea instead and tried not to think about what had been bothering her all through the night.

"Do you have his number? Why don't you call and ask him for dinner?"

"Because we said what we wanted to say on the boat last night."

"Sheridan, he's all alone out there on his boat. Don't you think he might enjoy a home-cooked meal?"

"I'm not much of a cook."

Bunny was so intent on watching Gavin, she didn't even lower the glasses to shoot Sheridan a look or tell her that wasn't the point. She just kept her equanimity and continued.

"I'll cook. Or Aggie will. It doesn't matter."

"I asked him to leave me alone."

Bunny gave her a look as if she was crazy. "Why?"

"Why do you think? I can't take any more pain. Please don't ask me again."

Sheridan found herself following Bunny's gaze across the water, staring at Gavin's boat. Last night he'd said he would have helped raise Charlie. She thought of the words now, a promise that could never come true. Yet often, during Charlie's growing up, she'd seen echoes of Gavin. He wasn't her son's father, wasn't in his life at all, yet there were ways Charlie seemed so like him.

Maybe it was because, like Gavin, Charlie had grown up without a father. Here at the beach, surrounded by kids with two parents, intact families, Charlie had always seemed tougher than anyone else. He would swim during hurricanes, ride the turbulent waves, test the sea. He'd always led the pack of kids that repainted the graffiti shark on the big rock over at Little Beach. She knew he wasn't exactly a stranger to pot.

Last night Sheridan had had to hold herself back from telling Gavin that Charlie was smart and tough like him. If Gavin had been part of their family, if he'd helped raise Charlie, would that have tempered her son's wild side or made it worse?

She had gotten through these last months telling herself that Charlie's death had been random. It could have happened to anyone. He'd had too much to drink, wandered down to the river. There'd been a confrontation.

But over what? Had someone wanted his money and his watch—the only valuables he'd had with him? Sheridan had been pushing down her own fears, that maybe Charlie had gone looking for trouble. Maybe he wanted to buy pot, or maybe he just wanted to claim the city for his own.

She hugged herself, looking toward Gavin's boat. Feeling pulled into the past and not knowing why, she just stared at the white hull shining in the sun. She and Gavin had been together for almost nine years, starting when she was fifteen. They'd grown up together, and she'd had to deal with her feelings about the way he loved to tempt danger. She remembered nearly passing out from the shock of seeing his scar. Brand new—raw, red, raised, running all down the length of his side. Looking at it, she'd felt sick.

"What did you *do*?" she'd asked.

"I just reacted, Sheridan," he'd said. "He came at me, and I fought back..."

"You make it sound like nothing, like it was no big deal. Gavin, if he'd cut you an inch closer to your heart..."

"He didn't, all right?"

"No, not all right..."

"You can't change people," he said. "People are who they are, Sheridan. Sometimes I get into fights..."

That had made her think. She'd loved him for a long time, had believed herself capable of accepting the true, real, complete Gavin Dawson—differences and all. She believed in peace and love, he believed in military solutions. She was against guns, he was never without his pistol. She sang tender songs of love and healing, he couldn't walk away from a knife fight. It made her feel insane.

"You know what I think?" she asked. "I think you want to push me away."

"The opposite," he said, reaching for her. "I want you right here."

"No," she said. "You say that, but I don't believe you. You're trying to get me to leave you."

"Sheridan—"

"I see it now," she said, feeling pressure in her chest, tears building. "I keep waiting, thinking some-day we'll be happy. You'll get out of the Navy, and we'll live together. You'll get the fighting out of your system. The anger. You'll...love me."

"I do love you," he said, his eyes wide. He was

scared—she could see it. He sensed the change in her, saw that she had given up on them. And she had; in that moment, she felt everything shift inside her. She was tired of waiting for something that wasn't going to happen.

"It's over," she said.

"Sheridan."

She shook her head, tears pouring down her cheeks. "I never thought I'd say that, and I never wanted it to happen. But I can't go on like this, Gavin."

"I only have three years left on this tour . . ."

"Three years."

"That's not so long," he said. "We've been together so long."

"I want a life, Gavin. I'd like someone to come home to, to have children with. I'd like to spend summers at Hubbard's Point with you right there with me. I'd like to sit on the porch and look out to sea without thinking of you on a submarine under a different ocean. I'd like to know we're going to grow old together instead of worrying you're going to die in a stupid fight."

"Okay, I'll never fight again," he said.

She'd stared at him, knowing he was lying. And in that moment, she felt it all drain away, the things that made love real and possible: trust, connection, the spark of belief that things between them would keep getting better.

The sensation shocked her: she'd been so at-tached to Gavin for so long, and suddenly she

doubted everything about him. She felt betrayed by
her own good sense—why hadn't she let herself see
the truth? She began looking back, noticing ways
she'd ignored the obvious, the way she'd fooled herself into thinking she could love him forever, just
the way he was—instead of admitting to herself that
she had needs, too. She'd been waiting for a change
that would never come.

Over the years since, she'd spent many sleepless
nights wondering whether she'd made a mistake—
whether her pride had gotten in the way. Should
she have been more patient? Could she have waited
longer, seen if he'd come around? Could she have
met him halfway? She knew the answer was no.

In spite of all Gavin's rough edges, she'd never
found anyone she'd loved more. The problem was,
she wasn't willing to give up the part of herself that
craved meeting on common ground to be with
him. He might not believe it, but loving him had
hurt her so much more than Randy ever had.
Randy had never had the same kind of power—not
even close.

Staring at his boat, she knew that Gavin would
have understood Charlie. He might have helped
him to know that what you feel as a young man is
different from what you feel when you get older.
He might have helped Charlie to know that he
had to survive, to learn these lessons. The what-ifs
were so impossible in a million ways . . . and still
too much to bear. Sheridan stood up and walked
into the house.

"Are you okay?" Bunny asked, following her.

"I don't know," she said.

"It's having Gavin here. He's stirring everything up..." Bunny said. "How can he not? Let's normalize the situation, just have him up for dinner."

"Bunny," Sheridan said.

"I always liked Gavin. Agatha did, too. We loved you two together... but we also just liked him so much. I guess, I don't know... honey, we'd just like to spend a little time with him, so we can see how he's turned out."

Sheridan stared out at the boat, rocking on its mooring. "I think he's settled down some," she said.

"I'm sure that's partly why he's come back to Hubbard's Point," Bunny said. "To let you know that."

"He named his boat after one of Sheridan Le Fanu's ghost stories," Sheridan said.

"Well," Bunny said. "That's like naming it after you."

Sheridan didn't reply, but she felt color rising in her face.

"Why don't you invite him? Agatha and I would love to cook. I could make my curried summer squash soup, and she would make those tiny lobster canapés, and we'd collaborate on the main course... let's see... maybe grilled striper with herbs from your garden?"

"Bunny..." Sheridan said again.

"Let us know when would be good, and we'll get here early and help you clean up."

Sheridan looked around her living room. Books

and music were piled everywhere. Her guitar cases were dusty. Cobwebs hung in the corners. The window glass was frosted with salt. She had done her best, but lately housework and everything else had been a little too much for her.

"Thank you," she said. "But I can't, Bunny."

"Why can't you?" her sister asked. "Listen to me now, Sheridan. You're my little sister, and I've been holding my tongue long enough. You have to be careful, or loneliness will do you in."

Sheridan stared at her sister. Her mother used to say, *You'll have many friends, but only two sisters.* She loved her two older sisters more than almost anyone. But sometimes she expected, or at least wanted, them to understand her a little more than they did. She turned toward the living-room window, looking at Gavin's boat, out by the breakwater. Her sisters were both happily married; they thought that love could cure or heal anything.

As a Nashville singer, Sheridan had made a good living on that very premise. But losing Charlie had knocked it out of her. She couldn't stand the idea of getting close to Gavin again.

Loving him so deeply had nearly destroyed her once. She couldn't afford to even get close to it again.

SUMMER DAYS WERE ALL THE SAME for the kids of Hubbard's Point. They were timeless, and if you looked from afar at the beach, you'd see kids sprawled on blankets and towels, working on their tans and listening to music, talking to their friends and falling in love. You might not have any idea of whether you were looking at this generation, or the last, or the one before that.

Nell lay on her back, using Billy McCabe's back as a pillow. Billy was Peggy's brother, and very indulgent of Nell. After the thunderstorm, the day had cleared up, and everyone who wasn't working had flocked to the beach. The sun was so hot, it dried the sand quickly. Nell had her eyes closed, listening to the waves and the voices of her friends.

"Nell..."

She opened one eye, saw Wes Stanfield crouched there beside her. He was tan and wore cutoffs; his body was wiry and hard from a summer of working outside.

"Hey," she said.

"I was wondering," he said. "You going to the movie tonight?"

Movies on the beach, Nell thought. She shook her head.

"No, not tonight," she said.

"Because I was thinking maybe we could sit together, and then head over to Little Beach afterwards. There's a party..."

Nell smiled. Wes was acting as if she hadn't just said no already. His hope and attention were sort of touching. But Nell's heart wasn't in movies on the beach or parties at Little Beach or anything else. She just shook her head.

"But..." Wes went on, touching her hand. He

started to trail his fingers up her arm, until she pulled it back hard, gave him a cold look. Sitting up, she stared at him.

"Didn't you hear me say no?" she asked, so loudly everyone heard and turned to look at her.

"Okay, Nell," Wes said, backing off. She could see she'd shocked him, hurt him, with her tone. She glanced around, saw all the other kids watching her. She started to stand, realized she was shaking, and stayed where she was, making herself be still.

Partying and hanging around with boys had been okay this summer, in spite of how much she missed Charlie. But suddenly it wasn't okay anymore. She stared across the smooth, calm bay at Gavin's boat. Now that he was at Hubbard's Point, Nell knew that everything was different.

Until Gavin came, Nell had been lulled into the acceptance that Charlie was gone forever. She'd felt mere grief, dull and aching. But what she felt right now was alive and wild, a frightening thing inside herself. Now, watching the film of Charlie brought home as never before the way he moved, sounded, touched her. Suddenly she felt as if she *had* to see Charlie again, and for some reason having Gavin here made that feel possible.

As if Nell hadn't hired Gavin to find Charlie's killer, but to find Charlie himself. The thought rocked her, made her feel she just might be losing her mind.

"You okay, Nell?" Billy asked, turning to look at her.

She nodded. "I just need a swim," she said. She

adjusted her pink bikini and stood up. Then she took off in a dead run down the beach, and without even stopping to feel the temperature of the water, dived straight in.

STEVIE MOORE LEANED on a tall stool in her studio, working on a painting. She was illustrating her latest book, *Three Blue Eggs in a Nest*. Having written children's books her whole career, it felt both odd and wonderful to be doing another one now, just as she was pregnant with her first child.

She painted the fine twigs, pine needles, and strands of hair woven together. When Nell was ten, and she and her father had just moved in here, Stevie and Nell used to take nature walks to Little Beach, the marsh, or, some days, to the Hubbard's Point cemetery. They loved the quiet there, the austere and aching beauty of the old lichen-covered granite stones. Sometimes they'd bring paper and charcoal, make rubbings of winged angels, carved names.

But not on the day Stevie was remembering now, that was coming to life on her canvas. . . . They were just taking a walk, spending time together. There'd been a bad storm, and they came upon a robin's nest knocked out of a tree. They looked inside, and there nestled three perfect, unbroken blue eggs. Somehow they had survived the fall.

Painting now, Stevie remembered how panicked Nell had been. They had to climb the tree, replace the nest in the crook of the branches so the mother would return to it. But which tree? Which crook of which branches? Crying, Nell had scanned all the surrounding trees. The graves were on an open hillside surrounded by woods of pine, scrub oak, and sassafras.

They'd heard the mother robin before seeing her. Her grief was unmistakable. She was flying around and around a thick white pine. Stevie and Nell stood on the ground, holding her nest. They watched the robin fly in circles, as if wrapping the pine in invisible thread, as if she could hold something together.

"She's showing us," Nell had wept. "She wants her babies back..."

Nell had wanted to climb up, put the nest back; but she was sobbing so hard, Stevie was afraid she would fall. Back then, still dealing with the rawness of her own mother's death, Nell could so easily break at the thought of any mother and child being separated...even unhatched ones. So Stevie had climbed instead.

Working on her canvas, she remembered holding the nest in one hand, using the other to pull herself up into the pine tree. The needles were thick and long, blocking out the sky. She was surrounded by tree, feeling the sticky black pitch under her fingers. The nest felt precarious; she tried to hold it on the very tips of her tarry fingers, to minimize the human touch. It was such a crazy idea, such a long shot, that they could replace a nest, to hope that the mother—however grief-crazed right now—would return to hatch the eggs.

If she could even find the spot in the tree. Stevie had always loved nature, especially birds. Her children's bird books had captivated millions, but writing about happy outcomes in the natural world was so much different from the ambiguity and harsh reality of true life. But Nell was right: the mother robin was a harbinger, guiding them to the spot. So Stevie climbed higher, scouring the trunk and branches for any sign of where the nest had been.

And she saw it: a few twigs and a strand of human hair, caught in the fork of two small branches. Glancing into the nest, she saw more hair beneath the eggs. Someone who lived nearby had cleaned her hairbrush while the robin had been nesting. Inching out the branch, arm outstretched, she placed the nest into the exact spot. It fit perfectly, the missing piece of a puzzle.

Stevie climbed down the tree. She had a lump in her throat, thinking of Nell missing her mother, Emma, so much, and wondering whether the mother robin would return to her nest. White pine branches grow nearly down to the earth, so she stayed in the green enclosure almost until her feet hit the ground. When she stepped out, Nell was smiling, pointing up.

"She went back," Nell said, grabbing Stevie's hand. "See? She's already on her nest!"

And it was true. Stevie stood there with Nell, staring up. The mother had disappeared into the tree, but they knew where to look; and there, through the long pine needles, they saw her small dark head atop the nest. It was a small miracle, a gift of summer. She and Nell had returned often, watching the robin's nest.

The babies hatched. They'd learned to fly. And they flew away. One day Stevie and Nell returned, and they were all gone: mother, babies, everyone. They'd scavenged beneath the tree, and found two blue eggshells: all that was left from the hatching. Nell had cried again, but in a different way. Some losses in life were easier to take than others....

Now, painting the nest, Stevie thought of Sheridan. Sheridan's son, Charlie, was buried in that same cemetery as the robin's nest. Nell went there every day, to be with him. Sheridan, too.

The baby kicked inside Stevie's stomach, someone she didn't know but already loved. Her new book was mixed up with all of them: Nell, Charlie, Sheridan, the new baby, Jack, Stevie herself, and the robin family. Jack was so upset with her, and she loved him so much. Where did any of it begin, and where did any of it end? Life was one big love story, and you couldn't really separate any of it.

Lost in her work, she suddenly heard footsteps on the stairs and a voice calling her name.

"Stevie? Are you up here?"

Looking over her shoulder, she saw Sheridan poking her head into the studio door.

"Come in," she said, putting down her brush, wiping her hands on a rag.

"I knocked," Sheridan said. "But I guess you didn't hear."

"I'm sorry," Stevie said, leading her to a wicker

loveseat near the big, arched north window. "I'm glad you're here."

"You're working," Sheridan said. "That wonderful state where nothing else exists but you and your ideas and the art flowing from your fingertips."

Stevie smiled. Not too many people got it like Sheridan. "You know," she said. "I do it with a paintbrush and canvas; you do it with your guitar and your voice."

"The reason I came..." Sheridan said, then stopped.

"You never need a reason," Stevie said quietly.

Sheridan tried to smile, getting herself together. Stevie waited, gazing at her old friend. Like so many of their other friends here, they'd grown up together at Hubbard's Point. They'd known each other as babies, before they could talk. Now they were going through life together.

Stevie noticed how beautiful her friend was: she was ethereal, and it was the white hair. It made her blue eyes spark, made her pale skin glow. But it also accentuated the sorrow. Stevie had heard of people shocked into going gray overnight; until Sheridan, she had never seen it happen.

"The reason I came," Sheridan continued finally, "was to apologize for the other day."

"Sheridan, you never have to..."

"I do," Sheridan said, stopping her, hand on Stevie's wrist. "You brought me that beach plum jelly, and I was really rude."

"No you weren't," Stevie said, smiling. "But I heard the crash after I walked down your hill."

"Yeah," Sheridan said, smiling back. "I winged it pretty well."

The two women chuckled. Then Sheridan stared at Stevie's belly. Her hand inched close, as if she wanted to touch it. But she didn't.

"I'm so happy for you," Sheridan said, "and so jealous. That you're going to have your baby, and I've lost mine."

Stevie stared down at her friend's hand, still raised slightly. She thought of the mother robin flying in circles around the tree.

"I'm crazy with it," Sheridan said. "I can't stand to say his name, and I can't stand not to. The summer is filled with him, everywhere. I taste the lemonade I used to make for him. I hear his footsteps on the stairs at night, the way I used to when he'd sneak home from being with Nell."

"She still sneaks out," Stevie said. "She walks the beach roads because she wants to be with him. She goes where they used to walk together. She still wears that piece of towel around her ankle...."

"How can he not be here?" Sheridan asked. "How can someone so strong and alive not be here anymore?"

Stevie reached out and laced fingers with her friend, and they both were trembling. Inside, Stevie's baby kicked.

"People say I'll 'get past it,'" Sheridan said, gasping. "Can you imagine?"

"No," Stevie said.

"My sisters, I love them so much, but they're driving me insane. They brought me cookies . . . cookies!"

"Well, and I brought you beach plum jelly."

"I know," Sheridan said. "But somehow you're different. You know me in a way they don't. You know where the songs live . . . you know what a dark cave it is, because you go there, too, for your paintings."

Stevie held her hand, stared at her. She knew Sheridan had said she'd come over to apologize, but suddenly Stevie knew that wasn't true. She'd come over because Stevie knew about the cave, the place creative people had to live sometimes. Loss both drove you deeper into the cavern and kept you out of it.

"I was blocked a while back," Stevie said. "It was after my third divorce, and I felt like the biggest love-loser. Emma had died, and Maddie was drinking, and all I could think about was what's the meaning of life, and why are we here, and when will I meet my next husband? Everyone I knew had kids; I'd been writing children's books my whole career. No kids, no love . . . I was just a serial marrier."

"Don't say that. You believed in love so much, you had to keep test-driving it out. You were just kicking all those other tires until Jack came along."

"That's a nice way to put it." Stevie smiled.

"Well, you know I wrote 'Road Test' about you, right?" Sheridan asked.

"Really?" Stevie asked. She shivered to hear it. Everyone always thought writers' books were about them, singers' songs were about them, artists' paintings were their secret portraits. But the lyrics of one of Sheridan's ballads had reminded Stevie of life before Jack Kilvert:

> *I drove around the block a few times*
> *Baby, I took it down the road.*
> *You know I hit the open highway*
> *Pushed the pedal down, and I was gone....*

"Yeah," Sheridan said. "You were an inspiration to me. The way you kept believing in love, even after getting let down so hard. Especially after Sven."

"Husband number three, and a sociopath to boot."

Sheridan nodded. "Even so, love triumphs in your life. Me, after Randy—and well, especially Gavin—forget it. I haven't trusted anyone, or wanted to get close. That's why I had to write about you. You were so open to Jack."

"I was," Stevie said, shivering. "I still am. But he's not so sure."

"Jack?"

"Yep."

"He's not so sure about *what*?" Sheridan asked, sounding shocked.

"About me."

"Come on. He loves you more than anything."

Stevie nodded. "I know. I feel the same way about him."

"Then what's wrong?"

"He can't understand why I don't want to get married."

"Can I ask you something?"

"Sure."

"Why don't you want to get married?"

"Well, after being married so many times, I guess marriage just stops meaning very much. Love is all that counts, Sheridan...that's what I believe, anyway. Believe it with all my heart."

"What about Jack?"

Stevie stared down at her belly. "He wants to get married."

"Well, especially with the baby coming."

Stevie nodded. "I know. He's more conventional than I am. He really thinks we should make it legal before the baby's born."

Sheridan laughed. "Jack's not conventional—that's not it. He loves you. You're just falling back on the crazy-artist thing. We get away with a lot in the outside world because of that. 'Crazy artist'—license to be an idiot."

Stevie nodded, smiling. "No one blinked when I kept getting married—I think it was just another spectator sport here at Hubbard's Point: who's that nutty Stevie Moore going to bring home next? And now they don't blink when I'm pregnant and living with Jack, not getting married."

"You contrarian, you," Sheridan said.

"It's just, before I used to get married because, who knows why? I wanted to hold on to the person, I wanted the love to last forever, and I thought the piece of paper would help that happen. I was after security. Now I love Jack with everything, and I want it to last even longer than forever, and I know it will, but..."

Sheridan nodded. "But you know nothing ever does."

"Something like that. *Not* marrying Jack is how I honor our true love," Stevie said. Losing Emma, one of her best friends and original Hubbard's Point beach girls; losing her parents; and even watching Sheridan—and Nell—lose Charlie had made Stevie realize how short and precious it all was, how transient, how ephemeral. A marriage license meant very little compared to the enduring reality of love.

"Well, I do understand," Sheridan said. "I was married to Charlie's father for so short a time."

"From what I remember, he's not the one you really loved."

Sheridan glanced up. "Have you been talking to Nell?"

"You mean, do I know she called Gavin?" Stevie asked. "Yes."

"Have you seen him?" Sheridan asked.

"No," Stevie said. "I've been holed up in my studio, working on this book. I see his boat out at the breakwater...she looks like a beauty. Nell's seen him, though. She's gone out there."

"She hired him," Sheridan said.

Stevie nodded. She waited for Sheridan to get angry, but it didn't happen. She just stared toward the big north window, at the cool light pouring in.

"Maybe Nell is right, and we have to know about what happened. I don't know, Stevie—I don't know what difference it could make. But I know how he felt about her..." Sheridan paused. "Maybe I should have cared more about the police investigation, done that for my son. But all I really cared about was that he's gone. That's all that counted to me."

"That's how I would be," Stevie said. "But you know, Gavin's here now. Let him go looking. He'll find whatever there is."

Sheridan nodded.

"Good," Stevie said.

"My sisters think we should invite him for dinner at my house," Sheridan said.

Stevie stared at her, waiting.

"The worst thing that ever happened to me— before Charlie—was breaking up with Gavin. I swear, I wasn't sure I'd survive. He and I had been so close, and when we finally went apart for good, I felt as if my skin had been peeled off. I had nothing between me and—everything else."

"I remember."

"He was everything to me, Stevie," Sheridan said. "I grew up with him, and I saw the world through his eyes. I felt so alive and awake with Gavin. And I'd never imagined not being with him."

"None of your friends ever imagined that either," Stevie said.

"He's not...tamable," Sheridan said.

"Why would you want to tame him?" Stevie asked.

"I don't," Sheridan said. "But I can't live on the

edge. I couldn't back then, when we were young—and I definitely can't now." Standing, she walked over to Stevie's easel. She stood looking at the painting of the nest and the three blue eggs.

"Well, for whatever it's worth: you and he were really something."

"We were," Sheridan said. "But the differences between us were too much to take."

"Opposites attract," Stevie said. "To put it mildly."

"I know what you mean," Sheridan conceded. "I just couldn't take worrying that he'd never come home. He took so many chances. And he was away... all the time. Life on a submarine."

"I remember," Stevie said. "But he's not on a submarine anymore, is he?"

Sheridan stared at the painting for a few minutes, her back to Stevie. When she spoke, still not turning around, her voice was thick.

"You know how fast Gavin came down from Maine, as soon as Nell called him? He's here for Charlie... he didn't even know my son, and he's here to find out who hurt him. Something Randy never did."

"His own father," Stevie murmured.

She stared at Sheridan. She'd admired her so much, the way she'd raised Charlie all by herself. She'd made sure he had strong male role models, including Jack. She'd taken care to see he had good coaches, excellent teachers. While Randy, whom Stevie had never met, just stayed away.

"Do you and Randy ever talk now?" Stevie asked.

"Never."

"But you did, after Charlie died...."

"One conversation," Sheridan said. "That was it. I called to give him the news. He cried."

"Really?" Stevie asked, surprised.

Sheridan nodded. "He said Charlie had reached out to him, that he had wanted to finally have a relationship with his *son*. I sat there on the phone while he sobbed. But you know what?"

Stevie shook her head. "What?"

"He never even came to Charlie's funeral."

"I know," Stevie said. "Jack and I noticed...of course."

"He claimed he didn't want to upset me—he said he was afraid that if he showed up, I would feel worse."

"As if you could have."

"Those were crocodile tears he was crying," Sheridan said. "His crying was about Randy, about feeling sorry for himself. Not about Charlie. And here's Gavin, who didn't even know Charlie, wanting to find out what happened to him."

Stevie stood up, walked over to Sheridan, put her arm around her.

"Then don't you think," Stevie asked, "you should invite him for dinner?"

Sheridan didn't reply.

"I'll take that as a yes," Stevie said. "Just tell me which day."

"I don't know..." Sheridan said, still obviously in so much doubt.

It was a summer of turmoil for the women on the Point. Stevie's own stomach was in knots over Jack,

and she could see Sheridan grappling with not knowing how to be with Gavin. Stevie suddenly knew she
had to help her friend; Sheridan was gripped by the
past and old hurt, and it was time for her to let go.
There was nothing like a Hubbard's Point summer
dinner to help that happen.

"I do know," Stevie said. "Tomorrow."

"No," Sheridan said. "I can't—"

"We can," Stevie said. "You, me, and your sisters.
We're having a dinner party. Jack and I will be there.
We'll bring a pie."

"Stevie, I don't know..."

"But I do," Stevie said.

She took a deep breath, gave Sheridan a hug. The
truth was, Stevie had lied; she didn't know either.
Love was a mystery neither friend had been able to
solve. Sheridan and Gavin had crashed nearly twenty
years ago. Yet here they were, trying to connect with
each other.

The least Stevie could do was help Sheridan to be
brave.

And hope that maybe some of it could rub off on
her.

CHAPTER 9

VINCENT HAD OFFERED GAVIN ONE OF HIS
cars to take into the city, but Gavin was more
of a train guy. He didn't believe in being stuck in
traffic—it was against his nature. So early that morning, he took the Shore Line East from Old Saybrook
to New Haven, then switched to Metro North into
Grand Central.

The ride was nice and relaxing. It took him through
the marshes of the Connecticut shoreline, all green and
muddy and filled with herons and egrets and hunting ospreys. It meandered through the cities of New
Haven, Bridgeport, Norwalk, and Stamford.

He stared at old factory buildings and bustling
marinas. He brought coffee, a doughnut, and the
Hartford Courant, and he watched all the guys in
suits getting on at the suburban stops and felt glad he
lived the life he did.

He'd caught an early train because he wanted to
get back home in plenty of time for dinner. Last night

he'd somehow missed a call from Sheridan—maybe he'd been on another call. She left him a voice mail, almost reluctantly inviting him for dinner tonight. He'd planned to get together with Joe and his wife, but he canceled immediately and called Sheridan back—again and again.

She didn't pick up—even though she'd just called. He pictured her sitting by the phone, knowing it was him, not really wanting to talk. For some reason, she'd decided to invite him over, but her heart wasn't in it. Her voice had sounded so tentative in the message. He'd wanted to get her live on the phone, so he could hear what she was feeling, connect with her in a real way and convince her this was good and right, while at the same time trying to reassure her it was no big deal.

But she didn't answer, so he just left her a message saying he'd be there. He tried to put all that into his voice—all the rightness and goodness and no-big-dealness of it all. The whole thing made him feel a little off-balance—but it was just so much better than being asked to leave her alone.

After arriving in New York, he took the 6 train downtown from Grand Central, got off at Astor Place, and started limping east. At this time of morning, St. Mark's Place was still asleep. A couple of restaurants were serving breakfast; he picked up another coffee to drink as he walked.

His foot was killing him already. The only thing he could get over the bandage was a stupid-looking brown sandal. So it not only hurt like hell, it also made him look ridiculous right here in hipster central.

He passed Tompkins Square Park, saw people walking their dogs and moms walking with their kids, and wondered what was happening to New York. When he was young, this had been a haven for junkies and the homeless. He remembered the squatters with a sort of misty fondness.

Sheridan had gone through a phase of trying to fit into the Northeast's music scene. Her heart belonged to Nashville, but she hadn't made the move yet. Her band at the time had played at the Pyramid Club, as well as a place called 8BC. Located on one of the most decrepit and dangerous blocks in the city, the building had looked like something out of a war zone, and he'd always been amazed that it hadn't been condemned.

Now it was gone, and the East Village was condoland. Just like everywhere else, Gavin thought. Real estate developers deserved the tenth circle of hell as far as he was concerned. He headed south on Avenue B, past still-closed cute shops and restaurants. At least the neighborhood hadn't started waking up early— that would be the final indignity.

He walked down East Third Street, saw that the Hell's Angels clubhouse was still there. That both annoyed him and gave him a bleak sense of continuity: kick out the poor people, but let the bikers stay.

He retraced his steps, turned the corner, found Club 192. It was shuttered, as he'd expected. Posters of coming and past attractions were plastered to the steel grate and the brick wall, as well as to the plywood covering a neighboring construction site. Gavin stared at the tattered posters until he found Cumberland.

The photo showed a young woman holding a bass guitar, standing on a bridge over a muddy river. Gavin stared, recognizing the Nashville skyline behind her. Cumberland—the Cumberland River ran through the city. Obviously that explained the name, and the connection to Charlie's background gave Gavin a jolt of recognition, made his blood kick up a little. The woman's hair was short and dark; she had bright fire in her eyes, and Gavin found himself making comparisons to Nell. Had Charlie been drawn to the band because of this young woman?

His gut told him no, but maybe he was wrong. There was something poetic about her, the way she was staring into the water, lost in contemplation. Her pose, or that spark in her eyes, reminded him, a little, of Sheridan—at least when she'd been younger. After staring at her picture for a few more minutes, he eventually read the rest of the poster.

He saw that a second band, the Box Turtles, had opened for Cumberland. He jotted down a few details, then turned to leave. He walked along, wanting to get a feel for where Charlie had come, walk the route he'd taken just before his murder.

Taking out his cell phone, he called Joe.

"Hey, man," he said. "Do me a favor?"

"Sheridan gives you a better offer so you cancel

for dinner with me and Amy, but I'm supposed to be at your beck and call?"

"Yeah."

"Okay, what?"

"Come pick me up. My foot's fucking killing me."

"Where are you?"

"Avenue B and Houston."

"You're getting close to where you want to be. Hold tight, and I'll come get you."

"Thanks, Joe," Gavin said. "One last thing—can you pull anything the investigating officers found on Cumberland? And the band that opened for them? The Box Turtles?"

"What kind of band is called 'the Box Turtles'?"

"Never mind that. Just, can you bring me what your guys have on the bands Charlie heard?"

"I'll do my best," Joe said.

"Thanks." Gavin's foot was throbbing, and heat was starting to rise from the sidewalk.

"Be there soon, Gav."

Traffic poured off the FDR Drive, heading west onto Houston Street. Gavin breathed in the fumes, spotted an old milk crate between a bodega and a boarded-up bowling alley. "And I'll be right here waiting for you," he said.

Gavin sat down. He drank the rest of his coffee, sat back and watched the traffic pass by, coughed at the street sweeper churning up dust. A steady stream of people were coming up from the subway stop; some walked from apartments farther east. Must be nice to walk to work along the East River, he thought. If it involved seeing water, he'd be happy.

He found himself thinking about that picture of the young woman in front of the muddy river. He didn't try to weave her into the story, or even much wonder whether she had played any role in Charlie's life or death. He just let her drift in and out of his thoughts, her dark hair and bright eyes, and figured he'd find out what she meant to it all soon enough.

A few minutes later, Joe pulled up in an unmarked black sedan. Gavin climbed in, and they grinned at each other. Joe had lines around his eyes and mouth, but his expression looked the same as ever.

"Damn, good to see you," Joe said. "Even if you are a pain in my ass."

"Right back at you," Gavin said. Staring across the car seat, it seemed impossible to think of how much time they'd spent together under the sea, and how much time they regularly let pass before getting together.

"Well," Joe said. "Let's get to it."

"Sorry about tonight," Gavin said as Joe started driving. The car had been pointing west on Houston, but he did a U-turn right in the middle of the block and headed east toward the river.

"I know. So am I. But we'll do it again soon. That's for sure. That's an ugly sandal you're wearing."

"Thanks."

"What happened to your foot?"

"Stepped on broken glass. The bottom half of a jar,

shards sticking straight up. Cut right through my shoe."

"Ouch," Joe said. "Where were you, walking through broken glass?"

"Sheridan's yard," Gavin said.

"No comment," Joe said, driving down Houston, then taking the ramp under the FDR Drive. He rumbled down a connector toward the baseball fields, the East River flowing just beyond them. Again, Gavin's attention was caught by the river, and he thought of that woman in the poster. He shook the thought away, brought himself back to the present and reality.

Even in broad daylight, there was a deserted feel to the place. Gavin's heart beat faster now because he knew they were getting closer to where Charlie had died. He thought of Sheridan, and his blood started to pound.

He looked around as Joe slowed down, turning onto an access road. There was a sanitation truck moving slowly ahead of them. Gavin stared at the ball fields, green and shaded. The East River ran fast along this stretch—he looked across the fields at a red tug pushing a barge of concrete against the wild current. Waves thrashed out of the river, white against the low-riding hull. Joe parked behind a wire backstop, and the two men got out.

Heat rose from the pavement, summer in the city. Joe led Gavin straight to the bleachers. He stood still, catching Gavin's eye. Then he pointed at a spot on the ground.

"There," Joe said.

Gavin limped over. The field was covered with well-trodden grass, but in front of the bleachers it was all red dirt. He knelt down, put his hand flat on the ground. He knew from the police report that Charlie died here. His body had lain in this spot all through the night, until the sun came up.

All alone, he had died in a city brand new to him. The punch had killed him almost instantly, so he hadn't bled much. Even so, traces of Charlie's blood had soaked into this earth. Joe stood back saying nothing, and Gavin kept his hand pressed down. He thought of Sheridan, thought of her at home with the shades pulled, thought of Charlie dying right here. He stared at the ground, as if he could still see the footprints that had tramped around his body. Who had hit him, hard enough to kill him?

"The lady who found him . . ." Gavin said finally.

"A dog walker," Joe said. "Everyone in the city has dogs now."

"Did she see anything suspicious?"

"Nope. The city is so safe now. The murder rate's down even from last year; crimes like this don't happen anymore."

"This one did," Gavin said, his voice low.

"I know," Joe said.

Gavin stared down at the red clay. The sun was coming up over the trees, making the dirt brighter. He thought of all the days that had passed that Charlie hadn't seen. He thought of him lying here that night, and he just wondered: how long did it take, how soon before he died did he know he wasn't going to make it? Had his assailant run right away, had he stuck around to make sure Charlie was dead?

Why had it happened?

Young guys think they're going to live forever, Gavin thought. He and Joe had, for sure. But he remembered being stabbed, how he'd seen his own blood pumping onto the floor, felt blackness rising from within; and he'd had that moment he'd heard about, seeing his life pass before his eyes. Had Charlie experienced that? Had he felt afraid?

"Why did he come here?" Gavin asked.

"We don't know," Joe said. "There are two obvious possibilities."

"Drugs," Gavin said.

"Yeah, but we didn't find any in his system. And the other—a girl. Kids come down here to have sex at night."

"That wouldn't be it," Gavin said. His mind flashed on the Cumberland bass player, but then he thought of Nell. "He had a girlfriend."

"Come on, he was seventeen. Who knows who he might have met at the club? He had some drinks, maybe he forgot about his girl . . ."

"Say that did happen—did your guys talk to people at the club?"

"Of course. No one remembers seeing him."

"Well, another girl—that wouldn't be it anyway," Gavin said again. Then, after a few minutes, "So what else could it be?"

"I don't know. Maybe he just wanted some fresh

air. Had too much to drink at the club, and decided to come down to the river."

"And bumped into the wrong person," Gavin said.

"Like I said," Joe said. "It's just this: twenty years ago, that kind of crime wasn't rare, especially around here. But now..."

"The city's safe. You don't expect it."

"Right. Murders like this, we look at who knew the victim. The inner circle. Problem was..."

"Charlie was new in town," Gavin said, and Joe nodded. "He didn't have an inner circle here."

Gavin gazed out at the river, again seeing the brown Cumberland flowing under that bridge on the poster. Charlie had gone to school in Nashville for a while. Who was the girl? Had her path crossed his at some point? But if he'd known her, why wouldn't he have mentioned it to Nell? Unless Joe's theory was right, and this was about a girl after all.

After a few more minutes, Gavin was ready to go. He and Joe walked back to the car. Gavin had known there wouldn't be any clues to find here; he'd just wanted to visit the spot for Sheridan. And because it gave him a feeling about Charlie... The young man had been after something that mattered to him. And no matter what Joe thought, Gavin had met Nell— and he had a strong sense about Charlie's connection to her.

They drove back up Houston Street. They passed Katz's Deli, and even though it was early, on another day Gavin would have offered to take Joe to lunch. He didn't, though, and Joe just drove past.

Gavin stared at his old submariner friend and knew he hadn't wanted to be alone when he faced the place where Charlie had died. He opened his mouth to thank him, but couldn't speak. The truth of the boy's death, and the brutal terrible way he'd died, filled the whole car.

Joe asked him where he wanted to go. Gavin had thought he might stick around until Club 192 opened, but that might not be until well into the night, and he had to be back for Sheridan's dinner. Instead, he had Joe drop him off at Grand Central.

They said they'd see each other soon, that maybe Joe and Amy would drive out to Hubbard's Point for a day on the *Squire Toby*. Or maybe Gavin would return to the city, take Joe to lunch at Katz's. They said goodbye, and Gavin had started into the station when he heard his name being called. Turning, he saw Joe holding up a sheet of paper, so he went back, leaned into the open window.

"What?"

"I almost forgot. Here's the printout of those band lists—from both Cumberland and the Box Turtles."

"Thanks," Gavin said.

"No prob," Joe said.

It wasn't until Gavin was settled on the train, with a coffee in hand—on the water side, so he could watch the rivers and marshes and inlets of Long Island Sound—that he studied the lists.

Joe had printed them out from the Internet. From the looks of it, they came from the bands' websites. He read them both, focusing on Cumberland's:

Cumberland...direct from Nashville, featuring songs by Lisa Marie Langton.

Langton: bass, vocals.

Crispin: guitar, vocals.

Lance: keyboard.

Arden: percussion.

Gavin stared at the paper. Nothing looked familiar, but he was glad to have a name to put to the face of the girl on the poster. Lisa Marie Langton.

Folding up the paper, he stuck it in his pocket. He drank his coffee, staring out the scratched train window at the green marshlands and winding creeks leading to the blue Sound, on his way back to Hubbard's Point and Sheridan. He pictured her, and Nell, and then he brought to mind another girl's face, her dark hair and bright eyes, and knew that if she'd played a part in Charlie's death, he'd get her.

CHAPTER 10

GAVIN GOT OFF THE TRAIN AT THE SAYbrook station, took a cab across the Connecticut River to Hubbard's Point. As the car drove along, he felt he was heading home after a tough day, and the feeling was surprisingly deep. The salt air smelled so familiar, and the landscape had changed little over the years; the creeks and tidal marshes and beach pines and oaks were all the same. Paradise Ice Cream was still there, and the fish market, and the small boatyard on Black Hall River, and the pizza place, and the summer chapel. He felt melancholy mingled with happiness.

When he got to the beach, he paid the driver, climbed the seawall, and looked up at Sheridan's house. He stared for a long time; even though he'd see her for dinner in just a few hours, he wanted to go up there right now, hold her for a long time. He wasn't sure he had words for what he'd just experienced. He'd seen and touched the spot where Charlie had died.

Instead, he shoved his dinghy down the beach to the water, got his bandaged foot sandy and wet, and didn't even care. He rowed out to the *Squire Toby*, feeling good as he pulled on the oars, discharging pent-up energy. He tied the line to the boarding ladder, climbed aboard, ready to unlock the cabin, when he heard a shuffling sound up forward on the bow.

He held the stainless steel rail, inching along the wooden walkway up to the front deck; he winced, hearing the sand in his bandage scraping the finish. There, sunning herself, plugged into her iPod, was his client. Nell lay there on her back, eyes closed, face up to the sun. Gavin bent down, tapped her shoulder. She pulled the earbuds out and sat up.

"You're back," she said.

"You really shouldn't come on someone's boat if they're not here."

"Well, how was I supposed to know?"

"What'd you do, swim out again?" he asked.

"Peggy and Brandon dropped me off. They took his boat over to Shelter Island, so I asked them for a ride out here. And you weren't home, so I was stuck. I couldn't swim back to the beach with my iPod."

"Okay," he said. "I forgive you. So, what's up?"

"Well, I just wondered... I mean, I know you didn't take my money or anything, so you probably don't owe me any answers, but I just wanted to know what progress you've made."

Gavin stared at her. He was being asked for a

progress report by a teenager. Without replying, he turned and walked back to the cockpit. He undid the combination lock and let himself into the cabin, climbing down the ladder and tracking sand everywhere.

"Jesus," he said as a big pile of it showered from the gauze onto the floor.

"What's wrong?" she asked, following him.

"I don't want to scratch the teak," he said, sitting down and shoving an old newspaper under his foot.

"You're a bit of a neat freak, aren't you?" she asked.

"Try living on a boat."

"I guess."

He glared at her, unwrapping the gauze. The ER had sent him home with supplies, which he had stored in a plastic Tupperware container in the head.

"Let me help you," she said.

"That's okay," he said. But he told her where the bandages were, and she ran to get them. He managed to hop back up on deck, dunk a bucket over the side, and wash his foot in the salt water.

He remembered how Aphrodite used to tell them that salt water cured all ills—from cuts and scrapes to broken hearts. Her prescription for everything was a swim. Staring across the bay and up the steep rock cliff, he looked at Sheridan's house and wondered whether a swim could do anything, even the smallest bit, to heal her grieving heart.

Nell had brought the plastic container, but Gavin ignored it. He looked at his foot, at the black stitches.

The swelling was down, and the cut was healing. He decided to leave the bandages off.

"Didn't the doctor say you should keep that bandaged up?" Nell asked.

"Yes," Gavin said.

"Then you should do it."

Gavin didn't want to tell this impressionable young teenager that he'd gotten as far as he had—for good and ill—by not listening to anyone but himself. He stared down at her feet, at the ragged scrap of towel tied around her ankle.

"What's that?"

"Charlie tied it there."

"And you still wear it?"

"Uh-huh," she said.

Something about that made him like her even more than before. His mind flashed on the dark-haired Cumberland bass player. He frowned and hopped back down below, and she followed.

"So," she said, with no trace of young-girl tentativeness in her voice, "what progress have you made?"

"Have a seat," he said, gesturing at the settee. He gave her a towel to sit on. She slid in, waiting for him to boot up his laptop. "Tell me again. Why didn't you go to New York that night?"

She stared at him, seeming startled.

"You were his girlfriend, it was the last weekend of August," Gavin said. "So why didn't you go?"

"Because it was so hot," she said, trailing off. "I think about that, how I missed my chance to...be with him, maybe save him. I was selfish, and I didn't want to leave the beach to go into the hot city."

He stared at her, knowing he had to find out whether Charlie had steered her away, whether he had made plans without her and dissuaded her from coming. "Did he say anything?"

"What do you mean?"

"About your going or not going to New York. Did he seem to push you one way or the other?"

Pain crossed her face. "I told you—we argued. Are you trying to make me feel even worse about it? We usually spent weekends together, especially summer weekends. He wanted me with him. *Why* didn't I go?"

"Calm down," Gavin said. "Just tell me, how bad was the argument?"

"Not bad. He was upset at first, but then he called back and said not to worry—to stay at the beach, stay cool. He told me to take a swim for him." Her voice caught as she stared out over the water where she and Charlie had taken so many swims together.

"That makes sense to me," Gavin said, trying to ease her anxiety. "He was thinking of you, wanting you to be comfortable. Did he tell you what he was thinking of doing?"

"Not really," she said. "Just normal city stuff."

"Did you get the idea he planned to meet anyone?"

"No. He'd made some friends at school, but there wasn't anything definite. People were doing their own things, nothing organized. But that didn't matter... Charlie was good on his own. He liked to walk around, checking everything out and watching people. That's why he would have been such a good filmmaker..."

"He was an observer," Gavin said, watching her get herself together.

Nell nodded. "He was. He saw things no one else saw. He always picked up on the subtle things people were feeling, the ways they connected with each other. We'd go to Foley's for coffee and sit there watching everyone, and he'd make up stories of what people were doing. He'd see a couple of strangers and say they were spies, sent here to take the ferry from New London and take pictures of the submarines. Just stuff like that... He could tell a lot from looking at people."

"What about music?"

"Uh, he liked it," Nell said slowly.

"Did he have a lot of friends in the music world?"

"Some, from Nashville. But..." She bit her lip.

"What?"

"He mostly left that to his mother. He wanted to find his own way; he could sing, and he could have managed a band—he was really good with people and had lots of connections, because of his mother. But he didn't want to lean on her for that. He really wanted to do his own thing, something she had nothing to do with."

"But did he stay in touch with his friends from Nashville?" Gavin pressed. "Or mention going to hear any of their bands play in New York? Cumberland, for example?"

"Of course I know he went but I found out later, after he died," she said. "I used to tease him about that band. They had this really hot chick playing bass. I told him she was the reason he liked them. But he just laughed." A sad smile tugged at her mouth.

Gavin smiled back. "He didn't go to school with her or anything? Know her from Nashville?" He paused. "Did he ever talk about her?"

"No," Nell said, then frowned and tilted her head. "Why are you pushing about that?"

"I'm not sure," he said honestly. "You sent me his Talk2Me page, and he mentioned them as one of his favorites. And he saw them right before..."

"You're making me feel weird," she said. "As if you think something was going on with him and that girl."

"I don't," he said slowly. "I'm just looking at everything."

He stared at Nell, suddenly remembering how it had felt to see Sheridan with Randy, to know they had married, the wild jealousy, the utter anguish. He saw the hurt in her eyes, felt it resonating in himself, and changed direction.

"You told me he wasn't the kind of person someone would mug. But did he ever take risks? Go places you thought were dangerous?"

"No."

"Was he more careful when you were around? Did you keep him from taking chances?"

She glared at him, and Gavin knew his last questions had rubbed her raw. "Are you saying that if I'd been with him he'd still be alive? Do you think I don't already say that to myself?"

"That's not what I'm saying at all, Nell," Gavin said, realizing he was once again thinking of himself. Sheridan had always kept him steady and safe; he'd only acted like a wild jerk when she wasn't around . . . And that's why he'd pushed her away.

"I would have gone anywhere with Charlie," Nell said. "I would have done anything to protect him . . ."

Gavin nodded. "I know," he said, waiting for her to calm down.

"Look," she said, her voice shaking. "He was way more into music than I was. That's all it was. He probably stopped pressing me about coming to New York because he'd decided to go hear that band, and knew that I wouldn't be into it so much."

Gavin nodded. It was the first time she'd admitted, maybe even to herself, that Charlie had had plans to see the band—that it hadn't been random.

"What makes you think that?"

She shrugged. "I respected his taste, but it was different from mine. We had some bands in common, but not all."

"Cumberland?"

"They're okay. But I wasn't into them."

Gavin's computer had booted, so he Googled Cumberland. He saw the picture of the black-haired bass player standing on the bridge, staring into the river. Then he came up with the same list of band members that Joe had given him. He stared at the names, clicked through the site looking for band bios. Nothing that rang any bells.

"What are you doing?" Nell asked.

"You feel like looking at some names, see if any of them look familiar?"

Nell shrugged, slid onto the seat beside him.

Gavin watched her watch the screen; she scrolled down, reading the names. Then she clicked onto a page showing photos of band members. Some were head shots, others had been taken at shows; most were of the bass player, Lisa Marie Langton.

Nell paused at a crowd shot—a picture from a show two years ago, December. A Christmas fundraiser for a food bank in Memphis, the picture was of the crowd: people staring at the stage, faces upturned, watching Cumberland perform.

"Huh," she said.

"What?" he asked.

She brought her face close to the screen, staring hard. She looked at the screen for another moment, then shook her head. "Nothing."

"It looked as if you saw something..."

"Charlie was with me that night," she said oddly. "I remember the date so clearly—December twenty-first. The winter solstice. It was the shortest day of the year, and we went for a walk on the beach."

"Okay," he said, wondering why she would bring that up.

"We were all bundled up," she said, a haunted look in her eyes. "He wrapped his scarf around my neck

because once we got to Little Beach, stepped out of
the woods onto the open beach, the wind came howl-
ing off the water. We made a ring of stones, built a
fire out of driftwood. I told him...we needed
warmth and light, because the night was so dark."

"Nell..." he began, wanting to draw her back to
the website, get her to talk to him about what she
saw. "Tell me what's making you think of that night."

"Nothing," she said, her brown hair swinging as
she shook her head, giving him an accusing look.
"It's just a memory. Don't you have any of those?"

"Yes," he said.

"Then why are you pushing me? Just let me think
about Charlie!"

"Look," Gavin said, as gently as he could. "You're
the one who hired me. I have to ask you things, okay?
I want to figure out what happened."

"Not as badly as I do," Nell said.

Gavin stared at her. He thought of Sheridan, of
how he was doing this for her, too. Nell had asked
him about his memories. She'd made him think
of something—like Nell's, it had taken place in December. Only many years earlier, before she was
born. . . .

It had been the last time he'd seen Sheridan before
this summer. Sitting on that rock in her yard, shivering in the December cold as the snow fell on them,
she'd been eight months pregnant with Charlie.

Gavin remembered holding Sheridan's cold hand
in his. It was before Gavin had started working with
Vincent, before Sheridan had even decided for sure

to leave Randy. Gavin was a relatively new civilian, his hair still cut military-style; her long hair, tossed in the salt wind, dusted with snow.

He'd been kicked out of the Navy, but his old sub was in port up the Thames River in Groton. He knew they'd be shipping out in the morning for the North Sea, and he felt as if he'd destroyed every opportunity in his whole life. His head was spinning; he wanted to tell Sheridan everything, that he'd seen her with Randy, and had that fight, and gotten into so much trouble. He was reeling, just unable to tell her the truth of how he felt.

"Why did you come up here?" he asked.

"I had to see my grandmother," she said. "Nashville's been tough for me lately. I miss Hubbard's Point."

"What makes it tough?" he asked.

"My husband... it's hard to tell you this."

The word "husband" seared like hot metal, but he just kept his expression steady. "You can tell me."

"He's... I don't think Randy's very good for me."

"What's he doing, Sheridan?"

"Seeing someone else. And... I think he only got together with me for..."

"Tell me, what?"

"I'm supporting him. He takes the money from me, then looks at me as if he hates me. As if he resents me because he needs what I give him."

"Where is he now?" Gavin asked.

Sheridan raised her eyes to his; she'd heard the ice-cold tone in his voice and known that he wanted to hurt him. "That's not why I'm telling you. I just needed a friend...my old friend Gavin. Be that for me, please, Gav?"

"Okay," he said, trying to hold it together.

"I feel so bad about all this," she said, cradling her belly. "I'm the one who broke up with you, and here I am, leaning on your shoulder. But I needed so badly to talk to someone...you...about it all..."

"I want you to."

"It's just, I don't know what to think. Things with Randy were good at first, but it seems that once he 'had' me, once I got pregnant, everything changed. He's not the same person at all. He seems so resentful all the time, as if he'd rather be anywhere but with me."

"Then get out," Gavin said.

"I've thought about it...and I *have* left. But every time I move out for a few days, he comes to find me, gets me to come back. He seems so sweet again—like the man I fell in love with."

Gavin took the words like a body blow, just sat there. "Why are you supporting him? He looked like a capable guy."

"What do you mean? When did you see him?"

The snow was coming harder, blowing in from the east, starting to accumulate. Gavin slowly reached for her hand. "I saw you," he said. "One time when you didn't know I was there."

"When?"

"A few months after we broke up. I hitchhiked to Nashville to try to get you back."

"And you saw me with Randy?"

Gavin nodded. "I couldn't believe you could love anyone but me. So soon after we'd broken up." He stopped, then couldn't help himself. "After nine years together . . . didn't you think we mattered at all?"

"I thought," she'd said, and he remembered the way she'd fixed him with her gaze, her warm blue eyes so sad, "that we mattered too much."

"How's that even possible?"

"Stop, Gav. You know how I felt . . ." She corrected herself: "How I *feel*. You're the one who enlisted, and reenlisted, and you're the one who was gone for eight months at a time."

"I quit," he said.

"What do you mean?" Her head snapped to look at him.

"Okay, I didn't quit. They kicked me out."

"The Navy?"

His heart was pounding; he couldn't stand to tell her this, but he had to. "I got arrested for assault— it was a bar fight after . . ." He took a deep breath. "Never mind. I was dishonorably discharged."

"Gavin . . ."

Her eyes were filled with confusion and a strange sort of sympathy. He felt like the biggest disappointment in the world; she'd called him for help and comfort, and he was laying this on her.

"I'm sorry, Sheridan," he said.

"What are you fighting?" she whispered, tears in her eyes. "What are you *always* fighting?"

Putting her hand on his side, she'd traced the

length of his scar—the physical evidence of yet another altercation. The scar tissue pulled, and the
pressure of her fingers hurt. He stayed tough, not letting her see. He knew the scar felt like rope, and as
her fingers ran down it, he imagined her letting out
line between them.

He stared into her eyes, saw all the sadness there,
knew he was responsible for so much of it. Even
now, she was his best friend, the person he felt closest to in the world. They knew each other so well, yet
he'd never been able to keep from driving her away.
He didn't understand himself, the canyon he felt
inside.

"Forget everything," he said. "Start over with me."

"It's too late," she said.

"It's not..."

She put her hand up, cut him off. Then she cradled her belly. "I'm having someone else's baby."

"Why couldn't you have waited?" Gavin asked.
"We could have had a baby together...."

Sheridan had started to cry. She'd turned away,
then stood. Facing Gavin with pure despair in her
eyes, she'd said, "There was a time when that's all I
wanted. But now—I'm so confused. I'm married to
Randy."

"You don't love him!"

"I did," she whispered. "And I think maybe I
still do."

"Sheridan, don't do this. I don't care if it's someone else's baby. I want to be with you. Marry me,
Sheridan...I love you, and I love your baby."

"Stop, Gav," she'd said, weeping.

"Please..."

She looked up at him, touched his cheek with her hand. He reached for her, on fire, and she wrapped her arms around him, pressed her lips to his. Her mouth was hot and tasted of tears. The kiss made time stand still, filling him with desire. They held each other, kissing as if it would never end.

But it did. Sheridan pulled back. Staring into his eyes, she brushed his cheek again. He knew—he could see even before she spoke.

"Goodbye, Gavin," she whispered.

And then she walked away. He'd stood in front of the rock, watching her go. His body tingled from holding her. He swore he could still feel her, taste her, smell her hair. The air reverberated with the sound of her voice—but she was gone, returning to Randy. The man she'd married. The father of her baby. Gavin couldn't move. All he could do was think about her, know that she'd kissed him.

And know that it would be the last time.

He'd recognized the moment for what it was, their last kiss. Whether she stayed with Randy or not, Gavin knew she was never coming back to him. He'd lost her. He thought of that now, watching Nell sit there in front of his computer, the screen filled with photos of Cumberland fans, all staring up at the bass player. She stared at him, wiping tears from her angry eyes.

"Stop thinking Charlie had anything to do with her," she said. "Because he didn't."

"Okay," Gavin said.

"He didn't care about Lisa Marie Langton, or whatever her name is. You shouldn't be thinking that at all."

"I'm sorry."

"And *no* one wants answers as much as I do," she repeated.

And because Gavin, after years of fighting everything that moved, had finally learned how to stop, he nodded at her and let her win, and said, "I know. I know, Nell. No one."

THE EVENING WAS WARM and clear, the sky violet and filled with summer stars. The constellations seemed so close to earth, the Milky Way spreading a swath of white silk, turning the sky into a mystery. Agatha and Bunny had done everything: turned Sheridan's bluestone terrace into a scene out of the *Arabian Nights*.

They'd pulled out all of their grandmother's party things: bright paper lanterns strung from a corner of the cottage to the flagpole, lit with tiny tea-light candles; low Waterford vases filled with flowers and herbs cut from the garden, filling the air with scents of beach roses, honeysuckle, lavender, and mint; an old embroidered linen tablecloth and napkins.

While Bunny stayed in the kitchen with Sheridan, putting last touches on the meal, Agatha arranged the chairs around the table. It was a lovely night to dine in the open air. The sea breeze was just enough to keep away the mosquitoes, but not so strong it would blow out the candles.

Stevie Moore had made place cards, sent them over earlier in the day. Agatha admired their delicacy and whimsy, the way Stevie had somehow captured the spirit of each person.

As Agatha placed them—carefully, with true consideration and planning—at each seat, she said a prayer for each person. At Sheridan's and Gavin's places, kitty-corner, with Sheridan at the head of the table, she waved her hands and murmured an incantation.

"What are you doing?" Bunny asked, carrying out a pitcher of ice water infused with cucumber slices, lemon, and spearmint.

"Nothing," Agatha said, caught in the act.

"Don't let Sheridan see you doing that."

"What she doesn't know..." Agatha said, and Bunny smiled. The sisters stood together as Agatha reached into the pocket of her flowing green dress, pulled out a tiny multicolored silk drawstring pouch, and sprinkled what looked like grated nutmeg in the bottom of Sheridan's wineglass.

"Say it," Bunny urged.

"May the blessings of Aphrodite, our grandmother named for the goddess of love, and may the powers of this wild thyme, so lovingly planted and harvested from her garden, bring peace, love, and understanding to our sister," said Agatha.

"Amen," Bunny said, glancing down the hill. "Come on—they're here."

"Amen," Agatha said as they went to greet the guests.

THE EVENING WAS IDYLLIC, summer sweetness itself, as only a Hubbard's Point evening can be. The sound of waves gently breaking on the sand mingled with distant voices, people enjoying a walk on the beach.

A soft sea breeze blew up the hill, just enough so Jack slid his arm around Stevie's bare shoulders. The chairs were close together around the rectangular table; first everyone exclaimed about Stevie's place cards, then about Bunny and Agatha's excellent food.

They served chilled peach soup with a spoonful of crème fraîche and a sprig of sage; Agatha's lobster canapés made from crustaceans caught in local waters; filet of sole baked with buttered breadcrumbs; Bunny's roasted rosemary potatoes; and baguettes and Camembert.

Sheridan sat at the end of the table, with Gavin on one side and Nell on the other. She looked down the table, saw most of the people she loved in this world: her two sisters and their husbands, Stevie and Jack, Nell . . . She glanced at Gavin, saw him staring back at her. Caught, he gave her a big smile. She smiled back.

Eating her soup, smiling at Gavin, she felt as if she were practicing. She'd been so isolated for so long, she couldn't remember the last time she'd sat on her terrace with friends—something she'd always loved to do. Everything felt new.

The tea-light candles twinkled overhead, and the crinkled paper lanterns threw a warm, colored glow across the table. Sheridan ate, sipped her wine, remembered how much Charlie had loved his great-grandmother's paper lanterns. They were used only for the most special occasions. She took in a sharp, deep breath.

"You okay?" Gavin asked in a low voice.

Sheridan nodded.

"So, Gavin," Jack said from down the table, "Nell tells me that's your boat out by the breakwater."

"That's right," Gavin said, reluctantly turning from Sheridan.

"She's pretty," said Mike, Bunny's husband. "Chris-Craft?"

"Yep," Gavin said. "A Futura. The Jaguar of the Cruisers."

"I love all the bright wood," Nell said.

Everyone turned to look at her. Sheridan wasn't sure how much her sisters knew about Nell hiring Gavin, or what they'd told their husbands; in any case, she didn't want the conversation to go in that direction, and the thought of it made her catch her breath. Gavin must have heard or sensed it, because he started steering things right away.

"Nell, you're quite a swimmer," he said.

"Don't tell me you swam all the way from the beach out to that boat alone," Bunny said, gazing down at the water, assessing the distance. "It's almost all the way to the breakwater!"

Nell smiled proudly.

"Jack, remember when we used to swim from the beach out to the breakwater?" Gavin said.

"To go spearfishing," Jack said. "Fins, masks, and all, holding our spearguns out of the water and swimming with one hand. We looked like beach guerrillas."

"Cool," Nell said.

"Cool unless you drown," Bunny, the eternal mother, warned. "That's too far to swim without a boat along to spot you."

"This place is always the same," Nell said. "Kids do the same things their parents used to do, but the parents forget how much fun they had and tell them they shouldn't do it."

"Anyone care for seconds?" Agatha asked, passing the platter of fish.

"*Bien sûr,*" said her husband, Louis. Sheridan watched him serve first Agatha, then himself. She adored her brothers-in-law. Louis was French, from a small town in Bordeaux. He always brought the wine—tonight it was a St. Emilion from the vineyard of a friend of his; Sheridan thought it tasted delicious, but a little odd, as if parsley or sage had gotten mixed with the grapes. She watched Louis glance around the table, assess that another bottle was needed, go to the kitchen.

"This is beautiful," Gavin said in a low voice while the others passed the platters and talked about beach days past and future.

"It is," Sheridan said, sipping her wine and looking around. "I'd forgotten how much I love eating out here."

"Thanks for inviting me," he said.

She gazed into his eyes. They were hazel, flecked with gold. His hair was a little long, curling over the collar of his blue shirt. It was still brown, but going gray around his face, rugged and lined from a life lived in the sun and wind. She wanted to say "Of course," as if inviting him were the most normal thing in the world. But she knew it wasn't. It was a strange miracle that he was here at all.

"I'm glad you came," she said.

"So am I."

"Does Hubbard's Point seem the same to you?"

He stared at her instead of answering. She watched the color rise in his face, saw his eyes take in her eyes, her face, her hair, her hands. He gazed at her hands for so long, she felt him wanting to take them. Or maybe she wanted to take his.... The thought made her flinch.

"Yes," he said. "Because you're here."

"I've changed so much," she whispered. Emotions swept through her; she held his gaze, feeling her eyes fill. Her chest felt hot.

"Yeah," he said, his voice lower. "You're more beautiful than ever."

"No," she said. "I'm a wreck."

"You've had a lot to be wrecked about," he said.

"Everyone he loved is right here," she said. "And it's such a beautiful summer night...He should be here with us."

"Maybe he is," Gavin said.

Sheridan opened her eyes and stared at him. She felt him wanting to help her, trying to be close to her. He'd once known her better than anyone alive. He reached for her hand. She felt the pressure of his fingers; a long shiver ran down her spine. She wanted to lean into him so badly.

"More wine?" Louis asked, standing between them.

Sheridan didn't speak, so Louis took that as a yes. He started to fill her glass, but Agatha jumped up.

"Wait a minute!" she said, coming down the table. She picked up Sheridan's glass, held it up to the lantern light. Sheridan glanced up at her, then back at Gavin, who hadn't looked away.

Agatha murmured something about thinking she'd seen a moth in Sheridan's glass, Louis said, "*Merci, chérie*," and kissed his wife, and Sheridan kept staring at Gavin. He hadn't let go of her hand, and she felt growing panic, wondering what was happening to her heart.

CHAPTER 11

NELL SAT AT THE TABLE, UNABLE TO EVEN taste her food. She'd been shocked by Gavin's questions, thrown off-balance by the idea that Charlie might have kept something from her: plans to see Cumberland or, even worse, feelings for the bass player.

She'd started almost regretting asking Gavin to come. He didn't know Charlie at all, didn't know Nell. How could he think something so terrible? She stared down the table, burning with rage and thinking of things she could say to Gavin to make him realize how wrong he was. But suddenly something strange happened. Instead of staying furious over what Gavin was hinting at, she started thinking about it. What if it was true?

The thought was as bracing as cold rain. How well do two people know each other—even two as close as her and Charlie? What if he'd wanted to do something without her—not seeing another girl, but just going to the show on his own, not telling her? How bad would that be?

She glanced over at her father and Stevie. Seeing them reassured her—just knowing they were together, realizing that they loved each other so much in spite of their completely divergent lives.

Just because Stevie didn't tell her father every single thing, and he didn't run to her with every plan, didn't mean they weren't madly in love. In many ways, Nell looked to Stevie to show her how to be.

Sitting at the table now, Nell forced herself to breathe. She glanced at Gavin, wondering whether he'd found out anything more. Although no longer angry, she felt embarrassed that he could think Charlie might keep a secret from her. And why would Charlie do that, if it didn't have to do with some girl? She swallowed hard, unable to believe Charlie would do that to her.

She closed her eyes, trying to bring a picture of him into her mind. If only she could grab him now, shake him and make him tell her what had happened. Her fingertips burned—that's how badly she longed to touch him and connect with him. They had loved each other, they had had plans.

Real plans, life plans—not momentary, fleeting, confusing, not-being-honest-with-each-other-one-weekend plans. They were going to go to college together. Would Charlie have wanted her to be with him in New York if he had secrets to keep? That just didn't make sense, and was one of the worst parts about death: you couldn't talk things over, couldn't ask questions, couldn't explain the simple things that could so easily have been sorted out in life. It left so much unfinished business.

Nell tried to calm herself down, listening to conversation at the table, glancing around at everyone. She looked at all the adults. What did it mean to grow up? If Charlie had lived, would they have been able to make it together outside the enchanted boundaries of Hubbard's Point? Would she have been possessive and demanding? Had Charlie started feeling that about her? Had he started feeling trapped, maybe wanting to see someone else? The thought made her almost start to hyperventilate.

"Nell," Stevie said, catching her eye, "everything okay?"

Nell nodded, forcing herself to smile. Just the sight of Stevie made her realize she was being crazy; there was no way Charlie had felt trapped or held back by her. No way at all . . .

Except for Stevie, who was the very definition of an artist and free spirit and didn't care what people thought, and Sheridan, who was pretty much the same, Nell found adults to be constrained. It was as if sometime during their late youth, someone had drawn a box for them to step into. The box had four sides, a bottom, and a top; the adult would hop in— willingly, it seemed—and never get out again.

Like Nell's dad. As much as she loved him, he'd pretty much been in a box until Stevie had let him out. But then he'd fallen in love with Stevie, and she'd more than liberated him—they were proof, to Nell, that love actually set people free, rather than keeping them chained. Until this summer, with whatever was going on between him and Stevie, Nell's dad had been a happy man.

Looking around the table, Nell realized that pretty much all the adults here were in box-free zones. Agatha, with all her supernatural freakiness, was very cool; Louis was French and loved wine and had the most awesomely thick accent, you could barely understand a word he said.

Nell gazed at Bunny and Mike and wondered. With a name like "Bunny," you had to be kind of brave. But Bunny had the suburban mom thing down pat: even worrying about Nell's long swim out to Gavin's boat. Mike seemed nice; he looked like the only person at the table other than her father who might work in an office—his hair was trimmed in an office-friendly way, and he wore a striped polo shirt, and he had a heavy, kind of status-y looking stainless steel watch on his wrist. Any overt status symbol was an instant dead giveaway that the person wearing it was box-bound.

Gavin, on the other hand—and as mad at him as Nell still felt—was about as far from box-world as an adult could be. Nell looked him over, checking out the way he was leaning toward Sheridan. They were whispering, in voices too low to hear.

Since Charlie's death, Nell was used to seeing Sheridan super closed off and shut in, sometimes drinking a little too much. But tonight she seemed awake and alive, smiling into Gavin's handsome eyes. For an old guy, except for his disturbing theory about Charlie, he was all right.

"Everyone," Agatha said from the other end of the table.

Nell and the rest of the party turned to look at her.

"I think," she said, "a toast is in order.... If no one minds, I'd like to do the honors..."

"You are the oldest sister," Bunny said, smiling.

"But Sheridan is our hostess," Agatha said.

Sheridan laughed. "In name only. You two cooked the whole meal, and it's wonderful. Of course, Agatha..."

"Well then," Agatha said, standing. She took a deep breath, seeming to summon something from within. Nell leaned forward, watching. Agatha's eyes were closed, her lips moving silently. Then, "With the power of the stars, and the deepness of the blue, from the bottom of the sea, and the strength of me and you..."

"My God," Bunny said. "Is this a toast or a spell?"

"With Agatha, there is no difference," Louis said, only he made it sound like *Wiz Agate, zere ees no deeferance.*

Agatha went on, eyes still closed, as if there'd been no interruption. "With all there is, and all there was, may love touch each at this table tonight, may the wildest dreams come true, may it be done."

"Done and done," Bunny murmured.

"Hear, hear," Mike said, as if Agatha had just made a corporation-rousing speech. Bunny smiled proudly, whether at Mike or Agatha, Nell wasn't sure.

"That was some toast," Gavin said. "And I'll drink to it."

Everyone did, except Nell. She had no wine. They'd given her a glass of water, but she'd drained it. Glancing around, she caught Gavin's eye and gave him a cold stare. Smiling, Sheridan offered Nell her glass.

"Have a sip of mine," Sheridan said. "We wouldn't want you to miss out on your wildest dreams..."

"Thanks," Nell said, taking a big gulp. The wine filled her mouth and made her throat feel warm. As she swallowed, she felt all fizzy.

"Oh no," Agatha said from her end of the table, looking stricken.

"Don't worry," Jack said. "She can have a little. She'll be leaving the nest, starting college..."

And then everyone started asking about Regis, and saying how excited she must be to be going to college, but she wasn't...and all she could think of was Charlie. So she took another, bigger sip—and nearly spit it out. The wine had been fine going down, but now her mouth tasted like bitter herbs.

"Was that one of Aphrodite's toasts?" Gavin asked. And when Nell glanced at him, and saw him watching her, she knew he'd asked it on purpose—to get everyone to stop talking about college.

Stevie laughed. "If it came from Aphrodite, I think we can safely call it a spell, not a toast. I remember how she and my aunt used to go at it."

"Aunt Aida?" Nell asked. "What do you mean?"

"Well, they embodied each other's polar opposite.

Aunt Aida was an artist, but in some ways the most practical person you ever met. Whereas Aphrodite was so much of the spirit.... I used to think it was because she'd been blind since birth, it kept her from being attached to anything of this earth."

"That's true," Sheridan said. "She didn't care about anything material. I know she could have walked away from all her possessions in a second. But when it came to people, she was different...."

"Yes," Bunny said. "She couldn't bear to let the people she loved go. I remember when our grandfather died...she just couldn't bear not to have him with her. She refused to accept it."

"Yes," Agatha said. "She was so gifted, with such an ability to reach the ones who'd crossed over."

The words made Nell think of Charlie again, and her eyes filled with tears. The emotion, or wine, made her swoon. He'd crossed over. Charlie was gone, and she'd never—really—get the answers to any of her questions. Gavin might be right, or he might be wrong. Nell would never know. She hiccupped.

"Honey, you okay?" Stevie asked.

Nell squeezed her eyes tight. She found herself thinking of that picture on Gavin's computer: the shot of the crowd, everyone staring up at the pretty bass player onstage. She saw the kid in the crowd, wondered whether Charlie had been keeping secrets from her all along. Was it possible? Could he have been there? Dates raced through her mind, and she wondered whether she could have been mistaken

about the date of the solstice.... Or maybe the date
on the website was wrong.

"Cumberland," Nell whispered.

"Nell ..." Sheridan said, leaning forward. "What
are you talking about?"

"Oh," she said, putting her head in her hand. "I ...
I don't feel very good."

"Come on, honey," Jack said, walking around the
table, helping her up. Nell's legs practically buckled.

"Was it the wine?" she heard Bunny ask.

"I believe it was," she heard Agatha whisper.

"Nell, tell me what you meant ..." She heard
Sheridan press, and then she heard Gavin murmur-
ing something, soothing Sheridan so she wouldn't be
upset.

Nell let her dad lead her into Sheridan's cottage.
For a minute, Nell thought she needed to find the
bathroom and throw up, but instead she just wanted
to lie down on the wicker sofa. Her dad sat beside her
for a few minutes.

"Are you okay, Nell?" he asked.

She nodded, burying her head in the soft pillow.
Sleep was coming fast ... She closed her eyes, surrounded by the love of her father and everyone on
the terrace, by the fact that she was lying on Charlie's
sofa, that he had sat here so often, that he had been
right here, right here, right here ... He'd never lie to
her, they hadn't kept secrets from each other, so why
had he been in that picture?

Why had he gone to Nashville without her, why
hadn't he told her?

* * *

THE DINNER WENT ON, but Gavin saw the tension in Sheridan's eyes. Her sisters served coffee and tea, orange cookies and blueberry buckle and a peach pie made by Stevie, but Sheridan seemed preoccupied.

"What did Nell mean?" she asked while everyone else was asking Stevie about baby names.

"It has to do with looking into . . ."

"What happened to Charlie," she said quietly, and she sounded calm, as if something inside had settled differently.

"Yes," he said. "I'll tell you as much as you want to know."

"She wasn't talking about the river," Sheridan said. "She meant the band, didn't she?"

"He liked them . . . ?"

"You know he did. That's who he went to see that last night."

"Do you know them?"

She shrugged. "I know who they are. But not personally. Why?"

"There's a girl in the band," he said. "She's pretty. Supposedly she's an up-and-coming singer-songwriter."

Sheridan gave him a look. "Don't tell me you're going down that road," she said.

"Would it be so impossible?"

She nodded. "Yep," she said. "It would."

"Because—"

"You didn't see them together, him and Nell. They were in love, Gavin. Real true love."

"Okay," he said. "But . . ."

She shook her head hard. "Don't waste your time on this. I know for sure. My son was madly in love with Nell."

Gavin opened his mouth, but shut it again. He'd started to say something about young men, how sometimes their hormones took control, but then he remembered himself at Charlie's age. He'd been wild in plenty of ways, but there'd only been one girl for him.

A few minutes later, the party began to break up. Jack helped Stevie out of her chair. Mike asked when the wedding was, and Jack looked hopeful when Stevie said, "Oh, we'll see . . ."

Jack and Stevie got Nell up from the couch, thanked everyone for a great time, and headed home. Agatha and Bunny cleared the table and—in ways practiced for the last thirty years—washed the dishes while their husbands dried, all in record time. Sheridan started taking down the lanterns, but Gavin stopped her.

"I'll help you with that," he said, holding her wrist. "When everyone's gone."

She stared down at his hand on her skin, as if his touch were burning her. She nodded; they went in to help her sisters, but everything was done, and they were packing up to leave. Bunny took her casserole dish; Agatha took her cookie sheet; Mike held a stack of plastic containers; Louis left the rest of the wine on the sideboard.

"Thank you for a great night," Gavin said, hugging Agatha first, then Bunny. "It's so good to see you both again."

"You too, darling," Bunny said. "You haven't changed one bit."

"Neither have you," Gavin said, and they both laughed.

"Be careful of Agatha's words," Bunny warned. "She called them a toast, but you know they were really a spell."

"They couldn't touch him," Agatha scoffed. "He's already in too deep."

"Excuse me?" Gavin asked.

Agatha gave him a look; he knew what she was getting at, and blushed. She was right: she didn't need to bother putting a love spell on him. He'd been in love with Sheridan for most of his life; nothing had ever changed there.

The sisters all hugged, and Gavin shook hands with Mike and Louis. It seemed odd, a little sad, that they'd been brothers-in-law for so long, in this family Gavin had always wanted to be part of. But he toughed it out, slapped them on the shoulder, told them to row out to the *Squire Toby* for a day of fishing.

And then everyone walked down the hill, climbed into their cars, turned around in the cul-de-sac at the end of the Point, and waved as they drove past the house again on their way out of the beach.

Gavin stood beside Sheridan at the kitchen window, waving until they were out of sight. They were so close, their arms were touching. When Sheridan glanced at him, Gavin made a half turn and took her in his arms. It surprised both of them so much, he didn't know what to do next, and Sheridan stood on tiptoes to kiss him.

The heat of her mouth shocked him. Her hands felt cool on his arms. Or maybe it was just that her touch was so light, it made him shiver. They stood there in her kitchen kissing in the near-dark. One small light was on over the sink, but Sheridan's sisters had seen to it the room was otherwise without illumination.

He could have stood there all night, but suddenly she stopped. She looked up at him for a moment. He held her face in his hands, wanting her to stay with him, not close him out again, change her mind. He thought of the first night he'd seen her this trip: she'd looked like a sleepwalker. Lost, almost blank. Right now her eyes were bright, and she obviously had something on her mind.

"I know what I'm saying," she said.

"About Charlie and Nell?"

She nodded. "I mean it, Gavin. Thinking otherwise would be a waste of time..."

"You're pretty convinced."

"Don't you remember what it was like?" she asked.

"Very well," he said, holding her. "That was a long time ago, but you still look eighteen."

"No," she said, laughing. "Say something more convincing than that."

"It's true. You're the same Sheridan..."

"I'm a very different Sheridan," she whispered.

"Well, you don't look it," he said, staring past the white hair, meaning every word.

She shook her head as if he was hopeless. Taking his hand, she led him into the living room. The windows were open, and the sound of the waves rolled up the rocky hillside. She pulled him down on the sofa beside her, where Nell had just been sleeping a little while ago.

"Are you a different Gavin?" she asked, pushing the hair back from his eyes.

"Than when?" he asked. "That December when I saw you? I hope so . . . I was pretty angry that night."

"Yes," she said.

"Of course, what did you expect?" he asked. "You were sending me away. I couldn't stand what was happening between us . . ."

"Us," she said.

He watched the happiness drain from her face, saw the doubt and hauntedness come back. What was she thinking? If they'd been together, could he somehow have protected Charlie? Could he have helped Charlie find what he was seeking? If Charlie had had Gavin as a stepfather, would he have learned how to navigate the dangers of life better? Gavin knew how it was to grow up without a father.

She bowed her head, as if all the hope she'd filled up on these last hours was gone. He saw her hold her head in her hands, heard the waves outside, and suddenly there was nothing romantic about them. They sounded bleak.

He looked around. She might not be playing

music anymore, but the room was that of a professional musician. There was a Bose system, speakers mounted in corners of the ceiling. Shelves of CDs and loose, piled-up sheet music filled one wall. Another held racks of guitars—both acoustic and electric—and mandolins. Two huge Marshall amps were pushed into the corner.

"You know what I used to do?" he asked. "When I shipped out?"

"No, what?"

"Listen to Sheridan Rosslare. Wherever I was, there you were. On the radio, in my tape player, either way—you were always with me."

"Even when things were rocky between us?"

"Yes," he said. "Even then."

"But why?"

He had the sense that musicians felt about their instruments the way he felt about his boat: touch it uninvited, you're in trouble. Staring at the rack of guitars, he realized he didn't know a damn thing about them, but he picked one anyway—a big, classic-looking acoustic with golden-brown wood and mother-of-pearl inlay.

When he turned, he saw her watching him intently. Maybe she was afraid he would drop her guitar. He handed it to her. She held it as if she was about to start playing—but didn't.

"I listened to you," he said, "because some things are necessary."

"What do you mean?"

He crouched in front of her, his heart pounding.

Looking into her eyes, he saw the haze of sadness that had been there before tonight. It was back. He wanted to lift her up, carry her upstairs. Everything in him wanted her, was aching for it. But he looked into those blue eyes and knew she wasn't ready. Maybe she would never be.

He leaned forward, kissed her softly on the lips.

"Some things are necessary," he said again. He touched her face.

And then he walked out of the room and out of her cottage.

ON THE DECK OF HIS BOAT an hour later, Gavin sat staring up at Sheridan's house. The lights were still on; he saw her silhouette in the big front window. He'd hoped she would take the guitar he'd handed her, start to play. He'd hoped that would start to heal her. But she seemed to be just standing there.

He got to his feet. Stood looking up at her, and raised his hand.

"Come down," he said out loud, as though she could hear him across all that way. "Come down."

His heart jumped, because suddenly she stepped back from the window—into the shadow of the room. Had she seen him wave her out? Was it possible she would come?

He glanced around the boat. He was ready for her—and always had been. From the moment he'd bought the Chris-Craft, he'd imagined Sheridan on board with him. He'd seen it with her eyes: the warm, bright wood, the polished brass instruments, the small bookshelf filled with books he thought she'd like, books about nature and philosophy and old blues singers.

For a minute he thought about putting some music on. The blues, maybe—Robert Johnson. But who was he kidding? He'd told the truth up there on the hill, no lie: the only music he ever played on his boat or anywhere else was Sheridan's. He glanced at the stereo, knew he could fill the air with whatever CD of hers he had left in the slot.

But the sound of the waves hitting the boat seemed right. They echoed the feeling of the blood crashing through his veins—fast and steady, excited but sure. He played back each minute of the evening in his mind . . . Sitting beside her, arms brushing a little as they leaned closer. Her eyes, really looking at him again. He'd kissed her goodbye. If he had to, he could relive that kiss for the rest of his life.

Staring up at her window, he wanted more. Try *everything:* that's what he wanted from her, all of it. She'd reminded him of how they'd used to feel about each other—trying to convince him that Charlie had loved only Nell, that he'd have been completely faithful to her. Gavin wanted to believe that.

A cry from Little Beach made him turn his head: kids lighting a bonfire. He watched the fire, flames licking the salty wood. The sight filled him with desire; he found himself thinking of building long-ago beach fires with her, making love until the driftwood was a pile of embers.

He remembered one summer night, the middle of August, the peak of the meteor showers. The Perseids always signaled the end of the dog days, ushering in colder weather—as if the meteors themselves were harbingers of fall. The black sky would be filled with white sparks, and the temperature of the beach would drop and make the night just right for a fire.

The tidal zone was always full of driftwood—logs, sticks, branches, old boards from broken docks—soaked with salt water from their voyage from wherever. Gavin had dragged a bunch of the driest wood he could find, made a pile, and set it on fire. It had burned slowly, the dampness keeping the flames down.

Sheridan had sat with her knees drawn up, staring at the fire. Salt made the wood blaze burn blue, green, yellow, and red. The colors were a kaleidoscope, and the flames looked like faces. The air was chilly, making them sit close together. They held each other, sliding down onto the sand.

As Gavin kissed her, he felt the fire's warmth on her skin. The sand was cold underneath, and she snuggled against him, one blue-jeaned leg thrown over his. Their bodies entwined, pressing together and trying to be one. That's how he'd always felt with Sheridan—as if they were each other's missing part.

They'd struggled out of their clothes on the beach, naked in the cool air. Her skin was pale in the starlight, and the fire glowed in her eyes. They made love, holding each other's gaze, no need to say anything as the waves crashed at their feet. The salt spray coated their faces, and they tasted it in each other's kiss.

Gavin stood on his deck, staring up at her house now. He watched as she turned the lights out, one by one, and he knew that she wouldn't come.

"I'm here, though," he said out loud. "I'm here, Sheridan..."

SHERIDAN STOOD IN the dark, a few feet back from her window. She held the glasses to her eyes, pressed tight, watching every move Gavin made. She saw him sitting on deck, and then she saw him stand. He waved at her—thinking he'd actually seen her, she'd stepped back into the room. But still she watched....

He wanted her to come to him. Her head spun—maybe from the wine, and maybe from something else. Her house was filled with the aroma of her sisters' cooking, of the wonderful dinner they'd all just shared. But her senses were filled with other things: the scent of salt air, and of the smoke of a small fire burning over on Little Beach. She saw it glowing, just past Gavin's boat and the breakwater.

For a second she wondered if he'd made it for her. She remembered making love to him one August night, with shooting stars all around and the sparks of a driftwood fire crackling.

She shivered, thinking of how it would feel to hold him now, to lie on the sand while the fire burned beside them. But of course the fire she could see from her windows, across the bay, belonged to the kids. Nell's friends, probably—they'd lit a bonfire.

It was so crazy of Gavin to doubt Charlie's devotion to Nell. . . . Fires and stars and the sea: primal, elemental, the way her son had felt about Nell. The way Sheridan felt about Gavin. Right now, tonight: all she had to do was walk out the door. Head down the stone stairs, cross the footbridge, walk barefoot down the beach.

Gavin would be there to meet her—she knew it. But she couldn't move.

I'm here . . . She swore she heard him say it.

THE FIRE WAS SMALL, compact, ringed by the stones he'd collected from just above the tide line. He was conscientious about it all—he hadn't built a fire on the beach in many years, and wanted to make sure it didn't spread to the woods. This was a beautiful place, and the last thing he wanted to do was destroy it.

Mainly kids came over here at night. Little Beach was a haven for young lovers, and it always had been. They'd walk through the woods, sticking to the path that wound so magically through the tall trees, under interlaced branches, like the path in any one of a hundred fairy tales. In such tales, it always led to someplace magical: a witch's wood, a ruined castle, an abandoned rose garden.

Stevie had captured the essence of such paths. All her children's books were like charmed walkways—

gateways to her readers' hearts and imaginations. The woman could write and draw enchantment like no one else. She told stories full of love and connection, brought families together. So why was she driving their family apart?

That's how it felt to Jack Kilvert, huddled by the small fire. He had enjoyed Sheridan's dinner party so much—sitting there with all those old friends, with Stevie and Nell—he'd felt more comfortable than he had in weeks, maybe even months. He'd felt the security and continuity of being with people he'd known for so long; deep down, even though he didn't tell himself consciously, he'd believed that Stevie would feel it, too—and say yes without him even having to ask the question again.

But she hadn't. After the party was over, they'd walked home. Nell had gone straight to bed. Jack and Stevie had sat on the porch, talking about the evening.

"Wasn't it great to see Sheridan and Gavin together again?" she'd asked, rocking in the chair next to his.

"It was," Jack had said. "Made me wonder why they ever went apart in the first place."

"I guess it wasn't their time yet," Stevie said.

"Their *time*?" Jack asked, turning to look at her. He was aware of his tone—incredulous, annoyed. Because everything she said lately worried him. What was she thinking? How did she see life and the world?

"Yes," she said patiently.

"I have to ask you," he said. "What do you mean by that?"

"I mean, I guess they had to go their separate ways for a while. Maybe they each had to wrestle their demons before they were ready to finally get together."

"First, they're not really together," he said. "Sitting at the same dinner table is not the same as being 'together.'"

"I know that," Stevie said. "But it's happening. It's under way... I can feel it. They can't stay away from each other for long. There's going to be a big bang, and pow—they'll be as one."

"Big bang? We're not talking about the creation of the universe," Jack said.

"Ohh," Stevie said, turning to give him a glowing smile. "That's a great idea for my next book! The creation of the universe... I might call it *Worlds Collide*, and have it be about the evolution of creatures and beings and the birth of love!"

Jack just shook his head. Was everything books with Stevie? Had he missed something, falling in love with her?

"What's wrong?"

"Is it easier for you to write and paint 'the birth of love' than to figure out what you want to do with me?"

"I know what I want to do with you," she said, reaching across the space between their rocking chairs to take his hand.

"You could have fooled me," he said.

"Really? I think I'm pretty clear about it," she said. "I want to love and hold you and have our baby and live together in perfect happiness."

"Huh," he grumbled.

"What's the second thing?" she asked. "A minute ago you said, 'First, they're not really together,' implying there was a second . . . and maybe a third . . ."

"Okay," he said, taking his hand out of hers. "Second, what about us? We went our separate ways—just like Gavin and Sheridan. I married Emma, you married . . ."

"Three husbands," Stevie said. "What's your point?"

"The point is, I want you to be my wife!"

"Jack," she said, her tone suddenly cold, "I've told you. You are my one and only. You are my alpha and omega. You're singular . . . you're the sun. You're the moon. You're the Hope diamond. I will not make you number *four*. You are number *one*."

"I want to be number four," he said. "I want to be your husband."

"Not going to happen," she said stubbornly, shaking her head. "You are number one. The only man I've ever loved enough to not marry."

That's when Jack had stood up and walked away. He'd left their house—barefoot, without taking a jacket. Started walking, and wound up—without really having any idea of how he got there—at Little Beach. The night had turned cool, or maybe it was just that his blood was running cold. In either case, he was shaking. He looked across the water, at the warm lights on up at Sheridan's house, and assumed that Gavin had stayed.

They were making passionate love, swearing their lifelong devotion to each other, planning their marriage. Jack gazed up the hill and was positive that's what was going on. Gavin shows up on the scene and bang—he and Sheridan get married. That was the only possible outcome, considering how he felt about her. So why couldn't it be the same for Jack and Stevie?

Maybe because he felt so cold—or maybe because life felt so tough right now, and he just wanted to do something simple, Jack gathered stones, placed them in a tight circle. Then he dragged over smooth driftwood branches washed high by the tide, stacked them in a pile. He stuffed broken sticks beneath the pile, lit the dry tinder.

The fire had caught, and it was burning now. He felt the heat on his face and hands. Staring into the conflagration, he saw the smoke drift up toward the sky. A million stars blazed against black nothingness. The Milky Way, that huge and graceful white highway of stars, spread over everything.

He thought of Stevie and her new book idea: the big bang. Staring up, he knew that all this had come from somewhere. All this: stars, galaxies, the night, the sea, the fire, Hubbard's Point, the love he had for Stevie had all originated in space dust. So much from what seemed like so little.

He wanted to understand it all; maybe not the universe out there, but the one under his own roof. He wanted to help Nell make the big transition—leaving home for college, going out into the world. This should be a time of joy for her, but instead she was trapped in grief, in the obsession of learning what had happened to Charlie. He'd been the same way after Emma had died, and he knew what Nell was going through.

The fire spit and crackled, and Jack stared past the sparks into the sky, at a million stars. He tried to help Nell the best he could, and he'd do the same for the baby. Jack loved his family. When he thought about how eternal it all was, he knew that Stevie was right: a piece of paper, a marriage ceremony, didn't mean much.

But Jack tightened his arms around his knees and stared harder as his eyes blurred and a lump the size of a rock formed in his throat. Because he wanted it anyway; he wanted it so much. He knew how fleeting life was, and he wanted to hold tight to everyone he loved while he still had them.

CHAPTER 12

THE DAY AFTER THE PARTY, SHERIDAN SAT back on the couch, strumming the strings of the guitar Gavin had handed her. It was a big old Martin, a gift to her from Merle Haggard after a show they'd played together in Nashville.

From where she sat, she could see the *Squire Toby* at anchor. The boat looked miniature, so far away; she wondered whether Gavin might be on deck, looking her way as he had been last night.

She didn't have a hangover, but she felt the aftereffects of something. Her wine had tasted funny, but instead of a headache, she felt almost lighthearted. She remembered the taste of his kiss, and the sight of that fire on the beach behind his boat, and the knowledge that he was right there waiting for her.

Picking up the phone, she called Agatha.

"What did you put in my wine?" she asked.

"I thought perhaps you were calling to thank me," Agatha said.

"That, too," Sheridan said. "But I want to know."

"Darling, please. Didn't you listen to my toast? That's all I was doing...creating an atmosphere conducive to dreams coming true. Whatever they are. I wasn't focused solely on you—"

"Maybe you should have been. Poor Nell took a sip from my glass before I realized..."

"She's fine," Agatha said. "I called Stevie first thing this morning. Nell slept like a baby, that's all."

"Just tell me—what was it?"

"Wild thyme," Agatha said. "Perfectly harmless..."

Sheridan and Agatha talked a few more minutes, with Sheridan thanking her sister for dinner and the intentions. She hung up, staring down the hill at Gavin's boat. Wild thyme wasn't any big deal. It was an herb, grown right here in the garden, and Sheridan knew people used it in cooking all the time. Agatha was right—it was perfectly harmless. But their grandmother had always said "thyme for dreams..." She had told them to look right in their own dooryard garden, to find their own dreams.

Holding her guitar felt so good, a dream in itself. Last night Gavin had told her that some things were necessary; for her, that had always been music. Hearing it, finding the melody, composing lyrics had always been the way she'd made sense of her life. Her fingers picked the strings in old, familiar rhythms and repetitions.

She found herself staring at Gavin's boat, playing songs from the past. She'd never had to go searching for melodies—they found her. Her fingertips always knew what she most wanted to hear. Today that seemed to be songs for Charlie.

Her son had loved ballads. He'd been the original rough-and-tumble little boy. He'd climb trees all the way to the top, scramble into gullies, collect things that crawled. He'd loved snakes. He'd go to school in clean clothes, come home looking as if he'd been to battle: untucked, unwashed, scuffed, and torn. He'd watch the scariest movies without getting scared. But when it came to music, he loved ballads.

Sheridan had played him the classics, and she'd written plenty for him as well. Sometimes when he couldn't sleep, she'd let him stay up and he'd lie right here on the couch and listen to her play. She'd sing to him, the prettiest, saddest songs she could think of: Patty Griffin, Emmylou, Patsy, Lucinda, Loretta, Crystal, Dolly. That went on until the summer he turned twelve, and then he wouldn't do it anymore. He was too cool to let his mother sing to him.

His friends up here at Hubbard's Point were into their own thing, but Charlie stayed loyal to Nashville. He and she had been an anomaly down there: Northerners by birth, Nashville at heart. There'd been a few others, like Mary Chapin Carpenter and Maura Fogarty, but they weren't too common. Sheridan had been drawn to Nashville, moth to a flame, as a very young woman.

Maybe it was her unconventional family, the way they could outdo the Southern gothics with a glance and a spell; maybe it was her own sentimental heart, never cool enough for rock; or maybe it was just that she loved Merle Haggard, Loretta Lynn, and Loretta's little sister Crystal Gayle.

When she was young, right here at Hubbard's Point, she used to hold a candle and pretend it was a microphone, sing Crystal's "Half the Way." Mishearing the lyrics, she'd sung *Don't take me house away*. Agatha had had to correct her, but it hadn't mattered: Sheridan had felt the song's longing. She'd tapped into Nashville, and she'd tapped into herself.

Charlie had grown up commuting with his mom between Nashville and, during the years she'd signed with a major label in New York, an apartment in the West Village. She'd shown him the places she used to play: Kenny's Castaways, the Village Gate, the Pyramid Club, the Kitchen, 8BC.

"Mom, did you used to be cool?" he'd asked.

She'd laughed, because she knew what he meant: she had a reputation for writing about love, heart, family, mothers and kids.

"Sort of," she'd said. "I tried."

"Like how?"

"Well, I had a crazy haircut—cut short on one side, long on the other. I wore a motorcycle jacket."

"Sweet!"

"Not really," she said. "I had the look down all right, but I wasn't feeling it inside."

"Were you in a band?"

"Several," she said.

"Like which ones?"

"Well, ones you've never heard of. There was Five

Graves to Cairo, then there was Brass Ring...and let's not forget the Mothertruckers."

Charlie had loved it. They'd laughed, and she'd shown him pictures. Her mother had kept a scrapbook of all her clippings, and they'd looked through it. She'd shown her son the memory lane version of herself as a chameleon: with bleached hair, with black hair, with razored-short hair, and, finally, with the long wavy natural-colored hair she had today.

"Why'd you do all that?" he'd asked.

"Because I was a musician, and I wanted to make a living doing what I loved. Kids my age were listening to Madonna and Duran Duran, and that kind of music was happening in the city. The thing was, when I wasn't playing with the band, I'd be sitting home listening to Merle or Crystal...."

"You were living a lie," Charlie said gravely.

Sheridan had hidden a smile, loving to hear him say that; he was her son, all right: dramatic and emotional, right there with the big statement.

"Yes, I was," she said. "I remember playing a show at CBGB's. We were covering 'I Wanna Be Sedated.' Great song. I was playing it all downstrokes, Ramones-style, on my blue Stratocaster. When it came time for my solo, I did this crazy thing: I slowed everything way down, and I started playing the song like a ballad. All sad and brokenhearted, you know? And I looked up, and who do you think was right there in front of me?"

"Who, Mom?"

"Dee Dee Ramone."

"Holy shit!"

"Yeah," Sheridan said. She'd closed her eyes, remembering the moment. Charlie had jostled her arm.

"Mom, what'd he say?"

"Well, he took me out for coffee afterwards. There was an after-hours club everyone used to go to after the show, but Dee Dee steered me clear of that place. What he wanted to tell me was too important and private for that. So we went to the Empire Diner, all the way across town in Chelsea. Sat at a table with a black glass top. And I remember how he looked me in the eye . . . and he told me I had to change my life."

"Like how?"

Sheridan smiled. "Like play the kind of music I was born to play."

"He told you to go to Nashville?"

"Not in so many words. But he did tell me I wasn't punk, would never be punk, should stop trying to be punk. It was like being set free. I remember feeling as if a two-ton weight had just been lifted."

"And then you went to Nashville?"

"Yep," Sheridan said. "Sold one of my guitars and hopped a Greyhound bus the next week."

"And the rest was history?" Charlie asked.

Sheridan nodded. "Recorded a demo, did a showcase, got signed . . . and you know the rest."

"You met Randy and had me."

"That's the best part of the story," Sheridan said. "Having you . . ."

Charlie had never stopped smiling to hear her say that. Sitting on her wicker couch now, Sheridan kept her eyes on the *Squire Toby* as she played one of Charlie's favorite lullabies, "Gentle on My Mind." Her fingers hurt, and she realized that this was the first time since the year she'd started playing guitar that she didn't have calluses on her fingertips.

Mid-song she found herself switching to another song he'd liked, one Sheridan had written. It was called "Myth," and was about grandmothers in general and Aphrodite in particular.

> *"You told me love was my destiny*
> *Your words were always my prophecy,*
> *Goddess of love,*
> *Daughter of the king..."*

She strummed the guitar, singing softly. Her grandmother had prophesied love, that was true; she had even told Sheridan that the more she loved, the more she would be open to hurt. But Aphrodite's words couldn't compare to Sheridan's own experience. Now, nearly a year after Charlie's death, she still felt as if she'd been sliced open with a knife.

Holding the guitar hurt, but she was glad Gavin had handed it to her. Some things are necessary.... Playing the song, she softly sang the bridge:

> *"When your daddy is Zeus,*
> *There's such a long way to fall,*

You grew up in the sky,
Gazing down at it all
Seeing the world
With the eyes of your heart."

Charlie had loved that song, and he'd loved his own private family myths. The summer he was sixteen, Sheridan had heard him telling some of his Hubbard's Point friends that his great-grandfather was Zeus himself—king of the gods. Sheridan had laughingly corrected him, telling him that Aphrodite's husband was James, just a humble Irishman from the green hills of Wicklow and not Mount Olympus. And Charlie had laughed back.

"Don't you know, Mom? It's your song, but don't you know that's what myths are for? To tell something truer than true."

"Truer than true?"

"Yeah," he'd said, and he'd stopped smiling. She thought of the seriousness in his gaze now, and it made her lower her guitar. "James was a king, Mom. Because he was a good man. I never met him, but I know by the way Aphrodite talks about him. You can have everything in the world, and have nothing. Or you can have little and have it all."

They'd both known he'd been talking about his father. And that was the beginning of Charlie's quest to find out more about Randy. Sheridan had wanted to save her son from learning what kind of man his father really was; Gavin had wanted to protect her, too, but she knew. Randy's profession had been attaching himself to women who could take care of him. Sheridan had never openly faced it; she'd hoped that if she kept it buried, a secret even from herself, then Charlie wouldn't have to know.

She'd grown up with myths and magic, after all. And if you couldn't use those two things to protect your own child, then what good were they? Still, the time came when it was necessary to look at certain truths, at what Charlie said was truer than true. Sitting in her living room, a summer breeze coming through the open window, she played "Myth" on Merle's old guitar and gazed across the water.

LEAVING SHERIDAN'S HOUSE last night had been the second-hardest thing Gavin had ever done. The first hardest had been leaving her house that night all those years ago. But at least last night had left him with some hope—she'd kissed him. Their first kiss in over eighteen years.

That long-ago kiss had been "goodbye." Last night had felt like something else. It had felt like "hello." Gavin still sat in a deck chair on the *Squire Toby*, face turned toward her house. He'd slept there, just wanting her to know he was there, that he wasn't leaving.

Small boats passed, making his sway in their wakes. He was deep in a dream about Sheridan when the low throb of Italian engines caught his attention.

Vincent, driving a big white Donzi with a red

stripe down the middle of the bow, came around the breakwater. Gavin stared; more to the point, he listened. It was as if a Ferrari had just come to town. Vincent circled the *Squire Toby*, making sure everyone on the beach was catching sight of him.

Gavin knew Vincent had long since left Hubbard's Point for the fancier pastures of a summer house in Watch Hill—but he didn't really fit in there. The houses were big and gracious, the blood was blue, the circles were tightly closed. Vincent had more money than most of the Old Money, he'd done many of their divorces and was therefore loathed by fifty percent of the people at any given cocktail party, and he raised conspicuous consumption to the level of a travesty or an art form, depending on whom you asked.

"You can stop now," Gavin called. "I'm pretty sure everyone at the beach knows Vincent de Havilland is back in town."

"Just think, when my family used to come here, we had the smallest cottage—out by the railroad tracks. Well, it's all waterfront now, baby!"

"You want to anchor that thing and come talk to me?"

"Sure, but you come to me," Vincent said, making Gavin laugh at his huge ego. Gavin shook his head in amusement and climbed down into the dinghy, sculling the short distance.

"Okay, I'm here," Gavin said, climbing aboard.

"Check this baby out," Vincent said, gesturing all

around. "She's a twenty-two-foot classic, with a 454 Mag MPI. She's procharged with intercooler and five pounds of boost."

"Nice for the environment," Gavin said. "We both ought to get sailboats."

"Stop being a buzz kill."

Gavin shook his head. "You're so full of shit and such a winner in the courtroom, you think you won't get called out here in the real world. I'm serious. Don't you feel guilty? You should."

"Shut up. We got thru-hull exhaust, we got trim tabs, we got a four-blade Propco Slingshot, we got GPS..."

"What did you bring me?"

"You're an asshole, you know that?" Vincent asked. "I take the day off to come over here to give you a ride in my sweet new Donzi, and all you can think about is work. Sheridan giving you the business about having a powerboat?"

"Nah," Gavin said. "I give myself enough of that."

"How was your dinner last night?"

"Great."

"Nice of her to invite me," Vincent said. He glanced up at Sheridan's cottage, and for a moment Gavin was thrown back in time. Vincent hadn't always had this swagger.

Summers at Hubbard's Point, growing up, he'd always been a little bit on the outside. His family had rented at first, just the month of July. Then they'd bought a cottage, but by then all the solid, lifetime, since-birth friendships had been forged. Vincent had always had to work extra hard to fit in.

Gavin had liked him from the start. Vincent hadn't been athletic or cool—couldn't swim very well, never went drinking with the other kids when someone was able to swipe beer from their parents; he'd had a curfew and pretty much kept to it. He'd worn white socks.

His mother had made him wear a real bathing suit instead of going swimming in cutoffs. Rumor had drifted down from West Hartford that he was on the honor roll at Conard High School. He had sometimes disappeared for a few days, and when it was revealed that he went to debating camp, the other kids had teased him without mercy.

Like a whole lot of other men who'd felt unpopular as kids, Vincent was working overtime to make up for it now. He had to have the fastest car, the fastest boat, the biggest house, the richest clients. Gavin overlooked most of it, because he knew where Vincent was coming from. But every so often, he just wanted to tell him not to worry so much.

"She kept the dinner pretty small," Gavin said. "Just family and a couple of friends."

"Her weird sisters?"

"Bunny's not weird."

"But Agatha . . ."

"The word's 'eccentric.'"

"No kidding. Who else was there?"

"Jack and Stevie. And Nell."

"Huh. Your client. Well, interesting that Sheridan invited Jack and Stevie and not me. I mean, I did her divorce."

"You ever stop to think that's maybe why she *didn't* invite you?" Gavin asked, getting impatient. "Look, quit being so sensitive. What brings you over here, other than to show off your boat?"

"Oh," Vincent said. "Judy did a little research for you. You must have mentioned this when you called in for messages the other day. She wanted to bring it herself, but I dissuaded her. I know you have eyes only for Sheridan, and I don't want Judy getting her hopes dashed."

Gavin thanked him, taking the folder from his hand. It contained printouts from various Internet sites, all mentioning the bands Cumberland and the Box Turtles. He paged through them, stopping at one highlighted section.

The bass player—and lead singer—of Cumberland, Lisa Marie Langton, was twenty-three, originally from Memphis. She was one of the best female bass players in the business, and also one of the fastest-rising singer-songwriters. When asked her greatest inspiration, she replied, "Sheridan Rosslare."

"Did you highlight this?" Gavin asked Vincent.

"Yep."

"Uh, I hate to tell you, but Sheridan's probably inspired every goddamn singer-songwriter in the country."

"I would think. But read on . . ."

Gavin narrowed his eyes, focusing on the next paragraph. The name stood out as if in bold, black print.

"You're fucking kidding me."

"Nope."

"Charlie had to know this, right? It couldn't have been a coincidence. He had to have known about this connection."

"I would think."

"How could the cops have missed this?"

"You'd better take that up with Donovan."

"Is it possible they really didn't catch this?"

"The connection's not obvious, unless you've got the inside track on Sheridan—which, thanks to the fact I did her divorce agreement, I have."

"Huh," Gavin said, impressed. "Good job."

Vinnie shrugged, looking pleased with himself.

"So Charlie went there to meet . . ."

"From where I sit—yeah. You know I don't believe in coincidence. People never meet by accident."

"Why didn't Charlie tell Nell about his plans?"

"Who knows?" Vincent said. "He was a kid, on his own in New York. Maybe he wanted to stir up some trouble he didn't want his girlfriend knowing about. What do you think the meeting was about?"

"I don't know."

"Did the girl have anything to do with it? She's really pretty."

Gavin's stomach fell. He stared at Vincent, knowing his friend was probably right. Nell, and even

Sheridan, had been so adamant about Charlie loving only Nell, being faithful to her.

"Sheridan's divorce papers," Gavin said, taking another tack. "I'm thinking about that trust we set up."

"Ironclad," Vincent said.

"Really? But who did the money go to? Since Charlie didn't get it?"

"It reverts to Randy," Vincent said. "I see where you're heading, but come on. Not even he's that low."

"I don't know," Gavin said, staring at the page. "Why didn't the police look at him closer?"

"For one thing, because he kept his name off the company," Vincent said.

"Right. But you know and I know what 'Randecker' means," Gavin said, looking at the name of both bands' record label.

"Look," Vincent said. "Give Joe a call and see what he says. Keep me in the loop."

"I will," Gavin said.

"Tell Sheridan I say hi." He checked his watch. "I'd better get going. I'm meeting a client for drinks in Watch Hill in an hour."

"Well, you'll have forty-five minutes to spare, heading there in this thing," Gavin said, giving his friend a pat on the back, climbing into his dinghy.

"You take it easy," Vincent said. "Don't do anything stupid."

"I've been through anger management, remember?"

"Whatever."

Vincent took off slow—not wanting to capsize

Gavin. But the moment he got past the breakwater, he opened up the engine and took off for Rhode Island in a rooster tail of macho white water. Gavin couldn't help glancing up the hill at Sheridan's house, wondering if she was watching.

And wondering what she'd think when she realized who owned Cumberland's record label.

CHAPTER 13

THE DAY AFTER SHERIDAN'S DINNER, NELL slept till noon. She'd dreamed all night, and they'd been dreams of fighting. Wrestling with demons, sparring with black-masked ninjas, kickboxing everything that moved. She woke up exhausted. Lying in her bed, she checked herself for bruises. The dreams had been so real, she was sure she was black-and-blue.

She walked into the bathroom, washed her face and brushed her teeth. Her head felt thick, as if she had a bad cold. That wine last night had done something strange to her, even though it had hardly been more than a sip.

Thinking of Agatha's toast, about dreams coming true, she figured last night's selection wasn't exactly what Agatha had had in mind. Nell wanted to go back to bed, but her dad was leaving for a business trip to London, and she wanted to say goodbye to him. Then she had to go to work.

She liked her summer job at Foley's, working behind the soda fountain. Nell and Peggy usually managed to get the same shift, which made it pretty fun. They'd gone shopping at the Nearly New Shop, found some vintage dresses that they used as their waitress uniforms.

Today Nell wore a pretty yellow-striped sleeveless dress, and Peggy wore a pink-and-white flowered one. The lunch hour was busy, but since there were so few items on the menu it wasn't too hard: hot dogs, hamburgers, grilled cheese, sandwiches, lemonade, sodas, and milk shakes. Tyler and Brandon had come in for lunch—they were both painting houses for the summer, all tan and covered with paint streaks. Nell purposely gave Peggy their table; she couldn't take Tyler smiling at her today, and she was glad when they left.

She ran back and forth between the counter and the tables, the old wood floors creaking under her feet. She had the tables all the way in back on the left, near the old-fashioned wooden phone booth. Two people—obviously a couple, from the way they were holding hands—walked in and sat down.

It should have been simple: just another table, just another order. But it wasn't. Because the couple was sitting at the table that had been Nell and Charlie's. He had carved their initials there three summers ago: NK + CR. It was such a long-standing Hubbard's Point tradition, young couples proclaiming love for each other right here on the tables of Foley's Store. Nell didn't begrudge these two their seats; other customers had sat there during the summer, and she hadn't had any problem.

But this couple was young. They were teenagers—twenty at the most. They must have been in love, the way they leaned into each other, talking and laughing in low voices. The girl wore a sundress over her bathing suit; the boy had on shorts and a Boston College T-shirt. They were college kids, and it made Nell's heart hurt to see them together, to think of what she and Charlie were missing.

"Hi," Nell said, walking over with her pad. "What'll you have?"

"Um," the girl said, grabbing the menu, laughing and a little embarrassed because she'd been too wrapped up in her boyfriend to even look.

"I'll have a lemonade," the boy said.

"It's good," Nell said, nodding, unable to keep herself from glancing down at the initials Charlie had carved. "We make it fresh."

"I remember," he said. "My family used to come to Hubbard's Point when I was a kid. We're just passing through. I wanted to show my girlfriend Foley's..."

"The famous Foley's Store!" the girl said.

"Glad you came," Nell said.

"I'll have a lemonade, too," the girl said.

"And a grilled cheese," the boy said.

"Tuna salad for me," the girl said.

"Okay," Nell said, writing it all down, heading to the counter. She handed in the order just as Peggy came back from refilling coffees.

"Who are they?" Peggy asked, placing the coffeepot back on the burner.

"Just some kid who used to come here. He wanted to bring his girlfriend to Foley's."

"You should ask him about BC."

"BC?" Nell asked.

"His T-shirt—Boston College. You'll be at Regis soon, right down the road . . ." Peggy smiled, encouraging her to make a new friend. Nell knew she was right—summer was speeding by, and soon they'd be at college. The boy seemed nice, and if Nell were on top of things, she'd ask him about college life in Boston.

But she couldn't. Turning to glance at the table, she saw the boy reach into his pocket. He pulled something out, small and compact enough to hold in the palm of his hand. Without even looking, Nell knew what it was. He caught her watching, smiled sheepishly, waved her over.

"Hey," he said, blushing when she approached, showing her the pocketknife he held in his hand. "I remembered this thing here, where people . . . My parents grew up at Hubbard's Point, and they put their initials right here, at this table—"

He pointed to time-darkened letters: AL + DR; they were above and to the left of Nell and Charlie's; she remembered, sitting there with him while he'd worked at the wood, how they'd read all the other couples' initials, wondering who they all were, feeling a bond with all the people who'd ever marked their love at this same table.

"And you wanted to carve yours?" she asked.

He nodded. "I just wasn't sure it was cool," he said. "Considering that Jen and I really aren't from Hubbard's Point."

Nell was shaking, but she couldn't help smiling. He and Jen were holding hands, looking up at her so hopefully, as if she held the fate of their wildest dreams in her hand. "Love is love," she said. "Doesn't matter where you're from. Besides, if your parents fell in love here, there's some kind of grandfather clause."

"Really?" he asked.

She smiled wider, letting him know she was kidding. Then, leaving him to start carving, she went to the counter to get their order. She felt light-headed, as if instead of standing in the old beach store, she had suddenly climbed a mountain a mile above the earth. Her mouth was dry, and every breath made her wonder where the oxygen had gone.

Filling tall glasses with ice and lemonade, placing a circle of lemon on the lip of the glass, arranging napkins on the tray, waiting for the cook to slide the sandwiches across the counter, she couldn't help looking over her shoulder. The boy was deep into his task, concentrating as he formed each letter. The girl had her hand on his shoulder, delight in her eyes as she watched him immortalizing their love.

"They seem nice," Peggy said, coming over to wait for her order.

"Yeah," Nell said.

"Are you upset about what he's doing at 'your' table?"

"No," Nell said. "It's fine."

"I wonder where she goes to college," Peggy said. "Maybe you could..."

"Ask," Nell said. "I know. I was thinking of that." She smiled at her best friend, touched by her concern. This fall they'd all be heading off in different directions, and Nell knew Peggy would feel better if she was sure Nell was going to be okay.

And Nell *was* going to be okay. She told herself that as she loaded the sandwiches onto the tray, as she hoisted it up and started over. She had the questions all formed, things about college in Boston; she even planned to tell them she was getting ready to start Regis, in Weston, just a few miles from the Boston College campus.

She crossed the room, saying hi to Tyler and Brandon before stopping at her table. And when she got there, she was fine, she really was. She started placing the napkins down, making sure not to let her eyes fall on the new initials—somehow she knew that would be a little too much. Just take it one little step at a time, she told herself. Just let it all unfold, it's fine...

She had the words all ready.

"Boston College?" she asked, setting the plates down—the girl's right in front of her, but his off to the side, out of his way. "Do you both go there?"

"Yes," the girl said, because he was so lost in what he was doing. "Where do you go?"

"I'm about to start," Nell began. She was about to say "Regis," but just then she couldn't help herself:

she looked straight at where the boy was carving, and she saw that the tail of the "J" from "Jen" had cut just slightly but directly into the very outer edge of the "C" for "Charlie."

She heard herself cry out. And she saw the tray teeter and tilt, and heard the glasses crash, and saw the lemonade pour all over the table, and all over the couple. They jumped up, to keep from getting soaked and sticky, but Nell had already turned away. She ran over to the counter, buried her head in her hands. Peggy's arm came around her, and she felt herself shaking hard under her friend's embrace.

Peggy was whispering, and the young couple—Jen and her boyfriend—were asking if she was okay, and Tyler and Brandon had hurried over, to make sure she hadn't cut herself on the broken glass.

She hadn't, and she said she was okay, she was sorry about the spill—about the scream—about everything. And then she'd said something to Peggy about covering her tables and her shift and how sorry she was to leave her with everything—and then, because she really didn't have a choice, she just started running.

SHE LEFT FOLEY'S, but she didn't go home. Instead of heading down toward the beach and the Point, she walked up the road to the woods just before the railroad trestle, and as she did, she felt as if she were coming down from the mountain, returning to sea level. Her lungs were exploding, as if she hadn't had oxygen for a long time, as long as that couple had been sitting at that table. She relived the moment of her dropping the lemonade and cringed. She felt heat rising from the tar, but then shadows from the trees fell across the road and she cooled off.

She took a right on the dirt road that led into the wooded glade, into the cemetery. Her head was pounding, and her mouth was dry. She craved a drink of fresh water, so she stopped at the old pump. Back when Hubbard's Point was first settled, before there was a water system and when some families weren't able to dig their own wells, this was where everyone came to get water.

It was such an old-fashioned pump, tall and graceful, with a curved spout and a handle. Every winter it rusted in the salt air, and every June someone gave it a fresh coat of white paint. Nell pumped the handle a few times, priming it, then held her hair back as she drank the cool spring water.

The water soothed her a little. As she walked along the road, into the cemetery, she thought about those people at Foley's. They'd seemed so nice, so innocently in love. She'd overreacted, of course. The tabletop was scored with so many initials, all of them crowded in and bunched together—the boy hadn't had any real room to fit his and Jen's.

Nell figured Peggy would fill them in. Two strangers, just passing through, wanting to do something sweet and romantic, would hear about what had happened to Charlie. Peggy was so intuitive— she'd look at the table, and see that the "J" was touching the "C," and she'd know that's why Nell had gone a little crazy. She'd tell the kids, but in a nice way. A way that would make them understand and not feel bad.

Nell felt so tired. She wasn't thinking straight. The wine, and missing Charlie, and those crazy dreams last night . . .

As she walked through the cemetery, she said hello to the people who were buried there. Some of the gravestones were very old; the autumn she was nine, she and Stevie had come here and made grave rubbings.

They'd brought charcoal and fine parchment paper, knelt in the dry grass and gently pressed the paper to the stones. They'd rubbed the charcoal across the paper, and the names and dates and images carved in bas-relief on the gravestones had suddenly materialized onto the paper; it had seemed like ghost art to Nell. And it had helped her know something about each person buried here.

That's the thing, she thought, walking through now: it's so easy to look at cemeteries and think of them as one big mass of dead people, all blurring together. But that's not how it is. Each person still matters. Every single person here existed, had a life, had people who loved them.

There were children buried in this ground, with angel heads and wings on their gravestones. A woman who'd died very young, just twenty-two, who had spent her summers sailing: she had a sloop on her headstone.

And Charlie. She walked along the dirt road, heading toward his grave. Sheridan had had an angel carved into the stone, but not just any angel: she was playing a guitar. Because Charlie had loved music, and Sheridan had wanted him to know he wasn't alone, had wanted the pure, sweet notes she'd played for him since he was a baby to follow him always, even now, where she couldn't go.

No one had ever explained that to Nell: she just knew. She'd lost her mother when she was young; that made it easier for her to understand why Sheridan had needed a guitar-playing angel for her son.

But as she rounded the corner, coming into sight of Charlie's gravestone, Nell stopped dead. Someone was standing at the grave, his back to Nell. He was tall and muscular, and his head was bowed. Nell inched closer, her heart in her throat.

The young man seemed lost in contemplation or prayer. He didn't move, barely even breathed. Nell knew she should hold her breath, stand perfectly still, not scare him away.

But she couldn't hold it in anymore—she was shocked out of her mind and skin, and all she could do was open her arms and run toward him.

"Charlie!" she cried.

The young man froze. He turned straight toward her, facing her head-on. She saw his bright eyes, straight nose, sharp cheekbones. His hair was darker, and he looked as if he'd been lifting weights. For a moment she hesitated—she'd made a mistake. It wasn't Charlie at all.

But then he turned away, and she caught his profile—identical to the boy she'd loved so much—and she knew: it was him. Charlie had come back. There'd been a mistake, he wasn't dead at all, and he would explain everything.

"You've come home," she said, starting to sob as she stumbled toward him. The young man hesitated, and in that split second she saw tears pouring down his cheeks. Then he pushed past her, brushing her arm as he fled, and ran as fast as he could away from her.

HE HAD PARKED HIS BLUE car not far from the cemetery, on the dirt road, deep in the woods, but he ran in the opposite direction now, trying to get away from her and not let her see his license plate. The graveyard was small and hilly, filled with trees. He ran between two rows of old gravestones, dodged behind a stand of pines. Behind him, he heard her calling.

"Charlie, Charlie!"

The name cut him, but he couldn't react. Crashing through brush at the cemetery's far end, he jumped over a low stone wall. She must have been in good shape, because she was keeping up—he heard her footsteps on the ground, heard her intake of breath as she took the wall. A dog barked in someone's yard; he went the other way.

She kept calling and calling, crying now. He wanted to turn around, but he couldn't. Everything depended on her not catching him, not even *seeing* him—how had he let that happen? His heart was pounding—he was running full-out now; there'd be time to think of the mistakes later.

Up ahead, a steep, wooded hillside—he flew toward it, using branches and vines for handholds. He tore upward, up and over and around boulders. Connecticut was the rockiest state he'd ever been in; he skinned his knee on a slab of granite, just kept going. Toward the top he heard a car pass by—he'd come to a road.

Jumping over the guardrail, he ran along the narrow lane. He was still in Hubbard's Point, just the other side from where he'd driven in. The road was lined with little beach cottages. They all had pretty gardens and a car or two parked out front, but he didn't care. This was where he was in most danger. This was Hubbard's Point, where everyone knew his face. He kept his head down, pretended he was sprinting, training for a race or something.

He hadn't lost her, but she'd fallen behind. He heard her cry out, fought the urge to glance back. Maybe she'd fallen on the hill, or hit herself on the same boulder that had gotten him. His shin was bleeding hard now, the blood running into his sneaker. When he reached a fork in the road, he instinctively took the left one—it led into the shade, more trees, less light.

Now he looked over his shoulder—she was nowhere in sight. He slowed down—what if she'd gotten injured? What if she'd twisted her ankle, or blown out her knee? Or really cut herself badly? She was so beautiful and delicate, and he'd hurt her so badly. He'd already done enough, he knew that, and he hated himself for it.

Seeing her at the cemetery had been such a shock—but why should it have been? How could he think she wouldn't visit the grave? No, he was an idiot for coming here—he deserved to get caught. But that wasn't going to happen—and he just started running again.

His mind kept going backward. That's how it had been for almost a year now—as if the future didn't exist. Mainly his thoughts were dragged back, night after night, to last August thirty-first. But right now they had a new focus: ten minutes ago.

Ten minutes ago he'd seen Nell. Their eyes had locked—a split second before he'd taken off—but in that time, he'd seen all the spark and sorrow and passion and life he'd always known was there. Her love for Charlie had flooded into him—he'd felt it filling his mouth and lungs, veins and muscles. Love like that, the kind of love that made a person cry out and run faster than she'd ever run before, chasing him with all her might because she wanted him so badly . . . He shivered, because he'd felt that love coming from her, and he didn't know how he could live without that kind of love. He'd had it once. . . .

His head was a mess; he'd had a plan, to go back for his car and just drive away, but now he knew that wasn't going to happen. He couldn't leave, not yet. He told himself he had to just see Nell one more time, make sure she was all right. Just then, jogging along, he happened to look up at a passing car.

The man driving waved, and he waved back. That made his stomach drop—had he been recognized? Yes, the car was turning around, coming back for another look. He started to panic, knowing he had to hide in a backyard or somewhere, and fast.

There were more beach cottages along the road, and he studied them as he ran. They were small and quaint, close together. It was high season for Hubbard's Point—midsummer, when everyone was using their cottage, enjoying the sun and fun. At midday, people were starting to head home from the beach for lunch. Moms and kids were strolling along the road. He kept his head down.

He began making calculations, thinking of where he'd parked the car, wondering the fastest way back to it without running into her. He heard a train whistle and the Doppler effect of a locomotive speeding past, here and gone close by, and he went in that direction, glancing back to see if the car was coming yet.

There was an old overgrown field, surrounded by an Anchor fence. The faded sign said *Harry Anderson Recreation Area*. Too bad for the kids—looked as if it hadn't been used in some time. He saw a shed behind the fence, as well as a rusty old swing set and seesaw. A jungle gym had become a perch for crows—there were five big ones on the metal bars, watching him.

He looked around, ready to vault the fence. But just then the car came along, slowing and rolling down the window.

Jesus, he thought. *This is it.*

"Hey," the man called.

"How're you doing?" he asked, continuing to walk. The car rolled alongside, and he felt the man studying him. He just kept walking, as if he had somewhere to go. The man in the car didn't say anything, so neither did he. His chest was exploding. Any second, Nell might come tearing over the top of the hill, and it would be all over.

"Can I help you?" he asked, just to get this over with.

"My mistake," the man said. "I thought..."

He looked at him now, through the open window.

"You know something," the man said, "you are the spitting image of someone I know. A boy who used to live here."

"Yeah?" he said.

"It's uncanny," the man said. "You had a double."

Had. He heard the past tense, but ignored it and just gave the guy a smile as he drove away. As soon as the car disappeared, he started for the fence again. He had his eye on the shed, his mind was racing, figuring it all out, when just then—out of the corner of his gaze—he caught sight of something.

Newspapers on a front porch.

That's all it was, but that's all he needed. He'd been good at his work, his job, his craft, whatever you wanted to call it. He knew what to look for, knew the signs, didn't make many mistakes.

Papers, a week's worth of papers. Piled up on the front porch. Flowers in the garden wilting, tomatoes heavy on the vine in the little strip of vegetables along the side of the house. He was already looking both ways. Not taking the front walk, the concrete embedded with sea glass and beach stones, not taking the side door, arched over with a rose-covered trellis. Some of the roses were dead, needed water.

He went around back. Tall hedges that needed pruning separated the narrow yard from the neighbors. The privacy couldn't be better. He heard the Doppler effect again—the train tracks ran right behind the property, and here came another train, this one heading in the opposite direction from the last.

If he'd had more time, he would have checked under flowerpots, in window boxes, under the garden gnomes for the spare key. People in houses like this always hid a spare key. But he didn't have time. He heard the voice again, Nell's voice calling "Charlie, Charlie!" Still in the distance, but at least she was on her feet—he felt a split-second flash of relief as he bent down to pick up a brick, a loose brick dislodged from the chimney, maybe in a storm or something.

If he'd brought his tools, he wouldn't have to break the window. But he hadn't planned on staying around here. So he edged close to the back door, right up alongside, and gave the pane closest to the knob a good tap.

Bang: all it took.

He reached his hand through the shattered glass, taking care not to cut his wrist, clicked the lock open, turned the brass knob.

He was in.

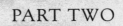

PART TWO

CHAPTER 14

WALKING UP THE STONE STEPS TO RETURN Stevie's pie plate, Sheridan noticed the little sign saying *Please go away*, the letters faded, the sign nearly overgrown with ivy. It seemed more like an artifact than anything else, causing Sheridan to reflect on how times had changed.

Not so many years ago, Stevie had been the official Hubbard's Point hermit. Young fans of her children's books would stop by to visit or get them signed, and Stevie had done her best to keep them away.

Knocking, Sheridan noticed a new sign taped to the screen door: *I'm painting in my studio—come on up!* She let herself in, left the pie plate in the kitchen, and headed upstairs. She smelled oil paint and turpentine, walked into Stevie's studio and found her standing before her easel.

"Hello," Sheridan said. "I don't want to interrupt you—I just returned your dish, and I wanted to check on Nell. How is she?"

"She's fine...slept a little late, and then went to work. I think Agatha's wild thyme disagreed with her."

"I'm sure my sister didn't expect Nell to drink from my glass; I'm immune to her potions, she should know that by now."

"Uh-huh," Stevie said, raising her eyebrow. "I'm glad you're here—come in, keep me company."

Sheridan walked over to the loveseat, sat down. She glanced up at Stevie, laughing quietly.

"What's so funny?" Stevie asked.

"Well, I don't mean to laugh. I'm actually just happy for you."

"For what?"

"You just seem...so content. It's such a change, walking up your steps and seeing that sign all covered with vines. And then to come to your door and find, basically, an open invitation for anyone to just walk inside and visit with you."

"Things do change," Stevie said, smiling as she worked on a painting of three baby robins lined up on a branch.

"You were such a recluse," Sheridan said.

"I know," Stevie said. "I was a love-wreck. I was so sick of making mistakes, falling in love with the wrong guy...I had to hide out from the world for a while. But sometimes I think back even further, to when we were kids. I was so happy then, so carefree; that's how I feel now. So what does that mean?"

"I'm not sure," Sheridan said.

"I have nothing profound to say," Stevie said. "I

think life is full of circles. That's all I can think of. Maybe because I feel I look like a beach ball..."

"You look great," Sheridan said. They smiled at each other. Sheridan knew there weren't many people she felt like visiting with, and even this felt touch-and-go. Seeing Stevie's pregnancy reminded her of when she was pregnant with Charlie.

"That's debatable," Stevie said. She put her brush down, wiped her hand with a rag, and came to sit with Sheridan.

"I was hoping to catch you while Nell was at work," Sheridan said, choosing her words carefully. "Gavin's been hinting at something, and I wonder what Nell's said about it."

"What's he hinting about?"

Sheridan shrugged, shook her head, knowing she had to just spit it out. "Well, that Charlie might have been seeing someone else."

"Besides *Nell*?" Stevie asked.

"I know," Sheridan said. "Crazy, right?"

"Completely. He didn't know them together— didn't know what they were like, how they drove us nuts needing to be with each other twenty-four/ seven... he'd never say something like that if he had. Where did he get that idea?"

"Something about the band Charlie went to see that night. Gavin thinks Charlie might have had plans he didn't tell Nell about."

"So? They don't have to tell each other every-thing... who does that? What couple in the world tells each other every plan they make? He must think there's more to it . . ."

"A beautiful bass player," Sheridan said.

"Well," Stevie said, "I'd like to think our old friend Gavin is a little more enlightened than *that*. A young man goes to see music, and just because there's an attractive female musician, he must be lusting after her? Or *sleeping* with her? What's wrong with him?"

"So there's nothing to it, right?" Sheridan asked. "I'm not the only one who knows he's barking up the very wrong tree?"

"The *totally* very wrong tree," Stevie said.

Stevie didn't speak, just sat there gazing into Sheridan's eyes. In the silence, Sheridan felt their long friendship. She saw the fine lines in Stevie's face, the strands of gray in her hair, and she thought of how different it must be to be having a first baby now instead of when Sheridan had Charlie. She saw the relaxation of tension in Stevie's being, the ease that had come over her since falling in love with Jack, becoming like a stepmother to Nell.

"Aside from the fact he's so wrong about Charlie and Nell, how was it having Gavin at the house?"

"It was . . ." Sheridan said. She trailed off, because she didn't know how to answer. She thought of the stress of sitting there with a man she had once loved so much, the strange betrayal of him being unable to change his nature for her. She thought of the wrong direction he was taking, thinking of her son as being so cavalier with Nell's heart. And then she thought of his kiss, and the thoughts pulverized into nothing.

"Like that, huh?" Stevie asked.

"Pretty much."

"I guess it's never smooth sailing. Jack . . . well, he disappeared for a while last night. He's had a lot on his mind lately, and after dinner he went to think things over. It was hot, and I couldn't sleep without him here . . ."

"Is everything okay with you two?" Sheridan asked.

"Yes," Stevie said, nodding. "It's great. Only Jack won't believe that. He's stuck on the marriage thing."

"Ah."

"Anyway, I went to look for him. I knew he'd be somewhere on the beach."

"Did you find him?"

"Yes," Stevie said. "I met him as he was coming back from Little Beach. He'd built a fire."

"That was him?" Sheridan asked. "I saw it, thought it was kids . . ."

"Nope. It was Jack."

"Pretty romantic gesture," Sheridan said.

"Speaking of romantic gestures, you should have seen Gavin last night. Jack and I walked along the water, and looked out to his boat. He was standing on deck, staring right up at your window, as if all he wanted to do was go up the hill to you. We could see it in his body—he was just holding himself back."

"How can you know that?"

"Because he was thinking the same thing at dinner last night . . . the way he sat there right next to you, looking so protective. He's in love with you. Sheridan, he always has been."

Sheridan stood and walked to one of the west-facing windows. She looked down at the beach, gazed across the bay at the *Squire Toby*. The sun was hitting the white hull, making it gleam. She peered at the deck, trying to see if Gavin was there, but it was too far away.

"And in spite of what I just said about it never being smooth sailing," Stevie said, "I think you're in love with him, too."

"Nothing has ever really worked between us. How could I be crazy enough to fall in love with him again?"

"How crazy would you have to be to get struck by lightning?" Stevie asked, laughing.

"It's not the same thing," Sheridan said. "I have no power over what lightning does."

"Well, waves then. How crazy would you have to be to ride a long, unpredictable, possibly rough wave?"

"That's nature," Sheridan said, starting to laugh as well. "That's not falling in love with someone you know is wrong for you."

"Can you work with me on this?" Stevie asked. "Don't you get what I'm saying? You and Gavin have known each other forever. You grew up together, you fell in love young, made a ton of mistakes, then went your separate ways. But what's meant to be is meant to be. It's the power of nature—you can't stop or change it."

"You mean like you and Jack?"

"Yes," Stevie said. "Like us. We all grew up together here at Hubbard's Point, and you know what they say...people fall in love here. The air is an aphrodisiac."

Sheridan smiled at her friend. It was true, that people said that. "Well, if you're so in love with him—and it's obvious you are—then why *aren't* you two getting married?"

That made Stevie stop. She gave Sheridan a smile, picked up her paintbrush again, stared at her canvas. Sheridan watched her other hand go to her pregnant belly and rest there.

"I'm sorry," Sheridan said.

"Oh, that's okay. We all have our sore subjects," Stevie said. "Interesting that for us, you and me, they so deeply involve men. You know what I wish?"

Sheridan shook her head.

"That I could just wipe the slate clean. Go back in time and just be with Jack. Skip right over the others. Don't you wish that for you and Gavin?"

Still standing at the window, Sheridan looked down at the beach. Did she wish that? She shivered, to think of kissing him last night, and she wondered how different everything would be if she'd had a lifetime of that. But she wouldn't have had Charlie—he had come from Randy. Just as Nell was Jack's daughter with Emma; if Jack had been with Stevie all this time, Nell wouldn't have been born.

"Scratch what I just said," Stevie said, hand still

on her belly. She'd obviously been thinking the same things.

Sheridan kissed Stevie, glanced at the painting—so beautiful and tender—of the three baby robins about to fly.

"Looks like us," Sheridan heard herself say.

"What do you mean?" Stevie asked.

"We're all about to fly," Sheridan said. "Everyone who's ever been born, at every moment. Trying to fly . . . Always stepping off the branch into something new. Feels like such a long way down . . ."

"That's a song, Sheridan," Stevie said sternly, giving her a hug. "Now go home and write it."

STEVIE STOOD AT HER EASEL getting lost in work, just as she'd always done. She'd never found anything to both take her mind off her problems and help her solve them like painting. And not just physically applying paint to canvas, but all the preparation that went into it: coming up with the right subject, making sketches, letting her imagination follow the threads of what would become her next children's book, going to the lumberyard and buying wood, stretching the canvas, applying gesso, starting to paint.

She spent the late afternoon working on the baby robins, already starting to think about her next book, *The Big Bang*, listening to notes drift through the privet hedge from Sheridan's house. Had Sheridan actually listened to her, gone home to work on a song about trying to fly? If so, Stevie would be first in line to buy the CD. She really needed some lessons in getting brave enough to spread her wings and take the leap.

Jack had left for London. After she'd met him on the beach last night, she'd smelled the smoke. He told her he'd built a fire to keep himself warm—the implication being that she was making him cold. Then he said something about just needing a chance to think, to commune with the stars—a most un-Jack thing to say.

Jack was an architect. He was about precision, meticulousness, exactitude. He specialized in bridges, spanning rivers, currents, and roadways. He worked with concrete and steel—not spells and ablutions.

"Why did you need to commune with the stars?" she'd asked, stunned.

He'd just stared at her—as if he had no idea of who she was, of why she had to ask that question. He'd said very little after that. They'd walked along the water's edge, gazing out at Gavin's boat. This morning he'd packed in silence, then kissed her and left for the airport.

Stevie heard the door open downstairs. She listened for Nell, heard nothing. What did Nell think of Gavin's theory about Charlie? Stevie couldn't imagine she could feel happy about it, and wanted to talk to her about it.

"Nell, I'm up here!" she called.

A moment later, she heard a heavy tread on the

stairs—a man, definitely. She tensed up, but then Jack stepped into her studio.

"What are you doing here?" she asked. "Why aren't you at the airport?"

"I'm not going," he said, dropping his bag on the floor. He stood in front of her, dressed for his trip. He was one of the most sought-after bridge architects in the world. He wore a dark suit and blue silk tie, he was the most elegant man Stevie knew, but when she looked into his eyes she saw the young man she'd always loved, the boy she'd met right here at Hubbard's Point.

"Why aren't you going?" she asked.

"Because I have to talk to you." He grabbed her hand, gently pulled her away from the easel, led her to the loveseat where she'd been sitting with Sheridan just an hour earlier. Pushing the hair out of her face, he stared into her eyes. "What are we doing?" he asked.

"We're living life," she said, catching hold of his hand. "We're having a baby."

"We're wasting time," he said, his voice hard.

"Jack, I don't know what you're talking about," Stevie said. "You're supposed to be meeting the Lord Mayor tomorrow, right? He wants you to build the newest London Bridge, and you're here worrying about *us* wasting time?"

"You know what I'm talking about," he said.

"No, I really don't."

"Aren't you paying attention?"

"Of course I am, Jack."

"Last night, going to dinner at Sheridan's ... then seeing Gavin afterwards, just sitting on his boat, staring up at the light in her window. Seeing him like that ..."

"She was over here earlier," Stevie said. "I told her, he's in love with her."

"Gavin's not the only one who's in love," Jack said.

"I'm in love with you, too," she whispered.

Stevie felt butterflies in her chest. Jack's eyes glittered. She'd almost fooled herself into thinking he was happy with things the way they were. They had so much to be blissful for; she held his hand, trying to reassure him of how much they had.

She knew he thought she was being contrary, being unconventional for its own sake. But couldn't he understand how afraid she was? She'd been married three times, and each of them had ended in divorce. Why did the piece of paper matter so much to him when she felt so much more secure without it?

"Stevie," he said, leaning forward.

"Jack, please ... don't."

"Explain it to me."

"I have," she said. "Again and again. You don't understand ... I love you so much, but I don't do marriage well."

"You've never been married to me."

That was true, and she knew it. She stared into his beautiful blue eyes and knew she never wanted to look into anyone else's, knew she never wanted to be with anyone else, knew she wanted to grow old with him.

"You're having my baby," he said. "We're a family. I want you to be my wife, and I want you to be Nell's stepmother. You've been that to her all these years, but I want to make it official...."

"'Official,'" she said. "What does that *matter*?"

"It matters, okay? Stevie, you think you're being nonconformist, is that it? Miss Artist? I'm telling you, I love you and I want to marry you."

"Jack, I can't just see the world the way you want me to!"

He stood up, eyes blazing. "I'm the one wearing the suit, and you're the one wearing a paint smock, but you know what? *You're* conventional."

Stevie reacted as if he'd slapped her. "What are you talking about?"

"You're walking the straight and narrow here. Sticking to the path you've set for yourself. So what if you've made some mistakes—you think I haven't? If that happens, we'll get through it together."

"We don't need a ring to prove anything!" Stevie said.

"Maybe I do," Jack said. "Have you ever thought of that?"

She stared at him, the butterflies-in-the-chest feeling getting stronger.

"I told you," he said. "Last night really affected me. Being at Sheridan's house, looking up and down the table, missing Charlie. My friend lost her son; my daughter lost her boyfriend. Stevie, life is really short. Don't you get that?"

"Of course I do," she said, shocked by his tone.

"Didn't you hear what Agatha said, about dreams?"

"That was for Sheridan's benefit!" Stevie said. "Sheridan and Gavin, giving them a little push..."

"Maybe they're not the ones who need it!"

"I live with you, Jack! I'm having your child. We don't need a push!"

"Here's what I'm going to do," he said, standing in front of her, taking her hand. "I'm going to ask you one more time. And that'll be it."

"Are you giving me an ultimatum?" she asked. "If I don't say yes, it's going to be over?"

"Do you really think that's what I mean?" he asked. "It can never be over. I love you forever, Stevie. I'm just getting really tired of proposing. I was halfway to JFK when I realized I had to come back here and ask you..."

"You could have waited till you got back."

His blue eyes filled with tears. It took a few seconds before he could speak again. "But what if something happened? To me, to the plane? God forbid, to you. Everything feels so fragile and precious, Stevie. When I die, I want to die as your husband. Please, don't make me go to London without knowing that's going to happen...."

Stevie held his hand, looking into his eyes. She thought of Sheridan here just an hour ago, of the grief she'd suffered this year. She heard music coming through the trees, and knew it was a new song, about learning to fly.

She glanced down at her easel, at the young robins poised and ready to spread their wings. Her chest was full of butterflies now—they were flying around, bumping into her ribs—and she wasn't at all sure she wasn't about to pass out.

"Stevie Moore," Jack said, his eyes still wet but his tone so strong, "will you marry me?"

At first she couldn't speak. She opened her mouth and tried, but the words were stuck. Outside the window, a sea breeze blew through the trees. Only when she looked down toward the beach, she saw the flag absolutely still—not a bit of wind was blowing. Yet up here, on the hill, right in front of Stevie's cottage, the leaves rustled.

She stared right at Jack, and the butterflies were gone.

"Stevie?" Jack asked.

She felt herself nod. She knew—she had always known, and now she knew something else, too: it was time.

"Yes," she whispered, looking up into the face of the man she'd always loved. "Yes, Jack, I will...I'll marry you."

NELL HAD CHASED the young man through the cemetery, over the wall, and halfway up the hill before she'd tripped on a root and lost him. She'd finished scrambling up the hillside and run through the beach roads calling after him, feeling like a maniac, scaring everyone she saw. She'd even run into Mr. Belanger, who'd heard her and stopped her to say she was wrong—he'd seen the same young man, made the same mistake, thought it was Charlie Rosslare.

"But it wasn't," Mr. Belanger said, sounding sad. "He said I'd made a mistake. And I told him he had a double."

Nell had thanked him, but she refused to believe she was wrong. She'd seen Charlie with her own two eyes. And even though Mr. Belanger had been in charge of the beach, and the lifeguards, while Charlie had worked there, he didn't know him the way Nell had. So she walked back to the grave to wait. Surely Charlie had seen her, had heard her calling, and regardless of what had made him run from her, he would come back.

She lay down on the grass to think. Her mind raced, running over the events of the last couple of days. The strangeness had started out on Gavin's boat, looking at that website for the band Cumberland. She'd looked through the pictures—mostly fan-type photos of the band, but also some shots of the crowd. That's when she'd first seen Charlie.

The image had been hazy. She'd squinted and stared, unable to believe her eyes. She'd told herself she had to be wrong. Gavin's computer screen was scratched; also, it was coated with that thin film of salt, those little white crystals that seemed to get on everything around the water. She'd leaned closer, looking more carefully at the photo, and, like Mr. Belanger, had thought she was wrong.

Like him, she'd thought Charlie had a double. Or

maybe an identical twin, separated at birth. One far-fetched explanation after another had flooded her mind. The date, December 21, had been so clearly labeled, and she remembered being with him that night. But labels could be wrong, websites full of mistakes.

Gavin had been sensitive, prying into whether Charlie might have lied, whether he could have been seeing someone else. Nell had nearly snapped his head off. But lying here now, knowing she'd just seen Charlie . . . what else could she think? They'd buried his body, though—she had to be going crazy. Could a mistake have been made? Could that boy who'd died by the river been someone else, while Charlie was still alive?

No, she told herself. No, Charlie would never do that to her, to them. Never, never. There was another explanation. Just as she knew, deep in her heart, that Charlie had not been in Nashville that night.

That night, the December before he'd died, he'd been with Nell right here at Hubbard's Point. They'd built a fire and snuggled together in the falling snow. It had been the most romantic winter solstice any couple had ever had, and she'd never forget it. So one thing was definite—the person in the picture was one hundred percent not Charlie Rosslare.

The person who'd been here at his grave, however—that *was* Charlie. Nell was exhausted from seeing him and chasing him. Her eyelids were heavy, and her body felt so tired. She was eighteen years old, and she wanted Charlie.

She wanted her love.

She thought of Agatha's toast about dreams coming true. She wanted to close her eyes and be with Charlie. It seemed impossible to imagine the days and nights she'd spent without him so far; the concept of eternity was too terrible to accept. And now she didn't have to—because he was back.

She pressed her cheek into the ground at the foot of his headstone. Birds sang in the trees, and shade from the robins' white pine fell across the hill. Nell and Stevie had saved those baby robins, delivered the nest and eggs back to their mother.

Why couldn't she have another miracle, right here in this spot? Why couldn't Charlie come back to her? She was Catholic, and although her family didn't go to church much, she believed in resurrection. She knew that Charlie's bones were in the ground, but she had believed that he had risen from the dead and was in heaven.

Was it possible that she'd seen his ghost? That could explain everything. . . . She'd seen his spirit earlier today. He wasn't alive after all . . . he was a ghost, and he'd come back to haunt her.

Her tears flowed into the dirt and grass. Suddenly everything made perfect sense. How could heaven be anything better than what they'd had? They'd loved each other so much; she'd always wondered whether she could find someone to love as much as her father loved Stevie, but she had, and it was Charlie. So of course he would come back. . . .

She'd wait right here, so he'd know where to find

her. She had to stay awake, make sure she was vigilant, so she wouldn't miss him. Her eyelids flickered as she felt sleep tugging her down. Thoughts drifted through her mind, random things about Charlie. She remembered those pictures on Gavin's computer. Something bothered her—not the photo of Charlie's look-alike, but something else. What was it?

One of the other pictures . . . she could almost see it now, one of the band shots. Cumberland, Box Turtles, which band was it? And what difference did it make? Who cared about someone in the band, when Nell had just seen Charlie?

The breeze blew through the trees, through the tall oaks and the robins' white pine, and it whispered to Nell, and she reached up to trace Charlie's gravestone with her fingertips—the angel, the strings of her guitar, the dates of Charlie's birth and death— and she whispered his name over and over to keep herself awake, keep herself ready.

CHAPTER 15

THE YOUNG MAN STOOD IN THE BATHROOM of the house he'd broken into, washing the cut on his leg. His shin was skinned raw and stung like crazy, but most of his senses were busy being alert for the sound of anyone approaching. He didn't want to ruin the homeowners' towels with his blood, so he dried the scrape off with toilet paper. Rummaging in the medicine cabinet, he found first aid cream and put some on. There were Band-Aids, but the small kind, and his cut was pretty big. So he left them untouched.

Walking around the house, he tried to take stock of where he was and what he was going to do next. First, he had to assess how long he had before the owners came home. Looking around, it didn't take much to figure out the place belonged to a retired couple.

There were a few glaring clues: a wheelchair pushed into a corner, some big old terrycloth slippers in front of it. Lots of pictures, snapshots, of a gray-haired couple surrounded by kids and grandkids. There was a plastic pill-holder, the seven-day kind that got you through the week, on the old enamel kitchen table. Coupons had been clipped, stuck into the napkin holder—something clearly handmade, probably by a kid. Shells and macaroni glued to the wood spelled out "Grandma." He took it all in without sentiment; he had to stay cool and not get all wrapped up in personalities while there were plans to make.

He didn't really want to be here, in these circumstances. It had been a while since he'd broken into a house. He hadn't had to recently, plain and simple. His needs were pretty much all met, at least in the material realm. But right now, he knew he had to stay close to Hubbard's Point. He'd wanted to get away as fast as he could, but the more he thought about Nell, the more he wanted to stay—just a short while longer.

A calendar hung on the wall, by the phone. It was one of those make-it-yourself-at-the-photoshop calendars, with a different family photo for each month of the year. Just glancing at August, he saw a group shot on the boardwalk that included several faces that looked familiar from the pictures in the living room.

He scanned the dates, and saw what he needed: written on the past Monday were the words *At Billy's*, followed by a long, shaky line and arrow all the way through Labor Day. The same spidery hand had written flight information. They'd flown American to

Chicago; they would return Labor Day on a flight that got into Bradley at six-thirty at night.

Why would the old folks leave this beach paradise in the middle of the summer to go see Billy, whoever he was? Retirement, he thought. Gave you plenty of freedom to do what you wanted when you wanted. Just like the artists in the music business, retirees could make their own schedules, pretty much. He wondered who Billy was. Probably their son. Maybe the dad of the kid who'd made the "Grandma" napkin holder. Perhaps the balding thirty-something guy in the family photo. Someone they loved enough to visit in Chicago for two weeks in the heat of August.

He'd been to Chicago, just two weeks ago. The tour had taken them there, and to Ann Arbor, Detroit, and Milwaukee. It had been hot as blazes, heat just rising from the pavement without even a whisper of wind; so much for the Windy City. So why would these people choose to spend hot summer days there unless it was to see someone they loved very much?

Loved very much.

Those words still felt phony to him. He felt like a fraud saying "love" out loud, or even thinking it. It seemed like a word from the movies, or a greeting card. He'd tried believing he had it with Lisa, and look what happened. Thinking it now, even about this family, felt fraudulent, and if he got caught at it, he'd be made fun of or run out of town. Run out of the house.

Then he remembered: it wasn't his house.

He was hungry and tired. Walking to the refrigerator, he opened it to check things out. The people were very careful—they hadn't left any milk or bread, anything that would spoil. That's why he was surprised they'd forgotten the newspapers—they should have called to stop delivery. Save themselves a few bucks, and keep people like him from knowing there was no one home.

He scanned the shelves, seeing jars of pickles, mustard, mayonnaise, big bargain-size bottles of Coke and ginger ale, a package of individually wrapped slices of American cheese, a big jar of peanut butter, some small jars of homemade grape jam. He hadn't eaten all day, not since he'd left the motel outside Philadelphia—his three-quarters point on the drive from Nashville—at dawn, and that cheese would have tasted good. But he wasn't going to take any.

He'd wait till dark before heading back to his car, then go to the grocery store, buy his own supplies. Before too long, he'd measure the window, fix the pane he'd broken. He hadn't always been so conscientious or concerned about the people whose houses he'd broken into, but people changed. They really did. It might seem like a dumb thing, but to him it was big: he wasn't going to eat these people's food. Picking up an envelope off the kitchen counter, he checked the name: Herbert Martin.

Glancing around the house, he checked to make sure the shades were all drawn. They were dark green, cracked with time—old-fashioned blackout shades from World War II, when everyone had been on the lookout for enemy planes and ships. A lady like Mrs. Martin wouldn't want her rugs and furniture getting all faded from the summer sun. That was good. The shades would keep anyone from looking in while he stayed there—not long, just a few days.

Just long enough to see Nell . . .

And maybe talk to her.

NELL SLEPT, AND HAD a dream so real, she thought she must be awake. It was just getting dark; she had dried grass stuck to her cheek. Fireflies glowed in the trees and tall grass around the edges of the cemetery. She lay on her back, looking up at branches in the sky. Through the leaves, she saw stars scattered in the deep blue sky.

She felt thirsty, and even in her sleep she knew she wanted to drink from the pump again. Stretching, she arched her back and reached behind her, to touch Charlie's gravestone. Instead, she felt a leg and a canvas sneaker. She jumped, but strong arms eased her back down.

"Shh," the voice whispered. "There's something I have to tell you."

Blood was rushing through her veins, and she felt scared and disoriented. What time was it—how long had she slept? Was she still dreaming? She was . . . his touch was filmy, as if his hands were made of air. But he'd eased her down with such gentle force, as if the strength came not from his arms, but somewhere deeper.

"I dreamed of you," she said, her voice coming out in a croak.

"I always dream of you," she heard him say, and she felt his ghost-hands stroking her hair, the side of her face. She half turned, saw Charlie sitting there, leaning against his gravestone.

He kissed her, their lips parting, and she felt the most intense shock of connection—he was there but not there. Her hands tried to grasp his hands, his wrists, his forearms, but she couldn't take hold. He was vapor, just a shape in the air.

She twisted around, knelt in front of him. He was wearing an old blue T-shirt, one she knew so well, with *Hubbard's Point* in white letters. Her hand hovered over his heart, wanting to touch him. She did, and her hand passed through, straight to the stone behind his back. She raised her gaze to meet his eyes. They looked so clear and bright, but filled with the hugest sadness she'd ever seen. And then she knew the truth.

He was dead, and this was a dream. She pulled back, kneeling eye to eye with an apparition; and even though she realized that she was asleep, she stared deeply into his eyes, knowing she would find the truth there.

"You ran away from me before. And you weren't wearing that shirt . . ."

He didn't speak, but kissed her forehead, her eyebrows, her eyelids. The kiss felt like a whisper.

"Not me..." Was he talking? Or was his voice in her head, as it always was?

"It was! I saw...and you ran away. I couldn't believe you ran away from me."

"You know, don't you? He just looks like me..."

There was so much she wanted to know. Her body trembled, thinking how terrible it was that she didn't know what to believe. She was wrestling with herself, her thoughts, the awful ideas Gavin had raised.

"We never had secrets before," she said.

"Death is full of secrets," he said. "And I can't stay long. But you whispered me back. You fell asleep here, saying my name. It called me..."

"I love you," she gasped, trying to hold him. If she could grab on, find a way to touch him, he couldn't go; she wouldn't let him leave.

He reached for her, kissing her, and in her dream she felt it. She melted into his arms and body, the angry fire dying down. She felt like liquid inside, as if she were becoming part of him. She tried to hold on, but again there was nothing there—it was like trying to embrace vapor. Staring, she saw his outline—his head and body, his strong shoulders—dissolving.

"Don't leave me!" she begged. "Tell me what to do."

"He just looks like me," he whispered. "He just looks like me..."

And then he kissed her again, the longest, sweetest kiss in this or any other world, and then he wasn't there anymore.

Nell sat bolt upright. The cemetery was dark and deserted. The crickets were chirping, and overhead bats and night birds were swooping through the trees, on the hunt for moths. She rubbed the sleep out of her eyes and realized: she'd been dreaming. That's all it had been. Just a dream.

She felt frantic, confused. *Death is full of secrets.*

She felt as if she'd been presented with a choice—Charlie as a dream ghost, or Charlie alive, running away from her. Either one broke her heart, made her feel crazed and lost. She sat very still as the night birds flew all around, and the wings of bats and moths clicked and murmured overhead.

Just then she heard a car start. It had been parked over by the maintenance shed, where the beach crew parked the truck, and Nell saw its headlights come on. She didn't know how she knew, but it was him.

She sprang up from the grass, started to run. Hiding behind the trees as he pulled out, she waited to see for sure. He stopped at the entrance to the drive, looked both ways. She caught sight of his profile, and felt adrenaline: it was Charlie. But even as her heart leapt to see him, she thought of the words from her dream . . . *he just looks like me, he just looks like me.*

Tyler always hid the keys to the beach truck in a little magnetic box in the right front wheel well. Nell felt for it, found the key, and climbed into the truck. She was barefoot and had left her license at home, but none of that mattered. She started the engine, pulled out onto the road, and followed his car under the trestle and onto Route 156.

Fifteen minutes later, they were at the A&P. She hadn't been quite awake at the start of the drive, but now she was as alert as she'd ever been. Slouched down behind the steering wheel, she watched him get out of the car and stride, head down, into the grocery store. Cruising past his car, she jotted down the license number—it was from Tennessee. *Nashville*, she thought.

Parking across the lot from him, she ran into the store. She caught him in the baked goods aisle, hung back as he loaded bread into his basket. She watched him pick up milk, cheese, sliced bologna, a can of peanuts. As he took his time picking out a box of cereal, she studied his face.

And here in the fluorescent glare, she heard the words again: *he just looks like me*. He wasn't Charlie, not at all. The shape of his face was similar, and so was the way he stood—tall, but with a slight curve to his spine, as if he didn't want to be the tallest boy in the room. Where Charlie's features had been so fine, almost chiseled, this person's seemed a little more rounded, a little softer. He was slightly heavier, and there was a lack of grace in the way he moved.

Nell had planned on tailing him some more, to see where he'd go after the grocery store. But suddenly she became a Mack truck that had lost its brakes, and she started barreling down the aisle, unable to stop or hold herself back, and she crashed right into him, punching him in the chest with both fists.

"Hey!" he said, shocked.

"Who are you?" she asked, grabbing his shirt and shaking him. "What do you want?"

"Jesus, get off me," he said. "I don't know what you're talking about!"

"Right," she said, shoving him away. "I've made a *mistake*!"

"Yeah. You have."

"Try again. That might have worked with ancient old Mr. Belanger, but it won't with me. I chased you up the hill, remember? I saw you get *that*—" She gestured angrily at his skinned shin, wanting to kick it.

"I swear," he said. "You've mistaken me for someone else."

"Charlie," she said.

"Uh," he said, starting to turn red, as if he were embarrassed for her. "I don't know what you mean."

"Charlie Rosslare," she said. "That's who I mistook you for."

"Well, I'm sorry I'm not him."

"No, you're not. But you were at his grave."

"Girl," he said, putting his basket down on the floor and backing away, "you're all confused. Look, I swear, I'm really sorry. I can tell you're upset, and I wish I could help you out. But . . ."

Suddenly she felt dizzy, almost the way she had earlier, when she'd seen those kids sitting at the table with her and Charlie's initials. Was she losing her mind? If she'd just dreamed of seeing Charlie, could this be a dream, too? A dream of the A&P, fluorescent lights and all, and a young man who reminded her so much of Charlie? She swooned slightly, felt him catch her by the elbow.

"Hey," he said. "You okay?"

"Not really," she said.

"You want to sit down?"

She glanced around; they were right in the middle of the cereal aisle. People were passing by, pushing grocery carts along, looking at them. He held her arm, helped her toward the front of the store. Just before they got to the electric door, he put his basket down. Then he walked her out.

After the air-conditioning, the night felt muggy. It made Nell's head swim. Moths flew around the orange parking lot lights. She looked up into the young man's face. She nearly tripped over her own feet because his eyes were Charlie's eyes. Out here, away from the much brighter lights inside, she felt crazier than ever. She heard herself whisper his name.

"You got to stop doing that," he said, shaking her lightly. "I'm not him."

"But you . . ."

"My name's Jeff," he said.

"No, you're . . ."

"What's yours?" he asked, cutting her off.

"Nell," she said.

"Good to meet you, Nell," he said. And when he said her name, his voice broke. She had no idea why, but he was overtaken by emotion and had to stop. He looked away, staring up past the parking lot lights at the sky.

"Will you tell me what's going on?" she asked.

"I didn't want it to be like this," he said. "I wanted to find you . . . and talk to you."

"You know me?"

"Know of you," he said.

"But how?" she asked.

"My brother told me. He talked about you . . ."

"Your brother?" she asked, her heart starting to race, waiting for his answer, although, of course, she already knew, it was what Charlie had been trying to tell her in the dream.

"Charlie," he said, his voice cracking again. "Charlie was my brother."

AFTER THAT, once she realized he wasn't going to run away again, Jeff went into the store to buy his stuff. He didn't want to let her know where he was staying, so he made up something about an inn in town. She'd guessed which one—the Renwick Inn, because it had housekeeping cottages where he could cook his own meals—and he'd just nodded. Lying was so easy with honest people. They never thought you weren't telling the truth, even after you'd lied repeatedly and they'd caught you at it. It was as if they just didn't believe in lies.

Jeff felt no pleasure or triumph in lying to Nell, or in having her believe what she was starting to want to believe: that he was all good. He could see it in her face—an almost-glow in her skin and eyes, just knowing she was in the presence of a blood relative of Charlie's.

They drove in a two-vehicle caravan down the street to the stop light—the only one he'd seen in town. Luckily, he had had Nell lead—otherwise he'd never have been able to find his way to the inn where he was supposedly staying. She led him into a circular drive, and they parked in front of a stately yellow colonial house with big white columns. He noticed there was a bar inside and another in a barn out back. Instead, they walked down by the river.

Several rustic benches had been set along the banks. Jeff let Nell pick one, and he sat down beside her. She was beautiful and seemed nervous. She brushed the long dark hair back from her face, and he felt her staring at him, taking in every detail. He could only imagine how she felt, seeing the strong resemblance to Charlie. Meeting him had been like looking into a mirror.

"Charlie knew he had half-siblings," Nell said. "He said his father had had kids with other mothers, before he got together with Sheridan . . ."

"Yeah," Jeff said. "There are—were—three of us."

"Who's the other one?"

"His name's Clint. But I don't know him much. He grew up in California, lives there still."

"Does—did—Charlie know you?" Nell asked, and from the way her pretty mouth quivered, turned down, he could tell the question came from a very tender place.

"No, I can't say we really got to 'know' each other," Jeff said. "Not so much."

"But did he ever meet you?"

"Yes," Jeff said, unable to tell a lie to that question. "That he did."

"That must have made him so happy," Nell whispered. He saw her shoulders start to shake; she was crying.

"Nell," he said, unable to help her, wanting to comfort her, "what's wrong?"

"I thought we knew everything about each other," she sobbed. "I thought he told me everything...I never thought we kept secrets."

Jeff sat paralyzed, watching her bury her face in her delicate hands. He wanted to push her hair back, touch her cheek, but he couldn't.

"Something as important as having a brother..." she cried. "How could he not have told me about you?"

"Like I said," Jeff said, "we didn't really know each other. We would have gotten to, I'm sure, but we never got that chance....He would have told you, Nell."

"If there'd been more time?" she asked.

"Yeah," he said.

She nodded, as if that made sense. He watched her wipe her eyes with the back of her hands. She stared into the slow, dark river. It was all country around here, with rushes growing a little farther along the bank, with stars reflecting in the water. He saw little rings and bubbles, fish swimming down below, heard the croak of a bullfrog from around the river bend.

"When did he—or when did you—get in touch?"

"Well," he said slowly, not wanting to make a mistake, "you might have known Charlie was looking to get to know our father some."

"I do know that."

"That's pretty much how it came about. My father introduced us."

"When?" Nell asked. "And where?"

"In New York, right after Charlie got to college," Jeff said. "Seemed like a good place to meet—Randy didn't want to have us come on up here, to Connecticut, not with Charlie's mom around and feeling the way she does about him."

"She has good reason," Nell said, giving him a steady gaze.

"I know," Jeff said quickly. "So does my mother. Randy wasn't exactly...well, he wasn't exactly a model dad when I was young. Same for Charlie, I suspect."

"That's for sure."

"But Randy's different now, Nell. He's sorry for not being there for us when we were young. He had a heart attack a few years ago, and it showed him what was important in life. He vowed to be there for us."

"Be there for his sons?" Nell asked.

Jeff nodded.

"But he wasn't! Not for Charlie! As time went on, Charlie began to hold it more and more against his father. He was going to make a documentary about 'missing' parents—fathers who choose not to be there for their kids."

Jeff felt a quick surge of anger. She didn't know Randy, everything he'd put himself through, and everything he'd suffered—because of his own mistakes—just like he was suffering now, all over again. But he quickly calmed down. She just didn't have all the information. He could easily forgive her for that—just as he could forgive Charlie for wanting to expose something on film, something that wasn't there anymore.

"Randy would be the first to admit he hurt us," Jeff said. "But he's not that way now. That heart attack really changed him, made him see the light."

"Okay," Nell said. "If you say so. I wonder whether Charlie would see it that way."

"I think he did," Jeff said, unable to stop the lie.

"You say that as if you talked about it!"

"Well, not exactly. Not in so many words. But Charlie was pretty friendly to him. To us . . ."

"How long had you been in Randy's life?"

"Just three years," Jeff said. "Three. I was twenty-two when he first got in touch with me. We had some rough patches, but . . ." He paused, thinking. "It's good to have a father. I even changed my name back to his."

"Changed your name?"

"Yeah," he said, and he felt a pang, thinking of his mother and her reaction. "I took his name—Quill. Jeff Quill, that's me."

Jeff remembered Charlie's reaction when he'd heard the same thing. The memory was charged and made his pulse race, but he didn't let it show. He calmed himself right now, letting himself realize he was sitting next to Nell on a bench by a river. Their arms were pressed together, and she was looking up at him with such need and trust in her eyes, as if he held the answer to every single thing she needed to ask. Maybe, if he was careful, he could make things right for both of them.

"Why did you run before?" she asked.

"I told you... I wanted to see you, but I wasn't ready." He swallowed, staring into the weeds along the riverbank. "I needed to visit my brother's grave. I just... to know him so short a time, and to lose him. It's huge."

"I know," she said.

"He talked about you. It's weird." He looked deeply into her green eyes, felt as if he'd been staring into them for years. "I looked up and saw you there, and I felt as if I knew you. I was going to introduce myself, but then you called his name."

"Charlie."

He nodded. "I... kind of freaked out."

"I guess I can see why," she said slowly. "I did, too."

"I know we look so much alike. And man, when I met him, I realized we were alike in so many ways. So having you call me by his name..."

"It must have been unsettling."

"To say the least," he said.

"I still can't believe he didn't tell me about you," she said, sounding stunned. "And if he kept that from me, oh God." She drew in a sharp breath, then looked up at him. "Maybe there were other things."

"I don't think so, Nell," he said quietly.

"Would you tell me if you knew?"

He nodded.

"There's a girl," she said. "I ... don't think they ever met. But it's possible. Maybe they did. Someone ... well, this guy Gavin thinks maybe there was something between them. Charlie and the girl."

"What's her name?"

"She's the bass player for Cumberland," Nell said, looking into his eyes.

"Lisa Marie Langton," Jeff said slowly. He caught the shock in her expression, and he realized she'd taken his answer for assent—that yes, there'd been something between Charlie and Lisa. Jeff felt stabbed by the thought of it.

Nell gasped and jumped up. He felt her trying to read his face: did she see in his eyes the fact he was trying to hold himself back from telling her he had a picture of Charlie with his arm around Lisa? It had been taken ten minutes after they'd all met, such an innocent, exuberant moment. Remembering it made Jeff close his eyes, weave in his seat.

"What is it?" she asked, grabbing his shirt, just as she had in the grocery store. "What happened? Tell me there was nothing between them—I know Charlie, know he wouldn't do that to me ..."

Jeff wanted to tell her the whole story, but he couldn't. He knew it would devastate her, it would destroy him. So he just kept his eyes closed, lowered his face into his hands, heard himself moan out loud.

It must have been more than Nell thought she could stand. Whatever she thought he was about to tell her, she wasn't ready to hear. She took off, running barefoot across the inn's lawn. He heard her truck start up, pull away, gravel flying.

She thought he was staying here, a guest at the inn, in one of the cottages. But of course he wasn't, so he got into his car and headed down the road behind her. If she looked in her rearview mirror, there he would be. She'd see his eyes, Charlie's eyes. She'd know he hadn't finished his story, he still had something to tell her, almost none of it about Lisa.

And he hoped she wouldn't think too carefully about the timetable of what he'd told her already. He hoped she wouldn't catch him in one of the few lies he'd dared to tell to this girl he'd cared about even before they met.

Cared about a lot. His brother had loved Nell.

And in spite of everything, that mattered to Jeff.

SHERIDAN WAS SITTING in the living room, feeling the night breeze coming through the open window, as she strummed her guitar. The white curtains moved like ghosts, dancing in the sea air; staring across the water, she saw lights on Gavin's boat. She'd been working on a new song, inspired by Stevie's painting and parting words. She had the verse and chorus, and she was playing with the bridge, working it out, when she heard a noise just outside.

"Is someone there?" she called.

No one answered. She felt prickles on the back of her head, wheeled around and saw a shadow just outside the window. Was it her imagination, or was someone hiding out there? Ever since last night, she'd felt her family's magic swirling around. Her grandmother had said magic was seasonal; it diminished in autumn, and hibernated in winter, and renewed in spring, and became powerful in summer.

Still holding her guitar, she walked into the kitchen, peered out the window at the backyard. Summer was in full bloom: the night smelled of jasmine, beach roses, pine, and salt. She felt the sea breeze blowing her hair, and she thought of going out for a walk. But her skin tingled again, and she stayed inside. She had the feeling someone was watching her.

Standing at the door, she heard footsteps on the path up from the beach. Someone was hurrying, coming fast. Sheridan stared, waiting for the person to come around the corner. She felt tension building, and when Gavin came into sight, she let out a long breath—so glad to see him, but still rattled by the sensation of being watched.

"Did you pass anyone?" she asked.

"No, why?"

"I thought I heard someone," she said, staring down the dark path. Then she looked up at Gavin and smiled. "Hi."

"Hi," he said. "I saw your light."

"I saw yours, too."

"I wanted to come up and say goodnight."

She smiled, opened the back door to let him in. He wore jeans and a black T-shirt. Seeing him in the glow of her kitchen nightlight, she thought he looked the same as he had twenty years ago; she stood there mesmerized, caught in the past.

"You haven't seen Stevie tonight, have you?" he asked.

"No," she said, suddenly worried it could be the baby. "I visited her this afternoon. Why? Is she okay?"

"Fine," he said, quickly. "Better than fine."

"What, then?"

"I ran into her on the beach earlier; she was taking a walk, and she gave me some news. She said she wanted you to be the first to know, but she wanted me to be the one to tell you. She sent me up here. . . ."

"What is it?" Sheridan asked.

"She and Jack are getting married," Gavin said.

"That's good," Sheridan said softly, thinking of the talk she and Stevie had had earlier. "I'm so happy for them. Wow, she changed her mind pretty fast. I wonder what happened between our visit and her seeing you?"

"I think Jack talked to her," he said. "In a different way. And she was ready to listen—also in a different way." He paused, gazing into her eyes.

"People change their minds," she said.

"I'm counting on that," he said, staring at her. The intensity of his gaze made her take a step back. She felt suddenly on guard, folding her arms across her chest, looking down at her feet. He came closer; her heart started pounding.

"Don't, Gavin," she said.

"Sheridan, look at me."

She shook her head slowly, keeping her head down. He stood right there, so close she could feel the warmth of his skin. He touched her shoulder, running his hand down her arm. She could barely breathe.

"You just said it yourself," he said. "People change their minds."

"Not us," she said. "We had our time."

"Yes," he said. "And we're having it again."

His words broke her heart open. She didn't want to look into his face, but she couldn't help herself. His eyes sparked, reflecting the light. She watched the way he stared at her, not smiling, as if he was as full of regret as she was. She wanted to say something, to make sense of the moment, but she couldn't speak.

"I've been wanting to do this since last night," he said, taking her face between his hands, kissing her. She knew she should pull back, but instead she stood on tiptoes to meet him. His body pressed into hers, and she pressed back. His lips were on hers, and he touched her tongue with his, and everything dropped away.

They moved into the living room, holding each other. She pushed her guitar aside so they could sit on the wicker sofa. They kissed again, and she leaned into him. His body felt so solid and hard; his chest was a rock. He held her tight. His touch wasn't light—he gripped her. But somehow it felt like the most tender and gentle touch she'd ever felt.

She opened her eyes while they kissed, to look at him. Maybe she needed to make sure this was really happening. She'd dreamed of love her whole life. She'd once had it with Gavin, but she'd let it go, and she'd made a mistake that had brought her Charlie, and then Charlie had gone, too. She held Gavin and saw him, and she knew this was real and she was wide-awake.

Music of the water and wind came through the window, and the leaves on the trees rustled in the breeze. Sheridan closed her eyes again, wanting to be lost in the kiss. His arms were around her, his hands trailing down her back. His touch felt like fire, and she arched into his body. She traced his upper arms, feeling nothing but muscle, and his kiss was soft, aching, and intense.

The kiss ended, but he kept his forehead resting against hers, stroking her cheek with his hand. They stared into each other's eyes for a long time. Waves broke and broke on the beach below, one after the other. It would go on forever. The sound was a blanket, holding Sheridan and Gavin in the eternity of Hubbard's Point.

"Why did I mess things up before?" he asked.

"You?" she asked. "It was me. I didn't believe..."

He waited for her to finish her thought, but she wasn't sure exactly what she meant to say. She hadn't believed they could be together, she hadn't believed they could overcome their differences. He'd been on the submarine, she'd been in Nashville, and she'd moved on. Randy had come along. And even after she'd figured out the truth about him, she hadn't trusted that Gavin could settle down, really love her and another man's son. That they could all make a good life together.

"It's okay," he said. "We're here now."

"Close your eyes and listen to the waves," she said. He did, and so did she, and she leaned back into the circle of his arm. They sat there quietly for a few minutes. She wanted to say, *Isn't this the same as it ever was?* It was almost possible to believe that no time had passed at all.

"Familiar sound," he said after a while. "I've been at a lot of beaches, on a lot of waterfronts, but I'd know Hubbard's Point waves anywhere. It's Long Island Sound, so they're smaller than ocean waves; but it's the eastern end of the Sound, Orient Point is just across, so there is less protection and some oceanic action. And it's a sand beach down below, not rock...so the splash is soft, not hard."

"I've listened to those waves every day this year," she said. "At first the noise sounded so harsh. I'd think, another wave Charlie won't hear. And another, and another. But now..." She trailed off.

"What?" he asked.

"They bring me peace. I think, Charlie swam in those waves. He walked the beach so often, loved it so much."

"It's the same sand, the same water. It doesn't change."

"Yes," she said, looking at him. "Having you here made me realize that."

"Me? In what way?"

"I've been thinking about the past," she said. "How we used to be together. I had those thoughts about the waves and beach—about you. It's all the same, the exact same water and sand, as when you and I were young. The beach kept us together, even when we were apart. So it will keep me and Charlie...together, even though he's not here anymore."

"I was afraid that my coming here was too hard on you," he said.

"It was, at first," she said. "For all sorts of reasons. Seeing you reminded me of how badly I'd screwed things up....But also, knowing you were here to look into Charlie's death." She stopped, shivering.

"I don't know how much you want to hear about what I'm finding out."

"I want to know," she said, gazing at him hard. "But I have to tell you something, too."

"What, Sheridan?"

"Charlie loved Nell. No matter what you say, I'll never believe he would have done anything to hurt her."

"Understood," he said.

Did that mean he believed her, agreed with her? Or was he just acknowledging what she held true for herself? She realized how much she needed him to see Charlie through her eyes.

"The police stayed in touch with me the first few months," she said. "They told me they'd keep me up to date. But after a while, they stopped calling. And I never followed up."

"Some people want to know every detail," he said. "Seeking justice makes them feel they have more control."

"I can understand that, even though it's taken me a while. I want justice," she murmured, a huge wave of grief overtaking her. "But not as much as I want Charlie back. I want you to know him."

"I want that, too."

"He was a great boy," Sheridan said. "One of the all-time wonderful kids."

"I believe you. We'll get justice for him," Gavin said, hugging her even more tightly. "I promise you, Sheridan."

She leaned back and he kissed her. She felt as if they belonged to each other in a whole new way. He'd just made her a promise, and until this moment, she hadn't realized how much it mattered to her: justice. It had seemed so abstract, an ideal for someone else, when all she'd wanted was the solidity of having her son back.

Gavin held her hand, pulled her up. He started toward the stairs, and he led her up to the second floor, into her bedroom. She knew she should fight it—this wasn't right for her, for him; in spite of what she'd said about people changing their minds, she knew that she was too broken to go back, to love Gavin the way she once had. But he held her so firmly, and she wanted him so badly. All her thoughts and reason fell away, and she was swept along by her feelings.

Everything had changed since they were young.

Sheridan and her sisters had slept in the small rooms across the hall. Now she occupied the big bedroom that had been her mother's. It faced the beach, had a big bow window with a window seat overlooking the curved crescent of white sand, the half-moon bay, the heavily wooded rocky point that led to Little Beach.

They pulled each other down onto the big bed. Sheridan had bought it for herself a few years ago; no one else had ever been in it with her. But looking into Gavin's eyes, she admitted to herself how often she'd dreamed of him here. She'd needed him all these years. Her heart had longed for him, her body had craved him, and even though she knew they could never make it right, she knew she'd never needed anyone more.

"I've wanted you for so long," he whispered. "More than you can imagine."

"I think I know, because I've wanted you so badly."

They clung to each other, undoing buttons and zippers, not caring whose was whose. There must have been a moon in the sky; she couldn't see it yet, perhaps it hadn't quite risen over the trees. But ghostly blue light streamed through the skylight and windows, painting their bodies in white light.

Sheridan kissed the shadows on Gavin's body. The dark edges of his muscles, the hollow of his stomach, the long, crooked scar down his side. It represented all his past mistakes, which made her love him more—because she'd made so many of her own. He rolled over, to hold her close above him, her hair falling into his face. They kissed through it, too passionate to push it away. She eased off, onto her side, then her back, and he entered her.

Every inch of her body came alive. His touch made her shiver. She writhed and ached with love, and felt nothing but joy. And then she tumbled into exquisite longing for more, something like sorrow, a feeling that she only wanted this, forever, and she knew she couldn't have it, that it would have to end, that she would hurt him again, and that was too much to bear.

Gavin kissed her on the lips, his mouth hot, scorching her, making her arch her back so there wasn't an inch of space between them. He slid his arms around and behind her, holding her closer than two people had ever been. Sheridan blinked, looking up at him, saw that he was watching her so closely, as if he could never look away.

She knew this was an interval of time. Charlie's death had taught her something about forever, and she felt bittersweet knowing that she and Gavin couldn't go on. But she held his gaze, wrapped in his arms, wishing life were different. They moved together, holding tight. The blue moonlight bathed them like water, and they were swimmers, cutting through the waves, the gentle waves so particular to Hubbard's Point, toward the beach that had always been their home.

CHAPTER 16

THE NEXT MORNING, GAVIN SWAM FOUR miles. He felt he could have kept going, all the way to Orient Point and back. He hadn't slept, but he was filled with energy; just before diving in, he'd stood on the deck of his boat staring up at Sheridan's house—he'd left early, returned to the boat to check for updates from Joe—wondering why he wasn't still there especially because the fax tray was empty. Being with Sheridan was the first thing that had really made sense to him in years.

As Gavin powered through the water he turned everything over in his mind. He swam parallel to the shore, from Hubbard's Point to the mouth of the Connecticut River and back. He'd been the rescue swimmer on his first vessel, when he'd first joined the Navy. He'd liked the long training swims, designed for endurance. But he'd always excelled at short competitions—brief bursts of speed. In life, he'd found he had to do both.

When he returned to the *Squire Toby*, before pulling himself out of the water, he hung onto the boarding ladder, breathing hard as his heart rate slowed. Wiping salt water from his eyes, he stared up at Sheridan's house, wondering what she was doing.

Even after his long swim, his body still felt her. She had lain in his arms long after they'd made love. The bed, her house, had felt solid; Gavin had been sleeping on boats for so long, he didn't know how to sleep with nothing moving beneath him. So he'd stayed awake while she slept.

Sometime around dawn she'd woken up, and they'd made love again. The sun rose behind Hubbard's Point, falling on the crescent beach and curved bay slowly. He hadn't wanted to leave, and he wouldn't have if he wasn't so anxious to complete the investigation. He worried she wouldn't let him back; she was bothered by the direction he was taking. He'd felt it last night, when she'd wanted him to back down from what he was thinking about Charlie. It was a subtle thing, because he wasn't really onto anything solid—he just had to stay open to what had happened, and he knew that meant seeing Charlie through his own eyes. The dynamic had come between them before—a way she had of viewing the world, and wanting him to see everything the same way.

From her bed, holding her as the sun came up, he'd been able to see this boat. This was his home, and he loved it, but he would have liked to stay up there with Sheridan and never come back here—

keep the moment going forever. Standing in the cockpit, he toweled himself off. Shaggy-haired and dripping, he looked up and saw Nell coming around the walkway from the bow.

"I thought we'd talked about this," he said. "You call first, and . . ." Then he really saw her, the acutely troubled expression in her green eyes, and he pulled a deck chair open for her. She glared at him, dark crescents under her eyes. She paced, refusing to sit down.

"Where were you?" she asked.

"I went for a swim."

"Last night I called and called you!"

"I'm sorry," he said. "I had my cell phone turned off. Weren't you celebrating with your dad and Stevie?"

"I saw Charlie," she said, her voice thin and high, stretched like a wire about to break.

"What are you talking about?"

She was tense and crackling, her skin glinting with salt from her swim out from the beach. A small runabout puttered out of the channel under the footbridge, heading for Wickland Reef. Two teenage boys were laughing and joking; when they spotted Nell, they changed course and came closer. Gavin saw them both staring at her. He watched for her reaction, but she had none. She didn't even see them.

"Hey, Nell," called one. "It's my day off—come with us. We might head over to Shelter Island."

She ignored him, staring at Gavin, her fists tightly clenched. Her chest was rising and falling with quick, shallow breaths. She looked as if she hadn't slept and was about to pass out. Gavin walked over to ease her down into the deck chair, but she shook him off. The boys waited a moment, their boat idling. Then they drove away.

"Didn't you hear me?" she asked.

"I heard," Gavin said.

"But it turns out it wasn't him at all," she said. "It was his exact double."

He stared at her, holding both ends of the towel draped around his neck. "Okay," he said. "Start at the beginning."

"I'll start with the fact he has a brother. Did you know that?"

"Yes," Gavin said. He'd known about the two other boys, as well as the fact that Randy was a deadbeat dad and never bothered to participate in their lives, ever since he'd investigated him during the divorce.

"Well, one of them looks just like Charlie. His name is Jeff Quill. And he's here."

"Here? In Hubbard's Point?"

"Not right now, no. He's staying in town. But he *was* here, at Charlie's grave. I saw him."

"How do you know his name?"

"I chased him," she said. "And I caught him, too. I made him tell me everything."

"Jesus, Nell!" Gavin said.

She glared back at him. "What was I supposed to do?"

"Not go chasing after someone you don't know.

You know nothing about this guy—you could have gotten hurt in more ways than I can count."

"Gavin, he knew Charlie," she said, the fight going out of her as she sat down in the cockpit. "I didn't get to hear it all, because I . . . well, I sort of got upset and ran away. But he told me some. You were right about something."

"I was?" he asked.

She nodded. "Charlie did keep a secret from me. Or Jeff said maybe he just didn't get around to telling me. But they met—"

"Did he tell you when?"

"Right after Charlie got to NYU."

"How did that come about?"

"Their father introduced them. Randy. See, that's what's so confusing to me," Nell said. "I knew that Charlie wanted to see his father! He told me that, we used to talk about it all the time. He even wanted to make that documentary . . ."

"Yes," Gavin said, watching her growing agitation.

"So why wouldn't he tell me about this?"

Gavin thought of the website printouts, and had his own theory. He knew that timing was central to everything, and he had to put it all together. Right now Nell's distress was so deep, he figured that moving slowly would be his best bet. He sat down beside her, put his arm around her shoulders.

"It'll be okay, Nell," he said.

"You know what upsets me most?" she asked. "I thought that this was a mystery about how Charlie died. But it's turning into a mystery about his life. I thought I knew everything about him. But I don't."

"Nell, that's the thing they don't tell us. Everything in life is a mystery. I read something somewhere once. Can't remember who said it, but he talked about 'the dark unknowability' in every one of us."

"There's nothing dark and unknowable about me," she said, sounding defensive.

"Yeah, there is," he said. "And it's not bad. It's just life. We all have our hidden corners. I know you won't believe this, but even I do."

She laughed, snorting through tears. "*That* I have no problem believing." But then despair took over again. "But Charlie! He was just like the sun to me— so open and bright. We told each other everything. I'm . . . hurt that he wouldn't have talked to me about his father, and even more . . . what if there was something between him and that girl in the band?"

"You don't have any reason to think there was."

"I do, though. Because when I mentioned her to Jeff last night, he acted upset. And he seemed really evasive."

"Did he tell you why he's here? What he came for?"

"To visit Charlie's grave," she said.

Gavin took that in, tried to process it with what he'd been thinking about Randy. Could Randy have put the kid up to something, dragged him in? Gavin was thinking of bank accounts and trust documents, social security numbers and passwords. To know Randy Quill was to check to make sure he hadn't lifted your wallet.

"You mentioned that Jeff's name is Quill," Gavin said. "Did he make it sound as if Randy's been in his life all along?"

"No," Nell said. "I wondered that, too. He said he's known him three years, since he was twenty-two."

"So why's he calling himself Quill?"

"I don't know. He seemed..." Nell thought for a minute. "Surprisingly happy to be Randy's son. I told him I knew Charlie would never take his father's name."

"What did he say to that?"

"Nothing. That's when we started talking about the girl."

"Where's Jeff now?" Gavin asked.

"At the Renwick Inn," she said.

"What do you say we take a ride over there, to talk to him? I'd like to meet Charlie's brother."

She nodded, wiping her eyes. "You want me to drive?"

"That'd be great," he said. "Because I don't have a car."

AND SO THEY HAD A PLAN. Gavin went down below, pulled jeans and a shirt onto his damp, salty skin. He rowed them into shore. Instead of beaching the dinghy, he rowed under the footbridge into the creek, tied up at the steep steps. They walked up the stone steps to the path that led to Stevie and Jack's. Nell picked up the car keys, and they climbed in.

She had to stop at Foley's to ask Peggy to cover her

for the lunch hour. Gavin was glad, watching her go through the paces of her everyday life, grounding her as they prepared to confront Charlie's brother. The more Gavin learned about Cumberland, the more he suspected that Randy had been in New York on August 31. He wanted to ask Jeff what he knew about that.

Charlie's father had the most to gain from his death. That was just a raw, immutable fact. If the father was anyone but Randy, Gavin would have dismissed it as unbelievable. But tigers don't change their stripes, and Randy had been so greedy and so disinterested in his son at the time of his birth, he couldn't believe he would have suddenly stopped caring about the trust fund scheduled to be paid to him on his eighteenth birthday.

"I'll be just a minute," Nell said.

"No problem," Gavin said, following her inside.

The store looked like an old barn. Huge, drafty, it had been supplying provisions to Hubbard's Pointers for generations. The gas pumps had been modernized, but that was about it.

Foley's brought a whole new realm of memories back to Gavin. He'd come here with his grandmother when he was little. When he got older, he'd come with his friends on rainy days. They'd buy comic books, penny candy, and Mountain Dew. As teenagers, they'd go into the Hangout and play the jukebox and pinball machines.

The plank floors creaked with age. Gavin followed Nell to the soda fountain in back. He'd come here for lunch a thousand times. They made the best lemonade in the world. Sheridan had liked strawberry ice-cream sodas.

He walked over to a square table near the phone booth. Running his hand over the weathered surface, over all the initials that had been carved there over the years, he came to rest on the ones he'd put there himself, with his Buck knife, one rainy day a million years ago: GD + SR. They were black with age, but the message was still clear: Gavin Dawson and Sheridan Rosslare.

"Here are ours," Nell said. She led him to a table across the room, pointed at a set of initials—not as black as his and Sheridan's, but obviously weathered by a year or two of salt air. CR + NK.

"Charlie carved them?" Gavin asked, and Nell nodded.

Gavin knew they both loved Rosslares, and it made him feel even more bonded to the young woman.

"Nell."

They turned around, and a red-haired girl stood behind them, holding a tray of food.

"Peggy, I was just coming to ask you to cover for me at lunch," Nell said.

"Sure," she said, looking troubled. "But I have to talk to you. Let me just drop this off, okay?"

They watched her run over to a table, place the coffee and pancakes down, and return. She looked from Nell to Gavin and back.

"You're the detective, right?" she asked.

"Yes," Gavin said.

"I forgot, you haven't officially met yet!" Nell said. "Peggy, this is Gavin Dawson. Gavin, this is my best friend, Peggy McCabe..."

"Bay McCabe's daughter?" Gavin asked.

"Yep," Peggy said.

"Tell her I say hi," Gavin said.

"So, what's up?" Nell asked.

"Okay. I'm just going to say it," Peggy said. "Someone saw Charlie. Mark and Ally were on Oak Road, and they saw him coming out of a yard there."

"A yard, on Oak Road?" Nell asked.

"*That's* the part you find surprising?" Peggy asked. "Not the part about seeing Charlie alive in the first place?"

"Well," Nell said, "not as much as you'd think. It's not Charlie."

"But Mark said!"

"Peggy, Charlie has a brother. And I've met him."

"You're kidding!" Peggy said.

"No," Nell said. "They look so much alike, I couldn't believe my eyes. And Oak Road...that's where I was chasing him yesterday. That's probably when they saw him, right?"

"They came in this morning, and the way they talked—they were so worked up—I had the feeling they'd just seen him," Peggy said.

"It had to be yesterday, Peg," Nell said. "Because that's when Jeff was up there. He'd have no real reason to go back today."

A customer called for a coffee refill, and Peggy

said she'd be right there. But first she gave Nell a hurt look. "When were you going to tell me?" she asked. "That you met Charlie's brother, that no one knew he had?"

"I've been running a little crazy," Nell said. "But I planned to tell you at lunch today . . ."

"Okay," Peggy said. "Whatever."

She went to grab the coffeepot, and Nell and Gavin walked out of the store. Nell gave a backward glance, as if she wanted to run back inside and make things right with Peggy. Gavin didn't have kids of his own, so he deeply enjoyed this chance to deliver such an obvious life lesson.

"See how easy it is?" he asked.

"What do you mean?" she asked, frowning.

"For a 'secret' to happen? And come between people?"

"I wasn't keeping a secret! I just didn't have time to tell her."

"Exactly," Gavin said.

And she seemed to think that over as she started the car and began driving under the train bridge, toward town and the Renwick Inn.

CHAPTER 17

NELL TOOK IT ALL IN, DRIVING GAVIN TO meet Jeff. She knew exactly what he was saying, making a parallel between Peggy's hurt feelings now and what Nell had been feeling about Charlie. But was it the same? She knew her own heart, knew that she would have told Peggy as soon as she could.

Had Charlie felt that same way, hardly able to wait to tell Nell about meeting his father and brother? She'd never know, and that hurt more than anything. That's why she pressed on the gas a little harder, speeding along Route 156, taking McCurdy Road past the country club. Because the person best able to tell her about what she needed to know was right here in town, barely a mile away.

The tall white steeple of the Congregational Church loomed ahead, and she took the turn onto Main Street, hardly noticing the graceful white sea captains' houses, the art galleries and ice-cream shop, the lovely brick library with its curved porch and elegant white columns. Past the art academy, under the highway bridge, past the house and grounds where the Black Hall art colony had originated a century earlier.

Nell turned into the Renwick Inn's driveway, parked in the shade of a sprawling elm. Last night the scene had seemed enchanted—sitting on the riverbank with a young man who'd looked just like Charlie, seeing the starlight reflected in the river's smooth surface. The fact that he'd so badly wanted to talk to her, share with her his feelings about Charlie, had made everything all the more powerful.

Today she felt ready for almost anything. She wanted to hear whatever Jeff had to tell them. The Renwick Inn was regularly voted "Connecticut's Most Romantic Inn" by everyone who visited. Painted classic Black Hall yellow with gleaming black shutters, sparkling windows, screened porches, and a sprawling back wing flanked by rose gardens on either side, it was surrounded by tall, ancient oaks, elms, and maples. Shade fell everywhere, but sunlight shone through the leaves, making it all so summery and bright.

"Should we go inside and ask for him?" Gavin said.

"I don't see his car," Nell said, looking at all the vehicles parked along the curve of the wide circular drive. "But he must be staying in one of the cottages—he bought groceries to cook for himself."

"We could go back and find him ourselves," Gavin said.

"Sure," Nell said.

They walked down the gravel path toward the river. Nell scanned up ahead, trying to see his car parked beside one of the small, perfect country cottages. They were set apart from the main inn, and she knew they were usually occupied by guests staying a week or more. That made her feel happy—to think of Jeff here for a while, so they'd really have the chance to get to know each other. She felt a little embarrassed about running off last night, about her jealous thoughts about Charlie and the bass player. She'd be glad if he could put those to rest.

"What kind of car does he drive?" Gavin asked.

"A Ford," Nell said. "With Tennessee plates."

"Okay," Gavin said. "You see it here?"

They walked from cottage to cottage, looking at all the cars. She didn't see it. Two parking spots were empty—maybe he'd gone out. Just in case, she led Gavin all the way to the end of the path, where it stopped at the river. She looked left and right, to see if Jeff might be sitting on one of the benches.

He wasn't.

Without a word, they started back toward the inn. Nell found herself picking up the pace. She wasn't sure why, but she felt anxious. He'd probably just gone for a ride. Or maybe he'd gone back to Hubbard's Point, to visit Charlie's grave again. When they got to the main entrance, Gavin held the wide screen door.

They walked up to the reservation desk. A tall, elegant woman was on the telephone; Nell recognized her as Caroline Renwick. Her father had been a famous artist, and somehow, probably because of the painting connection, she and Stevie were friends. When she finished her call, she gave them a friendly smile. Nell didn't want to waste time introducing herself, but she needn't have worried. Gavin took over.

"Hi," he said. "We're looking for one of your guests. Jeff Quill."

"Let me check," Caroline said. She opened a large leather-bound book and began running her finger down a column of names. After a moment, she looked up. "I don't see him registered here."

"But he is," Nell said. "He's staying in one of the cottages."

"I don't think so," Caroline said. "Those get booked up a year in advance by families who come back every summer. I know pretty much everyone..."

"Maybe he's using a different last name," Gavin said.

Caroline raised her eyebrow and gave him a questioning look, but Gavin didn't seem deterred. "Just check for anyone under the first name Jeffrey, or Jeff, or letter 'J.'"

Obliging, Caroline tried again. "Nope," she said. "There's a John and a Jonathan. No Jeff or Jeffrey. Or letter 'J.' Do you have the make of car he drives? We could check that way."

"Ford," Gavin said.

"Ah," Caroline said. "Three guests have Fords. You don't happen to have the license plate, do you?"

"Yes!" Nell said just as Gavin shook his head. He looked at her with surprise and admiration. She fumbled in her pocket, found the slip of paper she'd written it on while she was tailing him to the A&P yesterday. She read it off, hopes rising.

But Caroline dashed them. "I'm sorry," she said. "We don't have that plate listed here. Maybe you misunderstood, and he's staying across the street, at the Black Hall Inn?"

"No, it was here," Nell said stubbornly, even as Gavin thanked Caroline and steered Nell outside to the car. Tears were rising, and she thought she might lose it. How could this be happening? Had Jeff lied to her? Had she dreamed the whole thing?

"Give me that plate number again," Gavin said as they climbed into her car. She handed him the slip of paper, and started the engine.

He made a phone call. She heard him as she forced herself to keep her eyes on the road. Her mind raced, going over everything about Jeff. The way he'd looked, the things he'd said. She'd been positive he was being straight with her; she'd sensed his sadness about Charlie, his need to connect with her—because, as he'd said, Charlie had talked about her.

"That's right," Gavin was saying into the phone. "Tennessee tags." He repeated the number.

Nell's chest hurt. Her eyes welled with hot tears, and there was nothing to do to stop them. They pooled and spilled down her cheeks. She felt as if she'd lost Charlie a second time. Not that she thought Jeff was anything like him, but she'd been so happy about the chance to talk to his brother, to hear more about the boy she loved so much. She felt betrayed by a stranger who just happened to be Charlie's brother.

"Yeah?" Gavin asked, sounding fired up at whatever he was hearing. "You sure?"

Nell glanced at him. He was making notes on the scrap of paper. She heard him say he had a trip to take. Driving along, she swallowed down grief. She made herself concentrate on the road. When Gavin hung up, she waited for him to speak.

"I'm going to track him down for you, Nell," he said.

"Who was that?" she asked.

"My friend, a cop. You did a good job, getting that license number."

"It doesn't matter," she said.

"Yeah, it does. It tells us a lot."

"The car's Jeff's," she said. "But Jeff's not staying at the Renwick Inn. He lied to me. . . . We sat there by the river, talking about Charlie, and he looked me in the eyes and lied."

"The car's not registered to Jeff," he said. "It belongs to a corporation down in Nashville."

"That's where he's from."

"It's a record company," Gavin said. "And you know what band's signed to them?"

Nell shook her head. She didn't care.

"Cumberland," Gavin said.

* * *

DRAGONFLIES HOVERED OVER the birdbath, wings iridescent in the sun. Sheridan sat reading in a lawn chair under the oak tree, and felt a breeze come up from the beach. It rustled the leaves overhead, cooled the skin on her bare arms. After last night, all the joy she'd felt to be with Gavin, today she felt her old familiar melancholy return.

She heard a car coming up the street and she looked up from her book, hoping it would be the blue car again, but it wasn't. Early that morning, she'd looked out the kitchen window, seen someone who looked like Charlie driving by. She was losing her mind.

She turned back to her book, Rilke's *Sonnets to Orpheus*. They were love poems, and beautiful. She understood Rilke to mean that separation was part of love, as valid and true as coming together. The whole experience, whether two people were as one or driven apart by circumstance or renunciation or death, was what mattered. Love was bigger than the human heart could understand, or sometimes bear.

Sheridan held the book on her lap, but closed her eyes. Too many words, too much explanation, could get in the way. She had to read in the spaces between lines, to fill in with her own experience. She had lived so long without Gavin. Just as in Rilke's Sonnet XIII, their parting had introduced her to winter. An endless winter, one she'd never expected to pass—especially after losing Charlie as well.

The breeze blew across her skin, reminding her of last night, the way Gavin had touched her. It had been so long since he had, but it had immediately felt good, wonderful, familiar, as if no time had passed at all, as if there'd never been time or distance between them. Perhaps that was a nighttime state.

Because today, she felt empty again. She didn't want these feelings; she wanted to reclaim last night's joy. In bed, it had seemed impossible that they could ever be apart. Today she realized, with bottomless sadness, that separation had become a habit; she couldn't open herself up to someone else—to him—again. She'd gotten used to the idea of being alone; it suited her, even as she ached to change. But too much loss, too many goodbyes, had frozen her solid.

Earlier that day, she'd looked down the hill, seen a small blue car driving past. She'd looked up just in time to see the driver's face turned toward her: a young man who'd reminded her, shockingly, of Charlie. She'd jumped up to call to him, but he'd just driven past—maybe even sped up.

Sheridan must have imagined it—not the car and the man, but the resemblance to Charlie. She thought of him every day, all the time. But having Gavin here, knowing he was working on the case, had stirred everything up in deeper ways. Sheridan felt exhausted by the turmoil. She wanted to be the kind of woman who could heal, not by conjuring up visions of her dead son, but by letting love back into her life again. But she wasn't.

Hearing footsteps on the steps from the beach,

she raised her eyes. Gavin came shouldering through the overgrown path, brushing wild bamboo and jasmine out of the way. She stared up at him. He was the same man she'd been with last night, but inside she was different. He couldn't tell by looking at her—he grinned to see her, and leaned down to kiss her on the lips.

"I missed you," he said.

She nodded, but she couldn't say the words. She'd missed him, too, but the feelings were too raw and dangerous to trust.

"Last night . . ." he said, trailing off as if there weren't any words to describe it.

"I know," she said.

His expression changed; something about her tone, her reticence, the emotion she couldn't keep out of her eyes, had put him on notice that something was wrong.

"Sheridan," he said.

"We're not back together," she said in a low voice, almost too quiet to be heard above the wind in the leaves overhead.

"Yes, we are," he said, crouching down.

"Gavin, I don't know what to think," she said, holding the book. "Last night . . . it was wonderful in ways I never thought would ever be wonderful again. Just being with you, after so much time . . ."

"Almost as if we were never apart."

"But we were," she said. And what if they were again? How could she bear it, opening herself to all the ups and downs of love, even the best of it? What if she had nothing to give?

"Don't you believe we've learned our lesson?" he asked, taking her hand.

"I'm not sure it's that simple."

"But it is," he said with a stubbornness that reminded her of how he'd always been. And she knew: love was a cycle that didn't end. She stared into his eyes and remembered the boy he'd been and saw the old man he'd be. She knew she'd love him, as she always had. But the heart had gone out of her.

"It's too hard," she said, her eyes filling with tears.

"Is it because of what I said about Charlie last night? Because I wasn't seeing him exactly the way you were?"

She shook her head. "I know my son," she said. "You don't, so you're trying to get a picture of him. He was rock-steady when it came to certain things . . . when it came to Nell. You'll learn that if you find out more about him."

"So that's not it," he said. "It's us?"

She shrugged. "Or it's me," she said. "I'm not who I used to be. There was the me before . . . and then there's after."

He stared at her with piercing eyes, waiting for her to explain.

"After you and I broke up," she said, "I still believed I could have love. I tried with Randy . . . and Charlie was born. Having a son like him, well—I had more love than I ever thought possible. That 'after'—

the after you and I broke up—was hard, but I got through it. This one..."

"The 'after' Charlie's death," Gavin said, and she nodded.

"It's too hard for me," she said. "I tried last night. Or, I didn't even have to try. I just...loved you. But today I feel different."

"You don't love me today?"

She stared at him. She did, but she couldn't tell him, because it would give him too much hope. She knew that love was just as strong when the person wasn't there, even when you chose not to be together— sometimes it was even more powerful. She didn't want him to stay here, crouched before her, so she shook her head.

"I don't believe you," he said.

"I thought I could try, but I can't," she said.

He just stared at her long and hard, without changing expression. She had the feeling he was taking her in, letting her know he was with her no matter what she thought or felt. The sensation affected her down to her bones; she wanted to lean into him, have him hold her, but she couldn't. She was still frozen.

"I'm going to give you some space," he said.

"You're leaving?" she asked, and the thought jolted her.

"Not for long," he said. "Just for the day."

"Where are you going?"

"Nashville," he said. "I'm flying down and back."

"Why?" she asked.

"A young man came to Hubbard's Point," Gavin said. "Nell talked to him. He looks like Charlie, and he says he's his half-brother Jeff."

"He looks like Charlie," she said, shocked, thinking of the man in the blue car.

"Yes," Gavin said, frowning at her tone. "He hasn't been here to see you, has he?"

"No. But I think he might have driven by," she said, suddenly gripped by the thought, trying to picture him, the way he'd looked, the way their eyes had met for a second.

"When?"

"Early today. Why was he here?" Sheridan asked.

"I don't know, but I'm going to find out."

"You don't have to do this," she said, as if the territory had changed, as if her declaration that she couldn't love him would mean he'd stop investigating Charlie's death.

"Yes, I do," he said.

"Because Nell's your client?"

He shook his head. "No. Because Charlie is your son. And in a way I can't even explain, that makes him mine, too, Sheridan. I might not be his biological father, but he's your child, so I love him. I'd protect him if I could. I would have while he lived, and I'm going to do my best, now that he's dead."

"Gavin," she said.

Again, he gave her a steady look. He took her hand, held it for a long time. She stared down at their fingers clasped together. They'd been holding hands in this yard since they were fifteen. He would go away, and he would come back, and one way or another he would go away again. She stared at their hands, and thought of how life broke your heart slowly.

"You're going to feel better," he said. "I know you don't believe it this second, but you will. You're crashing today because of last night. But I won't let you, Sheridan, not really. I won't let you really crash."

Still staring at their hands, she felt the tears spill over.

"I've got you, kid," he said, his arms coming around her as she sobbed quietly into his shoulder and the breeze made the oak leaves rattle in the tree above them. "Believe it or not, I've got you."

CHAPTER 18

VINCENT DE HAVILLAND ENJOYED THE MANY perks of his law practice; one of his favorites was having access to a G4 jet nearly any time he wanted it. An extremely grateful client, the ex-wife of a billionaire venture capitalist with his own investment firm that happened to be one of the largest stakeholders in the Light Years media conglomerate, made it available just for the asking. One call to the private aircraft hangar at Groton–New London Airport, and the jet was fueled and ready.

Gavin had been moving fast since encountering Nell after his swim that morning. She'd told him about Jeff Quill; they'd gone to the Renwick Inn, then Nell had dropped him at the boat to pick up some paperwork—including a faxed note from Joe saying the NYPD had missed Randy's connection to Cumberland. Then he'd gone up to see Sheridan. He'd wanted her to be as happy as he was about last night, but he'd found her sitting under a tree, looking haunted. She'd seemed so closed off, almost regretful about last night.

He felt thrown by Sheridan's retreat, by how it seemed almost as if last night hadn't happened at all. She had taken a step back into the shut-down state of mind she'd been in when he'd first arrived, full of hurt and mistrust. Gavin knew he had to keep moving, just to stay sane. If he lost her again now, he didn't know what he'd do. But did he even have her to lose?

He'd told her that Charlie was like a child to him. He'd really said that: like his own son. Now, walking up toward the trestle from the beach, he cringed at how presumptuous that sounded. What would she think of him daring to say that after keeping his distance all these years? He'd lost his chance to really know Charlie—to spend time talking to him, hearing his thoughts and watching how he made his way in this world. That was over—not just for Gavin, but so profoundly for Sheridan. She'd never see her son again. So why had he said that to her?

The truth was, he felt it. He loved her so much, and that meant he loved Charlie, too. He was going to fight for him now, find out what had happened to him that night a year ago. Even if it was the last thing he could do for Sheridan—if she really didn't want him in her life—he'd do this now. His foot throbbed from the long walk from the beach, and he settled down to wait just outside the railroad bridge at Hubbard's Point, in the post office parking lot, until

Vincent's Bentley came humming over the hill and around the bend.

"Thanks for doing this," Gavin said, climbing in.

"I'm just glad I was free," Vincent said. "Opposing counsel canceled a deposition at their offices in Greenwich. The little wimp's afraid of having his ass kicked in front of his client again. I've already won the case—survival of the fittest. It's just a matter of him deciding it's time to say 'uncle.' So it'll be fun— you and me on the road."

"Do you ever think," Gavin said as Vincent sped down Route 156, "about the ethics of you using some client's corporate Gulfstream as a favor to me?"

"Not corporate—private," Vincent said. "We're playing in the big leagues now. This woman's feet never touch the ground; she wants to play golf at Farm Neck, she flies the G4 to the Vineyard. She has a date at Nick and Toni's, she takes it to East Hampton."

"Why's she letting you take it today?"

"Because I got her everything she wanted and more. Nearly half. She has full custody of their two kids—he can't leave the state with them without the court's permission, and he'd been threatening to move to Los Angeles. She's thankful to me for getting him to see reason."

"How'd you do that without my help?"

"You've been elusive lately—hiding out in Maine, working for other people, whatever. I didn't really need an investigator... just needed to let the other side know I wouldn't be backing down any time soon. I wore them down. They were just like bald tires when I was done. . . ."

"Bet her husband hates you."

"They all do," Vincent said, chuckling. And his women clients—he specialized in getting good deals for women—loved him.

"You don't have to come with me," Gavin said.

Vincent started to smile, as if he were going to make a joke. But then he stared, dead serious. "You might need my help."

"I think I can get the answers I need."

"I want to make sure you get them without getting yourself in any trouble."

"You mean you want to keep an eye on me, make sure I don't use deadly force on one of my least favorite people alive," Gavin said. He wasn't joking, and Vincent didn't take it as if he was.

"What's the deal?" Vincent asked.

"Randy sent his son Jeff up here," Gavin said. "I want to find out why."

"You mentioned that on the phone. What makes you think Randy sent him? Why couldn't the kid have come on his own?"

"He's driving a car registered to Randecker Studios," Gavin said. "I've always believed it's about the money. Randy didn't want to pay out Charlie's trust fund. Maybe he promised Jeff a piece . . ."

"And maybe he didn't. That's a stretch, Gav."

"Jeff Quill's been in trouble," Gavin said. "I had Joe check him out."

"And?"

"And he's got a record. His juvenile records are sealed, but as an adult he's been in trouble for breaking and entering. Randy could have enticed him into doing something to Charlie."

"So what's your theory?"

"I think Randy was in New York with Cumberland that night. Maybe Jeff, too."

"And what? They lured Charlie to the club, then down to the river so they could kill him and keep his trust money?"

"Something like that," Gavin said.

"And what about the girl? That Lisa? She was the bait?"

Gavin had wondered about that, thought it was a possibility. But that was before he'd known about Jeff. Besides, Sheridan and Nell were so persuasive about Charlie's loyalty. "I'm not sure. It's one of the things I plan to ask Randy."

"Where's Jeff now?"

"On his way back to Nashville, I hope. Joe sent out a bulletin all down the East Coast to pick him up. Nell was sharp, getting his tag numbers."

"What was her take on him?"

"Well, at first she was sentimental about the fact he was Charlie's half-brother. Apparently he's a dead ringer, and I'm sure that didn't hurt his cause. But once we figured out he'd lied to her about the Renwick Inn, she got wise very fast."

"You think he might be hanging around the area?" Vincent asked.

"No," Gavin said. "I think he's on his way out."

"Well, why would he come to Connecticut in the first place?"

"Maybe curiosity, wanting to see Hubbard's Point, where Charlie came from; maybe Randy sent him to Sheridan's bank."

Vincent nodded. "Black Hall Savings," he said. "I remember it from the settlement papers. They administered the trust. But you realize the whole thing became moot after Charlie died."

"Yes, but maybe Randy had to make sure."

"Let me have Judy call over there and see what's going on."

Gavin nodded. He was hoping Vincent would say that. They headed east on I-95, and Gavin stared out the window, listening to him on the phone. Vincent held while Judy made the call, then thanked her and hung up.

"You were right," he said. "Judy talked directly to Sam Peyton, and he said that two days ago a young man was there, asking about a trust set up by Randy Quill. Specifically, he wanted to know whether it could be liquidated or dissolved or assigned to another party."

"Charlie's trust?"

"That's the strange thing," Vincent said. "The trust is no longer in Charlie's name. It was reassigned after Charlie's death, to be split evenly between Randy's other issue."

" 'Issue'?" he asked.

"Randy's two surviving sons: Clinton Alderson of

Encino, California, and Jeffrey Quill of Nashville, Tennessee."

"What was he wanting them to do?" Gavin asked, thrown off by the mention of the other son.

"Sam didn't know," Vincent said. "Jeff Quill didn't say."

Gavin was silent as Vincent drove across the Thames River and the Gold Star Bridge, toward the Groton–New London Airport. As promised, the jet was ready. He parked in front of the hangar, and the two men boarded the aircraft.

NELL SKIPPED WORK and went back to the cemetery. She ran down the dirt road, under the spreading tree branches, into the bright sunlight of the open graveyard. The sun was high in the sky, and none of the trees was casting long shadows. It was one big patch of sunlight filled with grass and gravestones.

She walked straight to Charlie's grave, sat in front of it. She stared at the headstone as if it were a door. If she knocked, would he come out? If she fell asleep, would she dream of him again? Her hair was sleek and salty from her earlier swim out to Gavin's boat; she wore her bright green bikini beneath her T-shirt and shorts, the one that had always been his favorite. She ran her fingers over the carvings on the stone.

The letters of his name, and the dates of his birth and death, were scored so neatly and deeply into the granite. Leaning her head against the stone, she felt the coolness in her skin. She wanted to embrace the marker because it was the closest she could get to embracing Charlie. But she didn't.

Right now she was filled with hate. She'd never felt anything like it before. It tasted like poison in her mouth, pure hatred for whoever had killed Charlie. She stared into space, wondering what she would do if she came face-to-face with that person. She would attack whoever it was, and make him or her suffer for what had been done to Charlie.

Meeting Jeff, she'd almost forgotten what she was doing, that she'd hired Gavin to investigate Charlie's death. She'd been so swept away by Jeff's likeness to Charlie, by the fact she'd found him at the grave, the way he'd almost seemed to be praying. Their short time together had been so intense; she'd cut it off, she realized now, not really so much because of the mention of Lisa Marie Langton, but because she'd been unable to withstand being in the presence of Charlie's half-brother.

On Gavin's boat, she'd felt so excited—ready to lead him to someone who might be able to help them piece together the clues that would lead to Charlie's killer. It had never crossed her mind that Jeff might have had anything to do with that. How could it? He was Charlie's flesh and blood. But now, learning what a liar he was, that he'd led her on for some reason, and for some reason disappeared, she began to wonder whether he was connected somehow.

What was he doing, driving a car owned by Cumberland's record label? Had he lured Charlie to the club that night—or had Charlie merely stumbled in?

Was there any way in the world Charlie had planned to see Cumberland and not known they were connected to his father and half-brother? Had he known them from Nashville? She closed her eyes. She was back to the most painful part of all: why hadn't he talked to her about it?

"Charlie," Nell said out loud.

He didn't respond, and she was really listening for anything—the wind in the pines, a bird singing overhead, clouds spelling out words. She wanted a message from him, she so badly wanted to be with him again. In her dream, Charlie had told her he'd come because she'd whispered his name. So she tried that now: "Charlie, Charlie, Charlie..."

The wind was still, and the pines didn't move, and the sky was blue and cloudless, and Charlie Rosslare stayed in his grave. He didn't answer her at all.

But Jeff did.

HE'D SPENT THE WORST NIGHT of his life in that little house up by the railroad tracks, and he'd spent some pretty bad nights. There was a long stretch when he was twelve, when the court sent him to juvenile hall for assault. He'd come home one night, found his mother passed out with a guy who had previously beaten her up, and gone crazy. He'd grabbed an empty bottle, swung it at the sleeping man, broken his jaw in three places.

The court had sent him away for that. His mother had begged the man not to press charges, but he wasn't coming back to her anyway, and his jaw and teeth were damaged for life. So Jeff had done two years in a place with bars on the window and rats in the walls and the meanest kids in Tennessee in the bunks around him.

Later, when he was fourteen, he'd gotten out just in time to go to his mother's wedding to John Thorpe, a man with three kids of his own: two boys and a girl. Jeff's mother had been so happy; Jeff remembered how she'd bought him a suit, pinned a boutonniere on his lapel, and told him, "Jeffrey, you'll have a father now."

"He's not my father."

"He'll be good to you, Jeff," she'd said. "He's a wonderful dad to his three kids, and he wants to be that to you."

"He won't be," Jeff had said.

"You're wrong," his mother had said, smiling so hopefully. She'd had her hair dyed blonde, the curls all ironed out. She'd had her nails done, and she was wearing a pink dress that could have been made for a princess. Jeff couldn't remember seeing her so bright and lucky before, so he'd just shrugged. But he'd known.

And he was right. But so was she—he was a good father. To his own three kids, he never said no, he bought them presents, he drove them to their games. He called his daughter "Angel," and he told Jeff that she was an angel, a real one, blessed from above, and that if he ever caught him even looking at her, going near her, just taking one step toward her, he'd cut off his balls.

His sons were going to go to college. Maybe even law school. They got new clothes and shoes at the end of summer in preparation for school. When winter came, John bought them warm coats from the best store in town. He praised them for their schoolwork, which he always read. He went to their ball games, cheering louder than anyone there.

Jeff and his mother moved into the Thorpes' house after the wedding. Even though each of the other kids had their own room, and even though there was a spare room that had been their mother's sewing room—after she died, they'd just started using it for storage—Jeff had to sleep on the TV room couch.

John said that the kids would be too traumatized to see their mother's sewing room turned into a bedroom. Their poor dead mother had loved them so much, and she'd always been sewing for them, making them clothes, had been sitting right there in front of her big black Singer almost every day when they got home from school. So he just couldn't let Jeff's mother clean the room out, move in a bed and dresser and all the belongings of a teenage boy.

Because of Jeff's past trouble with the law, John wrote him off as a student and as anything much besides a delinquent. He didn't think Jeff should do the same after-school activities as his kids, like sports and clubs, because they cost money. Better for Jeff to get an after-school job, start earning, and prove himself. If he wanted to be treated like part of the Thorpe family, he had to gain respect.

Jeff had felt angry for a long time. He'd like to have blamed it all on the state home, and the way he was treated there; or maybe, going back, on the guy he'd attacked, the one who'd given his mother two black eyes and some broken ribs. The way John Thorpe acted toward his kids made his rage grow. But when he looked way back, all the way through grade school and kindergarten, all the way back to when he was just a little kid, he knew he'd started getting angry every time he saw someone with a father.

People were supposed to have two parents to protect them. And not just that—to do things with, teach them, have fun with them. Activities for kids were best done with mothers and fathers. Going to Six Flags, you wished you could go with your dad. Or having a hot dog at a ball park, you knew it would taste better if it was bought for you by your father. That's the way life was supposed to be.

Jeff had always known that. From the time he started school, he knew he lived in a single-parent home. Other kids did, too. But he didn't think of them; it didn't reassure him to know he wasn't alone, even though some of the others had it much rougher than he did. At least he and his mother were comfortable; his grandfather had owned car dealerships, and he'd paid all the bills.

There were stories that Jeff's father had been after his mother for the money. His grandfather loved to throw that at her, whenever she had to ask for a little extra to buy something nice for herself or Jeff. "Too bad you were so free with my money before this one came along," his grandfather would say. "You waved it around, and you attracted the wrong kind of guy, and now you're paying for it."

By "paying for it," Jeff knew his grandfather meant him. His mother had gotten pregnant, had to get married. She and Jeff's father had had a shotgun wedding, then lived together in a seasonal hunting cabin owned by her family. Jeff's father had stayed married to her for two years, running around with every girl in Nashville. Just to get rid of him, Jeff's grandfather had paid him off: given him a good sum just to disappear and get out of their lives.

His name wasn't ever to be mentioned again, but Jeff knew it: Randy Quill. Jeff had been born Jeffrey Quill, but after the ugly divorce, he and his mother went back to using her maiden name. He'd sign Jeff Easton on his school papers, but inside, he was always Jeff Quill.

He liked the name. It reminded him of an eagle feather, something with grace and nobility. He pictured a quill pen and an inkwell, the kind of writing instruments Ben Franklin would have used. It was old-fashioned and strong: his father's name.

From the time Jeff could tell stories, he had one going about his father. Mainly he'd imagine it himself, but sometimes he'd tell the kids in his class. His father was a long-haul trucker, crisscrossing America. He came home, sure, but never for long. It wasn't that he didn't want to stay—it was just that the company relied on him to deliver the goods from Richmond to Seattle, and then from Portland to Miami, endlessly.

His father would arrive home at night, after dark, when the neighborhood was asleep. That's why no one ever saw him. He would let himself into the house, wake up Jeff and his mom, tell them everything that had happened since they'd last been together. Jeff's mother would cook him his favorite foods, and they'd let Jeff stay up with them, talking and planning the day his father could quit and they'd all live together.

Gifts were bought on the road, sometimes from truck stops, sometimes from gift shops in small towns. Jeff would bring the things to school, show them to his friends. That's how he'd started stealing. He'd needed items to prove his father had been home, had loved him and his mom, had brought them things.

It was odd, and Jeff would never understand this, but even though he'd become a thief who sneaked into neighborhood houses to rifle drawers and cupboards, jewelry cases and silver chests, part of him believed that the objects he stole were gifts from his father. He knew it was crazy. It was after he'd taken a diamond ring, a very large one, from the red velvet case of a widow named Mrs. Grace Pleasant, and brought it to school to show his friends the beautiful ring his father had gotten for his mother, that a teacher saw and sent him to the principal. Who called the police.

That was another stay in reform school, before his mother married John Thorpe. So that's what John meant by Jeff's having to prove himself, and earn the family's respect. John used to say he'd as soon turn his back on a cottonmouth than on Jeff. He just knew Jeff couldn't be trusted.

Well, he'd been right. After Jeff had gotten out of reform school, he'd continued breaking into houses. And then Randy had come along—really stepped up to help Jeff, just like in his dreams and fantasies— and Jeff had stopped getting in trouble. Or he had until late last summer . . .

Jeff, standing in the grove of pines up behind Charlie Rosslare's grave, looked down at Nell and knew that John had really known what he was talking about. In spite of Randy trying to help him feel good about himself, Jeff couldn't be trusted. That was a given. Now Nell knew, too, and she'd know even more before the day was over. Jeff cleared his throat and said her name one more time.

"Nell."

"I heard you the first time," she said.

"You're just going to ignore me?" he asked.

"Why shouldn't I?" she asked.

"I was hoping . . . I still want to talk to you."

"Like we talked out behind the Renwick Inn? Where you're *staying*?"

"You found out," he said.

"Uh, yeah. You must think I'm pretty stupid, that I wouldn't."

"I don't think that at all," he said. "I just thought I'd find you again before you had the chance to go looking for me. You okay?"

"What do you care?"

"Well, you were pretty upset last night. After you ran away, I wasn't sure you'd want to talk to me again anyway."

"You really think that?" she asked. "Considering you're Charlie's brother?"

He shrugged. Where he came from, the brother bond—or half-brother or stepbrother—didn't count for much. He'd always wanted it to, and staring at Nell, he told himself she might have been his sister-in-law if Charlie had lived. Nell and Charlie could have gotten married someday. Jeff could have been best man. He stared at her, into her magical green eyes, and could see why Charlie had been in love with her. It reminded Jeff of how he'd felt about Lisa....

"What's wrong?" she asked. "Why are you turning red?"

"Just," he stammered, "I'm glad I found you here. I told you, I still want to talk to you."

"Where did you sleep last night?" she asked.

"I—" he said, looking for a good lie to tell.

"Don't bother trying to come up with something I'll believe," she said sharply. "You either tell me the truth, or I'm out of here."

"I slept by the railroad tracks," he said.

She peered at him, shook her head and turned on her heel. "See you," she said.

"Okay, wait," he said. "I'll tell you. It is by the railroad tracks . . . up by that overgrown recreation area."

"On Oak Road," she said, her eyes glinting. "Someone saw you. You were staying up there?"

"Yeah. I found a house."

"You 'found' a house?"

He nodded, ashamed. She was glaring at him, just like a cop. He'd gotten caught pretty much in the act, and he was going to pay for it.

"Show me," she said.

And because she'd left him no choice, he shrugged and started leading her through the graveyard, up the steep hill where she'd chased him yesterday, and through the beach roads to the house where he'd spent last night not sleeping—just thinking, thinking and planning, planning.

NELL FOLLOWED JEFF through the familiar landscape of Hubbard's Point, but somehow, being with him made her feel as if she were in a dangerous dream. Anything could happen—monsters could jump out from behind trees, fissures in the earth could open and swallow her whole. This was exactly the kind of thing her father would warn her against: don't go places with strangers.

But he'd also taught her to trust her instincts, and right now her inner guidance was telling her to see this through, spend this time with Jeff and listen to what he had to say. They walked up Cresthill Road, turned left where the road branched, veered north toward the houses built along the railroad tracks. Heat rose from the tar, but the more they walked, the taller and thicker the trees grew, and Nell began to feel cooled by the spreading shade.

This part of Hubbard's Point felt almost like being in the woods. Nell had always loved the different sections of her beloved beach hamlet, and she knew Charlie had, too. There was the rocky Point, the sandy strand, the marshy swale, and this forested section. When they got to the fenced-in and no-longer-used Harry Anderson Recreation Area, she stared, remembering.

"What's in there?" Jeff asked, seeing the expression on her face.

"A big swing set," she said. "All rusty now . . . Charlie and I used to climb the fence, and we'd go on the swings at night, try to get going really high, our feet trying to kick the moon."

"Why's the fence there, to keep kids out?"

"Because one boy, back when Charlie and I were about eleven, played on the tracks—just what parents always warn you not to do."

"Did he get hit by a train?" Jeff asked.

Nell nodded. "It was terrible. I wasn't here that day, but Charlie was. He never stopped thinking about him. The beach shut down the recreation area after that—no one was ever allowed to play here again. Charlie and I . . . we just ignored the fence, and went in anyway. We'd never go near the tracks, but we liked those swings. I think being there made Charlie feel close to our friend, the one who died."

"What did Charlie do when he saw that kid get hit?" Jeff asked, seeming stunned by the image.

"He told me he climbed down the bank," Nell said. "The train...dragged Steven. Charlie was yelling, and the train brakes were screeching. That's what he remembered, the sound. And he got to Steven, and tried to pull him out...but he was already dead. He wouldn't leave him. Even when the train crew tried to get him away, Charlie fought them off and sat there with Steven."

"How long did he sit there?" Jeff said, his voice thick.

"Until Steven's mother came. His sister had seen what happened, and she'd run down Carrington Road to get her. Only five minutes away...Charlie said that Mrs. Mayles came right away, and just knelt beside Steven, holding him. That's when Charlie knew it was okay for him to leave."

"He stayed with his friend," Jeff said, staring through the wire- mesh fence as if he could see Charlie and Steven down by the railroad tracks.

Nell nodded, then gestured to Jeff that they should keep moving. Without another word, he led her through some backyards, behind the common hedge that separated them from the hillside sloping down to the tracks. Both she and Jeff glanced down at the rails; she wondered whether he was hearing those brakes scream.

When they got to a hole in the overgrown privet,

Jeff ducked through and Nell followed. They stood in the backyard of a small cottage. Nell didn't really know the family who lived here—they didn't have kids her age. But she recognized a typical Hubbard's Point backyard: picnic table on the patio, the beach chairs and umbrella leaning against the house, gardens overflowing with flowers and vegetables.

Jeff tilted a flowerpot back, picked up the key there, and inserted it into the door. As he did, Nell noticed a recently replaced windowpane—the wood frame around it was scored with chisel marks from being pried off. She recognized the signs because she and Charlie had once had to break into his house—his mother was on tour, and he'd forgotten his key, so he'd had to take a glass pane out of the door so he could reach in and unlock it.

"How'd you know where they hide the key?" she asked Jeff.

"I don't even want to tell you how easy it was," he said. "Just remember this when you get your own house: don't hide your key under something right next to the door. Everyone does it, and burglars know it."

"So, you're admitting you're a burglar?"

"I used to be," he said, opening the door and putting the key back. "And I guess I am again. Come on in."

"Inviting me into someone else's house. Very nice," she said, glaring at him and refusing to enter.

"You might as well come in. At least we can have privacy. Out there," he said, gesturing toward the street, "people will see us and think you're with Charlie."

"Yeah," she said. "You're right. You are attracting a certain amount of attention." She followed him inside.

The shades were down, and the house was dark but for slices of sunlight coming around the dark green panels. Nell's eyes got used to it, and she saw that at least he'd kept the place neat. She could see he'd slept on the couch—a sheet was folded on top of a bed pillow. He moved them aside so they could sit down.

Now that they were still and sitting next to each other, she was able to focus on his face. Its sweet familiarity was both comforting and jarring. She forced herself to breathe evenly. She didn't have to remind herself that this wasn't Charlie—he was too rough-edged in just about every way. But if she stared into his eyes, she could go into a little trance that made it seem, just very slightly, as if Charlie had come back to life.

But after a few long moments of silence, she began to feel uncomfortable. This wasn't Charlie, and she couldn't kid herself that it was. Jeff was gazing at her with such intensity, and a kind of longing that made her wonder what the hell she was doing in this house with him. His arm reached across the sofa back, almost as if he wanted to touch her. She inched away.

"Okay," she said. "So what do you want to tell me?"

"I don't know," he said.

"Why did you come here?"

"I wanted to see where Charlie came from. To meet you . . . and, well, at least see his house. See where his mother lives. And I had some business in town, too."

"You're from Nashville, Tennessee. What business could you possibly have in Black Hall, Connecticut?"

He fell silent for a moment, then reached into the back pocket of his jeans. He pulled out a folded piece of paper, smoothed out the wrinkles as he laid it on the cushions between him and Nell. She recognized the Black Hall Savings letterhead.

"That's where everyone in town does their banking," she said. "Why do you have it?"

"My father set up a trust for Charlie," Jeff said. "A long time ago."

"I know," Nell said. "Charlie told me about it. He . . . he didn't care anything about the money."

Jeff gave her a skeptical glance.

"Everyone cares about money," he said.

"Nope. Not Charlie."

"How can you say that?"

"Because I know. He was going to use the trust to finance a documentary he wanted to make, about growing up without a father. He didn't want to compromise his principles, but he thought there was a fitting symmetry to the whole thing."

"Which was?"

"Well, using money his father was forced to pay, to film a documentary that would basically expose him—and absent fathers everywhere. That's why I don't get the whole Charlie-going-to-meet-him-and-keeping-it-secret thing. He was curious about his father, but he didn't respect him."

"People change," Jeff said. "Like I told you yesterday, even Randy."

"Think that if it makes you feel better," Nell said, "but I doubt Charlie did. He spent his whole growing up without a dad. So did you, right?"

"Yeah," Jeff said.

"Besides," Nell said, tapping the bank letter between them, "forget all that. What do you have to do with Charlie's trust?"

"It stopped being Charlie's trust," Jeff said, his voice dropping. "After he died. But because Black Hall Savings had set it up in the first place, Randy left the account there. It just seemed easier than moving it down to Tennessee. Only one of the beneficiaries lives there anyway."

"Beneficiaries?" Nell asked, and he nodded.

Nell watched Jeff fidgeting, his color rising, and his whole demeanor seeming more anxious and uncomfortable. That made her own blood start to race; and she stared at him, wondering what was going on.

"If it stopped being Charlie's," she said, "whose did it become? Who has the trust now?"

"It will be going to my other half-brother, Clint," Jeff said. "And to me."

"That must make you happy," Nell said, not taking her eyes off him. The moment felt charged, full of sparks, and she wondered if she might explode, if she should just run for the door, if he was confessing to having murdered Charlie for money.

"It doesn't," he said, shaking his head. "It doesn't at all."

"Come on—" she said. "You get all that money... is that why you came here?"

"Randy changed things up. The bank won't pay till we're thirty."

"Well, that must suck."

He buried his face in his hands. Sobs tore from deep inside his chest, and he howled, almost like something wild, a creature locked in a cage. Nell couldn't move. She wanted to run for the door, escape and get as far away as she could from whatever this was. But instead she felt herself pulled, sliding across the couch, the slipcover's nubbly fabric on the back of her bare legs, to put her arm around Jeff's shoulders.

"Why are you crying?" she asked. "What is it?"

"I did a terrible thing," he said.

"What?" she asked, her pulse thudding in her ears, in her mouth. She felt herself choking on her own heart.

"I was there," he whispered.

"What are you talking about?"

"That night, with Charlie."

Nell's throat closed up and she felt as though she were suffocating. Her mind went blank, as if every thought, every memory, had been erased, just wiped out as if they'd never existed at all. Sitting in the house of strangers, in the dark, a house broken into by Jeff Quill, she felt walls caving in around her. She was buried under rubble, and she couldn't breathe or talk or move.

"You already knew that, didn't you?" Jeff asked, tilting his head to look at her with tearful red eyes.

She shook her head.

"I could have sworn you did," he said. "The way you looked at me, back at Charlie's grave."

"I know about your car," she said. "That it's registered to Randecker Records. And that they're Cumberland's label."

"My father owns the label," he said. "It's his car. He let me borrow it . . ."

"Does he know you're here?"

Jeff shook his head. "No. He thinks I was going to meet up with the band. With Cumberland, the band Charlie came to see. I was there, I was with him at the club, I was with him by the river."

Nell's mouth must have dropped open, because she felt herself closing it. Lips tightening, a solid line, no words could flow out. They were stuck in her throat anyway, all the words, and a scream, and all the emotions in the world.

"You understand, don't you? It's why I came to Hubbard's Point. Why I went to his grave. It's because I had to explain . . . You talk about my father, saying Charlie, well, basically hated him. You're right. He did, and he said so to his face that night. . . ."

"At the club?" she asked. "Your father was there that night?"

Jeff nodded.

"And was he with him at the river?"

"Yes."

"What happened?"

"Charlie lost it with Randy. He...told him what he thought of him."

"And he what? Randy *killed* him?"

"I want to tell you, Nell." He stopped, closed his eyes, spoke again. "When you talked about Charlie and Steven, Charlie being with that boy after he died...I knew what that was like. Because I was there with Charlie..."

"Shut up," Nell screamed. "Don't you dare say it's the same thing! Tell me what Randy did to him!"

"I want to explain. But to someone else, too. There's someone else who needs to know the whole story. I owe it to you...and to her."

Nell had heard about people losing it. She had herself, lost it big-time, after her mother had died. She wasn't afraid right now—that wasn't it. It was more that she was numb, exhausted suddenly, unable to stay upright on this sofa next to this man who'd been with Charlie the night he died. Nell's mind was ringing with the words *Charlie lost it with Randy.*

She wondered if he'd saved up all his eighteen years of outrage, let them loose on his father that night. She thought of the footage he'd already shot, the things he'd said, captured forever on film, about growing up without a dad. Had that triggered his father somehow? How could a man attack his own son?

Nell's cheeks were wet, and she couldn't stop thinking of Charlie. She felt herself rise, as if she were a spirit, and float out the front door of the house. Jeff didn't try to stop her. He didn't seem to care who might see her leaving this supposedly vacant house he'd just invaded.

She sensed him standing in the doorway behind her, but he didn't make any moves to follow as she walked down the road, the familiar shady road that she and Charlie had walked so often—the same road Charlie had walked down after seeing Steven killed by the train—and Nell walked, then started running, straight toward the Point and home.

CHAPTER 19

VINCENT HAD OFFERED TO GET A CAR AND driver, but once they touched down at Nashville International Airport, Gavin took over. They went to the Hertz counter, just like regular people, and he rented a midsize sedan. Vincent gave him a look out in the parking lot, somewhere between dismay and disbelief, that he was being expected to ride in a rental car.

"Just get in," Gavin said.

He drove toward the city, remembering previous visits. He had come here, either with Sheridan or to visit her, many times. She'd taken him all over—to the Ryman Auditorium, the big brick concert hall at 116 Fifth Avenue North, that had once been home to the Grand Old Opry.

"It's the Mother Church of Country Music," she'd told him. "Everybody's played here."

"Yeah? Like who?"

"Elvis, Emmylou Harris, Loretta Lynn, Johnny Cash, Patsy Cline, Hank Williams..."

"What about Sheridan Rosslare?"

"Someday," she'd said, grinning.

And she had. She'd played on the Ryman stage that same year, and many other times. Gavin had seen her twice: once when she knew he was there, once when she didn't.

That second time, on leave from the *Crawford* in dry dock at the sub base in Norfolk, Virginia, he'd traveled to Tennessee just to see her. Being here in Nashville again brought it all back.

She'd told him he belonged to the Navy, not her. She needed real love in her life—someone who was there to hold her and be with her, not someone who'd rather serve in the military and see the world. He'd tried telling her he felt a sense of duty to his country. She'd told him he was good at excuses, pointed out that he'd already finished one tour, had just signed up for a second.

Gavin hadn't been able to say much to that. She was right. At that time he'd never been to a psychologist, never gone to a shrink, but even he knew he had a problem with settling down. He had, in the words of the shrink he wound up going to after he beat a guy nearly to death for attacking a shipmate, started "acting out" right after his father's funeral, when he was six.

He knew he had a violent streak in him. He felt so angry at his father for dying, at God for taking him. He'd get into fights wherever they docked, and Joe

Donovan would have to haul him back to the boat. Gavin couldn't rest, couldn't stay ashore. The only peace he felt was when he was with Sheridan. But he didn't trust his own ability to be as good to her as she deserved. He was afraid he couldn't sustain a life on shore with the most gentle woman alive.

So he reenlisted in the Navy, to keep from finding out. And she'd had enough—broke up with him, stopped writing to him. The only way he knew she was performing that weekend was that he happened to see a listing in the Norfolk paper.

She was headlining at the Ryman, complete with a full band. Gavin hitchhiked to see her, felt the same thrill seeing her up on stage. He'd hung around afterward, his excitement building. He was going to make everything right, ask her to come back to him.

Then he saw her embracing some stagehand. Tall, thin, the guy acted as if he owned the place, like he belonged with Sheridan. And she acted as if she belonged with him.

Gavin turned and left before she even saw him. On the way back to the ship, he went to a bar near the dock, got into a fight—something completely unrelated, with someone he'd never seen before. He had nearly killed the man—got thrown in the brig, and got kicked out of the Navy for it. Gavin didn't care what happened to him—he'd have rotted in jail if it were up to him. All he'd cared about was losing Sheridan.

But Joe had heard plenty over the years about Vincent—by then a young litigator in his uncle's law firm. Joe tracked Vincent down; Vincent flew south from Connecticut to Norfolk and worked with the Judge Advocate General officer to get Gavin off on the worst charge, attempted murder.

Gavin had left the Navy with a dishonorable discharge. Driving into Nashville, he was reminded of what had set it all in motion: his reaction to seeing Sheridan with Randy Quill.

The Cumberland River flowed, reflecting the city skyline; he thought of the picture on the band's website, showing the bass player standing on a bridge over this river, and he spotted it straight ahead. Right behind the Ryman Auditorium, he turned into St. Cloud Alley. This was the place. He parked the car in a small lot, stared at the sign: *Randecker Studios.*

"You ready for this?" Vincent asked.

"Yeah."

"We beat him fair and square in the divorce," Vincent said. "We did that for Sheridan..."

"I know. And Charlie."

Vincent let that pass. "Don't screw things up by..."

Gavin pictured Sheridan as he'd first seen her this summer: drunk, disheveled, white-haired with grief. He saw Nell as she'd looked that morning outside the Renwick Inn: wild-eyed, crazed, betrayed. Gavin hadn't figured it all out yet, but so far signs were pointing to Randy Quill knowing something about it.

"I know what you're saying," Gavin said. "You don't want me getting arrested for assault. But if I find out..."

"We'll cross that bridge when we come to it," Vincent said, steely-eyed and ready for battle, in full litigator mode. He straightened the cream-colored linen jacket he'd had custom made in Milan, and climbed out of the rental Ford. The August heat was brutal—steam was rising from the riverbed. Vincent walked ahead of Gavin, through the door of Randecker Studios.

The reception room was small, with posters and photos of bands on the wall and a tight seating area with two black leather chairs and a matching loveseat. Gavin saw that pictures of Cumberland got the most wall space: there was the bridge shot of Lisa Marie Langton and her bass, blown up and framed.

It was a low-budget operation: the air-conditioning was broken, or kept on low. Either way, the receptionist looked ready to pass out. Young, dressed in a pink sundress, and dripping with sweat, she sat at a black metal desk, a fan blowing directly into her face.

"May I help you?" she asked, already sounding defeated.

"We're here to see Randy Quill," Vincent said, smiling. "Is he in?"

"Mr. Quill . . . uh . . ." she said.

"We'll take that as a yes," Gavin said, staring down a hallway behind her desk. It was lined with four closed doors, and he was already figuring out which one was Randy's office. "Which is it?" he asked.

"Let me handle this," Vincent said, his voice low. Turning back to the young woman, he gave her his best smile.

Gavin watched him in action—it was something to see. Vincent had had his teeth whitened by some New York dentist-to-the-stars. His teeth were of a whiteness not found in nature, and while *Esquire*-handsome, they were also somewhat menacing. "Young lady," he said, "we are here on official business."

"Official?" she asked.

"Yes. I am an officer of the court, and this man is . . ."

"I'm Gavin Dawson," he said. "I'm looking into the death of Charlie Rosslare. Mr. Quill's son . . ."

"He doesn't have a son named Charlie," the woman said, frowning. "His sons are Clinton and Jeff . . ."

That was all Gavin needed. Randy's receptionist didn't even know he'd had a son named Charlie, or that Charlie had died. It was wrong on too many levels to even contemplate, so Gavin just walked around the desk and started trying doors. He heard Vincent calling him, and the woman protesting, but he just turned and gave Vincent a "stay back" look.

The first door he opened was a large, vacant recording studio filled with state-of-the-art equipment. The second was a smaller studio. He skipped the third and went straight to the fourth and last, at the far end of the hallway.

Turning the knob, he pushed the door open and was greeted with a blast of icy air. The walls were covered with more band pictures, and Randy sat at his desk, paperwork and demo tapes spread out on the surface in front of him.

He looked gaunt, his reddish hair thinning and receding. Gavin was not unhappy to see that the boyish-roadie look didn't age well. Gavin's shoulders filled the doorframe, and he flexed his muscles as he closed the door behind him.

"You make your receptionist wilt in the heat while you crank your AC in here," Gavin said. "Still a prince."

"You're trespassing," Randy said. "I want you out of here."

"I'm sure you do," Gavin said, giving him his best showdown stare. He moved his gaze to the phone as if daring Randy to pick it up. Randy instinctively cradled his wrist, the one Gavin had broken last time. Gavin wondered if it still hurt. He kept staring, figuring Randy knew he'd hit him if he picked up that phone.

"What do you want?" Randy asked.

"I want to ask you about Charlie."

"What about him?"

Gavin glared at him. That was all Randy had to say? He took a step forward, and Randy flinched back.

"I went to see the place where Charlie was killed," Gavin said.

Randy didn't reply. Two dots of red appeared on his cheeks, starting to burn. Something was going on inside him, but Gavin couldn't read it yet.

"A deserted ball field," Gavin said. "On the bank of the East River."

"It's a tragedy," Randy said.

"In so many ways," Gavin said. Randy narrowed his eyes, stared a moment, then looked down.

"Leave me alone," Randy said.

"He wound up taking a walk by the river at three in the morning," Gavin said, "after spending the day in the city. You know what he was doing there?"

"Kids his age like to explore New York," Randy said. "I did when I was eighteen, that's for sure. A lot to see in that city."

Gavin watched him; why was Randy suddenly unable to meet his gaze? Gavin pulled a chair from a table across the room, dragged it to the desk and sat down at eye level with Randy. "He'd just started college," Gavin said. "Freshman year at NYU."

Randy stared at the desk.

"You know that? That your son was in college?"

"What was between me and my son is none of your business."

The words jolted Gavin—mainly because of the way Randy said them. He was full of emotion, as if there *had* been something between them. Randy was strung tight, tension in his face and shoulders.

"You know he wanted to be a filmmaker?" Gavin asked, and Randy nodded, his mouth quivering into a near-smile. "Make a documentary about his lost parent?"

"I wasn't lost," Randy said, the almost-smile disappearing.

"Charlie wanted to get to know his dad," Gavin said.

Randy didn't reply. He stared down at the papers on his desk, shuffling them around.

"Do you mind doing that later?" Gavin asked.

"I do mind."

Gavin just stared at him. As tough as he'd been trying to act, he knew he couldn't force Randy to do anything. But after a minute, Randy slid the papers away and looked up.

"Do you think I don't care what happened to him?"

"Randy, I'm just not sure."

"Well, I do. Sheridan and I talked, right after he died."

"She said you didn't go to the funeral."

Randy sighed and ran his fingers through his hair. He gave Gavin a contentious look, but it quickly drained away. "I don't like having to explain myself to you," he said. "Especially because of what I felt you did to me. Back then, when I was with Sheridan, you helped her see and think the worst of me. I've changed."

"Yeah?"

"Yes, I have. I was young and foolish back then— I'm the first to admit it. Made a lot of bad choices, and hurt people I care about. I nearly died a few years ago, and it showed me that life is short. I started paying attention to what matters."

"Life was short for Charlie," Gavin said.

Randy closed his eyes, and Gavin thought he moaned under his breath.

"I asked you about Charlie's funeral," Gavin said, unmoved.

"No, I didn't go," he said. "Partly because of how Sheridan feels about me. I didn't want to add to her pain by showing up there at the church."

"Wouldn't you have wanted to go for yourself?" Gavin asked. "Since he was your son?"

"Yes," Randy said, his voice low. "Of course."

"So why didn't you? Didn't you realize that no matter how Sheridan feels about you, she'd understand a father wanting to be there for his son? Maybe the last thing he could do for him?"

"I didn't think that, no."

"Show up to bury him," Gavin said. "That's what I'm wondering about . . . why you didn't go up there to Connecticut to be there for him, especially since you say you've changed."

"He was already gone," Randy said. "Any peace I might make with my son is between me and him now, no one else. I don't care what you think about it."

"You have to make peace with Charlie?" Gavin asked. "For what?"

"For not being there for him when he was little. For being absent for most of his life," Randy said.

"Try all of his life," Gavin said. "Sheridan and Nell told me about that."

"We were making an effort to spend time together, at the end," Randy said, his voice thick. "He was starting college, away from home for the first time. I wanted to get to know him, and I think he would have wanted that, too. We never got the chance."

"But you almost did, right?"

"What do you mean?"

"Club 192," Gavin said. "Last August thirty-first."

"No," Randy said. "I wasn't there."

Gavin stared at him. Randy had been a better liar when he was younger. He was sweating now, reaching into his top drawer for a pill case.

"What's that?" Gavin asked.

"I take aspirin, keeps the blood thin," Randy said.

"You know how I know you were in New York the day Charlie died?"

"I wasn't," he said. "None of us were."

Gavin's ears pricked up at the phrase, but he set it aside for later. "The cops missed it," Gavin said. "They knew that Charlie had gone to hear Cumberland . . . they probably checked out the band, part of their investigation. Probably saw they were signed to Randecker Studios, too. Funny you named your company after your first name instead of your last. The cops wouldn't have made the connection, seeing 'Randecker.' Only I did."

"Good for you."

"Yeah, it is. I saw it there on the Cumberland website and knew. 'Randecker' was one of your phony names, for one of your marriages, just another way to keep the IRS off track."

"That's old news," he said, sweating harder. "I'm square with the IRS."

"Maybe, but are you square with the NYPD? They might have caught it if you'd named your company 'Quill Records.' They probably knew Charlie's parents' names, and that would have triggered an investigation. But you're a wily old dog from way back, aren't you? Why put your real name on anything?"

"It's not a secret I signed Cumberland," Randy said, ignoring the question, gesturing at the framed posters on the walls of his office. "I'm not saying they're not my artists."

"It's not a secret here in Nashville," Gavin said. "But New York's another story. People up there don't know the connection. You mind if I call the cops right now? Put them in the loop?"

Randy shook his head. "Go ahead."

"I have another question before I do that," Gavin said. "That earlier marriage I mentioned just now. Was that to Jeff's mother?"

"Jeff?" he asked, color draining from his face. The physical change was instant and dramatic, and Gavin knew he'd hit the trigger point.

"Your son Jeff."

"What does he have to do with anything?"

"You tell me," Gavin said, leaning closer.

"He's . . . he's a good kid. Works for me now; he has for the last few years. He's on the road most of the time, looking after my business interests."

"Actually, he's in Black Hall, Connecticut—or he was. He went to Black Hall Savings—you know, the bank that administered Charlie's trust. Jeff went there two days ago, asking about dissolving it."

"He did not," Randy said. "He's in Ohio."

Gavin shook his head. "He was at Charlie's grave, and Nell—Charlie's girlfriend—met him. She said he looks just like Charlie—had her confused there for a little while. But they had a long talk, Randy. It's an ugly situation you're in. You and Jeff, well, you're a lot alike. You both like money; I've always known that about you, and I found it out about Jeff when I checked and learned about his record, breaking and entering. Taking other people's things . . . I think you got him to help you with Charlie."

"No," Randy said. "You're wrong."

"You were in New York with the band, and Charlie was right there. You saw your chance, and you got rid of him. Probably promised Jeff a piece of Charlie's trust."

"Gavin, you're wrong," Randy said, standing up. Clearly agitated, he started pacing. "Jeff's a good kid. He had a tough life, thanks to me. Yes, he's been in trouble, but that's all in the past. I promise you, he is working for me, trying hard . . . I'm there for him, and I can vouch for him."

Gavin didn't want to say what he thought Randy's promises were worth. He just stared, watching him walk over to the window, where he stood looking out into the back alley.

"You say you weren't in New York last August," Gavin said. "But Jeff was, wasn't he? Did he think this up on his own? Maybe he learned about Charlie's trust, felt it should be his instead. Make up for that bad childhood . . ."

"No!" Randy said. "And he's not in Connecticut right now, either. You're all wrong. I'll call him myself, right now. He'll tell you—he's in the Midwest, on the road with one of my bands."

"Prove it to me, Randy. Give him a call."

"I will," Randy said, as if Gavin had just handed him a solution.

Gavin watched him reach for the phone. His hands were shaking as he dialed the number. He stared at Gavin with defiance, as if he expected vindication any moment. After a few seconds, Jeff answered. Gavin stared at Randy the whole time. At first his expression was lighter, happy to hear Jeff's voice. But as the talk went on, his face turned into a knot of worry, and he turned his back on Gavin, to have some privacy in the conversation.

After a few minutes, Randy hung up, sat heavily down in his desk chair, head in his hands.

"He's not in Ohio," Gavin said.

Randy shook his head, and Gavin waited. After a few seconds, Randy looked up.

"He went to Black Hall, to try to get his name taken off the trust fund. He tried to convince the bank to do that."

"What are you talking about?"

"He never wanted the trust fund," Randy said. "The truth is, I didn't know what to do with the money. After Charlie died, and I found out the funds would revert to me . . . it just seemed like such a waste. I thought about giving them to Sheridan, but she wouldn't have taken anything from me. So I figured I'd put them in trust for my other two sons, Clint and Jeff."

"A windfall for them."

"Neither one of them will touch it. I had the trust

officer change the payout date, put it off a few years, till they turn thirty. Maybe they'll change the way they feel. Clint won't take it because he hates me, never wanted to even meet me. And Jeff... because of what happened to Charlie."

"What did happen to Charlie?" Gavin asked, feeling his stomach knot.

Randy just sat at his desk, shaking his head.

"Tell me, Randy."

"You've got to understand, Gavin. Jeff's... well, he's lost so much over this. He's already punishing himself more than I ever could. He was living with Lisa..."

"I don't give a shit about Lisa—you tell me what happened!"

Randy seemed not to hear. "She's a nice girl, and she loved him, too. But after... after last August, Jeff just stopped believing he deserved anything good."

"Did Charlie come between him and Lisa? Is that what happened?"

Randy looked at him as if Gavin were crazy. "Of course not. Charlie loved Nell, he was devoted to her. That came through in the short time we had together. He showed us her picture, told us about how she'd be coming to NYU after she graduated from high school. He would never have looked twice at Lisa. Oh God."

"What, Randy? You'd better tell me..."

"You were right. Jeff's in Connecticut, not Ohio. He's in Hubbard's Point..."

That didn't come as a shock to Gavin, but the

panic in Randy's eyes scared him, and he froze, waiting.

"He tried to tell Nell, but she ran away. So he's going to talk to Sheridan . . ."

"*What* are you talking about?" Gavin felt like he was about to explode.

"He didn't mean to do it," Randy said, breaking down. "It was an accident. I was there, Gavin. It broke my heart . . . but Charlie was gone. I had to protect my other son. I had to protect Jeff."

NELL HAD LEFT JEFF standing in the doorway of the cottage he'd broken into, and walked home in a daze. Like a sleepwalker, she moved on instinct, cutting through the hedges and side yards. She heard bees in the privet, but she didn't get stung. As she walked along, she noticed the light changing and the temperature dropping. It was late afternoon, and the entire landscape of Hubbard's Point began to shine with luminous light.

Stevie had stepped outside to watch. Always an artist, she was fascinated by light. Nell wasn't in the mood to talk, but Stevie had already seen her.

"Isn't it beautiful?" Stevie asked, beckoning Nell over. Nell went to stand with her, and Stevie put her arm around her; Nell hadn't realized how much she needed the comfort, and leaning into Stevie, she felt a violent shiver run down her spine. She needed to think.

They gazed down at the beach. A bank of fog was

rolling off the Sound, the front edge just reaching the breakwater and Gavin's boat. The sun, still far above the horizon, seemed to illuminate the fog from within, and the moisture intensified the light, giving it an otherworldly, amber glow. Since meeting Charlie's brother, everything seemed supernatural. Had such light ever been seen on earth before?

"When's Dad coming home from London?" Nell asked. She glanced up at Stevie, not wanting her to notice how nervous she suddenly felt about the two of them being there alone.

"Tomorrow," Stevie said. "He's just there for a quick meeting. . . . Nell, are you okay?"

"I'm fine."

"I mean, about your dad and I getting married. I love you, Nell, just as if you were my own child. I could never take your mother's place, could never even try. But I'm so glad that you're going to be my stepdaughter . . . I love just saying that. . . ."

Nell tried to smile. She wanted to celebrate—she would normally be jumping for joy, and she knew how happy this must make her father—but she felt too sad and anxious to say anything even slightly coherent.

Stevie took Nell's hand. She gazed deeply into Nell's eyes, in a way that made Nell feel like crying.

"This isn't an easy time for you," Stevie said. "About to leave for college, with the anniversary of Charlie's death coming up . . . I know you loved him so much."

"*Love* him," Nell whispered, correcting the tense.

"Yes," Stevie said. "You never stop loving someone; death can't take the love away. It must be hard for you, seeing your dad and me..."

"That's not it," Nell said. "Missing Charlie doesn't make me feel less happy for you and Dad. I love you, Stevie. You're already my stepmother—you have been since the beginning. I guess I just take it for granted. When will the wedding be?"

"Before the baby is born," Stevie said. "Which means soon, sometime in September... Nell, I'd like you to be maid of honor."

Nell had been standing on the brink of tears since walking away from Jeff, but Stevie asking her to be maid of honor pushed her right over the edge. Nell stood there sobbing, with Stevie clutching her and telling her she loved her, that they were family, that it would all be okay.

Nell pressed her face into Stevie's shoulder. When she pulled back to dry her eyes, she saw that the beautiful glowing light was gone. The fog had completely rolled in, covering the entire Point in gray gauze, making it impossible to see the breakwater or Gavin's boat, or even the beach.

The sound of a car driving down the road made them turn; it was Agatha's old green Hillman. Nell saw Bunny riding with her. Sheridan's two sisters waved up the hill at Nell and Stevie, calling out "Congratulations!" Stevie waved back, gave Nell a smile and a once-over gaze of assessment.

"I'm fine," Nell said. "I promise. I'm just so honored that you asked me to be maid of honor. With all your friends . . . They'll all be jealous."

Stevie laughed. "No one would expect me to ask anyone but you. There's no other choice in the world."

"If you say so," Nell said. She saw Stevie's gaze drift down the hill, to the sisters. "They'd probably love to hear the details of how Dad got you to cave in—you should go over to Sheridan's."

"You want to come with me?"

Nell shook her head. "Not right now."

"Okay, then," Stevie said. "If you're sure."

"I am," Nell said, kissing her, then running inside. She walked upstairs, all the way to the attic, where she and Charlie used to go. She wanted to lie on the mattress and think about everything. But staring out the window, into the fog, pulled by emotions she didn't understand, she felt the uneasy sense that she was missing something.

CHAPTER 20

THE DAY HAD BEEN CLEAR, BUT SUDDENLY A fog bank rolled in from the east and blanketed coastal Connecticut. It was just before dinner, and Sheridan stood staring out the screen door in the kitchen. Her sisters had stopped by, and then Stevie had walked over to talk about the big news in person.

They'd all had a good visit, feeling so happy for Stevie, and Sheridan had been glad of the distraction—she felt haunted by seeing that young man in the blue car; she found herself standing by the window, wishing he'd drive past again. Gavin had told her he was Charlie's half-brother Jeff, and seeing him had felt almost like a visitation from Charlie himself; as the anniversary of his death approached, she felt her son shimmering close by.

Feeling restless, she wished Gavin were back from wherever he had gone. She hadn't liked the way their meeting that morning had ended. Her emotions were all over the place, and she was afraid she'd driven him away. The words he'd spoken about Charlie, about feeling the same way he would about his own son, had been almost too much to bear. Now that her sisters and Stevie had left, she kept checking his boat, looking through binoculars to try to see if he'd returned. But there were no lights on—or maybe the fog was just too thick to see.

Aphrodite had been superstitious about fog: she'd told the girls never to pick roses in the mist, to not stand with their backs to a mirror, and to beware of dreams dreamed on foggy nights. She'd told them that animals seen in the haze were often "wanderers"— ghosts trapped in the earthly realm, unable to say goodbye and get to heaven.

Sheridan gazed out the screen door at one of the Hubbard's Point rabbits. They were an old family, living in warrens under the rock ledges. She watched it hop across her yard, heading toward a privet bush. Billows of fog blew up from the beach, and the rabbit disappeared.

Walking into the living room, she felt the damp darkness closing in. Her hands were trembling as she reached for a candle and lit it. The light wasn't enough, so she lit another, and another. Her family had always gathered by candlelight. She felt comforted by the warm glow, and sat down on one of the two slipcovered loveseats flanking the stone fireplace.

Just five minutes after she'd settled down, she heard a knock at the door. Rising, she hurried through the house. Her heart was beating as if she'd run a race, and when she got to the door she felt breathless.

He stood right there on the top step. Sheridan stared at the young man's face: such beautiful wide eyes, angular cheekbones, soft mouth, hair falling across his forehead.

"You look so much like Charlie," she said. She had to hold herself back from touching him.

"Can I talk to you?" he asked.

"Of course, Jeff," she said. "I saw you drive by earlier, and I've been hoping you would come. Come in..."

JEFF STEPPED PAST SHERIDAN as she held the screen door, and when he turned around, he saw that she was watching him. He felt prickles on the back of his neck—wondering if she knew. But then she smiled and took his hand.

"You really do look..." she said, pausing for a moment to study his eyes. "You just look so much like my son."

"Thank you, ma'am," he said, feeling so shy and uncomfortable. He was always a little awkward around people, and Sheridan was so famous. But the funny thing was, the longer she held his hand and gazed at him, the more he felt himself relaxing. He wasn't exactly comfortable, but there was something about the way she was looking at him that made him feel—well, it sounded crazy—as if he belonged.

"How old are you, Jeff?" she asked.

"Twenty-six almost," he said. "Getting old."

"That's so young," she said softly. "You're still very young..." Then, as if it took a big effort, she let go of his hand and looked at him expectantly.

"I'm sorry to bother you," he said. "I really didn't plan on barging in this way, but there's something..."

"Come into the living room," Sheridan said, cutting him off before he could say it too soon. Jeff got those tingles on his neck again—as if he and Sheridan were in a strange sync, he felt as if she knew what he was going to say, maybe even what he'd come there for, but wasn't quite ready to hear.

She led him through the downstairs into a wide room, dark except for one corner where three candles burned on a table in front of the fireplace. Picture windows overlooked the fog-shrouded beach. A cool breeze blew through the side door into the room. Sheridan led him to a big window, gesturing at the subtly beautiful mist-obscured panorama.

"We're lucky to have a spectacular view," Sheridan said. "On clear days."

"Do you get a lot of your inspiration from writing right here, gazing down at the water?" Jeff asked.

"I used to," Sheridan said.

That caught Jeff's attention, and he squinted into the fog, pretending to admire the view, just to hide the fact he was dying inside, that he knew Sheridan wasn't writing anymore and it was because of what he'd done.

As soon as he could, he turned away from the window, taking in the room. It was real warm and homey, nothing fancy about it. Filled with furniture that looked as if it had been there a long time, all sun-faded and comfortable, barely illuminated by those three candles.

He stared at a big armchair covered with a blanket kind of thing and thought how welcoming it looked.

"That was Charlie's chair," Sheridan said, coming over to stand by him.

"It was?" he asked.

She nodded, hand on his shoulder. "Sit down in it, why don't you?"

"No," he said, freezing. "I couldn't."

"I insist," she said, and although her voice was gentle, there was steel in her blue eyes. Jeff's legs were shaking as she pushed him down into Charlie's chair.

"There," she said, seeming satisfied. She gave him a warm smile.

"Let me get you something to drink. What will you have?"

"Oh, nothing for me," Jeff said. "I don't want to trouble you. I just have to talk to you."

"Seriously," Sheridan said, cutting him off and again giving him the idea she wasn't ready to hear what he had to say to her. She locked eyes with him and smiled. "It's no trouble. I'll be right back with some iced tea."

So Jeff sat in Charlie's chair and covered his face with his hands. Out in the kitchen, he heard the clink of ice and glasses. After a minute he looked out the window again.

The fog was so thick, now completely impenetrable; he couldn't see anything, but the sound of waves gently lapping the beach came through the open windows, slightly disconcerting because he couldn't see the source, couldn't see the water at all. It seemed as if the waves were coming from nowhere. He shivered in the damp chill, but it felt sharp and refreshing.

Sitting in Charlie's chair made him feel too terrible, so he stood up. There were guitars in racks on one wall, and another—a big old Martin—leaning up against the desk, as if Sheridan had been playing it when he'd disturbed her. He reached toward it, his hand hovering above the strings. He thought of Lisa and remembered how he used to feel the energy of her playing quiver through her fingers when she touched him.

The room was rustic, built of varnished pine. The finish brought out the wood's grain and warmth, making the room glow with a dark golden-hued burnish. A rough-hewn stone fireplace at one end of the room was flanked by two loveseats facing each other, across that table with the candles burning. The setting was so romantic, especially with the sound of the waves washing over anyone who sat there. Lisa had admired Sheridan's music, and he knew she'd assume a lot of Sheridan's love songs had been written in this place.

A gallery of family photos lined the old wood mantel. Drifting closer, Jeff saw pictures of Sheridan with two women who looked like her sisters, with two older women—probably her mother and grandmother. Peering at the photo, Jeff couldn't resist lifting it up. He gazed at the tiny old woman— her birdlike frame, soft white hair, wrinkled face, brilliant smile.

"My grandmother," Sheridan said, coming in from the kitchen with a tray bearing a pitcher and two glasses. "Was there something about her that interested you?"

"I don't know, ma'am," Jeff said, gingerly replacing the photo.

"Well, what made you pick it up?"

"Just thinking of Charlie being raised here. Lot of women."

"Yes, there were."

"Didn't you ever get married or anything? Didn't he ever have a stepfather?"

"No," Sheridan said. "He had me and his aunts, and his grandmother, and his great-grandmother. We did our best."

"I think you did a good job," Jeff said. He thought of his mother and John Thorpe, and then he turned away from the mantel.

"Thank you," she said, gesturing for him to sit in the loveseat opposite her, pouring iced tea into the glasses. "You . . . knew my son?"

"Not well," he said, settling down across the table from her. "But I did meet him."

"After he went off to college," she said, and Jeff

tensed, thinking *This is it*. But then she backed away again. "What about you? Who raised you?"

"My mother," he said. "But I did have a step-father."

"Did that make up for not having your father around?" she asked, and Jeff was surprised by how curious she sounded, as if she really wanted to know.

"Nothing could make up for that," he said, his voice coming from deep down in his chest.

"Boys really need their fathers," Sheridan said. "I tried to be both to Charlie, but it's impossible. He knew it, too. He had good male role models—his cross-country coach, mainly. And the dads of some of his friends. His girlfriend's father, Jack..."

"Nell," Jeff said.

Sheridan glanced up. "You know about Nell?"

"I met her," he said.

"When?"

"Yesterday," he said.

"How did that come about?" Sheridan asked.

Jeff held his breath. They'd just been playing at having a nice visit, and they both knew it. The moment had come, and Jeff stared into the candlelight. His voice cracked, and he had to wait for it to work.

"I was visiting Charlie's grave," he said.

"Why?"

"To find a way to tell my brother I'm sorry," he said.

"Sorry about what?" she asked, still smiling.

"The worst thing there is," he said, staring at her.

"You took his life," Sheridan said. The friendliness was gone—her eyes were suddenly hard, and her voice came from deep in the Arctic.

NELL LAY ON THE MATTRESS in the attic. She'd fallen asleep under the eaves. Waking up, at first she had no idea where she was. But then she looked around, saw fog darkening the windows. She'd had a long nap.

She'd dreamed of a river flowing in slow motion. Overhead the stars were coming out, but they weren't like stars in nature: they were not simply constellations, not just shapes suggested by a few stars, but actual beings come to life. Orion was really a hunter, the Pleiades were really seven sisters, Gemini were two twins, and Ursa Major was a big bear.

Nell had been little in the dream, just a child. She'd been on her father's shoulders, taking a walk by the river, and she'd stared up, delighted: so many beings and creatures up in the sky! She and her father had laughed, watching the bear run. But suddenly it turned on them, bared its teeth and came at them.

That's what woke her up: the image of that bear in the sky, about to eat her and her dad. Lying on the mattress, Nell tried to catch her breath. She started out dissecting the dream, trying to separate all the images. But then something else, a recent memory, pressed into her mind.

Jeff . . . something he'd said.

Nell lay still, her heart pounding. She stared at her open window, saw tendrils of fog drifting past. The atmosphere felt thick and impenetrable. Living at the beach brought the clearest days, when you could see out to Long Island and beyond. But it also brought heavy air, laden with moisture picked up from the sea, when every breath tasted of salt.

She pushed herself up, rubbed her eyes and tried to wake up. Why did she feel so upset? Had her dream been about Jeff? Was he the bear, charging to attack? Looking around, she almost felt Charlie's presence. They had spent so much time up here. If only she could turn to him, ask him about Jeff. But knowing she couldn't, that he'd never come up here to the attic again, filled her with despair. She thought of Sheridan having to live in that empty house where Charlie had been so alive, and couldn't imagine how hard it must be.

And that made her remember: that was it, the thought pushing into her dream. Jeff had said he had something to tell her and Sheridan. The two of them together. Nell felt sick to her stomach. She should have gone straight there, to see Charlie's mother, instead of falling asleep.

Knowing she had to be with Sheridan, Nell stopped by Stevie's studio to tell her where she was going. But Stevie was lost in painting, completely immersed in her work, so Nell didn't say anything. She just walked downstairs and slipped out into the fog.

* * *

THE JET HAD MADE ITS DESCENT and was now flying in slow circles. Gavin pressed his head to the window and couldn't see the ground.

"Why aren't we landing?" he asked.

"I don't know," Vincent said, starting to push the button to call the flight attendant when he entered the main cabin.

"We're fucking WOXOF," Gavin said, staring down.

"Excuse me?"

"Indefinite ceiling zero, sky obscured, zero visibility," Gavin said. "*Fuck.*"

"The captain asked me to tell you New London is socked in," the flight attendant said. "We're waiting for the fog to clear so we can land."

"When does he think that will happen?" Gavin asked.

"Uncertain," the flight attendant said.

"Laney and I have tickets to Shakespeare in Westerly," Vincent said. "Outdoors, in the park, under the stars. Shit. The weather was supposed to be good." He shrugged. "She'll be pissed that I'm late, but at least if the weather's too bad to land, the production will be canceled."

Gavin glared at him. "You've been a divorce lawyer too long," he said. "Your thought processes are far too convoluted for anyone's good. Where can we land?"

"Sir?" the flight attendant asked.

"Fog is coastal. How far inland do we have to fly to get away from it?"

"I'm not sure," the flight attendant said. "I'll ask the captain."

He walked forward, disappeared into the cockpit.

"Shit," Gavin said out loud. He had tried Sheridan's number repeatedly, but each time the call went straight to voice mail.

"I know," Vincent said.

"What do I do?"

"We'll get there as soon as we can. Look, I bet Jeff won't go see Sheridan at all. He'll chicken out."

"No he won't."

"He's not going to stand there right in front of Charlie's mother and confess to his murder."

"He's on his way to see Sheridan, if he isn't there already."

"Gavin, say that Randy was telling you the truth..."

"He was," Gavin said, remembering the scene back in Randy's office, the anguish in Randy's eyes as he finally told Gavin what had happened.

"Well, even if he was—and it's not a pretty story, sure makes Randy look bad, covering for Jeff all this time—say it's true, and he's right, why would it be bad for Sheridan to find out?"

"She has to find out," Gavin said. "But I need to be with her when she does. I don't know if she can handle hearing it alone. And, shit—"

"Shit, what?"

"The kid is a loose cannon. Something triggered

his anger that night, and he killed Charlie. What if Sheridan says the wrong thing? She's going to explode when she hears—what if she provokes him into hurting *her*?"

Vincent stared at him, nodding gravely.

Gavin pressed his head to the Plexiglas and stared out into murky nothingness. They were a few thousand feet up, and just a few miles east of Hubbard's Point. Once the plane landed, Gavin could be at Sheridan's door within fifteen minutes.

"I say as soon as we land, we call the cops. They can arrest him on suspicion of Charlie's murder," Vincent said.

Gavin thought of what Randy had told him, saw his sunken, troubled eyes. This had haunted him. He thought of Sheridan, of the last year. If someone had ripped her heart out of her chest a year ago in that city park on the river's edge, it would have been less painful than what she'd been through. He couldn't imagine her going through this, too.

"Excuse me," the flight attendant said, emerging from the cockpit. "The news is not good. The fog extends all the way inland to Hartford, all along the Connecticut River Valley."

"Any updates on how long he thinks we'll be circling?"

"No. It seems there was a sudden and unexpected temperature inversion—cold air from Canada that had been held up by a stationary front seems to have—"

"Can he land in Hartford?"

"Brainard Field, yes," the flight attendant said.

"Ask him to do that," Gavin said.

Vincent nodded his agreement. The plane stopped circling; Gavin felt it level off and thrust forward, northwest toward Hartford. Still staring down at the invisible ground, Gavin heard Vincent talking, trying to calm him down. He was saying that Judy always tracked his flights, that as soon as she realized they were diverted, she'd call the limo company they used in Hartford and make sure there was a car waiting on the tarmac at Brainard when they landed.

Gavin did the math: twenty minutes in the air, forty minutes—thirty if the driver was good—down to Hubbard's Point. Worst-case scenario, he'd be at Sheridan's within an hour.

CHAPTER 21

SHERIDAN SAT IN THE LIVING ROOM, IN THE damp breeze and flickering candlelight, with Jeff. She was home, but everything felt unfamiliar, as if she had allowed this stranger into her house and with him entered a brand-new country.

"You killed my son," she said steadily.

"Yes," he said.

The words seemed impossible, both from her lips and in her ears. This wasn't a conversation people had. It was supposed to happen in police stations, or at crime scenes, between two strangers, one of them a cop. It took place between characters in a movie. It wasn't supposed to be happening between a mother and the young man who'd killed her boy.

"Do you want someone to be here with you now?" he asked nervously.

She shook her head. "I need to hear straight from you what happened. I don't want anyone else getting in the way of you explaining it to me. That's why you came, isn't it? Because that's what you want, too?"

"What's it matter?" he asked.

"You're right," she said softly. "I don't really care what you want."

Sheridan and Jeff sat across from each other, on the loveseats tucked by the fireplace. A low table rested between them; Charlie had made it from a driftwood log that had washed up after a storm, its gray wood smooth and silvered by time in Long Island Sound.

In the center of the table, a shallow pottery bowl held shells and stones, all gathered by Sheridan and Charlie over the years. Things thrown out of the Sound—they'd survived countless storms and tides, withstood waves that had traveled across the whole ocean, and finally washed up on Hubbard's Point beach.

Sheridan leaned over and reached for a shell—a small moon shell, no bigger than a marble, faultless and without any chips. She ran her thumb over the surface, felt the tiny whorl, considered the perfect pattern that made it so like every other moon shell that had ever been created. After holding it for a moment, she handed it to Jeff.

He accepted it, his expression confused.

"Look how delicate that is," she said.

"Excuse me?"

"That shell is finer than china. Thinner...If you hold it up to the light..." For the first time, she reached over, turned on a lamp. When Jeff didn't move, she guided his hand up, so the incandescence illuminated the small shell. "You can see how fragile it is, can't you?"

"Yes."

"While Charlie was so...*strong*," she said. "So powerful. He ran cross-country at school, and in summers he ran on the beach. Loved to swim. He played basketball...worked out. His arms were muscular. Funny, I didn't always think he was that strong. When he was little, I was always afraid he'd get hurt, that something terrible could happen..."

"Ma'am," Jeff began.

But Sheridan cut him off with a look.

"I thought he'd fall off the monkey bars, or out of the tree he was climbing. I worried he'd dive off the raft and hit his head on a rock. Break his neck...I worried that he'd play on the train tracks, like his friend..." She trailed off, thinking of Steven Mayles.

"Maybe that's how it is, being a mother," she continued. "You have to consider the worst possibilities before you can learn to relax. But you know what?" When Jeff didn't reply, she went on. "Charlie wasn't breakable. He could swing from branches, dangle from the bridge, do a perfect swan dive. I knew his body was full of tensile strength...and he took care. He was brave, but he was cautious. I took comfort in that, and I began to trust."

Jeff tried to hand the shell back to her.

"Keep it," she said sharply. "Because I want you to think about something. That tiny shell, the size of a peanut...it was lashed by the ocean, thrown around the rocks and the sand, rolled in the tides—you know, the tides come in and out twice a day. High tide, low tide, high tide, low tide . . . every twenty-four hours. Day after day, that little shell survived. But my son . . ."

"Ms. Rosslare," Jeff said.

"My big, strong, smart, wonderful son," Sheridan continued as if he hadn't spoken, "couldn't even survive one day with his brother. Couldn't even survive the first—only—meeting with you."

"Please," Jeff said. "Let me—"

Sheridan exploded out of her seat. "*Let* you? I will *force* you to tell me. I want to know every second of what happened. Tell me, Jeff. Tell me how you killed Charlie."

"I will, Ms. Rosslare," Jeff said nervously, his voice gentle, as if he wanted to defuse the situation, as if he thought he could somehow soften what was coming.

"You did it," Sheridan said, nearly spitting at him. "You came here to Hubbard's Point, went to his grave. You talked to Nell, and you drove by my house. I saw you—didn't you think I'd react, seeing someone who looks so much like my son? You came up here, you sat in his chair. You looked at the picture of his great-grandmother on the mantel! While all the time, all this year without Charlie . . . I've been missing him every second."

The young man looked shocked, but Sheridan didn't care. Her grandmother had always told her that power came from three things: love, words, and the sea. Their use had to be undertaken with great care, because they could cause either joy or grief, salvation or destruction. These last twelve months she'd known only grief, and it came pouring out in her words now.

"So," she said, never taking her eyes off Jeff, her whole body shaking. "Tell me what you did to my son."

AND JEFF DID. This was what he had come here for. He could see Sheridan's rage, and he was ready for it. He'd grown up in the South, and he felt the way he did on hot August afternoons when you knew thunderstorms were coming. The low pressure would sit over the county like a big headache, just tightening and squeezing till you thought your skull would crack.

That's what his guilt had felt like. Building all this year. Coming between him and Lisa; her wanting him to hold her, say her songs were good, ride with her in the bus on the way to the next show, share with her his deepest feelings about losing his brother. She'd met Charlie at the same time as Jeff—that night, right after the gig. They'd all stood on the street, taking pictures and saying how good it was to get together, how important family was.

Then Lisa had headed for the bus with the rest of the band. The plan was for Randy and Jeff to drive home to Nashville to meet with some studio musicians, and then Jeff was going to fly up to Boston, continue on the road with her.

That never happened. Once the news of Charlie's death hit, Jeff had done just what Randy had told him—acted as surprised as anyone. Lisa had comforted him, crying in shock and sorrow at the random, terrible killing of his brother. She'd been told by Randy that he and Jeff had headed south right after she'd left, as planned. They'd heard the news from Sheridan—when she called a day later, after the New York cops had found her.

All through this last year, Jeff and Lisa had drifted apart. Grief and guilt just chipped away at what they'd had. He couldn't touch her. Couldn't stand letting her touch him. It was as if seeing his brother die, seeing what became of a human body—watching the life whisper out of it, watching the soul leave the eyes and skin, seeing how strength was so temporary, seeing Charlie just lying there in the dirt—had made him renounce everything in the physical world. He couldn't hold or be held, couldn't kiss or be kissed.

Talking, too. He'd never been much of a confider. He'd learned early, during his painful childhood years, to keep the worst of what he felt bottled up inside. Juvenile hall had intensified that tendency, as had being the outsider in the Thorpe family. Once Randy had come into his life, Jeff had found himself opening up a little. Randy had wanted father-son talks, and the more he tried, the more Jeff realized that he wanted them, too. He'd had a lot to say; at first he'd held back the parts about feeling angry and abandoned, but Randy had told him to let it all out.

That if he kept his feelings bottled up, he'd wind up having a heart attack before he was fifty.

So Jeff had tried. He'd started figuring out how to match words with feelings, even his deepest and darkest ones. And nothing in his life had ever made him feel more loved than the fact of his father wanting to hear them. Sitting there in the office, across the desk at Randecker Records, Randy's face grave as he listened to Jeff tell him how much he'd wanted a dad, how seeing his stepbrothers with John Thorpe had made him want a dad so badly he'd wanted to die.

Once he and Lisa got together, he'd started talking more. She loved words, loved putting them together in the songs she wrote, and even more, she loved lying in bed with him and getting him to tell her stories. They both did, about places they'd been, people they'd known, things they dreamed of doing someday. She'd taught him that words were connection, that talking was music.

But after that August night, Jeff couldn't talk to her anymore. He was full of secrets. It wasn't even as if she probed him for what had happened with Charlie—she never suspected anything. She'd taken Randy's and his story at face value—she was a trusting girl, and she loved them both, and it would never occur to her that Jeff would ever hurt his brother.

It had never occurred to Jeff, either. He felt bewildered by it, which only added to his storm of confusion and guilt—and it had been getting worse as the anniversary came around, feeling like the hours before a huge, tree-ripping, barn-destroying, river-flooding storm: "yellow-sky storms," his grandmother had called them, the kind that spawned tornadoes.

Sheridan had been holding her fury in so long, she was like a yellow-sky Southern storm, all jagged lightning and torrential rains, and sitting across the table from her, he was glad it was starting. It made him feel as if the pressure on the outside finally equaled the unbearable pressure inside, and it gave him some strange relief.

"Tell me," she commanded.

"I didn't mean to do it," he said softly.

"That doesn't matter to me," she said. "Tell me what you did—whether you 'meant' to or not."

He swallowed, his heart right in his throat, the taste of blood in his mouth from where he'd bitten down hard on the inside of his cheek. He felt jangled and wracked by emotion—sort of like how he'd felt the night he met Charlie. As if he didn't know what might happen next, and all he wanted to do was keep a little control over everything, over himself. He dug his fingernails into the palms of his hands.

"We'd been at the club," he said. "I manage Cumberland, Lisa's band. She is, was, my girlfriend.... Usually Randy wasn't there at the gigs, but that night, well, it was our New York debut. So he came."

"Randy?" she asked, looking shocked.

Jeff nodded, realizing she hadn't known he was there that night. He wanted to protect his father as he had done for him, but right now it seemed most important to just tell the story, and tell it straight and true. "Yes," he said. Then, quickly, "But none of it was his fault."

"Did Charlie go there to meet him?"

"He did," Jeff said, staring at Sheridan. "I... was real surprised."

"Surprised?"

Jeff nodded. To his shock and shame, his eyes stung with tears remembering how his short time of being Randy's only son had come to an end. Clint, in California, hadn't really counted—he had long since written off Randy, said he didn't even consider him his father. Jeff wanted to tell Sheridan how happy he'd been to have found a brother in Charlie, how lucky he felt, but he couldn't lie, and he knew she saw.

"You didn't know Charlie existed?"

"Nope," he said, swallowing hard, getting past the sting in his eyes. He was okay now. She wasn't going to see that part of him; he wouldn't let her see him cry. Showing her his wounds might make her feel sorry for him, but it wasn't going to get the story told.

"How soon before that night had you met Randy?" she asked.

"Not long," Jeff said. "About three years."

"So you were new to the Quill family?"

Jeff nodded. "Yes, ma'am. But I was proud."

"You took his name?"

"Yep."

"What was your name before?"

"Jeff Easton," he said, blushing as he thought of

his mother, how upset she'd been when he'd changed it back to Quill. He pushed that thought away, cleared his throat. "I was happy, knowing my father."

"All boys need their fathers," she repeated, staring him in the eye. "Charlie wanted to know his father from the time he was old enough to realize..."

"That his dad wasn't around," Jeff said quietly, nodding, knowing because he'd felt the same way. The big things and the small things. He remembered being in the county home, a constant dream that had gotten him through the fear and loneliness: of walking down country roads with his father, kicking a rock ahead of them, not even talking. Just being together. That would have made him so happy. Maybe Charlie had dreamed the same thing.

Sheridan sat still, like a statue, just watching him till he could start up again. Jeff swallowed. "Anyway, Charlie came to the club. When we met—man, it was like looking in the mirror."

"I see that," she said.

"We laughed—and so did Randy, and even Lisa once the show ended and she'd finished up backstage. We were all standing around, deciding whether to go eat or get a drink, something to keep the night going. We were all of us charged up, almost giddy-like, the craziness of realizing we were blood. Three of us anyway—Randy, Charlie, and me."

"Your girlfriend was there?"

"She left," he said. "Cumberland was on tour, heading to Providence for the next night. The bus was ready to go, so she just said goodbye."

"But the rest of you?"

Jeff swallowed.

"Well, Charlie was only seventeen, too young to drink, so a bar was out. And no one was hungry, so we decided to walk."

"Down to the river?" Sheridan asked.

"Yes, ma'am."

"Why there?"

"Well, before she left, Lisa said something poetic, like she always does, about rivers keeping us all connected. How we were down in Nashville on the Cumberland, and Charlie was up in Black Hall, on the mighty Connecticut, and New York was surrounded by rivers—how it was such a fitting place to meet, on Manhattan Island between the Hudson and East rivers."

"That's why you went, because of something your girlfriend said..." Sheridan trailed off.

"Well, her talk of rivers started it..." Jeff said. "But it was because Randy wanted to show us where he'd played ball."

"Ball?"

Jeff nodded. He thought back to that night, to the way his father's eyes had sparkled that hot summer night, wanting to take them to the field, and how he'd choked up and hadn't been able to speak.

Sheridan couldn't stand the silence. "Please," she said. "Tell me..."

"I will," Jeff said. "Back when Randy was working as a roadie—on your band and others—they used to have a league. The sidemen would be on one team, and the roadies and sound guys would be on another, and sometimes the artists would join in, and they'd play, whatever city they were at."

"I remember that," Sheridan said.

"Well, in New York, they always played downtown—at the park where Houston Street runs into the East River. Randy talked about the ball fields along the river, how cool that had been. He wanted to show us both where he played. Seemed real important and symbolic to him."

Sheridan stared at him through the candles.

"He felt guilty," Jeff said. "Not ever playing ball with us. He had three sons, never once chucked a ball with any of us. That ate at him—once he got older, had that heart attack...he figured out all the crap he'd done wrong, found a better way to live. He started seeing how he'd let us all down."

"He did," Sheridan said.

"I didn't hold it against him," Jeff said, getting past a flash of anger. "I would have liked growing up with him, but it didn't happen. I'm not blaming him."

"Maybe you should..."

"All I'm saying," Jeff said, holding up both hands, to let her know to stop, "is that's why he wanted to show us the ball field. That August night, it was a real summer night, and Randy was thinking of pitches not pitched to us, hits not hit, balls not fielded. A lot of lost opportunities with his three sons. All of us grown now, no getting back the past."

Jeff bowed his head, the wave of missed opportunities nearly knocking him down. Sitting in Charlie's living room, holding the little shell in his hand, facing his mother, made him think of every minute of life Charlie hadn't lived and wouldn't live since that night—and how her words tonight were echoing his.

"So that's why we went to the field," he said, finally looking up.

Sheridan nodded, obviously steeling herself for the rest. He watched her gather her strength. It was just past eight here in Hubbard's Point, but in the story it was three in the morning, and Jeff and Randy and Charlie were all down there in the dark and deserted ball park.

In his memory, the East River was rushing by, a black torrent. Silver ripples were splashed on the wild surface by city lights. The chain-link backstop glinted in the lights of cars passing by on the elevated FDR Drive. Jeff remembered the heavy air, the oppressive heat. He closed his eyes, thinking of how he'd felt to see Randy walking along with his arm around Charlie's shoulders—as if Jeff had already been replaced by someone new.

But that's not even what did it, kick-started his violent streak. The emotions had risen up in him so fast. He'd hardly known what was coming. It was as if he'd swallowed an anvil—then been dropped off the top of a tall building. He couldn't have stopped his fall, even if he'd wanted to—which he hadn't. He had tilted, then started his plummet, and he'd wished it would be fatal.

"I don't know what happened," he said now, looking straight into Sheridan's eyes.

"Yes you do," she challenged.

"I know what I did," he said.

"Then tell me, Jeff. What did you do?"

"Charlie and Randy were walking along, up ahead of me. I . . . felt a little left out. I, well, I'd grown up on the outside of a family, and it felt like that. Like maybe Randy was going to start liking Charlie better. Something like that. I guess that's what got it started, working on me . . ."

"Okay," Sheridan said, listening.

Jeff nodded. "We were all just walking along. Me in back, Randy and Charlie up ahead. I was staring at the back of their heads . . . They were talking about Nell, Charlie saying how lucky he was to have some-one like her. Then Randy said something about him having had that once, with you. And how Charlie came from you and him, and how he was the son of such a great talent—you. All those great musical genes. How maybe Charlie would want to join the business, maybe even convince you to sign with the label, put old feelings aside."

"Randy said that to Charlie?" Sheridan asked.

Jeff nodded. "And I couldn't see his face, but if it was me, I'd have been eating it up. I started thinking maybe Randy was going to bring Charlie into the company, push me out. That's how things go, that's how my life's been all along."

"Charlie had plans for his life," Sheridan said. "He wasn't going to work for Randy . . ."

"I know," Jeff said. "But I didn't know then; I just said something stupid. Came out of nowhere, too—

just spit the words out of my mouth, no thought behind them. I said, 'Don't think you're gonna ride in,
take my place.' Something like that."

"But Charlie wouldn't 'ride in.' He'd never think of
taking your place."

Jeff shrugged, remembering the panic he'd felt that
night. His chest had felt constricted, as if a python
was wrapped around him, squeezing the air out of his
lungs, the blood out of his heart. Now he knew Sheridan was right; but that night, seeing Randy give all
his attention to his newest son, the latest in line, had
made Jeff know with every bone in his body that he
was about to lose what he'd had for so short a time—
the sense of mattering to his father.

"Charlie turned around," Jeff said. "I . . . I thought
he glared at me. But maybe he was just thinking I
was crazy. Because he didn't even speak. Just stared.
With his open face . . . and big eyes."

"Probably wanted to let you know he knew what
you were thinking," Sheridan said, her eyes glittering. "He'd know exactly what you felt. He'd been
abandoned by his father his whole life."

Jeff heard her words, but he couldn't let them in. If
he did, they would kill him, make him feel even
worse for what he'd misunderstood. "I took his silence as him wanting to throw down. He just stared.
And I . . ." He choked down a burst of grief boiling up
from his chest, ". . . started getting mad. Really mad."

"What did Charlie do?"

"He just turned away. Randy didn't see any of it. He
was too busy feeling psyched that we were all at the

ball field together. He got off the subject of Charlie working for the company, started talking about his regrets over missing our childhoods. He started saying that stuff I told you, about games not played..."

"Pitches not pitched," Sheridan said between clenched teeth.

"And Charlie changed," Jeff said. "He just stopped in his tracks, looking at Randy with this wild spark in his eyes."

Sheridan tensed; Jeff could see she understood, that she was drawing on everything she knew about her son to understand the moment Jeff was describing. It didn't come as a surprise to her; no, it was more as if she'd been waiting for it, conflict between Charlie and his father.

"Randy just stood there smiling, as if he'd never been happier," Jeff said. "And I understood. Charlie looked at me, as if we were on the same side. I didn't know where he was going with any of it."

"What did he say?"

"He . . . just lost it," Jeff said. "All of a sudden he attacked Randy—just started talking in this low, intense way. Saying it was more than a few missed ball games—that he'd abandoned you, left you to raise Charlie all on your own."

Sheridan's eyes filled with tears, and she covered her mouth with her hand.

"Randy was blindsided—he'd been feeling so good about bringing us together. But he started defending himself, saying it was half your fault for keeping Charlie away from him..."

Sheridan shook her head hard, as if saying Randy was a liar.

"Charlie lost it then—he shoved Randy away, told him he was full of shit. And Randy was in shock, hurt and mad, but trying to apologize, asking Charlie to try to see how hard it was for him."

"How hard for *Randy*?" Sheridan whispered, aghast.

But Jeff barely heard. He was remembering the night, the moment. "Charlie was in a rage, starting to walk away. Then he turned—I don't know if I thought he was going to jump on Randy, just start pounding him...or if it was that I...I couldn't take hearing Charlie talk to him that way...our father. After all the love Randy had just been showing him. I was jealous of Charlie—there was Randy giving him all that attention, and Charlie was just throwing it back in his face...All I know is," he said, his voice dropping, "I'm sorry, Sheridan."

"What did you do?"

"I went after him. One punch."

"You hit Charlie," Sheridan said.

"I did," Jeff said. "It—it wasn't...it came from somewhere else. My arm shot out, it was over so fast. I...hit him in the temple. He went down."

Sheridan crouched, as if she couldn't hold herself up anymore. Jeff heard himself speaking, knew that he was crying. He had the sensation of tears pouring down his face. He saw the scene in front of him— Charlie lying on the ground, not breathing.

So sudden, and so total: Randy trying to give him mouth-to-mouth resuscitation, then pushing on Charlie's chest with the heels of both his hands, Jeff pacing, his tread so heavy, the words "Oh my God, oh my God" ringing in his own ears as his fist throbbed, as his stone-hand came back to life and started to hurt from that one punch to Charlie's head.

"He was lying in the dirt," Jeff said. "That's all I could see. So I took off my shirt. I lay it under his head... There was blood coming out of his nose, his ears. He bled into the ground. Randy held him."

Sheridan's arms were wrapped around herself, and she'd slid out of her seat, and she knelt on the floor, rocking gently. Jeff kept speaking, but he saw that she wasn't listening anymore. She was kneeling on the sandy red earth by home plate, holding the body of her son. She was with him right now, soothing him and cradling him. Randy and Jeff might have been there that night, but she was with him now.

"Charlie didn't wake up," Jeff said quietly.

"My boy, my beautiful boy."

"Randy breathed and breathed into his mouth," Jeff said. "He wouldn't stop. But Charlie...oh, he turned cold. And then he was stiff." He stared at Sheridan, trying to gauge how much more he should tell. But Sheridan didn't stop him. "He was dead," Jeff said. "He must have died instantly. We tried, Sheridan, but we couldn't bring him back."

"Oh God," Sheridan whispered.

"We sat there with him all night," Jeff said. He

thought of Steven Mayles, of how he'd related to that terrible story Nell had told. "I wanted the police to come. I kept saying I wanted them to take me away. At first Randy said I deserved that. That he'd testify, so I could rot in prison the rest of my life. With my record, that's what would happen. We were going to call 911, we kept being about to dial, but we didn't. There was something about us there with Charlie alone—we were his family. For all the sorrow that brought him, we were his blood. And we couldn't let him go. At least, that's how I felt . . . I think we both did."

Jeff listened to his own words. He'd killed Charlie, but that night he'd been unable to bear thinking of anyone else touching his body. Strangers—cops, EMTs, the coroner. He shivered now, thinking of the moment the sun rose.

"Dawn came," Jeff said. "And that's when Randy had to decide."

"What to do," Sheridan said.

"I still wanted the cops to come. Wanted them to take me away, stick me in a cell," Jeff said. "Where I belong."

"You wanted that."

"I still do," Jeff said, looking Sheridan straight in the eye.

She finally let go of her knees, stopped rocking. She raised her head, gazed straight at him. He saw that her face was wet and sticky with tears, and he knew that his was, too.

"My father wouldn't let me call them then," Jeff said. "Said he'd already lost one son, he wasn't going to lose another. What I did was terrible, and I'd be paying for it the rest of my life—said that guilt ate people up like cancer, that I would have to live with what I'd done, that the guilt would slash me ragged. Randy said he'd help me however he could—he loved me, he'd get me help. We were his boys."

"Two of you still are," Sheridan said. "But Charlie..."

"I know," Jeff said.

"I'll never see my son again. He'll never see me, or Nell, or this place he loved so much. You took that from him."

Jeff couldn't speak. He stared down at the bowl of shells, hearing Sheridan's voice, feeling it rip him up.

"I'm sorry," Jeff said, his chest splitting open like a walnut. He held back sobs, because he saw the hatred in her eyes. There was force and velocity there, and it made him feel afraid of what she was about to do.

"Yes," she said, her voice cold. "I can see you are. Your father is right—guilt destroys people. It's killing you, isn't it?"

"Call the cops," he begged. "Get them here now."

"I will," she said, reaching for the phone.

But just then the screen door flew open, and Nell stepped in, green eyes blazing. Very methodically she slammed the door shut and locked it behind her—as if to make sure Jeff couldn't escape. His blood stalled—like a tidal wave hitting the beach, washing back onto itself. He felt stunned by the ferocity in her eyes. For a minute he thought she was going to pull out a dagger, stab him through the heart. Instead she took a few steps toward him, tears pouring down her cheeks.

"I heard you from outside," she said. "I heard it all."

"Nell, I'm so sorry," he said, his voice cracking.

"You killed Charlie," she screamed, throwing herself at him. Sheridan jumped up, to catch her, to keep her from—what? Jeff had no idea; was she guarding him, protecting Nell? Whichever, she lunged across the driftwood table, upsetting one of the candles. It teetered and tipped, but Sheridan didn't see. She went straight for Nell, trying to push her back out the door, away from Jeff.

Jeff stood stunned, staring at Nell. Papers, sheet music, a book, the beams and timber of the house itself, sparked and caught like tinder as flames started licking up the old wood walls.

"Sheridan," he said. "Tell her I didn't mean . . ." he stammered.

"Oh my God," Nell said, looking over Sheridan's shoulder, making her turn.

"No!" Sheridan cried, running back to the table, trying to beat the fire down, smother it with pillows from the loveseat.

"We have to get out," Nell gasped in the smoke.

"Sheridan!" Jeff said, grabbing her. His arms were around her, pulling her hard, away from the center of the fire. And whether it was out of hatred of him or sheer panic, he didn't know, but she cracked him on the head with her elbow, and they went down together, and the house was on fire around them, and the night went dark.

CHAPTER 22

GAVIN TOOK A RIGHT OFF THE MAIN ROAD, under the train bridge into Hubbard's Point, hardly slowing down for the stop sign. Vincent sat in the back seat while Judy rode up front, holding tight after a breakneck ride down from Hartford.

Having tracked the flight, Judy had driven from Hawthorne to meet the plane at Brainard Field in Hartford, and Gavin had commandeered her blue Subaru wagon, not even stopping to drop Vincent off at home. There was still no answer when he tried Sheridan again and again on his cell phone. He'd sped down the highway, making record time, nearly hitting a deer on Route 9.

"So, this is Hubbard's Point," Judy said, looking around with interest. Her tone was strangely conversational, considering how fast Gavin was flying down the winding road. "The legendary boyhood meeting place of Gavin Dawson and Vincent de Havilland."

"Jesus, Gav," Vincent said. "Slow down."

Gavin didn't reply. He concentrated on the curving beach roads, trying to see through the fog. Two rabbits scampered out of his way.

The fog thickened as they neared the Point. This close to the water, Gavin wasn't surprised. But the air smelled acrid, not salty; of smoke, not fog. When they got to Sheridan's house, he pulled the Subaru behind her car and got out. The smell of smoke was stronger here; it drew his attention up to the house. He noticed an orange glow in the downstairs windows and started running up the hill, ignoring his foot. Smoke was seeping out from the windows and seams of the cottage. A few neighbors had come out of their houses to investigate.

"Call 911!" Vincent shouted to anyone as he ran right behind Gavin.

"I'm on it," Judy yelled.

Gavin tried the kitchen door, but it was locked. He gave the window one quick pop with his bare elbow, cutting himself as he reached inside and fumbled for the lock. He turned the knob, let himself inside. Vincent was on his heels. Gavin heard coughing and wheeled around.

Nell came stumbling out of the smoke, eyes streaming, grabbed his arm and shook it violently.

"Sheridan!" she cried.

"Where is she?"

"In the living room," Nell said through a coughing fit, eyes red and burning. "I couldn't get them up."

"Where in the living room?"

"By the fireplace."

"'Them'?" Vincent asked as Gavin tore away.

"Sheridan and Jeff," Nell said.

Gavin headed through the kitchen, relying completely on memory as he made his way through the smoke. He heard flames crackling and someone choking and whimpering. Running with his head down, he stepped into the narrow, smoke-filled hallway and saw that the living room was engulfed in flames.

Holding his arm over his mouth, he barreled into the thickening smoke. It seared his eyes and lungs, made him blind. He felt his way along one wall, already hot to the touch. Smoke obliterated everything. He started feeling his way toward the two sofas under the eaves by the hearth, straight into the fire.

The entire room was scorching hot, the old wooden beach cottage going up like a stack of dry tinder. Gavin felt as if he was gulping smoke; it burned his skin and eyes, throat and lungs, made him feel as if he were melting both inside and out. He blinked back fumes the best he could, trying to gauge how far Sheridan was from where he stood: twenty feet? He took his last semi-good breath, and put his head down, and ran straight into the fire.

Flames had encircled one of the small couches, were licking up the walls and ceiling. Everything was burning, red-orange light everywhere. He couldn't see, so he got down on his hands and knees and felt. The floor was so hot it blistered his hands as he scuttled along, feeling for Sheridan. His lungs were searing, bursting. He felt dizzy and sick, and he knew if he took a breath now, he'd die. That bothered him, but not as much as the fact that Sheridan would die, too, so he kept going.

And he found her.

She lay in a heap, unconscious. With his lungs bursting, Gavin picked her up, held her to his chest, carrying her into the hall. Smoke poured out from behind him, making it impossible to see. His feet burned. He was completely disoriented, and his chest was exploding, and he needed to breathe. He didn't know which way to go, took a step right and banged into a wall.

"Gavin," he heard. He looked wildly from side to side, seeing nothing.

"Help him." A figure emerged from the smoke, a young man. He thrust out his hand, pointing, and Gavin saw that he'd missed Jeff lying on the floor. He crouched to half lift, half carry the dazed young man toward the door, his other arm supporting Sheridan. Gavin knew he was losing it, but he swore the stranger was Charlie. He felt sure of it. With all the trust he could muster, Gavin held on to Sheridan and Jeff, letting the shape guide him through impenetrable smoke.

Gavin held Sheridan tighter, pressing her face into his shoulder, not wanting her to breathe the burning air. They took one step along the hall, then another. The flames had eaten away at some of the floorboards; Gavin felt them singe his legs.

They cleared the fire; closer to the kitchen, the house hadn't yet caught. Smoke billowed, and it was still impossible to see; Gavin felt himself being pulled and guided. His thoughts were crazy; he was hallucinating. He heard someone whispering in his ear, Irish words he couldn't understand. But he'd heard the voice of that old magic woman before, and he knew she was telling him to stay strong, get Sheridan out. He thought he heard the voice of a young man saying "Mom, I love you."

He stood in the kitchen where the smoke was less thick, and he finally took a breath. He got some oxygen into his lungs, and looked around expecting to see Aphrodite and Charlie. Instead he had Vincent in his face, supporting Jeff, tugging on his hand, pulling them all toward the kitchen door.

And behind Vincent was Patrick Murphy, and behind Patrick was Lily, and behind her were the Healeys, and the Butlers, and the Devlins, and the Halls, and Miss Davis, and the Fitches, and the Glenneys, and the Johnsons, and the Wheatons, and Helen and Julian and Arnold, and Teddy, and the Potholms...

The residents of Hubbard's Point had formed a human chain to save Sheridan and Gavin. When he stepped out the kitchen door, he saw them all. They gathered around, pulling him and Sheridan into the yard, away from the house. Gavin heard a siren, looked through the fog, down the hill, in time to see the fire truck and a police car arriving.

"Here, Gav," Vincent said, putting his arm around him.

Gavin lay Sheridan on the cool, damp grass. The

fog swirled around them, soothing their burns. He touched her face. Under the soot, she looked so pale and still. He wanted to tell her he'd seen Charlie. He knew the neighbors had been there at the end, but he wanted to tell Sheridan that they'd been saved by her grandmother and Charlie.

"She's not breathing," someone murmured from behind.

Gavin bent close to Sheridan's face. He pressed his mouth to hers to give her mouth-to-mouth resuscitation, realized he didn't have any breath of his own to give, and passed out cold on top of her body.

NELL'S FRIENDS HAD ALL run to the Point when word of the fire got out. They'd come armed with buckets and garden hoses; some were soaking the neighbors' houses on either side of Sheridan's—the wooden cottages were so close together, they were in danger of catching on fire, too.

The neighbors and all the other residents of Hubbard's Point had worked hard, joining in to save whatever they could. The police and fire departments came, along with an ambulance. At one point Peggy gasped and pointed, and Nell turned to look at Jeff Quill, bent double and coughing madly. He'd revived, standing at the very edge of Sheridan's yard.

"Oh my God," Peggy said. "Charlie . . ."

Nell stared, mesmerized and horrified, at Jeff. She left Peggy standing there and walked over, stood right in front of him.

He still looked so much like Charlie, but he was covered with soot and ash. His face was streaked, and his shirt was torn. Standing in the dark, with emergency lights flashing, Nell took stock of his features. She still saw the similarity to Charlie, but what she saw mainly, now, was how haunted he looked, how ruined he was by what he had done to Charlie.

"Did they get Sheridan out?" he asked, his voice croaking.

"She's over there," Nell said, gesturing at the spot where she'd seen Gavin and Sheridan. "They're working on her."

"Oh God," he said. "If she dies, too . . ."

"You told her what happened," she said. "I heard everything."

He stared into her eyes, and nodded. "I know," he said. "You said that, just before . . ."

"The fire," Nell said, cringing. She stared at Sheridan's beloved house.

"It's not your fault. It's mine," he said, as if he could read her mind.

"Jeff," she said, feeling prickles race across her lips. She tasted the smoky air and felt as if she might pass out. "If you'd just walked away from Charlie . . ."

He didn't answer out loud at first. But he stared at her in such a long, deep, wordless way, she felt as if he was feeling anguish beyond comprehension.

"I'm ready to pay for it," he said.

Nell stared at him. Tall, blond, his face streaked with sweat and black ash, Jeff started coughing uncontrollably. Nell wanted to feel compassion for him, but her ears were still ringing with what she'd heard him say inside the house. She looked up, wondering how someone so normal-looking, so much like Charlie, could have taken away something so extraordinary as Charlie's life.

"I want you to pay for it," Nell cried, gripping the front of Jeff's shirt, tangling her hands in the fabric. She wanted to tear it, wanted to do damage, and she began to weep—pent-up wrath and grief pouring out as she hit him again and again. Nell felt hands grabbing her shoulders, trying to pull her off Jeff, heard Peggy crying, "No, Nell—stop!"

Struggling against the person trying to pull her away, Nell thought of Charlie. She knew that this was his brother, that Charlie must have trusted him, that he'd walked with him to the edge of the water, and that he'd gotten killed. Nell scratched Jeff's face, tried to claw his eyes out. She heard herself weeping, calling Charlie's name.

Suddenly Stevie was there, her arms around Nell—not pulling, but soothing, gentling her. "It's okay, Nell...you can stop now. I have you, sweetheart... Stop, Nell. Stop this..."

And Nell stopped. She could barely breathe, but the words exploded out. "Why?" she wailed. "Why did you do it? Why did you kill him?"

"It was an accident," he cried. "I hit him, yes, but I didn't mean for him to die. I know how that must sound to you, Nell. I'm not trying to get out of anything. I didn't mean for it to happen, but I did it, Nell. I killed Charlie. I'll pay for it forever."

Nell stared at him. He spoke in a low, calm voice that cracked with every word—the smoke must have seared his throat. She almost wished he'd try to make excuses, squirm out of the part he'd played, try to deny what had happened. She'd like to attack him again, accuse him of being a coward on top of everything else. She watched his gaze lift above her head, fix on the police car.

Nell turned to see Sheridan, supported by Gavin, walking over. Sheridan reached out one burned hand, took Nell's. They gazed into each other's eyes, and Nell's filled with tears.

"Now we know," Nell said. "Now we know what happened."

Sheridan tried to smile. She couldn't, but she hugged Nell.

"Jeff Quill. I hate him so much," Nell whispered. "He took Charlie's life."

"I know," Sheridan said. "Don't give up yours."

"Mine?" Nell asked, pulling back, surprised. "My life?"

"Don't hate him, Nell," Sheridan said. "It will eat you up. Charlie wouldn't want that."

Did that mean that Sheridan wanted Nell to forgive Jeff? Gazing into Charlie's mother's eyes, she saw sorrow and kindness. Nell looked past her at her burning house, and grabbed Sheridan's hands.

"I'm so sorry," she said.

"Shh," Sheridan said. "There's nothing for you to be sorry about."

Nell wanted to say more, but Sheridan was looking over her head. Turning, Nell saw Jeff walking straight toward the police car. Nell, Sheridan, and Gavin watched as he approached one of the Black Hall cops, started talking to him.

Sheridan kissed Nell and gently stepped away. Gavin nodded at Nell.

"I saw him in there," Gavin said softly.

"Saw who?"

"Charlie," Gavin said. "I know it sounds crazy, but he was there. And he saved Jeff."

Nell couldn't speak. She watched Gavin following Sheridan across the yard, straight toward Jeff. Cops were gathering around him, and Nell suddenly knew he was confessing.

The firefighters had surrounded Sheridan's house, were spraying their hoses in great arcs of silver water, but it was futile: the flames broke through the roof, leaping up to the sky. Hubbard's Pointers were in shock; some were crying. Nell clutched Stevie, watching Sheridan and Gavin standing with Jeff as what remained of Charlie's home burned.

And then Nell kissed Stevie, told her she'd meet her back at their cottage, and ran as fast as she could toward the cemetery. Gavin had seen Charlie. And now she had to.

CHAPTER 23

WHILE EVERYONE ELSE WATCHED HER house burn, Sheridan turned her back on it. She held Gavin's hand and watched as Jeff spoke with the police. People tried to get her to go to the hospital, but she just shook her head.

Jeff told one officer what he had done. At first the cop reacted with skepticism, calling others over to hear. Sheridan held back, watching. She saw the Black Hall police, used to dealing with speeders, accidents, and the occasional break-in, listen to this young man confess to killing someone in New York. Sheridan watched their faces, their expressions turning from doubt to suspicion. She'd had little to do with the police, and didn't know any of them well.

"Say that again?" one of the officers asked.

"I killed someone," Jeff said.

"When was this?"

"Last August thirty-first."

"In New York City, you say?"

"That's right."

"So why don't you tell me what happened?" the officer asked, his eyes hard as he started taking him seriously.

"I—" Jeff began.

Sheridan stepped forward. "Jeff," she interrupted.

He looked over at her, his eyes wide open. At the sight of her, his gaze flickered and his voice faltered.

"Sheridan, you're okay . . ."

She nodded. "Jeff, you need a lawyer," she said.

"No I don't," he said. "I did it . . . that's not in question. Let me get this over with."

Gavin was already halfway across the yard, looking for Vincent. The cops watched Sheridan and one of them stepped between her and Jeff.

"This is police business," he said. "And it sounds as if he knows what he's doing."

"Maybe so," Sheridan said calmly. "But he still needs to talk to a lawyer."

"He just confessed," the officer said. "So he's taking a ride. The lawyer can find him at the station, okay?"

Sheridan nodded, locking eyes with Jeff. Her emotions were too big to handle; the sound of her house burning filled her ears, and as she stared into the face of this young man who looked so much like Charlie, the young man who had taken him away, she felt the world tilt beneath her feet.

"What's the victim's name?" the cop asked Jeff, but Sheridan answered.

"My son," she said. "Charles Rosslare."

Gavin came running over with Vincent, and as the police put handcuffs on Jeff, Vincent was already asking questions and making arrangements to follow the car to the small police station on Route 156. Sheridan told Vincent that Jeff had tried to save her in the fire—that he should know that. Vincent hugged her gingerly and thanked her, and then he hurried down the hill to go to the station.

With Jeff and the others gone, Sheridan turned back to the fire. Gavin took her hand and started leading her in the opposite direction—through the Devlins' yard, toward the rocks. Sheridan's cottage faced the beach, but this side of the Point was rocky and wild, a craggy strip of glacial moraine sloping down to Long Island Sound.

"I think you should go to the hospital and get checked out," Gavin said.

"I think you should, too," Sheridan said.

But they just held hands tightly, limping through the Devlins' yard in the fog, onto the granite ledge. Sheridan's feet were burned, and they hurt. Her lungs felt as if they'd been squeezed by a giant. Every breath felt as if she'd swallowed a knife. Her head felt bruised, from where she'd hit it when she'd passed out.

"You did the right thing, getting him a lawyer," Gavin said.

"I know," she said.

"I don't know how you're doing it," he said. "Putting your feelings aside about what he did."

"No," she said. "I'm not that good. I just thought of what Charlie would want."

"Charlie would have wanted Jeff to have a lawyer?"

"Yes," she said simply.

When they got near the water's edge, Gavin eased her down one step, then another. Her muscles felt stiff, as if she'd been sleeping for a hundred years. He supported her as they inched their way down the rocks.

The tide was out. Gavin had said he loved the sound from Sheridan's house, of the waves washing gently over the sand. Here, on the other side of the Point, the waves sounded different: more turbulent and powerful, rolling straight in from the open ocean, through the rough waters of the Race—where Long Island Sound met the Atlantic—fetching up here on the eastern edge of Hubbard's Point. The waves splashed noisily, sucking stones and seaweed as they washed back to sea.

Gavin held her tight, helping her step into the first tidal pool. The water felt cold and wonderful on her burned feet. She stood still, waves swirling around her ankles. When she was ready, he took another step down, onto the ledge that dropped off into the Sound itself. Because the tide was out, the waves were breaking a few yards away, leaving them in peace here.

Sheridan braced herself against Gavin, and together they lowered themselves onto the ledge, sitting waist-deep in the cool, healing salt water. A hundred yards behind them were noises from the fire: axes hacking wood, water gushing from hoses, people crying out in distress. Gavin sat quietly beside Sheridan. He didn't ask if she was okay, didn't ask if she wanted to go back to her yard, be there with her house as it burned. He just sat with her.

"My grandmother always said salt water healed all wounds," she said.

"Well, it sure feels good now," Gavin said.

"When you put your mouth on mine, up at the house, I tasted salt," Sheridan said. "Even through the smoke. I think it woke me up."

Gavin laughed softly. "I swam early this morning, a hundred years ago; didn't have time to shower before heading to Nashville."

"Maybe it saved my life."

"Then I'm glad I swam."

The water splashed over their feet and legs, spray coating their faces; Sheridan watched as bits of ash were washed from their bodies and drifted out to sea on the waves' foam. She stared at one piece, circling in an eddy, then disappearing underwater.

"He told me everything," Sheridan said.

"I knew he planned to," Gavin said, putting his arm around her.

"Randy told you . . ."

"I wanted so badly to get back here, so you wouldn't have to be alone to hear. I wanted to be with you when he told you."

"I know," she said softly. "And I love you for it."

Had she just said that? Her heart, aching from all

that had happened, crashed around in her chest, and she couldn't bring herself to look at him.

"It must have been so hard to hear what he had to say," he said.

"Yes," she said. "And also good to hear. Because now I know what happened. Nell was right; we had to know."

He nodded. Sometimes resolution made things better. Not at first, but once it all sank in; it made it easier to accept and go on. She wondered whether that was why he'd become an investigator. Because knowing was better than not knowing.

"How did the fire start?" he asked.

"I'd lit candles...because I was tired of being alone in the dark. I was...thinking of you. And then Jeff came, and then Nell. I...really don't remember the rest. It was an accident. It happened so fast."

"Thank God we got you out."

"All of us," she said.

"Jeff, too?"

"Jeff, too," she said.

She felt Gavin looking at her, glanced up to meet his eyes. The water swirled around them, cooling her burns. She waited to see disbelief in his face, but he just gazed at her.

"That's my Sheridan," he said.

"I'm just thinking of Charlie," she said. "Of what he would want. He'd want his brother to be safe."

"I don't..." he began. "I never really believed in your family's magic. You know that, right?"

"I figured," she said. "You were always so practical."

"But tonight..." He shook his head.

"What?"

"Well, after I'd picked you up, leaving the living room, I couldn't see where I was going. I felt myself starting to pass out, and I swear I heard..."

"Charlie," Sheridan whispered.

Gavin nodded.

Sheridan stared at the shining black water. She had heard her son—and seen him, too. With the flames all around them, and Jeff lying on the floor beside her in that burning room, she'd seen a white shape, so graceful and true. The smoke was thick, obscuring her vision. He'd touched her, told her he loved her. But then he'd faded away.

"He saved us," Sheridan said.

"I know," Gavin said. "Charlie was there, right there with us. Aphrodite, too."

Sheridan sat on the rock ledge, half submerged, trying to hold the moment in her mind. If Charlie had been with them in the fire, why couldn't he be here now? Why couldn't her son come back to her? She cried softly, tears rolling down her face.

Leaning into Gavin, Sheridan felt the salt water washing around them both, healing their burns, and scars, and even her broken heart. She coughed, feeling her lungs start to expand. The fog cooled every breath, soothing her throat. And then she knew: the fog had brought her ghosts home to her.

Aphrodite had believed in so few rules, but she'd

always told them to be careful in the fog. She'd told Sheridan and her sisters not to step on fairy table-cloths—cobwebs stretched between blades of grass, silvery with fog's dew—and not to stand with their backs to a mirror, and that when they saw animals on foggy nights, they were really human ghosts. For the first time, Sheridan realized that Aphrodite's pro-hibitions had not been so much to protect her grand-daughters—as to protect the dead.

To give them rest, to not call them forth. She glanced up, saw scraps of fog breaking up, the first stars shining through.

"I hope they can save the house," Gavin said.

Sheridan didn't reply. She thought of her guitars and equipment, her stacks of sheet music, the note-books full of songs she'd been writing. She thought of Charlie's room, of all his things. And she thought of Aphrodite's kitchen, all the dried herbs and sea-shells and bits of sea glass. She thought of her grand-mother's book of spells.

"I don't care," she whispered.

"Don't give up," Gavin begged, hugging her. "Sheridan . . ."

"I'm not giving up," she said, gazing into his eyes. She wanted to explain it all to him, make him see: tonight was a beginning, not the end. A house was made of wood and glass and bricks and stone. It was filled with things—objects that mattered, but that were not the whole story.

Songs could be rewritten, guitars could be re-placed, the things in Charlie's room were just things, not Charlie himself. Sheridan had Charlie with her every minute of every day. He was in her heart and soul; she'd given him life, and he'd given it back to her.

She held Gavin's hand, rocking back and forth. Sitting in the water, she felt the power of the sea. Her grandmother had been named for the goddess of love, who'd been born out of the ocean, had come to earth in a beautiful scallop shell. They had all come from the sea, and would return to the sea; Sheridan watched as sparks from the fire drifted over the tree-tops, fizzling in the bay like drowning stars.

An ember landed beside her; Sheridan touched it, a charred piece of her house hovering on the water's surface. She watched, expecting it to sink, but it didn't; the small ember floated away, a small boat, borne by the waves until it disappeared into the darkness.

"Sheridan," Gavin whispered.

"I'm almost ready to get out," she said. "But not quite."

They put their arms around each other. Sheridan felt the warmth of Gavin's body through their wet clothes; she felt her heart beating against his, the rhythms melting together as if they were one, as if they'd always been together and would never be apart. Time away from the one you love disappears once you realize that distance is only in your mind, that it never really mattered at all.

She kissed Gavin on the lips. He still and again tasted of salt. They looked into each other's eyes and didn't have to say a word. Together they stood and, holding hands, stepped off the ledge into the cool, dark Sound. They swam side by side along the shore, buoyant in their home waters.

Sheridan and Gavin swam, their path illuminated by the stars in the clearing sky, their backs to the fire as the fog finally cleared.

ONE NIGHT PASSED, then another. A third, a fourth. The fifth day was August thirty-first, the anniversary of Charlie's death, and Nell returned to the cemetery. She had been so sure she'd see him in her dreams the foggy night of the fire. She'd left everyone standing around Sheridan's house as the firefighters tried to salvage at least something of the frame. She'd run up the street, her legs aching as she tore through the beach roads.

Hurrying to Charlie's grave that night, she'd almost expected to see him sitting right there waiting for her. But of course he wasn't. She'd sat on the grass, her back to the gravestone, willing herself to fall asleep. Minutes had passed, then an hour. She'd watched as the emergency vehicles drove away. Sometime in the middle of the night, exhausted and knowing that Stevie would be worried, she'd headed home.

Her father had returned from London. His joy at Stevie's agreeing to marry him had been tempered by his devastation over the loss of Sheridan's house. They'd grown up together here at Hubbard's Point, and her sorrow was his. Stevie tried to tell him what Sheridan had told her: that it was only a structure, that she carried everything important—the love, the memories, even the magic—in her own heart.

But Nell's dad was an architect, and to him structure was very important. He knew that Sheridan's house had been her home, that the complete reality of loss probably hadn't yet hit her. He'd asked Stevie to pull out all the photos they'd taken over the years, visiting Sheridan—for Charlie's birthday parties, for Sheridan's impromptu concerts, for visits with Aphrodite. He wanted to make sure they had them, to give to Sheridan when she was ready.

Today, five days after the fire, Nell had gone back to work. She'd just finished her shift at Foley's, walked up to the cemetery for her daily visit. Her throat still ached from breathing smoke from the fire; she'd brought a lemonade with her to sip as she walked. Coming down the dirt road, she saw shadows dappling the green grass. The sun was setting behind the trees, glowing orange through the leaves. One year ago tonight, Charlie had died.

Nell shivered. She remembered the first time she'd seen Jeff, right here in the graveyard. She walked over to Charlie's grave, stood staring at it for a few minutes. The guitar-playing angel looked so peaceful, as if she were playing Charlie a lullaby. Nell closed her eyes, wondered whether she had imagined seeing him the last time.

After a while, she sat down on the grass. She drank most of her lemonade, then set the cup down. A bee buzzed drowsily around the rim, then flew away. Overhead, birds were singing in a last burst before nightfall. Nell watched the robins hopping across the grass a few feet away; this year's babies were all grown up. Soon it would be autumn, time to fly south for the winter.

She stared at the lemonade again, thinking of how she'd spilled those two glasses on those people who'd carved their initials in the table at Foley's. So much had happened since that day. Now Jeff was under arrest for manslaughter. Randy was being investigated as well, and he was cooperating with the police. Nell had done what she'd set out to do: find answers.

Maybe Sheridan had been right all along: losing Charlie was what counted, not how or why it had happened. Nell stared down at her ankle, now bare of the scrap of towel Charlie had tied there. It had come off in the fire. She gazed at her bare ankle for a long time, then slid down and lay still, listening to the crickets. She'd dreamed of him here once—it had seemed so real, so she prayed for him to come to her again. Her eyelids grew heavy, and she drifted off.

"Charlie," she whispered, begging him to come. "Charlie . . ."

And tonight was the night, because he whispered back: "I'm here."

And when she opened her eyes, he was. He stood in front of her, solid and strong and tan and real. He had never gone away, never died. He was alive, and he was smiling, and he touched her and came to sit beside her.

Nell held him.

"Charlie . . ." she whispered.

He laughed, kissing her. "You're the Boy Whisperer," he said. "That hasn't changed."

"Where were you? I've come every day . . ."

"Shh," he said. "Let's not talk yet. I just want to be with you."

He caressed her with his strong hands, running them down her arms. They kissed, feeling each other's bodies. Nell tangled her fingers in his hair, traced the back of his head, touched the skin of his neck, ran her hands up under the sleeves of his T-shirt to feel his shoulders, touch his muscles.

Charlie eased her down onto her back; he lay beside her in the grass, brushing the hair back from her forehead, gazing into her eyes. He smiled; she reached up, touched his lips with her finger. He lowered his head to kiss her, parting her lips with his tongue. His cheek rubbed against hers, scratchy with scruff, as if he hadn't shaved in a few days. It felt so sexy, making Nell squirm and kiss him harder.

They lay on the grass, making out like crazy, as if a whole year hadn't passed. Nell knew every inch of his body, and it was clear he remembered every bit of hers. She squeezed her eyes tight, seeing stars, convincing herself that the last year hadn't happened at all—she had had a bad dream.

People had told her Charlie was dead, but he wasn't. He was here, alive, with her, and they were young, and it was summer, and overhead the first star was starting to glint in the twilight sky.

"Make a wish," she said, pointing up.

"Nell," he said, touching her face, unable to look away.

"Star light, star bright," she said, laughing. "Come on, let's make a wish."

He smiled, still staring into her eyes. She tickled him, and he laughed. "You first," he said, kissing her.

Nell closed her eyes. It was a long, slow kiss that made her spine tingle, filled her body with warmth all the way down to her toes. A wish came to her, but it seemed too easy. So she looked deeper, tried harder as the kiss grew more intense. Many wishes flew through her mind, all of them good. But she returned to the very first one. They kissed another few seconds,. and then Charlie pulled back, still holding her, looking into her face.

"Okay," she said. "Done."

"What was it?"

"If I tell you, it might not come true. Now you—your turn to make one."

He smiled at her as if being very patient. Then he closed his eyes. She stared up at his face for a long moment; her hand hovered close to his cheeks and chin, wanting to touch him but for some reason holding back. She watched the smile get bigger for a moment, then drain away. When he opened his eyes, he looked sad.

"Did you make your wish?"

He nodded. "I wished . . ."

"Shh," she said, putting one finger to his lips. "Remember, if you tell me, it won't . . ."

"It won't come true," he said.

"But only if you tell me," she said.

He shook his head. She saw anger in his eyes, then the glint of tears. "No, Nell. It won't come true no matter what..."

"That's not true," she said. "You of all people should know—coming from your family, with all the spells and magic—wishes are important! And if..."

"Nell," he said, stroking her cheek. "My wish can't come true...because I wished to stay with you. And I can't."

"Charlie, but..."

"It's time for me to go." He paused, kissing her forehead, her cheeks, her lips again. "This past year, I wanted to stay forever. I couldn't bear to leave you, Nell. Or my mom, either."

"Charlie...stay!" Nell said, gripping his hand.

For a moment she saw a flicker of hope in his eyes. Maybe they could live that way—love each other forever, live side by side, never seeing one another but counting on the other's constant presence. Maybe that would be enough...

"It wouldn't be fair to you," Charlie said.

"Oh, Charlie," she whispered.

"It's time, Nell," he said, taking her hand.

Nell stared at him, her beautiful friend, her only love. He was humble and dear, and she knew that she had to let him go, that it was time for him to sleep.

"Okay," she said.

"Are you sure?"

She wasn't, but she nodded anyway. "It's time..."

Something made Nell turn. There beyond the graves, in the tall grass filled with fireflies, she saw a fragile, evanescent form. Aphrodite, holding out her arms to him.

Nell turned back to him. He hadn't stopped gazing at her, even for a second. He took her hand, and they looked deeply into each other's eyes. Nell swallowed, trying to memorize everything about him. She traced the outline of his face; he grabbed her finger and kissed it. Then he put his arms around her.

They rocked, and he felt so solid, she almost changed her mind. He tilted her head back, lowering his mouth to hers. He tasted so good, so much like he always had; he tasted like summer. Overhead a night bird flew through the trees, its call deep and low. Nell never wanted to stop holding him, couldn't bear to pull back. She thought of her wish, and it welled up inside her, filled her eyes with tears.

"I have to leave," Charlie said, his hands gripping Nell's elbows.

"You know what I wished?" she asked.

"You told me you couldn't tell me...that it wouldn't come true."

"It won't anyway," she gasped. "But I want you to know."

"Okay," he said, nodding, waiting.

She swallowed hard. "It's dumb," she said. "But it's what I want more than anything..."

"Tell me," he whispered.

"I wish I still had that piece of towel you'd tied around my ankle," she said.

Charlie was practically holding her up; she felt as if her knees might buckle. Very gently he let go of her, then crouched down. He picked a long blade of grass from the edge of his tombstone. Still kneeling, he tied it around her ankle. Then he stood up.

"It's the best I can do," he said, smiling.

"I like it," she said, smiling back.

Then he kissed her. He took her in his arms, their feet in the shadow of his grave and their faces in the light of the stars, and he held her tight. She reached up to hold him, tasted his summery taste, felt his hot lips, and the feel of his cheek rough against hers, and the way his arms pressed her into his body, as if making them one and the same person.

When the kiss was over, he stepped away. She reached out to grab him, but her hand caught only air. He walked backward a few paces, holding her gaze with passion and intensity.

"Charlie, I love you," Nell said.

"I'll always love you," he said.

Then he turned and walked into the tall grass where his great-grandmother was waiting. Aphrodite smiled at Nell, said something in Irish that she couldn't understand. Then, side by side, Aphrodite and Charlie walked away. Nell stared until they disappeared into the silver starlight, until she was sure they were gone.

A truck rumbled by on the road outside the cemetery, and Nell rolled over, felt the cool dirt on her cheek, and woke up with a start. Her mouth was dry. Her mind swam with the dream she'd just had.

It had felt so real.

She cried to think of how good it had felt to hold Charlie, and she knew she'd sleep here every night if she could kiss him again, even in her dreams.

She looked up at the stars. Then she looked down at her ankle where she wore a thin green anklet of tall grass. Sitting up in pure shock, she stared at the grass tied there. Had she done that in her sleep? Had he? She touched her lips; she could still feel Charlie's kiss.

Nell knew that it was time to go. She turned away from the gravestone with its guitar-playing angel. And she walked out of the cemetery, onto the winding road that led toward the Point and home.

EPILOGUE

THE SKY WAS SEPTEMBER BLUE, CRYSTAL clear, without a cloud. A sharp, warm breeze blew off the Sound, making the flags snap. Most Hubbard Point families had gone home at the end of August, back to school, but many of them had returned for the wedding. It was to be held on the beach, right on the sand, at noon.

Agatha and Bunny had been busy all morning, preparing the buffet. With the help of Peggy, Tyler, and some of Nell's other friends, they set it up on the boardwalk, under the blue pavilion roof. They'd made lobster canapés, cucumber sandwiches, Hubbard's Point tomato soup—although the day was sunny, there was a fall snap in the air, and besides, there were all those late-summer tomatoes coming in on the vines. But the *pièce de résistance* was to be Coquilles St. Jacques— scallops served in their own shells—in honor of Aphrodite.

Sheridan and Gavin were staying on the *Squire*

Toby, and would be until Sheridan's house was re-built. Gavin hadn't exactly packed dress clothes for this trip, but he managed a blazer and a pair of not-too-wrinkled khakis. Sheridan had lost all her clothes in the fire, but she looked as beautiful as a bride herself in a soft-yellow dress she'd borrowed from Stevie.

Gavin pulled the dinghy close to the boarding ladder, helped Sheridan over the side and into the small boat. She moved gingerly, as if everything hurt. He knew it did—she had burns on her feet and hands, but every day she swam in salt water, healing a little more at a time. Gavin never let her go in alone; he swam right alongside her, feeling his own burns and cuts closing up.

Heading into the beach, he pulled on the oars, staring at Sheridan. The September sun glinted on her white hair; she'd never looked more lovely. He knew everything she had lost last month, wondered how she could stand looking up the hill from his boat, at the empty place where her house had stood. But she did; he came up on deck every morning, found her sitting there with a cup of coffee, gazing contemplatively up at the spot.

"You ready for this?" he asked her now.

"The wedding?" she asked.

He nodded. "The last time we saw all these people gathered together, it was..."

"The night of the fire," she said. "I know. It's okay, I'm fine."

"Really?"

"Yes." She smiled, and he knew she was telling the truth.

As strong and tough as he'd always wanted to think himself, his strength was nothing compared to hers. Every night since the fire, she'd huddled over the mahogany table in the main salon, writing songs. He'd gone down to New York, to her regular guy at Mandolin Brothers on Staten Island, bought her a Martin guitar just like the one Merle Haggard had given her.

Last night he'd asked her what she was writing, and she told him it was a surprise—a song for the wedding. Now, rowing her in to shore, he wondered why she hadn't brought her guitar.

"Forgot something?" he asked.

"No," she said. "Why?"

"Because if you're planning to sing that song you wrote, we'd better go back and get your guitar."

"I don't need it," she said.

"But it sounded so pretty," he said, "the way you were playing last night."

She just smiled, as if she had a secret. The look in her eyes filled him with more excitement than he could believe—amazing that just one little look could do that to him. He shook his head, smiling back. He'd never understand his luck, as long as he lived. He'd blown things with Sheridan so long ago, and here they were again, giving each other another chance.

"You know what?" he said.

"What?"

He stared, the smile growing on his face. He just

shook his head, because he couldn't tell her what he was thinking. What he wanted, more than anything, was to propose to her. They were on their way to the wedding of two of their oldest and best friends, and all he could think of was marrying Sheridan.

But she'd been through so much, he didn't think it was fair to lay this on her right now. Not just the fire, but the trauma of losing Charlie, and then finding out Randy's son had killed him. Sheridan knew that Jeff had suffered through childhood without a father, just as Charlie had. Tragedy had caused more tragedy, and she had bittersweet compassion for Jeff Quill. She'd told Gavin that when time had passed, she knew she would go to the prison, where he was being held in New York, and talk to him. Gavin knew better than to try to talk her out of it; she was doing it for Charlie.

Gavin knew he owed her a break before he started hounding her about being his wife. Let her get used to him a little longer, see how they did living together.

"You're not going to tell me?" she asked just as he rowed them up onto the sand, rolled up his pants, and hopped out into the shallow water to haul the dinghy up above the tide line. He helped her out of the boat, shook his head.

"Not right now," he said. "But I will, Sheridan. I'll tell you soon—and that's a promise. You got that?"

"I got it," she said, slipping her arm through his as they hobbled—old soldiers home from their own private war—down the beach they'd always loved, toward the wedding tent.

SHERIDAN CRIED. She didn't even try to hide it. The whole ceremony was so beautiful: Stevie nine months pregnant, Jack holding her hands and gazing at her as if no man had ever loved anybody more. Nell, their maid of honor, standing there so still in her pretty blue dress, wearing her mother's pearls. Maddie was Stevie's bridesmaid, and of all the guests, she and Sheridan cried the hardest.

The vows had come from several sources: Agatha had offered a prayer, and Stevie had asked Sheridan for one of Aphrodite's best love spells to incorporate into the vows. When the ceremony was over, Agatha, who as Eucharistic minister had officiated, said, "I now pronounce you husband and wife!"

Gavin waited, then turned with surprise to Sheridan.

"Aren't you going to sing?" he whispered.

She smiled and shook her head, wiping away tears. "No," she said.

"But . . ." he began, confused.

Then the reception began, and everyone filed through the buffet line, filling their plates. This was a most unusual wedding, in every way—at least to Sheridan. The bride and groom pulled her and Gavin aside. Instead of her giving them wedding presents, they gave gifts to her.

Stevie, dressed in a beautiful white lace maternity

dress, handed Sheridan the basket she had carried over to her house in mid-August, the night Sheridan had thrown the jelly jar at the rocks.

"Oh, Stevie," Sheridan said, lifting the cloth, seeing the portrait of Charlie.

"I painted it for you during the winter," Stevie said.

"But I wasn't ready for it when you tried to give it to me before," Sheridan said.

"No," Stevie said. "It was too soon . . ."

"And too unfinished." Sheridan stared at her son's portrait, so lovingly painted by her old friend. Stevie had caught Charlie's eyes, the sparkle and smile that had always been in them. Sheridan touched the canvas, as if she could brush his fine blond hair out of his blue eyes.

She tried not to think of Jeff, but he was part of their story now—part of their lives, part of their family. He was being held on Rikers Island, until his plea could be accepted and his sentence handed down. Gazing at the portrait of Charlie, she saw hints of his brother. Sometimes she prayed that they'd never met. But they had, and life had been forever changed.

"Charlie," she whispered, still touching the painting of her son. The canvas felt so stiff beneath her fingers; but Stevie had put such life into his eyes, into his being, and Sheridan felt him with her. She felt Charlie as he was, as he'd always be: her beautiful boy.

"We brought you these, too," Jack said, handing her an album. Gavin helped her open it, look through. The pictures were so vivid and alive—all of her house, many of Charlie. All different ages—at birth, when he was two, the day he got his driver's license, the summer he died.

"Thank you," Sheridan said, looking up at Jack. "I lost all my photos in the fire. These mean so much to me."

"Look," Gavin said. "Here's one of Aphrodite and your mother...and your sisters..."

Sheridan nodded. "And so many of Charlie."

"Also," Jack said, "of your house."

"Yes," Sheridan said, feeling a wave of sadness. "I said it didn't matter, but it does. I miss the place...it was so quirky, one of a kind. I'll never have my old cottage back."

"No," Jack said. "But you'll have one just like it. Or as close as I can make it..."

Stevie smiled, hugged Sheridan. "Jack is drawing up plans," she said. "From all these photos, he was able to do blueprints..."

"That's going to be our gift to you two," Jack said, shaking Gavin's hand.

"Yes," Stevie said, kissing him. "Congratulations!"

Gavin played it cool. He smiled, as if they knew what they were talking about. He accepted their good wishes, laughed, thanked them for their generosity. Nell called them over to the boardwalk, to get their scallops while they were hot.

Sheridan held the basket in one arm, the portrait of Charlie in the other. Gavin had the photo album in his hand. She stepped forward, and he put his other arm around her.

"What?" he asked, looking confused.

"That song I wrote last night? For the wedding?"

"Yes," he said.

"It's for *our* wedding," she said.

"Sheridan . . ."

"Stevie and Jack asked me the other day when you and I were going to follow them. . . . I didn't even have to think about it. I told them soon. I said you and I would be getting married soon."

"Is that true?" he asked, really starting to smile.

Sheridan nodded.

"Gavin," she said, "will you marry me?"

"Sheridan," he said, grinning, "you know I will."

She put down the basket and portrait, and he put down the photo album, so they could really hold each other tight. And Sheridan Rosslare and Gavin Dawson stood on the beach at Hubbard's Point, in the bright sun of the mid-September day, under the bluest sky they'd ever seen, and they kissed.

ABOUT THE AUTHOR

LUANNE RICE is the author of twenty-six novels, most recently *The Geometry of Sisters*, *Last Kiss*, *Light of the Moon*, *What Matters Most*, *The Edge of Winter*, *Sandcastles*, *Summer of Roses*, *Summer's Child*, *Silver Bells*, and *Beach Girls*, among many *New York Times* bestsellers. She lives in New York City and Old Lyme, Connecticut.

COMING IN HARDCOVER
August 4, 2009

THE DEEP BLUE SEA FOR BEGINNERS

by

LUANNE RICE

A legendary island steeped in the mystery and
wisdom of centuries . . .

A runaway heiress learning to trust life and love . . .

A mother and daughter, separated for years, searching
for a way to face the future together . . .

New York Times bestselling author Luanne Rice
tells a powerful story of love, family, and
friendship through the lives of two women who
reunite at a place where dreams begin—and
where they may be fulfilled at last. . . .

THE NEW YORK TIMES BESTSELLING AUTHOR OF
THE GEOMETRY OF SISTERS

LUANNE RICE

THE DEEP BLUE SEA FOR BEGINNERS

A NOVEL

THE DEEP BLUE SEA
FOR BEGINNERS

On sale August 4, 2009

Prologue

~

Lyra Nicholson Davis stood in the olive orchard at the far end of the walled garden overlooking the Bay of Naples. Bees hummed in the bougainvillea, and the morning breeze rustled the fine, silvery leaves overhead. The blue water of Capri was calm and clear, the surface scratched by white wakes of passing ships.

Max had gone to pick up Pell. He'd taken the small yellow boat, left before dawn, to wait at the dock in Sorrento. Pell's flight was on time. Lyra had checked online, had tracked the plane from New York to Rome, watched the tiny airplane graphic as it flew across the Atlantic.

The binoculars felt hot in her hand. What would she see when she looked through them at the boat coming across the water? Would she recognize her daughter? Of course, she told herself. Pell's school pictures were lovely; Lyra had tucked each one away, along with Lucy's, in a corner of her desk drawer.

She looked at her watch: ten a.m. Life was full of changes; every day was a coming together, a casting off. Small things: the white roses were blooming again, the full-moon tide swept a pair of oars off the rocks, you lost your glasses. Big things, too, that took your breath away, altered everything, exploded the course of life.

The joyful ones: she got married, she had two babies. The terrible ones: death, loss. So often the really huge moments came as a shock, a tsunami on a sunny day. It was rare to be given fair notice that the world you've built is about to change.

For Lyra, it would happen within the hour. She held the binoculars, wanting to lift them to her eyes. But she couldn't, not yet. The minute she did, started scanning the horizon for the yellow boat, she would be a mother again.

She would see a girl she barely knew. Brave, amazing child, to have flown all this way, to meet the woman who'd abandoned her and her sister. What kind of young girl would do that? Initiate this visit, get on a plane, come to Capri. What would their first hug be like? Or would Pell push her away?

Lyra couldn't bring herself to raise the binoculars to her eyes. Blue sky and sea surrounded her. Sky, blue sky. Deep, blue deep. Capri. Where she had come to escape herself and all she'd given away.

She wasn't sure she deserved to get any of it back.

One

I'd flown all night. Taking off from New York, banking over the Atlantic, the plane had headed east into the darkness, toward Rome. Stars filled the sky. Once the flight attendants dimmed the cabin lights, I stared out the window at a thousand constellations. I don't think I slept a minute. My thoughts were a web, swinging me from one star to the next.

I was alone. I mean, there were other people on the plane, but I was traveling by myself, without Lucy. You don't take little sisters on missions, especially when you are completely unsure of the outcome. My grandmother insisted I fly first-class. It wasn't even a discussion—once I told her that I was going to Italy to see my mother, as much as she disliked the idea, she put me in touch with the family travel agent, with the words "Pell Davis, you've always loved a lost cause."

Travis drove me from Newport, Rhode Island, to JFK. We didn't speak a lot. We each had too much on our minds. He had to get back to his job, I was thinking about what I'd set out for myself on this trip, and we both were considering the weeks of being apart looming ahead.

There were good reasons for this trip. I knew I didn't have to explain them to Travis. He's my boyfriend, but we have an unusual relationship. He's a football star at our school, and therefore tough, but sensitive in ways that belie outward facts.

He drove me through Connecticut, across the Whitestone Bridge, to the Alitalia terminal at JFK. We got there very early, with hours to spare. The June midday sun was hot as we stepped out of the car.

Travis lifted my bag and backpack from the trunk, and checked to make sure I had my passport. Twenty-four hours earlier, the maximum allowable span, he had printed out my boarding pass for me. I looked at my watch, calculating the time he would need to drive home to Newport. He had signed onto a fishing boat as a deckhand, and they went out at dusk.

We took care of each other, just as we took care of our sisters and, in Travis's case, his mother. Both of our fathers are dead. They died too young, beloved men. We are shaped by the loss of our fathers, and others. Perhaps that's what drew me to Travis in the first place, a sense that he understood that love and life's beauty are real, but any assurance they will last forever is a soothing lie.

The flight from New York was smooth. Flying eastward across Long Island at sunset, I looked down and saw the North and South forks, the curve of Montauk, the dark water of Block Island Sound be-

neath scratchy white wakes of fishing boats and pleasure craft. Could one of those boats hold Travis? I
chose to think yes, I saw him as I left, and he watched
my plane pass overhead.

Love is like that. You can see everything. All it
takes is the right kind of attention. When my father
taught me to play baseball, we'd stand out in the yard
until the light died and fireflies came out. He'd throw
and I'd catch, or he'd pitch and I'd hit. He'd say,
"Don't take your eyes off the ball, sweetheart. No
matter what, just keep your eyes on the ball." That's
how to see everything with the people you love—
keep watching, stay vigilant, watch the ball instead
of the fireflies.

So my last sight over the United States was of
Travis's boat. He and his family are looking after my
sleepwalking sister while I am gone. An ocean later, I
landed in Rome, was met by a driver, and taken to
Sorrento. Two and a half hours on the road, a chance
to think about what I am about to do.

The long drive from Rome to Sorrento, jet-lagged,
horns blaring, my grandmother's style of driver: uni-
formed chauffeur. I will be straightforward about
something right now, just so you will understand.
Gossip columns, before and after she left the country, referred to my mother as "Lyra Nicholson Davis,
heiress." Now they say the same of Lucy and me. Old
money, blue-bloods, heirs to the Nicholson silver for-
tune. We ignore what is said. They now say of my
mother, "reclusive heiress." We overlook that too.

My grandmother arranged to borrow the chauffeur from her friend Contessa Otavia Migliori, who

used to spend summers in Newport, at Stone Lea, the property next door to what used to be the Aitkens', parents of Martha Sharp Crawford, also known as Sunny von Bülow. Another tragic Newport family. I think of Cosima, daughter of Sunny and Claus, her father accused of trying to kill her mother over Christmas holidays by injecting her with insulin, then leaving her in a room with windows open to the frigid sea air. He was convicted, then acquitted.

This is the most terrible thing I ever heard, and it sticks with me over the years, but I once heard my mother crying, shrieking, that something was killing her, killing everything she had inside her. Even as a child, I knew she wasn't talking about a knife or a gun or a drug. She meant her heart and soul. She left us about a week later. And the really unjust, awful thing is, it took a few years, but my father is the one who wound up dying.

Anyway, the contessa's chauffeur drove me to Sorrento, an ancient seaside city filled with dark and crumbling beauty I felt too nervous to notice. Lucy would have—she loves antiquities, ghosts, and architecture. I felt pricked by guilt; perhaps I should have brought my sister. Will Lucy be okay without me this summer? We're very close. For so long, we've been each other's most important person.

But the alternative was to bring her along, without knowing what to expect. What if our mother rejects us all over again? I am strong. I have Travis. But Lucy is my little sister. I want to protect her.

The limousine snaked down the hill to the port. Bright boats lined the docks, reminding me of Newport. I opened the window to smell the sea air. The chauffeur seemed to know just where to go.

He drove along the quay, past shops selling shell jewelry, colorful pareos, and finely woven sun hats. I saw stalls of fresh fish, their glistening bodies packed in seaweed, yellow eyes flat and sightless. The smell of strong coffee hit me as we passed a café. I wanted some, but couldn't bear to stop until I saw if she'd come to meet me.

We drove through a pair of stone pillars, onto a wooden dock. It seemed like a loading zone—fishing boats and small cargo vessels were tied alongside, and trucks filled with supplies for the islands parked along the edge. Metal and wind: halyards clanging against masts, longshoremen swinging big iron hooks. We stopped at the end of the pier. I climbed out. It felt good to stretch my legs, but my chest was in a knot. Had my mother come to meet me? Was I about to see her?

The chauffeur lowered my bags into a yellow wooden boat tied to barnacle-covered pilings. An old man in a blue shirt and rumpled khakis, his face tan and wrinkled and hair pure white, grabbed the bags, stowed them under a varnished wooden seat. I stood on the dock, staring at the man.

"Hello, Pell," the man said in an English accent. "Come along now, and I'll take you to your mother."

"She's not here," I said stupidly.

"No," he said without explanation. I was upset, and he could see it. He stared at me with sharp blue eyes. He didn't fill the silence with excuses about a headache, an important phone call, an earthquake, a plague of locusts, any of the many things that could have detained her. Reaching up, he offered to help me down into the boat from the pier.

"*Buono viaggio*," the chauffeur said to me.

I thanked him. I didn't tip him, knowing my grandmother would have made arrangements with the contessa. Then I took the old man's hand, stepped down from the dock into the yellow boat.

"I'm Max Gardiner," he said.

"Her neighbor," I said. I'd heard the name before, in letters about Capri, the island's expatriate community, all the artists and intellectuals, the fabulous people, the thinkers and writers who so fascinated her, who'd moved to the island from the United States and England, who had become her friends, companions in her desire to insulate herself from the world. From her daughters, Lucy and me. Max owned the land next to hers.

"Yes," he said. "Now sit tight. Prepare for wonder."

Wonder. Had he really said that? I forced a polite smile that hid the pain I felt. I wasn't new to the sea. I'd visited islands before. I'd been on boats every summer of my life. Now I was on the way to force myself in, to spend time with a woman who'd never wanted me, who didn't want me now.

I untied the bowline to be helpful and show him I knew my way around boats, then took my seat as he cast off. The engine sputtered, and we headed out. Bright day, brilliant blue sky, sparkling sea.

It could have been Newport, this atmosphere of the sea, yachts, classic wooden workboats with nets glittering with fish scales; I thought of Travis, in a time zone six hours behind me. He would have returned from a night of fishing; he would be asleep in his family's cottage on the grounds of Newport Academy by now. I hoped my sister was sleeping as well. There was this incident, a dream-state walking-to-Italy kind of thing, that we hope won't repeat itself. I held my backpack tight to my chest. It felt compact, comforting. I had filled it with books, letters, pictures of the people I love.

We puttered out of the channel. I heard a breath come from the water just below the gunwale—a quick, happy intake of air, then a rushed exhalation. Dolphins swimming beside our yellow boat. I glanced over my shoulder at Max. Was this what he'd meant by "wonder"? He smiled at me, pointed dead ahead.

"You only get this chance once," he said.

"What chance?" I asked.

"To arrive on Capri for the first time. I feel privileged to witness it."

It's an island, I wanted to say. *Far from home. A mountain, a harbor. Marine mammals, yes, but no Lucy, no Travis.* I faced forward again, my posture stoic as the boat gained speed.

And as I stared ahead, I saw: the white rocks of Monte Solaro, craggy against the sapphire sky, a precipitous drop down to the radiant sea. I smelled lemons, verbena, and pine, their scents carried on the wind. Terraces of olive groves, leaves flashing silver in the sun. Capri rose from the waves, and I realized how often I'd dreamed of this. The island was

the most beautiful place I'd ever seen, and not because of the scenery.

Because my mother lived there.

MAX HAD LEFT THE VILLA just before dawn. He'd
crossed the broad stone terrace, made his way down
the steep, winding stairs, through groves of olive and
fig trees. The sharply pitched land was terraced, overlooking the Bay of Naples; he used a flashlight, but
he could have found his way blindfolded—he was
seventy-two, and had lived here over half his life.
There was such beauty on Capri; he wanted to shout,
wake up the island, tell Lyra, Rafe, all the islanders, to
open their eyes. *Love each other, be happy, life is short!*

Two levels down from the villa, he had passed the
small white cottage, saw one light burning. Lyra was
already awake, keeping vigil. Last night's almost-full
moon had hung low in the sky, casting silver light
across the water, pulling at the tides. Low tide was
treacherous twice each month, when the water ebbed
under the new and full moons, exposing rocks and
stranding sea creatures in tidal pools that wouldn't fill
until the lunar cycle came round again.

Now, steering his yellow boat back from Sorrento,
he had Pell safe and sound, on her way to Lyra. Max
saw his grandson walking the rocky shore, rescuing
invertebrates. Capri was a blue mirage, the massif of
Monte Solaro floating above the sea. Max looked up,
seeking out the whitewashed cottage on the hillside.
Sunlight glinted off binoculars held by Lyra, standing among olive trees.

"She's waiting for you," he said.

"My mother," Pell said.

"Yes," Max replied. He slowed the boat down, steered toward the private dock.

"Where?" she asked, shielding her eyes.

"Up there," Max said, pointing.

Pell's expression made his heart catch. He glanced up, wondering if Lyra could catch the full impact of her effect on her daughter through the binoculars. The young girl's head was tilted back, her mouth open. There was joy in hope.

As Max pulled up to the dock, the dolphins leaped and dove, swimming away. Dolphins were emotional creatures, just like people. They were capable of love, great loyalty, staying together for life. If ever they were separated from their children, one ripped from the other, the parents grieved and keened. He'd observed that in dolphins, just as he had in humans.

"Ready?" he asked Pell.

"Ready," she said.

He looked around, wanting help with the lines, but Rafe seemed to have disappeared. So Max climbed up on the wooden dock, and tied the boat fast.

LYRA BRACED HER ELBOWS on the wall, to steady them. She finally pressed the binoculars to her eyes. Max docking the boat. And up forward, in the bow, a lovely young girl. Shocking, stunning, take-your-breath-away beauty. Long, dark hair tied back, tendrils blowing around her face. Pell stared straight up the hill, as if she could see Lyra behind the stone wall, and maybe she could. Even as a baby she'd had an intense, seeking gaze.

The sight of her daughter made every muscle in Lyra's body jump, as if her skin had memories all its own. She felt pressure on, not in, her chest: a six-pound, seven-ounce weight. Pell, just born, wet and slippery, hot as a coal, bellowing. Lyra had held her daughter. Taylor was right there, standing beside them, but the moment was Lyra and Pell's. It's not every day you have a daughter, and as much as you might love her father, he'll never know the wild electricity you have with her.

Standing in her Italian garden, Lyra Davis stared down at the small yellow boat and thought of that tiny baby. She pictured the six-year-old girl that baby had become. Pell had been six, Lucy four, when Lyra left—ten years since Lyra had seen either of her daughters.

Lyra gazed down, watched Max help Pell onto the deck, hardly able to hold herself back. Her daughter was smart; Lyra knew because she received all her grades, scores, reports from Newport Academy. She had a brilliant mind; several of her teachers said so. But she was so young. At sixteen, she might believe in hope, in redemption, in the possibility of forgiveness. Lyra knew Pell would try to forgive, understand, put herself in her mother's shoes.

But the body remembered. Nothing could be done about that, about all the missed hugs and kisses, the neglected hair-brushing, the times Pell and her sister had needed comfort and their mother hadn't been there to provide it. The cold winters, without Lyra to help them into their snow jackets, and that December day when she had taken Pell to the bridge.

Lyra knew those feelings were lodged in Pell, even if Pell didn't admit them herself. This island was ancient, its mysteries millennia older anything imaginable in America, and it had taught Lyra some cruel things about time, illusions, and hopeless wishes.

She walked through a break in the wall, onto the stairs. Built centuries ago, they led up to Max's villa, and down to the dock. Thick pines, jasmine, and rosemary covered the steep rock hillside. Orange blossoms, waxy and fragrant, bloomed behind glossy green leaves.

Lyra hurried down. The steps, chopped roughly into the rocks, formed a precipitous descent. An iron handrail, rusted away in places, provided the only barrier to a sheer abyss. Voices carried up from the water: Max's, low and English-accented, and a girl's.

Pell's.

Lyra broke through the clearing, emerging from pines and vines, and stood at the top of the rock ledge. She saw Rafaele crouched in the shade by the boathouse, frozen in place; she walked right past him, and he ducked out of sight. Max and Pell were hoisting her bags off the boat onto the dock. Lyra hesitated for a second, watching them.

"Pell," she said.

Had she even spoken, made a sound? Everything seemed lodged in her throat—words, her daughter's name, her heart. Leaves rustled and waves lapped the rocks. Max and Pell looked in her direction.

"Pell," Lyra said again.

Lyra took a slow step toward the dock. Her eyes drank in the young woman standing there, so close now: tall, slim, fine dark hair, creamy pale skin, and mysterious blue eyes. Lyra caught her breath. Raised her arms, held out in front, embracing the air.

Pell's feet pounded down the dock—it seemed impossible that such a delicate girl could make such a racket. She bounded off the pier onto the sea-washed black rock, and only when she stood right there, inches away from Lyra, did she stop.

They stared into each other's eyes, and it wasn't easy, because Lyra's vision was completely blurred with tears. Then, as if remembering what to do from the farthest, most-forgotten past, Pell leaned into her mother's arms, and they held each other for a long time.